Praise for the novels of Rosalind Noonan

AND THEN SHE WAS GONE

"A story of optimism and encouragement, despite the heart-wrenching subject matter." —*Chatelaine*

ALL SHE EVER WANTED

"Noonan has a knack for page-turners and doesn't disappoint . . . a readable tale." —*Publishers Weekly*

THE DAUGHTER SHE USED TO BE

"An engrossing family saga and a suspenseful legal thriller. Noonan covers a lot of narrative ground, with a large cast of characters whose situations involve morally complex issues, as well as knotty family dynamics. This novel would fuel some great book-club discussions." —*Shelf Awareness*

IN A HEARTBEAT

"Complex, intriguing characters and an intensely emotional plot make *In a Heartbeat* compelling." —*RT Book Reviews*

ONE SEPTEMBER MORNING

"Written with great insight into military families and the constant struggle between supporting the troops but not the war, Noonan delivers a fast-paced, character-driven tale with a touch of mystery." —*Publishers Weekly*

"Noonan creates a unique thriller that is anti-Iraq war and pro-soldier, a novel that focuses on the toll war takes on returning soldiers and civilians whose loved ones won't be coming home." —*Booklist*

"Reminiscent of Jodi Picoult's kind of tale . . . it's a keeper!" —Lisa Jackson, *New York Times* bestselling author

Books by Rosalind Noonan

ONE SEPTEMBER MORNING

IN A HEARTBEAT

THE DAUGHTER SHE USED TO BE

ALL SHE EVER WANTED

AND THEN SHE WAS GONE

TAKE ANOTHER LOOK

Published by Kensington Publishing Corporation

TAKE
ANOTHER
LOOK

ROSALIND NOONAN

KENSINGTON BOOKS
www.kensingtonbooks.com

KENSINGTON BOOKS are published by

Kensington Publishing Corp.
119 West 40th Street
New York, NY 10018

All Kensington titles, imprints, and distributed lines are available at special quantity discounts for bulk purchases for sales promotion, premiums, fund-raising, educational, or institutional use.

Special book excerpts or customized printings can also be created to fit specific needs. For details, write or phone the office of the Kensington Sales Manager: Kensington Publishing Corp., 119 West 40th Street, New York, NY 10018. Attn. Sales Department. Phone: 1-800-221-2647.

eISBN-13: 978-1-61773-326-0
eISBN-10: 1-61773-326-1
First Kensington Electronic Edition: May 2015

ISBN-13: 978-1-61773-325-3
ISBN-10: 1-61773-325-3
First Kensington Trade Paperback Printing: May 2015

10 9 8 7 6 5 4 3 2 1

Printed in the United States of America

In memory of Ruby
My little shadow
Heart of gold

Acknowledgments

Special thanks to the marvelous ladies of the Ya Ya Book-lovers. I cherish your insightful conversation, rowdy jokes, and beautiful shared experiences. And the delicious snacks are a bonus. You are a testament to the power of books to bring people together.

PART 1

People are mostly layers of violence and tenderness wrapped like bulbs, and it is difficult to say what makes them onions or hyacinths.

—Eudora Welty

Prologue

December 2000

Two rivers of thought converged as Jane Ryan stared through the glass at her twin baby girls. One stream sluiced clear and cold with resolution to stick to the logical plan and take her firstborn; the other was a muddy pulse of doubt. Despite the decision that she had embraced months ago, her mind now jumped from one plan to another the way a monkey leaped from tree to tree. The monkey mind. She had to quiet the monkey brain.

Just choose.

Stick to the plan.

Or not.

She tried to envision her life beyond this hospital, but antiseptic smells and bursts of noise tugged at her consciousness. For a moment she listened to the conversation of the other people at the window, a new mother in a fluffy pink robe talking to a young couple.

"That's him. My Chad-man."

"So cute. Isn't he adorable?"

"Chad? Why'd you pick that name?" The young man voiced everything as a question. "You want him to be, like, a movie star?"

The woman with spiked hair smacked his shoulder while the mother defended her choice.

Their teasing made Jane ache for a simpler life with normal problems. Names could be changed. Some choices could be easily fixed, tempered, and shaved down. But not this.

Sweeping the dark hair from her forehead, she tried to shake off the haze of drugs and hormones, pain and exhaustion. Everything was distorted by the surreal bubble around her. She pressed one palm to the nursery window, as if the vibration of the glass would transmit the answer. Which baby? Which tiny girl would she bundle into the infant seat tomorrow? Which one would remain her daughter, her new family, light of her life? The other mothers who had stood at this window did not share her dilemma.

Twins. The power of one word, a single syllable that could ambush a carefully plotted route.

The pregnancy test had set the first alarm, casting the future into the wind and leaving her scrambling to catch the pieces and fit them into a semblance of order. She had said good-bye to her hometown, her family, her familiar life. She had escaped the man she had thought would be the love of her life. She had just begun to imagine a life for herself and her baby here in Seattle when her first sonogram had revealed the multiple heartbeats. That had cracked the foundation of her newly laid plans. Two babies. One would be a challenge, but two?

Marnie had come up with the idea, Googling the contact info of Seattle adoption agencies. That was Marnie, always prepared for mishaps. In grade school, she had carried an emergency dollar in her pocket. She had carried a fat cell phone in her backpack in junior high back in the eighties when most adults didn't have them yet. Marnie had been the only student in AP US History to turn her research paper in two weeks ahead of schedule. The skills of an event planner had shown Jane a way out, a light in the tunnel, a life with the one child she could handle.

But which one was that?

Her monkey mind wanted to renege on the agreement she had made with the adoptive couple and keep both babies for herself—an instant family. Her little girls could grow up together, sisters chasing each other through the backyard, sharing clothes and advice. But Jane had no backyard, no place to live as of yet. Marnie's guest room had been a safe haven, but you couldn't raise your children in someone else's household. There was no going home—that was too dangerous. She had refused to give her mother and sister her new location, for fear that they would tell him.

She hardened herself to the image of the double stroller. It would never work.

Just choose.

But she had already chosen Louisa, right? The baby named after Louisa May Alcott, author of *Little Women*. Jane would call her Lou.

Weeks ago, when she'd been in a quandary over which child to keep, Jane had decided to let fate choose. She had told the delivery room nurse that she wanted to hold only her firstborn. She had imagined the staff whisking the second baby out of her room and into Chrissy Zaretsky's arms, with Nick cooing at Chrissy's side. Jane had planned a simple, clean break.

Then came the C-section. Quivering on the table, splayed open like a rainbow trout. Her thoughts had run from panic to survival.

She shifted closer to the window, trying to ignore the tenderness in her abdomen, the angry incision that smiled across her belly.

She focused on her babies, one angel, and one little monster.

It had taken her a minute to locate them in the second row, toward the left of the room. The magnetic homing device of motherhood that she had anticipated had not taken hold, and the tiny loaves in rows of plastic bassinets all seemed strange and alien to her. She'd had to scan the cartoonish nametags to find two pink cards with **RYAN** marked in some nurse's quick block print.

Of course, her Harper was the only baby in the nursery on a crying jag at the moment. The pathetic bleating evoked both compassion and embarrassment. Perhaps it was a romantic notion to think that the baby would have strength and grace simply because she was named after Harper Lee, author of *To Kill a Mockingbird*.

Louisa and Harper...Jane had deliberately chosen rare names, having read an article claiming that an unusual name could raise a child's IQ.

Firstborn Louisa smiled in her sleep, a rosy-cheeked dream baby. The wails of her sister in the bin beside her didn't penetrate her peace. Such a sweet thing. So easy to love, if you could block out Harper's rant.

What was wrong with Harper? Shrieking and writhing as if in pain. A hot mess. With her infant acne and scaly scalp, she resembled a molting creature trying to escape the cocoon of her striped hospital blanket.

Tears stung Jane's eyes. So much anger and agitation. This little bean was going to be hard to love.

"What's wrong with her?" Jane had been asking everyone. She had begged an answer of the nurses, the pediatrician, and the aides who diapered the babies. "It's like there's a knife in her belly."

The pediatrician had given a sage smile, his eyes glassy and mystical, as if he were answering from a distant mountain in Tibet. "Babies cry."

The other answers were equally unhelpful. Hungry baby,

in need of a diaper change. Too hot, too cold. Blanket wrapped too tight or too loose.

"She just needs her mama to hold her," one aide had said as she placed the newborn in Jane's arms, where Harper had continued to squirm and cry herself hoarse. That was the myth—that a mother possessed the magic touch to calm her own flesh and blood. Jane had rubbed Harper's squishy little back and offered a bottle. She had rocked her and talked in a soothing voice. She had stroked her downy head and held her to her breast, but Jane was not capable of soothing Harper's distress.

Even now as Jane peered into the nursery, an attendant picked Harper up and began to sway. Silence came swiftly. Knowing that she would not be one of those mothers with the power to soothe, Jane simply stared.

A few minutes later, when the woman was called away, she carried Harper back to her bassinet and paused. Double-checking the baby's bracelet and the label, the attendant stepped over to Louisa's bassinet and, to Jane's surprise, tucked Harper in beside her sister.

"You can't do that." Jane knocked on the glass. "No!" They couldn't be together. Yes, they were sisters, but they couldn't get used to each other, accustomed to the warm contours of each other's bodies.

When Jane got the woman's attention, she was waved off with an omniscient smile. "It's okay," the nurse barked through the glass. "These baby girls are twins."

Jane stood watch as the nurse left the viewing area and quiet resounded. Nestled face-to-face with her sister, Harper was content.

A few minutes later, Louisa's open mouth was pressed to Harper's head, leaving a trail of saliva over her patchy skull. There was something primal about the sight, as if Louisa were trying to devour her twin. But Louisa's wet mouth soothed her sister. Both babies remained content.

Maybe they were supposed to stay together.

Suddenly, Jane wanted to keep both babies.

Or give them up—send them off together—so that they could remain as sisters.

She wanted both... or neither. Hormones swung her up and down, back and forth, like the creaking old playground swings that promised flight, but always pulled back down to earth at the last second. Both or neither. Louisa or Harper. Harper or Louisa.

Damned monkey mind.

Neither choice felt right.

Defeated, she returned to her room. Alone in her bed, she stared up at the bland vanilla tiles on the ceiling as guilt overtook her. It felt wrong to be apart from her children, and yet, when they were wheeled into her room for a feeding, Jane resented the loss of her freedom, the personal space she had spent a lifetime cultivating. She wondered if she would ever feel right again; she didn't think so.

Harper's howls scorched the room, prompting a disapproving sigh from Jane's roommate on the other side of the curtain. Jane got out of bed, picked up the crying baby, and began to pace with her, swaying in the silent dance the nursery attendant had shown her. After a few minutes passed, Harper's shrieks slowed to a whimper. Her mouth remained crumpled in a sour expression.

"You can't help the way you feel," she murmured in her baby's ear.

Louisa's little mouth was twitching into half a smile. Looking down at that perfect baby, Jane knew what she had to do. Louisa would be so easy to care for, so easy to love. And Harper... well, there was no way to be sure that the Zaretskys, or any adoptive couple, would have the patience for such a demanding child.

Turning away from the bassinet, Jane carefully eased herself back on the bed, careful not to awaken Harper, and pressed the call button. When the nurse answered, she asked her to take Louisa back to the nursery.

"Both of them?"

"No. Just Louisa." Jane faced the window, careful not to look at the baby being wheeled away—the Zaretskys' new baby girl. She stared at the dull bars of the window shade until she was sure Louisa and the nurse were gone. Until she knew it was over and done. A final decision.

She curled around her baby, her lashes grazing the vein that shone through the transparent skin at the bridge of Harper's nose. This tiny thing had her issues. The acne that begged to be scrubbed. The cradle cap. As Jane breathed in the delicate baby smell, her heart filled. Flawed and difficult to love, they would make quite the pair.

Chapter 1

The shadowed corridor of Mirror Lake High School was thick with new carpet smell—summer improvements—as Jane Ryan trudged along, trying to balance equipment that was awkward but not too heavy. Last week these halls had swelled with hundreds of students scrambling to reconfigure a schedule, pay fees, and score a better locker and a school photo that captured their best self. But registration was done, thankfully, and for the next two weeks the building was open for teachers and administrators to pull themselves together for the new school year. Hence the empty building.

This was one of Jane's favorite Oregon seasons, a time of lingering light and cool restful nights. Each year she contemplated taking on a different grade, and each year reaffirmed her love of freshman English when she met that startling batch of rambunctious new students, ready to blossom like autumn mums. This fall the excitement was amplified by her daughter's placement on the varsity softball team. The chance to dig her cleats in as varsity catcher had wiped out Harper's back-to-school blues, and the past three weeks of practice had brought her exhaustion, healthy color, and inner contentment. Harper didn't care that the position had opened up because last year's infighting had prompted most of the varsity players to drop the sport. Harper lived for the game—any physical game, really—and she took her satisfaction where she could get it.

Someone popped out of the science office, startling Jane. Mina Rennert looked more like a flower child than a buttoned-down biology teacher. Her hair hung loose over a tie-dyed tank top and peasant skirt, and Jane smiled when she spotted an ankle tattoo and a fat collection of toe rings. When the kids were away, the teachers did play. Jane had enjoyed her own play session while Harper had been away at camp, though she tried to keep her personal life tamped down and covered, probably more than most teachers. As an unmarried, single parent, she had always felt the need to guard her privacy and reputation. Originally, she had sought to protect her daughter from the stigma of being different, but now half of the people she met assumed that she had once been married to Harper's father and the other half didn't care.

"Hey, how's it going?" Mina revealed a pack of cigarettes in her hand. "I was just headed out for a smoke. And you look like you're going camping."

Jane adjusted the rectangular canvas bags that hung from her shoulders. "I'm in charge of the canopy for the girls' softball team. They've got a game today."

"Your daughter's on the team?"

"She's the catcher."

"Awesome." Mina shook a cigarette from the pack as she fell into step beside Jane. "Catcher is a key position. Most people don't realize that. They put all the attention on the pitching."

"You know your softball."

"I used to play the outfield. That's how I met my partner."

Jane paused at the turnoff, wincing as the canopy banged

into her hip. She would have walked outside with Mina, but her real intention was to stop off and see Luke. "Then you probably remember how games can drag on for hours."

"I mostly remember the excitement and the pizza parties. And the dirt. Dust and mud. We were mud people. That was such a pisser. Tell the girls I said good luck." Mina tucked the cigarette between her lips and strode away. Jane heard the rasp of the lighter even before the double doors popped open.

Sometimes Jane wished she could be a rule-breaker like Mina, unashamed and unfettered. But Jane reminded herself that she had more to hide and more to lose. Secrets, large and small.

She recognized the Grateful Dead tune emanating from Luke's classroom. Inside, Luke sat at his desk, singing along as he worked on his laptop. His face was a study in black and white. His dark hair was cropped neatly around the ears, though unruly strands fell over his pale forehead. Slender lines of charcoal hair etched his chin and upper lip. Bold black frames could not mask the smoky wonder of his eyes. Those chocolate eyes had been the lure that had pulled her over the brink three years ago when they had gone from being friends to secret partners.

She tried to tap on the door, but the bones of the tent rammed against the threshold as she wedged herself inside. "Mr. Bandini."

"Ms. Ryan. You seem to be in need of assistance." The strain around his eyes softened as he got up from the desk and came to her. At five-eight, Luke Bandini was smaller than many of the students, spare but strong, though what he lacked in stature he made up for in a powerful presence and a voice that could boom through a classroom like rumbling thunder. He slid the heavy canopy from her shoulder while Jane let the cargo from the opposite shoulder flop to the ground. "You've got to let me help you with this. It will only take a minute, and you know how I dig construction."

"True." While Jane had already pinched her hand assembling the damn canopy for a practice, Luke had mad physics skills. He could change a tire or bake flakey biscuits because he reveled in the science of things: the engineering of a simple lever, the chemistry of butter clumps in layered dough. "I don't know," she said. "I don't want to give the team parents any more information about us than they already have."

"Hey, nothing wrong with a fellow teacher lending a hand." He pushed the door closed behind her and took her hand. A daring gesture, here at school. "Besides, I think they know about us."

"They probably do." Her fingers curled around his hand, as if holding a glimmering seashell. "But I don't want to fan the fires." Her reputation was important to Jane; she didn't want to make a misstep that might start someone digging into her past. "It's already hard for Harper, attending the same school where her mother teaches."

"I know, and I can wait." Her nerves tingled as his thumb massaged her palm. "Three years." That was their new deal, forged this summer over cheese, crackers, and a bottle of red wine their first night at Diamond Lake while Harper was off at softball camp. Marriage. Jane ached to take that step with Luke, to make it legal and official, to stop sneaking around like teenagers. Oh, to share a bed, split the chores, cook for each other, and stay in their pajamas until noon on Sunday. But she couldn't do that to Harper, not while the girl was banging through the narrow tunnel of teen angst. To bring a man into the house—even a guru-saint like Luke—might derail Harper, who perceived threats in the most innocent of actions. In three years, Harper would be off to college, and there would be breathing room for all of them. Three years was the new mantra.

"I want to go back to Diamond Lake," she said suddenly.

One dark brow lifted. "I guess that means we're on for next summer."

"I'm so high maintenance. A single parent with a live-wire daughter."

"Complexity makes for a juicier story. You've got a great story, and a cute ass."

She squeezed his hand, then let it go. Maybe their mutual attraction was amplified by the need to keep things under wraps. Other parents got the occasional free weekend through shared custody or sending their kids off for a trip to Grandma's. Jane envied them the free time, but this just wasn't her season to leave the vine. "Three years," she said.

"With a few naughty nights in between."

"Let's hope so." She went to the counter, to the supplies that she always found so amusing. Cotton balls, Popsicle sticks, and paper cups to build crash crates for eggs. A fat jar of pickles, for snacking and zapping with electrodes to demonstrate properties of electricity. "So how do your class lists look? The usual crowds?" Kids were always trying to finagle a spot in Luke's conceptual physics class, and Luke, always a sucker for a good story, usually signed them in.

He sucked air between his teeth. "I haven't even looked. Angry Bird therapy got the better of me." He lifted the pickle jar to his chest. "Would you like a kosher dill?"

"I'm good. I'd better get out there. I just wanted to firm up plans for Friday night. Harper's got that sleepover." Although Luke had begun to join Harper and her for an occasional dinner, most of their time together coincided with Harper's time away from home.

"Friday works for me." He held up the heaviest canvas bag. "So do you want me to set this up on the field? No lascivious looks, I promise."

"Your very presence out there is an admission of guilt."

"And who is it we're hiding from again? Because the parents shouldn't care, and the kids already know."

They had been over this ground a thousand times, and Jane was beginning to wonder why she kept hiding the truth. Harper was fed up with the ruse. "Mom! Everybody knows," Harper complained, usually with a dramatic roll of her eyes. "Why are you making such a big deal of this?" Jane usually countered by saying that she valued her privacy and her reputation as a teacher. To which Harper would retort that Jane was "old-school" or "random."

Jane sighed. "What the hell. We can't hide forever."

"Let me remind you, we're not breaking any laws."

"Only the unwritten code of Puritan suburbia."

Humor sparked in his eyes. "I'll wear my scarlet letter like a badge of honor."

They stepped from the dim school corridors to a crisp landscape of cerulean sky and rolling green hills. Oregon summers held a distinct beauty, with sunny, dry days and cool, starry nights and oceans of sweet, fresh air. Summers reminded Jane of the best parts of California: green lawns and barbecues and the lemony sunshine that had lit her childhood.

Built into the green hills on the elevated rim of the lake, the school campus had one of the better views in town, though the fir trees had grown so tall in the last fifty years that you could no longer see the lake that nestled in the center crevice of the horseshoe-shaped formation of hills. The school track backed up to the grassy splendor of the municipal golf course, and now the new baseball "Field of Dreams" shared a fence with an assisted living home, which had received a few foul balls but only one broken window in the three years since it had been built. Jane had grown fond of the town that she'd chosen through an online search, plugging in "best schools" and "low crime rates" as her top priorities. Mirror Lake was a place where most kids lived close enough to walk to school and parents felt secure enough to let their middle-schoolers hoof it. It was not unusual to see a handful of kids on their bikes, riding to the ice-cream store, heading to the park, or going down to the river to do some fishing. These days Mirror Lake had more of a wholesome, hometown feel than Burnson, the California home of Jane's childhood that had crumbled into bankruptcy and depression in the past decade.

As Jane and Luke rounded the snack shack, the Mirror Lake girls came into view, their yellow and blue uniforms like sunflowers dotting the soccer field. Jane recognized Harper from the way she moved, graceful and strong, as she reached up to make a catch. This was Harper's realm: the kinetic game. Something clicked when she stepped behind home plate, replacing the wary, unsure teenager with a chiseled athlete capable of controlling the entire field of players.

"First game of the year with Hoppy as varsity catcher." Luke bumped Jane on the shoulder. "You must be proud."

"I'm so nervous." But Jane knew Harper wouldn't be ruffled. The girl might melt down over a geometry test, but she was in her element out on the diamond.

"She'll do fine," Luke said. "She's a natural."

"I know she is. Look at her, laughing with Emma. She doesn't get rattled by competition."

"When you come from a place of confidence, there's no need to stress. And for all other worrisome details, Harper has you to do the worrying for her," Luke teased.

"I'm glad someone appreciates me."

"Oh, I appreciate."

"Hi, Mom!" Harper shouted, waving before she whipped her arm back and shot a ball across the field to her warm-up partner. Hair the color of dark cider was pulled back in a ponytail, as usual, and Harper's new aviator shades resembled those of a Hollywood actress hiding from the press. Even her stern, tomboyish style of dress could not disguise the fact that Harper was a beautiful girl. But then, all the girls at Mirror Lake High possessed a distinct splendor, a signature movement or energy that they weren't quite comfortable with yet.

Jane waved back, glad that it was a good day. Since she'd started high school, Harper had vacillated between proudly owning her mother and pretending she didn't exist.

Many of the girls called greetings to "Ms. Ryan" and "Mr. Bandini."

"Hey there, Mr. Bandini." Olivia Ferguson turned toward him, ball in her mitt, and lunged to stretch her long haunches. "Are you coming to watch our game, too?"

The innuendo was not lost on Jane. Olivia never missed a chance to probe.

"Not today, Olivia."

"Aw. You should stay." When she stretched her arms overhead, her full breasts protruded against her tight jersey. A woman's body and an adolescent brain were a dangerous combination. Or maybe Olivia had matured since she'd been a student in Jane's freshman English class. "No one ever comes to our games." Olivia pouted.

Luke did not break stride as he flashed a pleasant smile. "Maybe some other time. Did you ladies have a good summer?"

The girls gave bland smiles, then turned back to practice.

Over at the ball field, the girls of the West Green team ran a lap around the outfield, a forest of thick, green giants. Local legend had it that everything grew bigger in West Green. The visiting coach was sharing her roster with the umpire, a stout, gray-haired man with a serious demeanor. It was always a relief to have a calm, seasoned person officiating; teenage umpires were so easily rattled.

Some of the parents had already set up chairs along the foul line. At the grassy edge of the outfield, Linda Ferguson lay on a blanket reading a book. One bare foot bent back over her butt as if she were a beach bunny. Linda's husband, Pete, hovered over the coach, who sat on the team bench working on the lineup. Legs crossed and head down, Carrie didn't seem interested in Pete's opinion, but no one in the Ferguson family read or respected body language. Although Harper had not played with Olivia yet, Harper had already been strong-armed by seventeen-year-old Olivia during practices. And Jane had been warned by a few of the softball moms that the Fergusons had been at the center of last year's varsity turmoil. A believer in education, Jane hoped that this year the Fergusons might learn a few lessons about teamwork.

Fortunately, two of Harper's friends since grade school were on the team with her, which gave Jane two instant "mom" friends, stable, capable women with a sense of humor and perspective. She headed toward Trish Schiavone, the most down-to-earth mom on the team. Trish squatted beside three grade-school kids, digging through a flexible cooler. "Did we really leave all the juice packs in the car? Kids, Mom is losing her marbles." Trish stood up and sprinted past Jane. "Be back in a sec."

Jane set her bag down and opened the canvas tote. "How are you kids doing today?"

"We're okay," Trish's daughter said, scratching her freckled nose. "But my mom is losing her marbles."

"I hate when that happens." As Jane set up her chair, she eavesdropped on bits of conversation: talk of a new wine bar in town, tales of summer vacation, and something about Olivia Ferguson. Summer camp? Jane recalled that Olivia had spent three weeks at a "superstar" softball camp, a pricey operation that promised amazing results. Harper had begged on her knees for the opportunity—"Please! Oh, please, please, please, Mama-dish!"—but Jane had explained that they couldn't afford a camp that would cost the same as a semester's tuition at the state university. The parent chatter was a bit more heated than usual today, with someone making a barb that "you can't buy athletic skill" and someone else expressing worry that the team would suffer. She sensed that the controversy swirled around the Fergusons.

Sinking into her chair, Jane tipped her face to the blue sky and vowed to remain neutral. As a teacher, she had to steer clear of the social dynamics that pitted parents against each other. Still, as a parent, she needed to advocate for her daughter. She walked a fine line, but wasn't life a series of choices and compromises? "Maintain balance," her yoga teacher said cheerfully. Such a good lesson for anyone.

Over by the team bench, Luke was just about finished working his magic, connecting poles and unfolding canvas to unfurl the canopy over the home team bench. Carrie still penciled notations on her clipboard, mindless of the tent rising over her as she fended off Pete Ferguson. It was unlike the two of them not to lend Luke a hand. Jane took out her cell and texted him.

Thanks. You're my hero.

The home team galloped over from the practice field, a herd of powerful, wild fillies. Some of the parents cheered, though most had their heads down, eyes locked on cell phones. Linda Ferguson had come in from the outfield, her blanket neatly folded under her arm as she talked with her husband. Clearly unhappy, they sat apart from the covey of parents.

When Trish returned with a carton of juice pouches, she was distracted, scowling toward the tiered parking lot that cut into the hillside. She leaned close to Jane, muttering under her breath. "There's some man sitting in a car down there."

Jane rose and turned toward the parking lot.

"A silver Chevy. Second tier."

Jane couldn't tell which car that was from here, and Luke had already disappeared.

Trish dug her fingers into the end of the carton and dumped the juice into the small cooler. "Okay, guys. You can each take one for now." The kids took their juice and scooters and headed toward the path. "And don't go down by the parking lot," Trish called after them.

"Should I call the police?" Jane said in a near whisper. "Or the office? Gray Tarkington will check him out." At six-foot-five, their vice principal was a tower of intimidation.

"He wasn't doing anything illegal," Trish said as they walked over for a closer look. The middle tier was a good hundred yards away, but from the ridge of the ball field they had a clear view. "It just gave me the creeps. I mean, he wasn't talking on a cell, and any parent picking up his kid goes to the front of the school."

"It is weird," Jane agreed. "We need to trust our instincts. It wouldn't hurt to get his plate number."

Sunlight glinted off a silver car as it backed out of a space and crawled up the hill toward the exit. It happened too fast and far away to make out any details.

"There he goes."

"Well. That's a relief." Jane promised to relay a description of the driver—a dark-haired, middle-aged male—to the administrative staff. "It's always good to report these things."

"Right? You never know," Trish agreed as they returned to their seats.

A few years ago, the report of a loitering dark-haired man would have sent Jane into a panic, but time had eased her fears. She still double-checked the locks at night, and her reserved demeanor kept most strangers at bay, but with each passing year the cloak of security grew stronger.

Without fanfare the game began as a West Green player grounded to first. Trish cheered for their pitcher KK Dalton, whose parents had missed most of last year's games.

"Come on, girlfriend," Trish shouted. "You can do it."

Jane smiled. Trish was way cooler than she was.

"Good afternoon, Jane." A chuckle came from beside her, and she found Keiko Suzuki squatting gracefully beside her chair. Jane had met Keiko when their girls were in the same preschool class, and over the years they had weathered a few parenting storms together. "You look like you're enjoying the sun, and I hate to bother you on this beautiful day."

"You could never be a bother," Jane said, and she meant it. She had always found Emma's mother to be kind, poised, and patient. Besides that, Jane was mystified at the way Keiko managed to hold down a job with a state agency, volunteer at school, and still attend every game.

"So much going on. Have you heard Pete Ferguson's new plan?"

"Tell me."

"Apparently, Olivia was told she is playing the wrong position for her body type." Keiko pressed a pale hand to her clavicle, wistful and respectful. Years ago, Jane had learned that a word for "no" did not exist in the Japanese language, and she saw that penchant for stating things positively in Emma and her mother. "That's what they were teaching at this softball camp. They said she is too tall and big-boned to be a shortstop."

"Really? Just like that."

"This is a new theory, but the Fergusons are taking it very seriously." Keiko gazed at the coach as she spoke. Linda had joined her husband, apparently double-teaming Carrie, who was not making eye contact.

"And they're badgering Carrie to switch Olivia's position," Jane said, narrating the scene before them. "What position did the experts tell Olivia she should be playing?"

"That's the concern," Keiko sighed. "I'm afraid she wants to be the catcher."

Chapter 2

Jane tried to stay in the moment and avoid falling into a pit of worry, but the game moved slowly for the first few innings. Foul balls and full counts. She watched for signs that Harper's performance was impaired by news of Olivia's plan, but Harper remained fluid and energetic, batting in two runs in the second inning. She couldn't have heard.

A breeze swept in from the west, brushing across the golf course that bordered the school grounds and bringing the scent of freshly mown grass with it. Jane took a deep breath and savored the moment; it was too easy to take Mirror Lake's beauty for granted and get caught up in small, biting worries that would pass.

In the top of the fourth, the tension thickened as the home team pitcher began to weaken and West Green loaded the bases with no outs. Crap. Jane squirmed as Harper stopped a wild pitch in the dirt. KK's face was beet red; the poor girl was falling apart. On the next pitch there was a bland chinking sound as the ball popped straight up. Harper scrambled to her feet, ripped off her face mask, and edged over to the chalk line by first base.

"I got it!" Sydney Schiavone called from first base. The ball seemed to hover in the air forever. At last, it looped down, right into Syd's mitt.

"Yes!" Jane cheered. But it wasn't over. Sydney shot the ball to home, where the runner was closing in on Harper. In one glorious motion Harper tagged the runner out and lobbed the ball to third base for a triple play.

"Out!" the umpire shouted.

"That's what I'm talking 'bout!" Trish high-fived Jane, who whooped with delight amid the thundering parent contingent. In the years of watching her daughter play ball, Jane had learned that you had to celebrate the great moments.

As the fielders met for a fist bump on their way to the bench, Jane saw elation in her daughter's face.

She's a great catcher, Jane thought as Harper scooped up a batting helmet. *Don't take that away from her.*

Maternal instincts ran deep, Jane knew that, but she thought she had honed hers down to her daughter's specific needs. She had to protect the light that shone inside her daughter, and for Harper that flame had always burned for activity. From the time Harper could move, she had been an active baby, rolling and crawling and pulling up on anything she could get a grip on. She had hated being cradled and insisted on being held so that she could face out and observe the world.

Those first few months had been a trial. More often than not, Harper would awaken from sleep screaming and writhing, as if someone were pressing a knife in her belly. Colic did not begin to describe the inconsolable crying jags, the harsh glare of pain in her periwinkle eyes, the long nights of pacing. Jane's stress had been increased by the fact that she was cut off from her family in California, living off her savings in the Seattle area as she cared for Harper and contemplated her next move.

Marnie had been a lifesaver. Even as she juggled a marriage, a child, and a teaching job, Marnie had managed to find the time to drop by with a dinner plate or to take all the kids out to the park after school. When Jane had asked Marnie and her husband Jason to be Harper's godparents, Marnie had thrown a celebration back at the house, including a small group of family and neighbors. Although Harper had slept through the church ceremony, stirring only slightly when water was poured over her head, she had awoken at Marnie's house in a blistering mood. The warmth of the kitchen, the noise level, and the food smells—it was all too much. Escaping out to the back deck, Jane had come upon an elderly man, staring out over the yard.

"Sorry," she had said, moving Harper to her other arm. Although the first blast of cool air had reduced the volume of the baby's wails, she was still whimpering. "You came out here looking for peace and quiet, and now you have a baby crying in your ear."

"I'm glad to hear it. Reminds me of the fierce emotion of youth." When he had turned toward them, she had noticed the folds of skin at his jowls and neck, like her Grandpa Harold had. The man looked to be every bit of ninety, but there had been a calm intelligence in his eyes. "Still sharp as a tack," Marnie had said. When he'd been introduced as Marnie's great-uncle, he'd teased that he liked that title. "Like Alexander the Great. You can call me George the Great, if you like."

He had touched the white bootee on Harper's foot, and she had given a sour yowl. "Yes, I know. At least when you cry, you've got a wonderful mother to comfort you."

Harper's face had puckered, and a sob had bleated past her rosy lips.

"I'm sorry. It's not you. She cries all the time."

"It's what babies do best. It doesn't make them any less magnificent."

She had switched Harper's position and begun rocking from side to side. "It's hard to see the magnificence when she drags you out of bed at four in the morning."

"An ungodly hour," George had agreed. "She's lucky to have you. I look at her and see what a good life she's going to have. With a loving mother, this little one will grow and learn. Ah, what joyous discoveries she has ahead of her."

Jane had smiled. "That's quite a prediction for such a grumpy baby."

"She's learning how to find her happy place, and you're nurturing her through this rough time."

Harper had been quiet then. Jane had thought she might have drifted off to sleep, but when she tipped her head down, Harper's periwinkle eyes had been shiny bright and wide as quarters. Both mother and child had taken to Uncle George; maybe it was the deep, raspy timbre of his voice.

"This is the most important job of your life," George had said. "I know it doesn't seem that way now. Time puts a golden light on some things. I wish I'd had an ounce of patience when I was raising my kids. But I loved them, and they turned out just fine."

"Harper doesn't have a father."

"And that will be her normal. No father, but who needs that when you've got a terrific mother like you?"

"You're too kind."

He had shaken his head. "Just observant. And a little jealous. My life is in the final act, and yours is just beginning. I envy you your future...such an important future as a mother. You just took on the biggest job of your life."

At the time, Jane had not seen the big picture of raising a child; the formative years and early development were lost in her focus on survival. One diaper change to the next. The rare moments of quiet between crying jags. The rewarding smiles and knowledge that these robotic days would pass were rare. But George the Great's advice had eased her through Harper's first year. She had a goal. She was raising a child, a new person.

Just days before her first birthday, Harper had risen for the first time in the middle of the kitchen floor and walked away from the pot Jane had given her to play with. She had simply walked off and disappeared into the living room. With a whoop of excitement, Jane had followed her in. Harper had dropped to all fours and rapidly crawled to the couch, where she pulled herself up to her feet, mouthed the arm, and tried to climb it. And just like that, Harper had graduated from baby to climbing toddler. Stairs, sofa arms, banisters . . . nothing was safe from the limber body of Harper scaling to the heights. But with the freedom of movement had come liberation. No longer trapped in a bouncy chair or stroller, Harper had stopped crying and traveled wherever she wanted to go.

Harper's fascination with basketball had emerged when she was barely three. When Jane had tried to interest her in the play structure at the park, Harper had ventured over to one of the basketball hoops and stationed herself under the net. On their cul-de-sac, loaded with Toys "R" Us's brightest trucks, wagons, and tricycles, Harper kept wandering to the Tullys' hoop, where one or two basketballs always sat on the edge of the curb. From her spot under the hoop, Harper would turn the ball in her pudgy hands, her round blue eyes searching its rugged surface.

"Honey, that's not your ball," Jane would say.

And then Nancy Tully would hurry out of the house and melt over Harper's adorability. "Let her play. Anytime. We put that hoop up so that we could have our kids right under our noses." Nancy's teenage sons had gotten such a charge out of seeing Harper with the ball. As days wore on and the little girl doggedly posted herself under the hoop, the boys had begun to work with her, grabbing the rebounds and demonstrating shots. Evan would squat down to be on her level. "We gotta make it a fair game," he had insisted. Carter used to hoist Harper up so that she could stuff the ball. "Slam dunk!"

Harper would say. The Tully boys had taught her well. They were grown now; Carter was nearly thirty with two kids of his own, and Evan was studying to be a physician's assistant. Jane would always be grateful to them, though Harper was embarrassed to see them now. "Mom, don't tell my friends those stories about Carter and Evan," Harper would say, pulling a hood over her shiny dark hair. "It's so embarrassing."

Jane had been awed by her daughter's determination. Where did her drive come from? Certainly not from Jane, who had suffered through high school PE, overweight and uncoordinated. She had been a bookworm by default, whereas Harper's blood ran thick with determination to move. In the early days, when you couldn't even see Harper's little head behind the basketball, Jane had figured the girl would eventually lose interest. She couldn't score a basket; she couldn't even hit the rim. But Harper had refused to give up. Determined to give the little girl some satisfaction, Jane had purchased a short plastic kiddie hoop...and the gaming began. Of course, Harper had scorned the kid-sized balls as inferior. Nothing but the real deal for her.

By kindergarten, Harper was taking part in clinics for older kids, and Jane had sat in the bleachers, intrigued by her daughter's fierce concentration on dribbling between cones and controlling bounce passes. In school, Hoppy lagged behind the other kids a bit, but she loved books, insisted that Jane read to her every night before bed. The poster Harper had made in kindergarten still hung on the bulletin board by the kitchen door. Next to a drawing of Dr. Seuss's Cat in the Hat, with his red-and-white-striped hat, whiskers, and amused smile, Harper had printed CAT IN THE HOP. The teacher had thought it was a minor mistake, but Harper had insisted that it was intentional. "That's 'cuz I like *Cat in the Hat* and *Hop on Pop*, both of them, so I wrote them together." Jane couldn't have been more pleased and proud; in that moment, she had realized that her daughter, though not conventionally brilliant, saw the world through a different filter.

By second grade, Harper had developed an unconventional left-handed hook shot that flabbergasted other "Little Hoopers." The parent coach had worried that Harper's unconventional shot might injure the developing arm muscles, but Harper had scowled at the idea of learning another way, and Jane had let her be. Basketball was Harper's comfort and joy.

When the third-grade coach convinced some of the girls to try softball in the spring, Harper had gravitated to the bulky catcher's equipment. She had told Jane that she felt safe behind the catcher's mask and padding, and she liked the position at the plate "so I can keep my eyes on everything." That had made Jane wonder if some of her fears had seeped into her daughter's psyche. Did Harper sense that she was being raised in hiding, camouflaged by a different name, a distant state, and a suburban landscape?

"You can't change the truth," Jane's therapist had said. "Someday, she'll need to know about her father."

Jane understood the power of the truth. It was the very reason she had held back the details about Harper's father for all these years. Would Harper want to know that her father was an avid surfer? The crash of a wave in Half Moon Bay came to mind, and now Jane wondered if that was true. Maybe Frank hadn't been a surfer at all. So much of his image had been built on lies, a wavering mirage designed for maximum appeal.

No, she would not credit him for passing amazing agility and athletic prowess on to Harper. Her steely concentration as she crouched behind the batters, her rapid response in the heat of a play, and the powerful connection between the ball and her bat. Harper commanded the field, inspiring awe. Other parents had mentioned her scholarship potential. "A girl like Harper will get a full ride," Coach Carrie had said, more than once. Jane just thanked them and hoped her daughter would develop the academic skills to make it into a good college.

The game was tied in the bottom of the ninth when Harper dug her cleats into the red soil at the plate and cocked her bat. That bat had given Jane pause; she'd been told that her daughter needed a three-hundred-and-fifty-dollar Louisville Slugger. "A bat that costs the same as a month of groceries?" Jane had asked Harper and her batting coach, who was already twenty-five an hour. "Why can't she keep using the team bats?" But the coach had explained how important the length, weight, composition, and balance of a fast-pitch bat were to the success of a hitter. He'd used phrases like "composite carbon fiber" and "good pop right out of the box." Seeing the plaintive look on her daughter's face, Jane had caved. And the coach had been right. "Blue Lightning," as the bat had been dubbed, had added a good twenty feet to Harper's hitting distance, and she reported no sting when she made contact with the ball. Blue Lightning had been worth a few ramen noodle dinners.

"Be a hitter!" Pete Ferguson barked at Harper from right behind the backstop. Bad form.

Harper connected on the first pitch, with a resounding clang of Blue Lightning. The ball soared out in a beautiful wide arc, sailing over the players' heads and the home-run fence. The home team roared. The West Green girls slouched on the field as Harper ran the bases, and then, the first game of fall ball was over.

Jane couldn't help but smile as she folded up her chair. She had been planning what to say to the coach, to defend Harper's position as catcher. But a triple play and a home run would definitely sweeten the conversation.

*   *   *

Afterward, the Mirror Lake contingent headed over to Pizza Kingdom for a victory dinner. The girls took over two large tables, and then fluttered like a flock of finches up the stairs to the loft, where pinball and air hockey and the claw beckoned. Jane was happy to settle into a booth with Trish, Keiko, and Cheree and Mike Berry, who had made it to the game for the last few innings. Cheree also taught at Mirror Lake, and over the years Jane had taken some pointers on parenting as she'd watched Cheree reel in her older kids, who were now in college. As Jane listened to summer stories of camping trips and Disneyland, chickens wandering from their coops and children fishing at Diamond Lake, she watched Pete Ferguson make the rounds. Beer in hand, he moved from table to table like a motivational speaker working a crowd. Jane was just finishing her first slice when he hit their table.

"So did you hear about Olivia's experience with the Starmaker people? What a great camp. You need to think about sending your girls there next summer. It was a transformational experience," he said with a lift of his beer mug.

"Our team is fortunate that Olivia had a chance to sharpen her playing skills," Keiko said diplomatically.

"It really showed tonight," Trish said. "Our girls played well together, didn't they? It's hard to believe they've only been a team for a few weeks. And when you think about it, they're absolutely remarkable for such a young team."

Jane chewed a piece of crust, loving the way Trish turned the conversation back toward the team.

"That's right," said Mike. "Olivia and Sarah are the only seniors. Pretty unusual for a varsity team."

"Yeah. True. But see, the Starmakers have this theory of softball that really works. It's all about body type. The way you're built dictates the position you play on the field."

"So it all boils down to genetics," Jane said.

"Exactly!"

Shades of eugenics, Jane thought as she plucked a mushroom from the platter. Trish arched an eyebrow, but kept mum.

"Here's the thing." Pete leaned in over the table so that no one could avoid looking at him. "Each position requires a specific body type. Second base and shortstop need a fast, wiry body to move fast. The first baseman needs height so she can snatch up those high throws to first. And your catcher needs to be big and strong to stop everything at the plate. Runners, pitches, you name it. I know, it may sound very basic, but the reality of it hit home with Olivia. She's got the perfect body of a catcher. It's all about genetics."

Jane was leaning away from his beer breath when he turned to her.

"And your daughter? She's a great player, but she's too slight to be behind home plate. Definitely an infield player."

"Harper's doing a pretty good job where she is," Trish said. "And I think we parents should stay out of it. Leave the coaching to the coaches."

"Carrie knows her stuff," Cheree agreed. "And the girls really like her." Carrie had coached most of the girls on last year's junior varsity team.

"Carrie is good people," Pete agreed, "but her best is only as good as her knowledge. That's why I'm sharing what we learned this summer. It's revolutionary." A spray of saliva blossomed over their table.

"Is that so?" Mike asked, sliding out of the booth.

"It's an absolute truth."

"My turn to buy the beer." Mike gestured for Pete to follow, and the two men headed to the counter.

Trish smacked her forehead. "Can you stand it? We're all genetically inferior to Olivia."

Jane and Keiko laughed.

"And that's quite a poor strategy," Keiko added. "To position Olivia against Harper, who is probably our team's best all-around player."

"That's kind of you to say, but I don't cherish my daughter's being the Fergusons' target."

"And he spit on our pizza." Cheree started dabbing at the remaining pizza with a napkin. "Did you see that? That's just gross."

The women chuckled.

"Oh, it's hopeless," Trish said. "The pizza, I mean. It's got cooties now."

"Your husband is a saint," Jane told Cheree.

"Don't let him hear that or he'll never unload the dishwasher again." Cheree was the chair of the high school English department, a strong, down-to-earth leader. Over the years, Jane had come to admire her for her unflappable, sanguine calm.

"This is going to be an interesting season." Keiko's eyes were dark with impending omen.

"I would like to have an exciting season," Trish said. "Fun. Even challenging. But interesting? Look, if I want to get burned, I'll add some cayenne to my chili. If I want drama, I'll watch *Housewives*. I don't need these shenanigans on my daughter's softball team."

"Same here," Jane agreed. "I swore off the adrenaline rush of drama a long time ago."

"Oh, I think we all get enough drama from our daughters." Keiko leaned back in the booth. "My daughter says she's getting her arms tattooed when she turns eighteen." She ran her slender hands down her arms. "Sleeves, they call them."

"No!" Trish gasped.

Keiko nodded. "Emma is emphatic about it. My husband says that this is not the thinking of a Japanese child, and Emma responds that she is American. I think she will kill her father before his time."

"She'll probably change her mind before she hits eighteen," said Cheree.

"Or maybe she'll compromise with a tiny tattoo on her butt," Trish suggested.

"Harper hasn't mentioned a tattoo," Jane said, "but if Emma is thinking about it, I'm sure my daughter isn't far behind. Here's a story for Emma. My friend Laura got a butterfly on her wrist the minute she turned eighteen. A few years later, the summer after graduation, when she was interviewing for teaching jobs, she had to wear long-sleeved shirts to cover the ink. Back then, the tattoo would have been a deal breaker for a teacher. It was a hot summer, and she really suffered. The principal who hired her later admitted that he wondered if she was covering up needle marks. Laura only got the job because the principal was personal friends with one of her references."

"See? That's the thing." Trish stabbed a finger in the air. "Our kids don't realize that people will hold things like a tattoo against you when you're trying to get a job."

As the gathering began to wind down, Jane was sorry to see it end. Although she had met most of these women through her daughter's sports, she enjoyed the "mom solidarity" she shared with them. There was some consolation in knowing that other teenage girls went crazy from time to time.

The women were sliding out of the booth when Cheree called to Jane. "Before I forget, there's something I wanted to tell you."

Jane didn't like the lines of concern on Cheree's forehead. "What's up?"

"I just wanted to give you a heads-up. Dr. Gallaway was going to tell you, but since I was there, I told her I'd speak to you. This afternoon a man came into the office looking for you. Very polite and clean cut, but he wasn't there on school business."

Fear curled through Jane, sickening, cloying. She forced herself to keep breathing, chest expanding, then compressing. "Are you sure he wasn't a parent?"

"At least he was honest about that part. Dr. G asked if he wanted to leave a message or business card, but he declined. When I asked his name, he just smiled and said he'd catch up with you somewhere else."

No, no, no. It couldn't be.

"Did you get a good look at him?" Jane asked.

"I did. I took notice because he was a good-looking guy and a bit of a charmer, too. He's about medium height, dark hair, broad shoulders, and in good shape. He was wearing khakis and a shirt with a collar. Office casual."

Tall, dark, and charming; it was him.

Jane could imagine him working the angles, schmoozing the office staff. Even Dr. Gallaway would have been intrigued, despite her demeanor of cool professionalism.

"Do you have a child in the school?" the principal would have asked.

His smile would have been apologetic.

"Can I ask the nature of your business?"

"I'd rather not say," he would have answered with a glint in his periwinkle eyes. As if he had a joyous surprise in store that he couldn't bear to spoil.

When the truth was that he had traveled hundreds of miles to find her. He had come to kill her. And if he found out about Harper, he would kill her, too.

Chapter 3

Dubstep music throbbed through the car as Jane drove home. After they'd discussed and dismissed Olivia's scheme, Jane had let Harper turn to her station, hoping that the music would keep the girl from noticing that her mother was shaken to the core.

Should she call the police? While it might be a relief to think of the Mirror Lake Police Department as a resource standing behind her, she wasn't sure she could impress the urgency of the situation upon them.

I'm afraid of a man who assaulted me fifteen years ago.

Would they tell her to file a police report back home in Burnson? Impossible. No one there would help her, even if she were crazy enough to go back. When it had happened, she had known many of the cops, his friends and coworkers. She had tried to imagine herself opening the glass and steel door to the precinct. Stepping right up to the sergeant's desk. Sitting with a cop as she provided dates and details. As she spelled out his name. "Frank, short for Francis. Yes, your buddy, Francis Dixon. One of your own."

"Say a word to anyone and I'll kill you," he had whispered in her ear. "And don't even think about calling the cops. They take this shit seriously now. You open your mouth and I could lose my job. If that ever happens, no one will ever find you. I know how to make people disappear into little pieces. Your parents will never know what happened to you. They'll never find you, because I have friends. I'm Tony Soprano." He'd laughed at that. "I know how to take care of business."

As Jane turned onto the street leading to their cul-de-sac, she wondered about their safety now, tonight, in their home. Did he know where they lived? Back at the pizza place she had called Luke and asked him to meet her at the house. She needed time to talk with Luke, time to assess the danger and risk, time to figure out if she was being prudent or paranoid.

"Why so mysterious?" he'd asked, and she'd promised to explain. She owed him that much, especially if he was going to brave this hornet's nest with her. He already knew some of her history—that she came with baggage—but she hadn't shared the worst of it.

She tapped the steering wheel nervously, thinking of her plan for the night. Jane would impose on another parent to take Harper, and she would go to Luke's place. The trick would be orchestrating this without arousing Harper's suspicions.

Jane lowered the volume on the radio.

"Hey! You said it was okay."

"I'm wondering if you might want to have a sleepover tonight. The summer is winding down fast."

"Really? Can I have two people over?"

"I was thinking you could stay with Sydney or Emma. I've got an early morning meeting tomorrow." It was a lie, but by morning it might be true. She could be meeting with the police. She might be meeting with her principal, warning Dr. G about her stalker.

"Emma! No, she has Japanese school all day tomorrow. Sydney. Call her mom. Only I want to bring some microwave popcorn over. They've got that air popper, and it tastes like cardboard."

"Okay. You can grab your toothbrush and pj's, and I'll shoot you over to her house."

"I need to take a shower first."

"You can do that there." Jane wanted her daughter out of the house as quickly as possible.

"Gross! There's a million little kids at her house."

Jane did not reply as she turned onto the cul-de-sac, checking for anything out of the ordinary. The Tiffany lamp inside their front window—the one on the timer—glowed in red and blue jewel tones. Luke's Volvo was parked in front of the Japanese maple. The Tullys' truck sat in their driveway. The Larsens had their spotlights on, illuminating the rock wall of their house and the fat trunk of the sequoia that filled their yard. Jane breathed in, trying to steady her rapid heartbeat. Okay, so far.

"Is that Mr. Bandini's car?" Harper's fingers were already pressing the button to open the garage door.

"It is. He's helping me with something."

For once, Harper didn't tease or question her about Luke. Jane gave the exterior of the house one last look, then rolled into the garage.

Jane popped the trunk so that Harper could retrieve her gear and then paused at the open garage bay. She wanted to run down the driveway and melt into Luke's arms. Solid, dependable Luke. But with Harper watching, restraint was a necessity.

"Hey, there," he said.

"Thanks for coming." She blinked back tears and hurried back into the garage to check the house. Inside the laundry room, the alarm beeped steadily—a normal signal. The panel of solid green lights revealed that there had been no tampering with doors or windows. Relief began to seep in as she disarmed the alarm and ventured inside. Everything was in its place: the key rack, the Cat in the Hop poster, the bowl of apples on the counter. The cookie jar contained its small stack of cash. Phoenix was asleep on her big slab of pillow by the family room windows, another sign that all was well. The golden retriever was fiercely protective of their home, and she usually met Jane at the door when something out of the ordinary—from squirrel activity on the deck to a package delivery on the porch—had occurred while she was gone.

Behind her, she heard the garage door rolling shut as Luke and Harper chatted. Harper stepped into the laundry room with her green-and-black-checkered backpack, recounting the game. Luke lugged in her heavy bat bag, and Harper showed him where to stow it in the laundry room closet.

"Mom? Did you call Mrs. Schiavone yet?"

"I'm calling now." Jane punched the contact on her cell phone and hurried up the stairs to check the bedrooms. Not that she doubted the alarm system; she just had to see for herself. As she squared things away with Trish, she patrolled upstairs. The windows were closed and locked, though Harper's bedroom looked like a laundry bomb had exploded.

"Mom?" Harper stood in the doorway of her room, hands on her hips. "What are you doing in here?"

"It's amazing that you have any underwear left with the collection scattered on the floor." Jane stepped over a purple-and-white-striped bra for emphasis.

Harper scowled as she tugged the band from her dark hair. "This is so random."

"Take your shower. Make it fast."

Jane waited upstairs until she heard the shower running, then went down to Luke.

He sat cross-legged on the floor, giving the dog a good rub-down. "Everything okay?"

"So far." When she sank down onto the floor near him, she realized her limbs were quivering. "I'm so scared," she whispered, leaning her head toward Phoenix to draw some peace from the gentle dog named after the mythological creature that had recreated itself. Jane was all about rising from the ashes. "I'm going to run Harper over to her friend's house, but while she's showering we can talk. I think my worst nightmare has caught up with me."

"Frank?" When she nodded, he patted the dog and shifted his hands to her knees. "Tell me."

She told him about the man seen in the school parking lot at the game, and then about the "charming" visitor who'd been asking for her in the office. "They described him as having dark hair, medium build. Friendly and amiable. It's Frank."

"Shit." His voice was hushed as he rubbed his knuckles over his jaw. "And why is he here after all this time? It's been... what? Fifteen, sixteen years?"

A shiver ran through her as Frank's words rattled in her brain: *Don't think you're going to get away. I'll hunt you down and kill you.* She shook her head. "I know he's vindictive. Maybe he's been busy with someone else until now. Maybe something set him off. He could have run into my mother in Burnson. Mom was always trying to get us back together."

"He really had her snowed."

"He was a skillful manipulator, and my mother wasn't very good at advocating for her kids. Besides, she was old-school. She believed that a woman could not be fulfilled without a husband." The wounds of the past still ached when Jane allowed herself to revisit those days. She had told Luke about that Sunday morning when Dad was off at mass. Jane had been asleep in her old bedroom, huddled under the blue and gold star comforter. She had escaped to the safety of her parents' house two days earlier, telling them she could never go back to Frank. Dad had accepted her decision, but Mom kept picking. "What could be so bad that you two can't work it out?" Sandra Flannery kept probing. "It's not all hearts and flowers in a relationship. Sometimes you have to make sacrifices to make things work." Pride had kept Jane from spilling all the details. The veiled threats. The manipulations. She had thought her parents would keep her safe because she was their daughter. She had been wrong. When the bedroom door had creaked open and Frank's hot breath had hit her cheek, a shrill alarm had torn through her.

"Get your ass out of bed, princess," he had said in a cloyingly sweet voice. "You're coming home with me."

When Jane had refused, he had reminded her that he had a gun, lifting the leg of his jeans to reveal the ankle holster containing his off-duty revolver. *But you won't use that on me . . . will you?* When she'd studied his face to see if he was kidding, the cold, impassive look in his eyes had been all the answer she needed.

The hour that followed had been surreal. Jane had been forced to sit at the kitchen table with a cup of bitter coffee while her mother served homemade coffeecake to Frank and doled out relationship advice. Jane had tried to get her message across without getting a rise from Frank. She had said she needed time to think. That she wanted to stay here at home. Frank's eyes had glowered, but Sandra hadn't picked up on the cry for help. Sandra Flannery had countered that Jane should appreciate having a man who cared enough to stand up for her. In the end, Mom might as well have wrapped Jane up with a giant bow and presented her as a gift.

"Just tell me what you need," Luke said, rubbing her shoulder. "We're going to keep you safe."

Jane leaned into him, scared but grateful. Thank God for Luke, her substitute family. Most people assumed her parents were dead when she said she had no family. She had shared some of the truth with Luke, but it wasn't a conversation topic she enjoyed. It was painful to admit that she'd had to cut her family off. She had sent a few e-mails to let her folks know that she was okay, but she knew her mother couldn't be trusted with an address or a phone number.

She had changed her name from Jane Flannery to Jane Ryan. And then, a few months after Harper was born, she had left Seattle. She'd figured any paper trail would stop there. She had closed out her credit cards and opened a few accounts in her new name. She had pretended that she was in the witness protection program and had tried to make a fresh start in a new place. A new person.

"I just wonder," she said, staring off at a piece of Harper's artwork on the wall. "Why now, after all this time? It's been years, and I thought I covered all my tracks."

"That's a good question." Luke rested his chin on his fingertips. "You've moved twice and changed your name. How did he find you?"

"He's a cop. Above the law. They can get into databases. The DMV. Phone records. God knows what else. And Frank can be very persuasive." She raked her toffee hair back with both hands. "I've gone soft these past few years. I let myself believe that I had gotten away, that he had moved on to some other obsession."

"You deserve to feel safe . . . to have a life. Don't beat yourself up for trying to live."

"It's not just me." She picked up the small leather mitt that Phoenix now used as a chewy toy. It had been Harper's first softball glove. "I've got a daughter to take care of—my greatest responsibility—and I can't put her in jeopardy."

Luke squinted, skeptical. "Do you really think Frank would go after a kid?"

"I can't even imagine what he'd do if he found out about Hoppy. He didn't want kids. During his rants he used to talk about ending the insanity of the human race. Stopping the madness. He set me up to have an abortion, but I slipped away before it could happen." She buried her face in her hands. "I can't let anything happen to her."

"We won't. Count me in on this. I got your back."

The shower shut off upstairs, replaced by the blare of the blow dryer. Jane scrambled to her feet. "I've got to get Hoppy over to Sydney's, and then maybe we can spend the night at your place. I feel like a target here."

"Sure. Whatever feels right." Sitting there cross-legged, Luke radiated confidence and concern. She had never loved him more than in that moment. "You do have an alarm system and a guard dog, but my place is a better bet. I doubt that Frank has tracked you there yet."

"Plus you've got a gun. A big plus." Despite Oregon's liberal gun laws, Jane had never been able to bring herself to buy a weapon. She'd always worried that it might be used against her, stolen, or discovered by Harper and her friends.

He took her hands in his. "Janie . . . your hands are like Popsicles." He sandwiched them between his palms and rubbed heat into her. "We'll get through this. Let me drop Harper off while you pack some stuff. We can bring Phoenix to my place for good measure."

Fortunately, Harper was okay with being chauffeured by Luke. "I need a hug," Jane told her daughter as she waited by the door, checkered backpack slung over one shoulder.

Harper wrinkled her nose, then opened her arms. "Why so weird, Mom?"

"Am I not allowed to hug my daughter anymore?" Jane closed her eyes as she breathed in the floral scent of shampoo mixed with a cake batter–scented perfume that Harper and her friends had all fallen in love with.

"Whatever. We've got practice at four, but some of us are going to the swim park in the morning."

"Just text me when you make a move," Jane said. "And no hanging here in the morning. I've got some work to get done at the school."

Harper groaned. "When am I going to be old enough to be trusted at home? Everybody else has friends over when their parents are at work."

"You're not everybody else. You're special, honey."

Harper rolled her eyes and ducked out the door. "Bye, Mom."

"Be right back," Luke promised.

Jane turned the deadbolt and peered out through the peephole, but she couldn't see them walking to Luke's car. The small tunnel of vision it afforded her was nearly useless. She sank against the door. She hoped she was doing the right thing, entrusting Harper to someone else's care. For years she'd walked in fear of Frank, making contingency plans and escape routes, but when a decade had gone by without any sign of trouble, she'd let her guard down a bit.

Stupid, stupid, stupid.

She hurried up to her room and pulled a duffel bag from the closet. Toothbrush, underwear, change of clothes and nightgown—the nice one, with ribbons woven through the bodice. Her usual T-shirt and boxers could stay at home. She was filling a small cosmetic bag with her medication and essential makeup when the doorbell began to ring.

Was Luke back already? A spiral of fear twisted in her chest. Luke would not ring the doorbell, and not repeatedly. Luke knew the garage code; it wasn't him.

He was here.

The doorbell chimed incessantly. He was not going away.

Her heart thudded in her chest as she bounded down the stairs, then stopped herself, falling back onto a carpeted step. She couldn't answer. But if she didn't, would he break down the door?

Call the police. She yanked her cell phone from her pocket as the bell pealed again, and then a knock came.

Indecision and fear tangled inside her. What if it was someone else . . . a neighbor or a friend of Harper's?

With a jagged breath, she crept to the bottom of the stairs and crossed to the door, sure that he could sense her movement on the other side of the door. Mustering her courage, she put her eye to the peephole. The man was turned away, and the damned peephole distorted things, but the thatch of dark hair and the broad shoulders were unmistakable.

It was him.

Frank.

Of course, he had stayed in shape, kept his muscles conditioned and strong enough to hold a woman down against her will or crush her windpipe.

The instinct to flee roared in her mind as she backed away from the door, which suddenly boomed. He was pounding on the door, rattling it in its hinges.

She wanted to beg him to go away, but she was afraid to reveal herself, and she knew her words would be powerless against him. Instead, she stumbled over to the bannister, hunkered down behind it, and tried to focus on the cell phone in her shaking hand.

Nine. One. One.

Chapter 4

The pounding on the door rocked the house like a barrage of gunfire. Pressed into the newel post for shelter, Jane had her arms wrapped around Phee, who had wandered over, curious and obviously concerned. Jane tightened her grip on the dog as she strained to hear sirens. She had told the dispatcher he was breaking in, and the woman had assured her that a car was on its way, but it seemed like an eternity had passed since the time they'd hung up.

There was a sound from the street—a squeal of tires? Yes, a car screeching to a halt. Afraid to approach the door, Jane crawled to the living room window, with Phoenix following curiously alongside her. She tugged the cord of the Tiffany lamp to plunge the room into darkness, crouched down on her knees, and lifted the corner of the silk shade.

Jane trembled in relief and fear. Luke had returned.

At the edge of the lawn, Luke stood in the firing position she'd seen on crime shows, his legs planted securely, his arms stretched in front of him, pointing his revolver toward her front porch. From behind him, the lights of his car carved an eerie silver path over the grass. The Volvo sat cockeyed on the street, the driver's side door hanging open.

"Whoa! Sir! Put the gun down." The order came from the front steps.

"Not a chance." Luke's voice rang out, a steel hammer. "Put your hands on your head and sit down on the porch step." She had never seen this side of him, not even when he was dealing with the most recalcitrant students. Because of the way the porch cut in, Jane couldn't see Frank from this window, but Luke's response indicated that he was complying.

"I'm a police officer," Frank said.

That was one of the things that made him so dangerous, Jane thought as she rose and steadied herself against the console table. She didn't dare open the front door, but she could go out through the garage. Phoenix barked behind her as she hurried through the laundry room and hit the button for the garage door.

"Luke!" she shouted, bending down to see that he had moved a few feet closer. "I called the police. They're coming."

He nodded without taking his eyes off Frank.

Phoenix spilled out behind Jane, barking at the intruder.

"Good dog." As Jane went to grab the dog's collar, she peered around the corner of the house to get a look at Frank. Instead, she saw an attractive Hispanic man with a strong jaw and sleepy eyes.

What? The pulse that had been pounding in her ears began to fade. He was dark-haired with a medium build, but not the man she feared.

"You're not Frank!"

The man winced, but he kept his hands propped on his head and his eyes on the man with the gun. "Please, tell him not to shoot."

Still compelled to keep her distance from the stranger, she hurried across the lawn to join Luke. "It's not him."

There was a fine sheen of sweat on Luke's forehead. "Are you sure?"

"Positive."

"Then who the hell are you?" Luke relaxed his stance, but didn't lower the gun.

"Name's Alvarez . . . Dennis Alvarez. I'm a police detective with the DA's office of San Joaquin County. I've got ID." Alvarez took one hand from his head to point down at his pocket, but he quickly clamped his hand back onto his hair when Luke waved the gun at him.

"Who hired you to stalk her?" Luke demanded. "You were at the school today, and now this. What the hell? Coming after a woman at night?"

"I haven't broken any laws. I have some questions for Ms. Ryan, that's all." He turned to Jane. "I was trying to be discreet, didn't want to make a scene in front of your friends. I didn't mean to frighten you, but you've been a hard person to track down."

Jane scowled. "And you didn't get the message? That I didn't want to be tracked down?" She had disappeared for a reason, and if this man could find her, so could Frank.

"I was doing my job, ma'am."

The whoop of sirens bounced through the surrounding trees and houses. The Mirror Lake Police would be pulling up any second. She turned to Luke. "Do you want to put the gun away before the police get here?"

Luke glanced from the gun to Alvarez. "Shit." He lowered the shiny black pistol. "Stay right where you are until the police get here," he told the intruder.

Jane called Phee in closer and together they kept a watchful eye on the detective. Alvarez remained sitting with his hands on his head while Luke tucked the gun away in his car.

"Mr. Alvarez, I have some questions for you," she said. "After the police run your ID, we'll talk." At a diner, perhaps. Somewhere neutral. She certainly wasn't going to invite him into the house. The neighbors were already getting an eyeful.

An armed standoff, and now two police cars that had burst into sight with lights and sirens exploding the darkness. It was enough of a disturbance to the neighborhood for one night.

She was conscious of the lights that had gone on in neighboring homes. Dave and Nancy Tully stood in their driveway, and Gary Larsen watched from his front porch, there for her, ready to help. She acknowledged Gary with a grateful wave and reassured the Tullys that everything was okay. Hard to believe, especially with the adrenaline that still sizzled in her veins, but it was true. Frank wasn't trying to kill her. Everything was fine.

She kept telling herself that, but she knew it would take hours, maybe even days, to come down from this frantic buzz.

Chapter 5

As they drove to the all-night restaurant to meet with Alvarez, the haunting refrain of "Building a Mystery" came on the radio, snapping Jane back to that fateful summer. She turned it off, craving silence.

"I feel like there's so much I have to tell you about the man I escaped from," she murmured, drained from the encounter at the house. "But then, the complete story is probably trite. Such a middle-class horror story."

"I can deal with trite," Luke said gently. "But give yourself a breather. We're almost there. After we're done with this guy, we can talk. No limits."

She nodded, sinking into the seat. Outside the air was cool, crisp. The temperature had dropped, but Luke had turned on her seat heater. That was Luke: thoughtful, protective. Although her trust in him was complete, absolute, definitive, Jane hadn't told him everything about her relationship with Frank Dixon. It wasn't easy talking about the biggest mistake of her life. Even years later, it burned.

When Jane looked back at the summer of 1997, she sometimes felt a pang of sympathy for the naïve young woman she had been after college graduation. Convinced that her life had been bland and ordinary, Jane was determined to set herself apart with some extraordinary adventures. Like most college students, Jane and her friends had been partying for years, but this was the first time they could imbibe in the local bar scene, a happening place in Burnson. In the apartment she shared with Marnie, she was free to skip meals and paint her toenails on the coffee table. Although their mornings were spent teaching summer school, they had the afternoons free to run along the river or take a ride to one of the beaches—"A perfect summer schedule," Marnie proclaimed. By the afternoon the marine layer that fogged the California coast lifted, leaving a magnificent shoreline of sparkling indigo water, sand beaches, and sheltered coves. Jane sported a bikini for the first time in years and, with her new, fit body, she actually enjoyed wading into the cold water and hanging with the surfers.

After an evening nap, Jane and Marnie showered and primped, giddy with the potential of another night out on the Docks, the string of bars and saloons that stretched along the river at the edge of town. Each night they met new urban professionals and reconnected with old friends. They scored free vodka tonics and lemon drops from guys who wanted nothing more than light conversation and a few laughs. They sang the angry anthems of Sarah McLachlan and Paula Cole, wondering "Where have all the cowboys gone?" They knew all the words to the Beach Boys tunes that peppered every beach party. But Jane and Marnie had agreed that their theme song for the summer would be Sheryl Crow's "All I Wanna Do." They were in it for the fun.

"We deserve it, after all these years of busting our buns in school," Marnie had declared.

Like the female singers who flung their bitterness through every jukebox and radio, Jane considered herself to be stoic and smart, exquisite and sophisticated. But beneath all the labels, some earned through years of school and some recently acquired through weight loss and exercise, Jane was mostly a romantic, a needy young woman in search of the hero who would sweep her off her feet. For the first time in her life she had a job, some money to play with, an apartment away from the folks, and the power to turn heads when she walked into a bar. Freedom was sweet, but coupled with a whiff of sexual attraction, it was a spicy dish, too hot for a timid heart.

And it had been the summer of fun. Marnie developed a crush on Jason, a bartender at one of their hangouts on the Docks. Jane remained unattached. But unlike the wallflower school days of awkward pity hookups, Jane's solo status now felt like a journey of independence. She had lost twenty pounds, and that made all the difference. Men gravitated toward her, and women wanted to be her friends. For the most part, Jane basked in the glow of male attention. Oh, there were vile, hungry looks here and there, but she found most guys to be polite. They enjoyed her little stories. They liked to laugh, as she did. And some of them were downright chivalrous, holding doors, giving up their bar stools, buying her a drink, or walking her to her car.

The golden days and indigo nights of summer passed all too quickly. Although Jane looked forward to her first year of full-time teaching, she hated to see her glorious lifestyle dwindle away. There would be no more trips to the coast for a while, and their obligation to chaperone school football games meant the nights at the Docks would be few and far between. "Our reign is ending," Marnie had said with a cute pout of her full lips.

When the summer began to wane, Jane and Marnie joined the other revelers in a countdown the last week of August. The town of Burnson had a darkly comic tradition of staging a Labor Day parade, during which marchers carried makeshift balsa-wood coffins to bury the summer. Most of the bars on the Docks entered a coffin in the legendary best-coffin competition. The bar where Jason worked, Smackdaddy's, was relying on patrons to decorate theirs. The owner had assembled it in his garage, and now the small wooden box was set up on a table in the bar. Tubes of paint, brushes, and markers were set up for customers to decorate the coffin as they saw fit.

"That is just pathetic." Marnie shook her head at the coffin, which sported a few poorly rendered flames and skulls. "A class of kindergartners could do better."

Jane pushed back the sleeves of her denim jacket. "Come on, Marnie. Let's show them how a proper art project is done."

They decided to cover the box with swirls and stars in bright colors, reminiscent of Vincent van Gogh's *Starry Night* painting. Jane focused on making a deep blue sky and a simple green landscape with pointed cypress trees while Marnie painted in glistening swirls of silver, white, and yellow.

It was a typical Saturday night, with music blaring, patrons gathering three-deep at the bar, and barely room to breathe out on the dock. But inside at their table, people gave Jane and Marnie room to work.

They were putting the finishing touches on their masterpiece when a customer came in and told Jason to turn on the television over the bar, reporting that something had happened to Lady Di. One of the guys remarked that he had never liked her, but Marnie defended the former princess.

As Jason turned the music down and clicked on the television, word spread through the crowd. Conversation dropped to a murmur as people turned to the TV over the bar. Paintbrushes in hand, Jane and Marnie pressed in toward the television screen, riveted as reporters showed the dark streets of Paris. They were talking about Princess Diana in the past tense; listening closely, the subdued patrons of the bar learned that she had died from injuries sustained in a car accident.

Jane and Marnie shared a hug.

"It's so awful," Jane said. "She was starting a new life."

"She seemed happy, being out of the restrictions of royalty," Marnie agreed.

Jane had always admired Diana, from the fairy-tale story of a young nanny plucked from relative obscurity to become a princess, to the survivor's tale of a woman who dared to buck age-old tradition and free herself from an unhappy life. Jane saw herself in Diana's struggles, at least in the first part, with an ugly duckling turning into a swan. And this was the summer when Jane had ascended from ordinary to something special. Pretty, popular . . . independent.

As Jane sat at the table and contemplated life and death, the way things could change in a heartbeat, Marnie brought over two frosty v-shaped glasses.

"Lemon drops, on the house," Marnie announced, handing one to Jane. "Jason said it's a gesture of thanks for saving Smackdaddy's coffin from coming in last."

Jane lifted her glass in a toast. "To Lady Di. I can't believe she's gone."

"It's like losing a friend. Does that sound deluded? I mean, it's not like we hung out with her."

"But we watched her become a princess. We saw her get married." The royal wedding had been one of Jane's earliest memories. The fancy carriage—just like Cinderella's—and the long train trailing down the aisle of the cathedral.

"My mom cut her hair short like Diana's. And those beautiful evening gowns. Sparkling and sleek. She was living every girl's dream of a life."

"Or so we thought." Jane took a deep sip from her drink. It was her second of the night; she'd been nursing a hard lemonade as she painted. But now she wanted more than the light social buzz. She took another drink as she wondered about the path of Diana's life. "Do you think Diana ever found happiness?" she asked Marnie.

"I don't think happiness is something you find. It comes in

fleeting moments. Like a flower in full bloom or a bubble floating along. Each moment of joy is short-lived. The bubble will burst. But there's always another one floating your way, eventually."

That was Marnie: poetic, ever hopeful.

There was more toasting to Diana mixed with conversation on the finite nature of life.

"You've got to live for the moment," Jason said emphatically, and the group gathered at the bar drank to that sentiment.

When Jason announced last call, Marnie turned to Jane and told her she'd be going home with Jason. "Are you okay on your own?"

"No problem!" Jane exclaimed, maybe a bit too emphatically. How much had she had to drink? She'd lost track. But she'd eaten a good absorbent dinner, and the drinks had been spaced out over time. She'd be fine.

As she stood up to leave, the periphery of her vision was dull and fuzzy, and it seemed to require a supreme effort to walk. One foot in front of the other, she told herself. One breath in, and then out. The mechanics of living could be so difficult. Especially when you were drunk.

"Are you okay to drive?" one of the bartenders called after her.

She lifted her hand in what she hoped looked like a dismissive wave. The cool air outside the bar sobered her up fast. Fresh air was what she needed. Her little Honda gleamed from its spot in front of the bar. She loved her little red car. Well, she had to love it since she'd be paying for it over the next few years.

After she bumped her head on the way in, she slunk down in the driver's seat, rubbing vigorously and wondering if she should call a cab. The worst case scenarios loomed large in her mind. She could crash like Diana, and that would be very bad. She could get a DUI, and that would be bad, too. She might lose her job, or even her teaching certification. A teacher had to set a good example, and breaking the law was not a good thing.

"Not good," she said aloud as she buckled her seatbelt. But the fresh air had helped her realize that she was upset and sad . . . tired, too. Not really drunk. Besides, she was a good driver, and the apartment was just down the road. "A straight shot," she said. Well . . . with a few turns. Gripping the steering wheel with one hand, she turned the key. She could do this.

The view through the windshield was surreal, a driving course on a dark video game as she accelerated slowly, steering carefully to stay on the track. The street by the Docks was well lit and fairly quiet, with only a few stragglers walking and the occasional car moving past her.

As the waterfront gave way to the industrial area, the lights dimmed, and she had to strain to see parts of the roadway. What a dark night! Was there no moon in the sky?

Just as the darkness closed around her, bright light bounced through her car. In the rearview mirror, the strobe of a police vehicle flashed red and blue. A cop. Oh, no! Right on her tail. The double whoop of the siren let her know that she had to pull over.

You're okay. You're okay, she told herself as she rolled to a stop on the gravel shoulder of the roadway and put the car in park. It was probably just a routine check. A glimpse in the rearview mirror revealed only the bright lights of the police cruiser behind her. Leaning toward the mirror, she was horrified by the fine beads of perspiration glistening on her upper lip. She swiped at her face and then shoved her trembling hands in her lap.

The beam of a flashlight hit her window, and she rolled it down and peered up at the dark form of a man.

"Good evening, officer." The calm teacher voice came through. "Is everything okay?"

"License and registration, please." The voice was gruff, brisk.

She handed him the driver's license from her wallet, but panic swirled as she wondered about the registration. The console. Of course. Her father would have put it there when he registered the car for her. She found the little leather folder that had come with the car, and the registration seemed to smile up at her. Phew!

"Jane Flannery." He moved the beam of the flashlight from the ID in his hand to Jane's face. "New car?"

"Pretty new."

"Have you been drinking, Jane?"

"Yes." Why had she said that? She was afraid to lie to him. He was such an ominous figure: dark uniform with a shiny badge, baritone voice, face obscured by that wailing beam of light. "But I'm not drunk. I mean, it was spaced out over hours and hours."

"Is there a reason you were driving with your lights off?"

"I . . ." She squinted through the windshield at the overwhelming night. No wonder it seemed so dark. She turned the switch, and the road was suddenly illuminated. "I didn't know. Sorry about that."

He moved away from the door. "I need you to step outside the vehicle for me."

She followed him to the brightly lit area in front of the cruiser's headlights. Panic seeped into her heart as she studied him. Thick black hair and chiseled features. A stern slash of a mouth. In his dark uniform, he was a wall of strength, solid and unforgiving. His name plate read: DIXON.

In the stark light, she felt exposed, naked despite her denim shorts and hot-pink T-shirt. She expected him to hand her something to blow in—a Breathalyzer test—but he gave her some tasks to do. Walk in a straight line. Stretch out her arms and touch her nose with her eyes closed. Nothing too hard, though she got a little wobbly when she had to close her eyes.

He asked her a bunch of questions, probably trying to see if her speech was slurred. She told him she was a teacher, gave her address, and talked about growing up in Burnson.

"Have you ever failed a student?" he asked.

"Not yet." She shivered in the cool night, unwilling to admit that so far her career had entailed only student teaching and summer school.

"So you're a nice teacher. Well, I consider myself to be a nice cop. I don't want you to fail, Jane. I could give you a Breathalyzer, but I can pretty much guarantee you're going to blow hot. Once you do that, I've got to take you in and press charges. Driving Under the Influence. You'll probably lose your license, a year minimum. And the arrest would be a public record. The local news can broadcast your mug shot. For some reason, they like to expose cops and teachers."

A sob wracked her words. "I could lose my job."

"Right. See how one failure affects so many people? I bet your husband would be upset."

"I'm not married." It came out in a whimper. "But my parents...they'll be mortified." She imagined her failure as another encumbrance to heap onto her father's shoulders, adding to the burden of supporting his elderly father and the scars of three tours in Vietnam, memories he kept sealed up tight under his wounded eyes. On the other side of the spectrum, her mother would be concerned about how such a scandal might reflect on her. Sandra Flannery would be afraid to attend church, worried that people were whispering about her daughter the "criminal." Jane sucked in a desperate breath. Her life was tumbling down before her, a row of dominoes, each one slapping the next to the ground.

"My hands are tied if I give you the Breathalyzer." The cop

paused, watching her, assessing. "If I don't give you the test, I have some discretion. I could give you a ride home, let you off with a warning."

Jane sucked in a breath. "Would you? Please? That would be such a relief."

"But I would need something from you. A promise that you're going to be a good girl for me. Can you promise that, Jane?"

"Yes. Yes, I promise. I'll never drink and drive again. Not even one drink."

"Yeah?" He assessed her, and although she tried to demonstrate her commitment, she found it hard to meet his eyes. His stern, iron-clad demeanor scared her, even as it excited her in a surprising way. Being in the presence of authority was like veering dangerously close to a fire. The closer you came to the flames, the more thrilling the dance. But the greater thrill also increased the danger of being burned.

"You're not just bullshitting me to get out of the charges."

"No. I'm an honest person. Please, I'll do anything for a second chance."

His eyes were smoky and unreadable; she sensed power and unleashed fury. Her knees began to quiver.

"All right." He nodded at her car. "Get your purse and keys, and then lock it up. You're coming with me."

She thanked God for mercy as she hurried to the car. Hitching her bag onto her shoulder, she locked up with the keypad. Back in the white shower from the headlights, he summoned her closer.

"Hold your hands in front of you like this," he said.

She followed his instructions, flinching when he snapped handcuffs onto her wrists. Wariness skittered up her spine. Was this a trick?

"I can smell your fear," he said.

"I . . . I don't understand. I thought I wasn't under arrest?"

"Just procedure. You'll need to ride in the back, too. It's tactical defense. A cop can't trust anyone."

"Oh. Okay." She tried to sound agreeable, though she knew she had no choice in the matter.

He opened the back door and pressed her head low so that she didn't hit it on the way into the squad car. A dank, salty smell assaulted her nostrils as she adjusted herself on the seat. How many hardcore criminals had ridden back here? Burnson was a nice place to live, but some parts had more than their share of gang-related crime and murders.

He leaned in, his eyes steely in the dome light of the car. "Let me buckle your seatbelt. Gotta stay safe."

She sat back, very still, as he veered close. He smelled of citrus and spice—much better than the car—and although he didn't touch her, she found the intimate proximity enticing. But he was all business. Once she was buckled in, the door closed, and he went around to the driver's seat.

Even through the screen separating them, his eyes were beacons in the rearview mirror. "I'll bet this wasn't the way you thought your evening was going to end."

"No," she admitted. Disappointment was draining her dry. The one true princess of the world had just died. Jane's transformational summer was fading. And she'd nearly tossed her future away with a poor decision. A tear slid down one cheek, and she lifted the onerous bindings to push it away with the back of one thumb.

As they drove away, passing her lonely red Honda, the radio erupted. A female dispatcher reported something happening on the 1200 block of Ortega, the sketchy side of town. Jane sniffed, telling herself to get over it. She had been given a reprieve. She was safe now.

"I live over on Figueroa," she said. "The Hillcrest Apartments."

"I saw that on your license," he said. "I know where it is."

The night streets of Burnson seemed sinister and gray from the back of the patrol car. Was that fear, casting shadows over the town she'd grown up in? Oh, to get home and step into a hot shower, scrub away the funk of her crime. She would wash away her sorrows, slip into clean pajamas, and fall to her knees beside her bed to thank God for saving her from doom.

Officer Dixon pulled the patrol car into the visitor's spot in front of the building. "Now let's do this quietly. We don't want to disturb your neighbors. Is there anyone else home in your place?" he asked. "A boyfriend? Roommate?"

"My roommate is over at her boyfriend's place."

Again, he put a hand on her head to help her out. This time, she felt his gaze sweep over her, down the length of her bare, tanned legs to her high-heeled sandals. It was awkward, getting out of a car in handcuffs, but when she straightened, his eyes lingered at the swell of her breasts. He was checking her out—definitely—and she enjoyed the slight shift of power, sensing that he liked what he saw.

Cocking one brow, she held up her cuffed wrists. "Will you take these off now?"

"Inside." He looked toward the building. "You don't want to make a spectacle out here."

She led the way, watching the windows, which were mostly dark. With any luck her neighbors were asleep and missing this fiasco. When she paused at the door, Dixon reached into the purse slipping down her shoulder and found the keychain with its little red ball. He unlocked the apartment door and gestured for her to go in. She breathed in the lemony scent of the familiar vestibule, flicking on the lights with her cuffed hands. Home. The familiar space restored her sense of confidence, her equilibrium.

"Nice place," he said, closing the door behind him. In the warm light of her apartment, he looked handsome and distant. His crisp navy uniform was a bold reminder of his authority over her. He paused at the collage depicting an ocean cove. "Did you do this?"

"I did." She noticed how he filled the hallway with a masculine aura, big and bold.

"Reminds me of Half Moon Bay. I'm a surfer." He folded his arms, biceps shifting where they touched the short sleeves of his uniform shirt.

She imagined his body in a wetsuit . . . or maybe just the bottom half with the top pulled off and dangling, the way guys hung out on the beach. Maybe she'd seen him at the coast. "You look like a surfer."

His dark eyes glittered as he reached for her hands. "How's that?"

"Tanned. Strong."

He unlocked the cuffs, folded them into small rings, and snapped them back onto his leather belt. "Let me see your arms." He turned her hands and ran his fingers over the smooth skin on the inside of her wrists. "Look at that; you might have some bruises. Sorry, Jane. If every perp was like you, I'd invest in cuffs lined with velvet."

She squinted at him. "Now you're kidding me."

"I am." He was still massaging her wrists, pressing into the tender pad at the base of her thumbs. The shift intrigued her. So Officer Dixon had a softer side. She didn't mind that he held onto her hands, finding the sweet spots in her palms and squeezing the tension away. She knew he was stepping over the line of procedure, and the fact that he was interested in her sounded a glad *ping* in her head. Men like him had always been out of her league—too good-looking and sure of themselves to give her a second glance. But Dixon wanted her— there was no question about that. Her heart raced at the realization that she had risen in stature; she was playing a woman's game now.

Here was a way to cling to her transformed self, the new

Jane who held court in the bar. The new Jane, attractive and entertaining.

When he pulled her into his arms and pressed his teeth to the tender spot on her neck, she let go and threw herself into the abyss. Dark and daring, wild and impetuous. His mouth was voracious, his touch heated by desperation. And the danger of it . . . the exquisite danger intensified every sensation.

There was no awkwardness, no grappling or miscommunication. He knew what he wanted. He knew how to get it. Jane followed his orders, moving to the couch, stripping off her clothes, piece by piece, until they were skin to skin. Her initial fear turned to intrigue and finally release as pleasure crashed through her body.

Afterward, he stroked her hair back, surprisingly gentle now. "Good girl," he whispered. "I knew you'd be a good girl."

Ordinarily she would have taken offense, but somehow his words filled her with pride. She had been good. It had been great—the hottest sex she'd ever had. Her heart purred with satisfaction.

He drew her hair back, pressed his lips to her neck, and sucked hard until she cried out in pain. What the hell?

"I always mark my territory," he said without apology.

Did that mean she was his girlfriend? The notion added sweetness to the afterglow. Apparently Officer Dixon was more sentimental than she'd realized. As the sting on her neck receded, she relaxed and reached for him, wanting the reassurance of his body against hers.

But Dixon was already sitting up, gathering his clothes. Contact over. She shivered and curled up on the couch as embarrassment cooled her skin.

When he asked where the bathroom was, Jane pulled her T-shirt against her breasts, covering up as she pointed the way.

"A little late for modesty," he said.

"I don't even know your first name."

"Frank." He picked up his gun belt and took it with him to the bathroom. "I'll be right back." He walked down the hall, brazenly naked.

While he was showering, she gathered her clothes and went into the bedroom to grab her robe. As she passed by the mirror, she dropped her clothes to the floor and took a good long look at herself. When had she become beautiful? Taut, rosy nipples and an hourglass shape. The tan lines from her bikini emphasized the dove-pale hue of her breasts and the healthy golden glow of the rest of her skin.

The slight embarrassment she'd felt at having sex with a stranger began to fade. She was a healthy woman, old enough to make her own choices. And given the choice again, she would definitely take another ride with Officer Frank Dixon.

Chapter 6

The trauma of Frank Dixon had nearly destroyed her. Fear might have overcome her if it hadn't been for the baby. Funny how she couldn't muster the strength to protect herself, but once she learned that an innocent life relied on her, she had found a way to escape. After she made it to Seattle and found an obstetrician to treat her, the news that she was expecting twins was even more incentive to stay away from California, remove herself from her family, and begin a new, anonymous life.

Like prey in the forest, she covered her tracks and always looked behind her. She got rid of her cell phone and used a pay-as-you-go phone for years. She changed her last name. And when Marnie got a call from Frank, who fished around for information about Jane, it became clear that Seattle could not be Jane's final destination. Marnie wanted her to stay, but she understood. If Frank was hunting her down, Jane had to keep running.

See Jane run. Run, Jane, run!

The old first-grade primer struck a macabre note for her in that first year or two, when her dreams were full of chase scenes. Frank popping up in the backseat of her car. Frank following her down the cereal aisle in the supermarket. Frank chasing her around the park while her baby sat, wide-eyed, on the bottom of the slide. What a relief to bolt up in bed and realize it was a dream. Even if her chest was exploding from fear, even if Harper was crying in her crib, the harshest reality was better than those nightmares.

For nearly a decade Jane had focused on making a life for herself and her daughter. Most people assumed she'd been married before, and she did not correct them. Harper had grown up believing that her father was dead—a difficult lie for Jane, but when she considered the alternative, she couldn't bear the possibility of Harper's one day tracking Frank down. That confrontation would certainly blow up in their daughter's face. Frank would toy with his daughter, torture her, harm her. No, Jane couldn't risk that.

With all her energy focused on her daughter and her teaching job, Jane befriended moms of Harper's friends and only engaged in family activities that involved Harper. While eating her bag lunch in the teachers' lounge, she shared amusing stories about raising her daughter, but she avoided asking personal details of her colleagues, and she did not join in the happy hour gatherings at local restaurants. Her body language clearly transmitted that she was not interested in a relationship, and people respected that.

Then came Luke. Scientist and teacher, philosopher and geek. He was as good at online gaming as any high school senior, and yet he was social, too. His tales often reduced faculty members to laughter, and other teachers in the science department sang the praises of the curriculum he created. Although Jane remained leery of men, Luke kept proving himself to be exceptional as she watched him studiously. It wasn't just his earnest attitude; Luke was transparent and unashamed of his past. He was on good terms with his ex-wife, whom he had met while they were both teaching at a college in Spokane, and his college-age son seemed to enjoy helping out at the high school when he visited. If Jane's past was sealed with Krazy Glue, Luke's was an open book, full of anecdotes about camping trips that went awry and Luke's own mistakes in the game of life, which always seemed comical when Luke was spinning the story.

While assigned one of the end-zone posts at a football game, they had a chance to speak one-on-one. The public setting kept Jane relaxed, while Luke's stories kept her smiling. By the end of the game, when he asked if she wanted to grab a coffee sometime, she reluctantly turned him down.

"I don't date. You know how it is when you have a school-age kid. They're so needy. And long ago I promised myself I would never give her any reason to feel threatened."

"Really? You're turning me down?" He pressed a fist to his heart. "I'm crushed. You probably don't realize it, but I've been working on asking you out for the past year. Refining my concerned but casual tone. Was I too pushy? Too cavalier?"

"No, no, it's nothing you said. It's me."

He groaned. "The old 'it's not you, it's me' line! Am I that hopeless?"

"If I dated, and I don't, you'd be at the top of my list."

"Wow. Not even a pity date?"

Jane couldn't help but chuckle as she looked toward the crowded bleachers. "Besides, we've got a few hundred sets of eyes on us. If we were seen together anywhere in Mirror Lake, we'd be a school scandal."

"It's hardly immoral for two coworkers to date."

He was right about that. Two of their colleagues, Ben and Mary Ellen Kitcher, had met right here at Mirror Lake High and married two years ago.

"Besides, we could get outta town. Go into Portland."

It was a sweet fantasy: a cup of hot tea at an outdoor table in the Chinese Gardens on a cool autumn day. Or wandering among the booths with Luke at Portland's Saturday Market. Or maybe a ride out to the gorge to hike the trail to the top of Multnomah Falls. She knew Luke was a hiker.

"Look, you don't have to answer now. Especially if your answer is no. Take some time and think about it. But I'm going to stay positive, Jane, and hope you'll eventually say yes." He winced. "Ooh, I'm starting to sound like a used car salesman. I think the nineties are calling, and they want their pickup line back."

"Yes." The word was out before she could check her impulse. After nearly a decade of following a strict code of behavior, she was caving, but with good reason. Luke made her smile. She had seen the mutual respect between Luke and his ex-wife, the camaraderie among Luke and his colleagues, the wonder in the eyes of his students. This was a good man, and wasn't it time to let a little light back into her life? "Yes, Mr. Bandini," she said aloud for the benefit of a handful of students passing by with soft drinks and hot dogs in hand. "I think we should try your idea."

"You . . . what?" His dark eyes brightened. "Really?"

"Incognito."

"Okay. Top secret." He grinned. "This could be fun."

They kept their secret for more than two years, getting together only when Harper was involved in an activity. They met in Portland and surrounding areas or at Luke's place, where Jane used a remote to open the garage door, pull her car inside, and close the garage door before any of the neighbors saw her.

"It's magic!" Luke would tease when she appeared in his kitchen. "Discretion can be so damned sexy."

From the start, they both agreed that sneaking around for their limited time together made things exciting. "You won't have a chance to get sick of me," Jane said.

Although she was sparing with the details about her past, once he learned that she had escaped an abusive relationship, he gave her breathing room. "You can tell me as much as you want when you're ready," he told her. "I'm not going anywhere. Unless you kick me out." That earnest, boy-scout quality won her trust. Luke had been in his late thirties, but she teased him that he still looked young enough to be in a boy band.

Her only problem with Luke was sleeping. To close her eyes and abandon all control—that required supreme trust. The first night they were together, she stared sullenly at the ceiling while Luke lay beside her, filling the space in her bed and in her life that had yawned empty for so long.

He would not pull her hair during the night; she knew that. He would not close his hands around her neck, squeezing until she lost consciousness.

He would not be standing over her when she awoke. Luke did not have issues with insomnia the way Frank had. Pacing through the night, sometimes cradling a baseball bat. Muttering. Frank's monsters came out in the darkness, though it took her months to realize the rants were not caused by alcohol. It was all Frank.

When he'd told her that he came from a family of crazies, she had thought he was joking. Another mistake.

Chapter 7

The Shari's Restaurant in West Green was one of the few places in the area that was open twenty-four hours. Usually Jane and Harper had trouble getting past the glass case of pies by the door: swirls of meringue or thick cream, sugared crusts, shiny dark berries, and wedges of dense cream custards. Tonight, Jane strode by the display to the man sitting at the table by the window.

Her fury must have been evident. Dennis Alvarez's small eyes opened wide as he dropped his menu. "You look mad, Ms. Ryan. Why don't you sit down and I'll buy you some coffee."

"I'm not here for coffee." She pulled out a chair and sat facing him. "Just information."

"I'll take some coffee." Luke was beside her, checking out the detective, up close and personal. He introduced himself simply as her friend Luke. Back at Jane's house, Luke had insisted that the Mirror Lake Police confirm the detective's identity. Two phone calls to California had confirmed that Dennis Alvarez was a detective for the San Joaquin County District Attorney's office, and that he was out of town on a case. Jane was relieved to have Luke at her side, thinking clearly.

They ordered two coffees and a chamomile tea for Jane. A truckload of chamomile wasn't going to help her sleep tonight.

"You want any pie with that?" the waitress asked. An older woman with a dry, smoker's voice. "We got Marionberry, just in."

"Ooh. Can't resist that." Luke ordered a slice, then turned back to Alvarez. "You know, I'm really glad I didn't shoot you. That would've freaked me out."

"Yeah? Me too."

"So how long you up here for?" Luke asked.

"Not sure yet. I'm trying to wrap up some business."

Jane dove in. "Involving me. I used to live in San Joaquin County. Is this . . . has something happened to my parents?"

He shook his head. "I spoke with Sandra and Ron a few weeks ago. And believe me, they didn't have a clue about your whereabouts. They're convinced that you're fine. I guess they got some messages from you. But they're not too happy with you for deserting the family."

She let that one slide off her back. It was amazing how family barbs could still sting more than a decade after separation. "So how did you track me down?"

"That's a long, dull story."

"Did you just find me today, or have you been stalking me for a while?"

"Just today, and there's a difference between surveillance and stalking."

"You were banging on my door. I thought you were going to break it down."

"Sometimes doorbells don't work. Look, I'm sorry I frightened you, but most people don't call the cops when someone rings their doorbell. Who'd you think I was?"

"No one. Nothing." The waitress arrived with their drinks. Jane tore open the wrapper on the teabag and started dunking. She wanted to run from the restaurant. She was grateful for

Luke's hand pressing into her thigh under the table. *Stay. Hear him out.*

Alvarez watched her as he took a sip of black coffee. "Look, like I said, I didn't mean to scare you. Sorry about that. If you're worried about Frank Dixon, you can relax. He's locked up right now."

Jane stopped dunking and let the teabag go. "*Officer* Frank Dixon? From Burnson?"

"That's the one. Burnson's most decorated cop. Well . . . he used to be."

Relief flooded through her. Frank was in jail. . . . No longer a threat. The unexpected news was hard to digest. "On what charges?"

"Sexual assault. He's serving seven years."

Seven years? Frank would not be a threat for seven years. . . .

"And that's just for one count, but there are other charges pending, based on a pattern of criminal activity. Dixon used to arrest a young woman for DUI, then offer to let her go in exchange for sexual favors. Apparently this went on for years, and no one came forward until two years ago. Dixon tried his scam with the wrong woman—my boss's daughter. We'll call her Jane Doe. After he raped her, she wasn't afraid to come forward, and the DA pressed charges. There are rumors that some young women had tried to file complaints before, but the cops at the precinct shit-canned them. After this story hit the news, two other women came forward." His gaze softened, and for the first time she noticed the half-moon creases under his eyes. "This Dixon is one bad apple, all right. My job is to find evidence to put him away for good."

While Luke questioned Alvarez, Jane retreated into herself and considered the string of assaults. Frank's abusive behavior had been no anomaly; after she had escaped, he had repeated it over and over again. What else had she expected from a true sociopath? She felt for all those women, she really did, but she had wrung the guilt out of herself over the years. If she'd had the strength and means of stopping Frank, she would have done so. As it was, she'd had nowhere to turn; her family and Frank's cop buddies had been in denial about his heart of darkness.

No wonder he didn't come after me, she thought. *He was busy hunting new prey.*

"You know," Alvarez said, "I'm surprised you didn't hear about this on the news. It's been a big deal, at least in California. The whole good-cop-gone-bad angle."

She shook her head. As a part of her therapy, she had stopped scouring media accounts of terrible things that happened to young women. The neurotic need to gather clues about the terrible hunters in the world had ruled her for years. The only way to quiet the roar of fear had been to stop devouring tragic news.

"I'm glad he's behind bars," she said. "But I don't understand what you want from me. To track me down here . . ."

"I'd like to ask you about Dixon. I know you were involved with him for a while. When the news of the trial hit, your father came to the precinct. He said that you left the state to get away from Dixon after the relationship went sour."

So her father had come forward; at last he believed her side of the story, though it was too little too late.

"I'm gathering evidence for a few other cases involving Dixon. One in particular involves a young woman who was involved with Dixon for a while. She's authorized me to share her name, hoping it will personalize her case for her. Lana Tremaine is her name. Just a kid, really. Tremaine can't recall a two-year period of her life. We believe that Dixon beat the memories from her."

Or he squeezed them out, his hands around her neck, clamping flesh and cartilage, cutting off air and life. Jane squinted into her tea, then looked up at Alvarez. "What is it you want from me?"

"I want to know everything you can tell me about Frank Dixon."

She shook her head slowly. "It was a long time ago. . . . I don't know how it would help you."

"With more information, with your deposition, we can pursue other charges. Assault. Possibly kidnapping. Did Dixon detain you against your will?"

"He did, but . . ." She covered her eyes. "I don't want to go there. I can't."

"Lana Tremaine can't testify because she doesn't remember."

Jane shook her head. "I have a daughter to protect."

"Don't you think you and your daughter will be safer with Dixon behind bars for years . . . maybe even for life?" When she didn't answer, he pressed on. "Lana was a nurse. Her parents said she was a wallflower when she met Dixon. Apparently, he's a charming guy, and she fell, hook, line, and sinker."

"He was a charismatic person."

"He was Lana's first boyfriend. That's probably why she was willing to overlook the charges he was facing, at least in the beginning. Her parents say that she left him once, and he coerced her into returning. Then, a month or so later, Beth Tremaine got a call from her daughter. Lana said she was calling in secret, afraid of what Frank might do if he found out. She said Dixon wouldn't let her leave the house for long periods of time. That he choked her until she passed out. That he patrolled at night with a baseball bat."

"That's all true. He used to clamp his hands around my neck, and he always kept the bat handy." Jane pressed her hand to her mouth as a vision of Frank filled her senses. The rank, salty smell of sweat. The way his bare chest glistened. The black snake tattoo on his arm that scowled at her, coiled and ready to strike. He had prodded her with the baseball bat and told her to get up. Get up and clean the floor. Get up and suck him off. Get up and go to work, even though it was the middle of the night and the school didn't open for hours.

"The Tremaines called the police. By the time they got to Dixon's house, Lana was gone. Dixon claimed she had left him to return home. Two years later, Lana Tremaine was found unconscious in a motel parking lot on the coast. Her injuries were consistent with blunt force trauma and strangulation. We suspect that she was held at another location by Dixon, but we haven't been able to identify where he might have kept her. We just don't have enough evidence to charge Dixon with Tremaine's kidnapping and assault. That's where you come in." The detective sounded tired. "Your testimony can make this case. It might be the difference between Dixon's getting out of prison in six years or sixty. Don't you want to do that for your daughter?"

It was more than Jane could have ever hoped for. Yes, yes, she wanted Frank out of her life, off the streets forever. But she wasn't sure she could dredge anything of value from her painful memories.

"I need to think about it. I don't know if I can help you. Not to make excuses, but those days are a jumble in my mind. I mean, I remember, but I don't know dates or times."

"Anything you can tell me might help our case." The detective handed her a business card. "Best-case scenario would be a deposition—an official statement that could be used in the trial. I can arrange to do that with you down at the courthouse in Oregon City or even in your home if that's easier for you. Just you, me, and the court reporter."

"Not at my house, please . . ." She couldn't let her daughter find out about this right now. She wasn't ready to tell Harper that her father was a violent criminal. "I need time to sort things out. I've spent nearly half my life putting Frank Dixon behind me."

"I understand." Alvarez's eyelids drooped in a wistful expression. "But don't drop the ball, Jane. You know this guy is a monster. He needs to be locked up for good."

Acrid memories seeped into her consciousness when she looked Frank up on the Internet during the car ride home. In the dozens of articles stamped with photos of his handsome face, his steely sapphire gaze had a piercing effect. The past still held power over her, a phantom wound with its curious aches. But back at the house, as she and Luke sifted through news accounts at her kitchen counter, the situation began to take on a new shape.

"He's been caught," she said. "Whether or not the DA can make other charges stick, Frank Dixon is behind bars. Not on my tail, not coming after me with a vengeance."

Luke closed a page on his iPad. "And that changes a lot for you, not having to hide. You must be relieved."

"A little. Right now I'm afraid to let myself feel anything." From her bed by the window, Phoenix snored quietly; a blissful sleep. "Still processing," Jane added.

"Do you want to go back? See your family in California? I mean, now that it's safe for you to go there."

She let out a grunt. "Absolutely not. There have been times when I pined for my lost childhood. Burnson was a great place to live before the city went bankrupt. But I have no desire to reconnect with Ron and Sandra. I'm glad Dad contacted the police, but that doesn't change the fact that my parents let me down when I needed them most. I mean, look at these accounts. Just about every article paints Frank as a serial rapist. My parents must know that the man they chose over me is in jail now. And did they reach out to let me know?

Did they send an e-mail? A short apology . . . or just a message to say they're glad I made it out alive?" She shook her head. "Nothing."

Luke put an arm over her shoulders. "I'm sorry you've had to go through all this."

"It's not your fault," she said, taking comfort in his arms.

"I know, but someone in the world should apologize."

Melting against him, she began to relax into the new reality of her situation.

She was free.

When Luke offered to make biscuits, she moved to the other side of the counter to continue her research. She focused on the coverage of Frank's conviction. The news accounts reported that the victim had gone to the emergency room immediately, and evidence collected through the rape kit had held up in court. Jane was grateful that this victim had possessed the courage and resources to pursue criminal charges against her attacker.

"I knew he was a wicked man, but I didn't realize he was a monster," Luke said as he cut frozen butter into perfect rectangular prisms. Luke's buttermilk biscuits were a vice that both he and Jane found therapeutic. "From his description in the media, it sounds like he's a sociopath."

"I've thought about that. Frank used to say that his family was crazy. In the beginning, I thought he was exaggerating. I was wrong about that."

"I keep thinking how lucky we are, that it's a miracle you got away." Luke rolled the dowel over the ball of dough, then looked up at her. "How did you manage that?"

"It was a matter of survival. Not for me, but for the baby."

The cool sting of Frank's eyes, the smug smile as he had handed her the slip of paper. "Here's your appointment. I told the nurse you were too nauseous to come to the phone, and you know what? She really didn't give a shit." Jane had unfolded the paper, unsure whether to be hurt by his comment or happy that he'd called the doctor for her. The fact that he was letting her see a doctor was a good sign, right? So he was softening on the idea of the baby. Jane had been sure that as time progressed Frank would find pleasure in paternity. Besides, she couldn't imagine any person withholding love from a child.

On the paper, an appointment date and time had been written in Frank's heavy script. He always pressed so hard—as if he needed to grind the letters into the paper—and his writing had a severe slant to the left. At the bottom was the doctor's name and, underlined twice, were the words Your Friendly Abortionist.

That snide cruelty had sparked the sterling moment: the transition. The possibility of someone's killing her baby had made something snap inside her.

As she told the story, Luke rolled the dough into a square, folded it into layers, and rolled again. Watching the process, knowing she was in a safe place, loved and protected, Jane let the horrible details spill from her dry throat.

"That was when I knew I had to get away," she told Luke. "Not just from Frank, but from the life I'd known. My family, my job. The town I grew up in. I think the worst part was leaving my students, but I was such a wreck at that point, I was afraid to connect with anyone. They were better off without me. I didn't have time to prepare. The next morning I drove to school and told them I wasn't feeling well. I waited until a substitute showed up, then I drove straight to my bank. Pulled out my savings in a bundle of cash and a cashier's check. I drove north and left my car parked at a shopping mall in San Jose. My little red Honda . . . I hadn't even paid it off yet. From there I took the train to Seattle, where Marnie and Jason let me stay with them until I was on my feet. That was risky, connecting with Marnie, but since Frank had never liked her, he had ignored the details of her life. He didn't know that she'd left Burnson. Didn't even know her last name, let alone Jason's." Jane closed the laptop and pressed one cheek to the cool tile of the counter. Luke was dabbing melted butter atop the biscuits on the baking sheet. How she loved watching Luke bake. "All these years, I worried about Frank's coming after me, and he was otherwise occupied. He turned his attention to new victims, other women. New prey."

Chapter 8

After twenty-four hours of research and soul-searching, Jane called Detective Alvarez to arrange a deposition. She didn't know if any part of her statement would be helpful in building a case, but she had to try. The meeting took place in Alvarez's hotel room, a generic business suite in a high-rise building along the expressway.

"The dates are fuzzy for me," Jane admitted as the court reporter set up her machine. "It's been fifteen years. But some events are still crystal clear."

"I'd like to hear anything you remember," Alvarez assured her.

A pink-faced woman with long, silver-streaked hair pulled back in a ponytail, the court reporter asked Jane to raise her right hand and swear that her testimony was true. Her smile seemed kind but professional, and she seemed to go into a daze as she began to record the detective's first question.

"How did you meet Frank Dixon?"

"He pulled me over one night as I left a bar on the Docks in Burnson," Jane said. Trying to stay as close to the truth as possible, she explained how he had told her he would not charge her and had given her a ride home. It was not rape; at least, not that time.

She explained how they began seeing each other, usually hooking up in the evenings, before Frank reported to work for a midnight shift. In the beginning, he had taken her out to dinner a few times, to quiet, inexpensive restaurants. Italian, Thai, California cuisine. Frank stayed in shape from surfing, or so he claimed. He didn't drink, and he called himself a "soldier in the war on drugs." Jane had been impressed, mistaking his sobriety for a grounded mental state. When she introduced him to her parents, Frank had been a model boyfriend. He had talked guns and ammo with Ron and complimented Sandra on her cooking. Granted, it was easy to impress her parents, but Frank knew all the right buttons to push. He always did.

After a few months, he had suggested that she move into his place so that they didn't have to "jump through hoops" to schedule time together. Despite his speeches opposing marriage and procreation, Frank's desire to be with her had won Jane over. She had moved into his house, eyeing the tiny room off the big bedroom as a possible nursery.

Once they were living together, their relationship began a gradual decline. Frank had wanted her to account for every minute she was away, and on the nights they were home together, his appetite for sex carved away at her precious sleep. Trying to talk it out, she had told him that she was not a sex slave. That had prompted him to lock her to the bed in handcuffs and keep her captive for the better part of a day. A joke, he had said. Couldn't she take a joke? That night, when she was about to begin packing, he had coaxed her out for a romantic dinner overlooking the river. Watching the way the waitress came on to him that night, Jane had been reminded of just how attractive and desirable Frank was. Doubting that she would ever do better, she had decided to stay and teach him the proper way to treat a woman.

In some ways the descent of their relationship had been

gradual. Frank had seized control over her in small ways, and she had allowed it, to avoid an ugly confrontation.

"Frank never could sleep," she said, explaining about the night monsters that possessed him. How some vile energy burned in his eyes at night, furious and wild. His patrols during the hours of darkness. The baseball bat. The bizarre demands. And his need to dominate her. That was what had driven him to close his hands around her neck. "It would be so easy for me to kill you," he had told her, pressing his thumb to her larynx. "A small amount of pressure in the right place. Doesn't take much. A minute or so, and you'd be dead."

Sometimes when the sun rose, the terror would drain from him, and he would actually smile and proclaim how lucky they were to be together. He would pull her to him and make tender love to her, as if the madness of the previous hours had never happened. Other times, he would simply snap into the daily routine, showering and brushing his teeth. She had begun to live for the nights when he would be away at work.

"When he was at his worst, he wouldn't let me leave his house." Those were the times when she had vowed to get away. Regardless of how much she wanted to love him, regardless of the fact that he was the best-looking guy she would ever land, regardless of his threats to kill her if she disobeyed him, she needed to stick to her resolve and leave this house and never come back.

And then when she was away from him her determination would wane. Was she being a prima donna, as Frank said? No relationship was perfect.

But the threat of violence . . . the manic control . . .

She had blamed herself for wanting too much time with him. Maybe they needed to include other people in their activities. Unfortunately, that could not include Marnie and Jason. Frank insisted that Jason was gay, and he thought Marnie was a corrupting influence. "After a few hours with her, your brain goes soft with thoughts of marriage and babies." Although Jane denied it, she knew there was a grain of truth in it. After all, that was what a woman in her twenties wanted: a partner in true love, someone to start a life and a family with. When Marnie had told Jane that Jason had found a job in Seattle, Jane hadn't been completely sorry to see her friend move to the Northwest. It would be one less source of contention between Frank and her.

Trying not to be selfish, Jane had suggested that she and Frank go out with some of the cops Frank worked with and their wives. "I'd like your friends to be my friends, too," she had told him. He had squashed the idea, telling her that he didn't want her meddling in his career. "You've got to learn how to keep different worlds separated," he had told her. She had met some of his coworkers once when she dropped in at the precinct, but the encounter had been awkward, with Frank glaring at her as if she had committed a crime. "Don't ever, ever come to my place of work," he had told her later.

"We'd been living together for more than a year when I found out I was pregnant." Jane paused as myriad memories bombarded her. The thrill of motherhood. Hope that the pregnancy might win Frank over. A sea of wavering doubts. Fear that the news might make his fury boil over. "He wanted me to have an abortion," she told Alvarez. "Actually, he *ordered* it. He made all the arrangements himself, assuming I'd go along with it. That's when I left. I knew I had to protect my baby from him. The only solution I could think of was to disappear. So I left town one day, and never went back."

When Alvarez looked up from his notes, compassion softened his eyes. He understood.

He had a few more questions, many pointing to Frank's hobby of surfing. "Did you ever go with him when he went to the coast?"

"Only once. I didn't know how to surf, and Frank didn't think I could amuse myself at the ocean. But in the beginning, I always wanted to go with him."

"*Going surfing,*" he would say in the morning. She always offered to come along; she wanted to be with him. But he refused. "*You'll just be bored,*" he told her.

"Do you think he really went surfing or was that some kind of ruse to step out? You know how guys do that . . . escape to watch a game, go to a strip joint, whatever."

"I've wondered about that, too." She explained that Frank had a board, and a few times when she saw it out in the garage, she noticed sand sticking to the tacky wax. "The one time when I went to the beach with him, he didn't actually surf. He took me up to the cliff overlooking a cove, and we watched the surfers out in the lineup. Frank was highly critical of them. It wasn't a good day. Frank was angry about something. We stopped in at his aunt's house. A small cottage. His Aunt Ginny was in a hospital bed in the living room, and there was some neighborhood woman who came in to take care of her. He teased his aunt about how she kept hanging on, and she stared at him, but I'm not sure there was any intelligence behind her eyes. He brought her salt water taffy, although she couldn't have it because of her diabetes. After we left the cottage, he was in a foul mood. He said Ginny should die already and leave the place to him." Jane frowned. "That was the one and only time I went to the beach with him."

When Alvarez asked about the level of violence Frank employed, Jane felt a twinge of embarrassment. Was the detective thinking that she could have just walked away? "It wasn't overt violence, but the threat was there. I had bruises from being manhandled and shoved around, and sometimes my neck was bruised from the choking."

He nodded, gentle encouragement. "The choking seemed

to be a pattern in his method of assault. We saw evidence of it with Jane Doe and Lana Tremaine."

I could kill you right now. It would be so easy. She shivered, trying to shake the harsh memory.

"Did he ever hit you with the baseball bat?" the detective asked.

"No. Never. He didn't hit me. That was one of the things that kept me in the relationship. I kept telling myself that he really loved me in his own way, and that he would never hurt me."

"I understand." The detective seemed weary.

Jane, too, was exhausted. She hoped they could finish soon.

"But you said earlier that he held you against your will?"

"Yes. He used those handcuffs. He wasn't shy about chaining me down. I don't know if they still have school personnel records, but I maxed out my sick days that year, mostly for times when Frank had me locked to the bed. And he forced himself on me." A tear slipped out, unbidden and unexpected. "He forced me to have sex. That's sexual assault under the law, isn't it?"

"Yes." Alvarez pushed a box of tissues over to her. "Yes, it is." There were a few more questions and then, at last, the deposition was over.

She was grateful to be finished. Energy had drained from her along with the harsh memories. Still, when she arose she felt so suddenly light that she had to steady herself with one hand on the table. Funny thing about painful memories—you felt so damned good once you let them go.

"There's one more thing." Alvarez's voice stopped her. "Off the record." He wrote something down on a notepad and tore off the page. "Some information for you on Frank Dixon's family history. I know he told you his parents were dead, but his father and uncle are serving life terms in Ohio for three counts of homicide. This is the link to a documentary that details their crimes. And we're looking into his grandfather, who also had a record of violent behavior back in the forties."

"So his family really *was* crazy."

He nodded. "Criminally insane, maybe. Or maybe just criminals."

"Why are you interested in this?"

"The prosecutor is planning to bring in an expert witness on genetics. If we can show that Dixon is a violent sociopath like his father and the other men in his family, we've got a better shot at keeping him locked up for life."

Jane pulled her thin, polka-dot sweater closed at her throat. Funny to be shivering when it was actually warm and stuffy in here. She tucked the paper into her purse and left the room, wondering if she would ever lose the chill between her shoulder blades, the feeling of being watched, the icy frost of his eyes.

PART 2

It's the ripple, not the sea
That is happening.

—Stephen Sondheim

Chapter 9

The call came at 4:22 a.m. Saturday morning, awakening Jane with a jolt of alarm. She sat up in bed and snatched her cell phone from the nightstand.

"This is Officer Pickett of the Mirror Lake Police Department."

"What? What's going on?" Heart-pounding panic gave way to disorientation as the voice explained that everyone was okay.

"Your daughter Harper is being cited for breaking curfew."

"Breaking curfew?" Somewhere in the back of her mind was the dusty, archaic rule that made outlaws of young people who went outside after hours. Jane realized that Luke's hand was still securely on her hip, and somehow that made her feel a little risqué as she spoke to the cop.

The officer explained that five girls, wanting some "fresh air," had taken it upon themselves to venture down to Palisades Elementary. Apparently, Harper had been the ringleader. "We have them down at the precinct now, on Tulip Avenue."

"In jail?" She scraped her hair back with one hand. "You've incarcerated teenage girls for a curfew violation?"

"They're waiting in the sergeant's office. You need to come get your daughter."

"Okay, officer." A sigh rasped from her throat as Jane extracted herself from the warm bed and rubbed the back of her neck. "I'm on my way."

"Is Harper okay?" Luke asked from the shadows of the comforter.

"She violated curfew. I need to spring her from jail." Although Jane made light of it, she felt a little sick. The early hour, the abrupt wakening, the panic of worrying that her daughter was in jeopardy, the lingering horror over the information Detective Alvarez had given her. She switched on the dresser lamp, sending soft amber light spilling through the bedroom.

"Do you want me along for moral support?" He rubbed the dark hairs on his chin. "You've had a rough week. And as you've seen from recent events, I can be quite the badass."

She gave a small laugh as she grabbed a scrunchie from her dresser and pulled her hair back. "No, thanks. Your presence would only expand the scandal. 'Teacher's daughter arrested. School teachers purged from love nest.'"

"Right." He pulled his jeans on. "But I can't stay in bed. Unless you'd like me to greet Harper with animal-shaped pancakes."

"Sorry. My brain is sleep-deprived."

He slipped on his shirt as he crossed the room. "I get that. A lot has been dumped on you, but it looks like the really bad shit is in the past. Frank is in jail. That's a gift."

"It is." She yawned. "But now Harper is in jail, too."

He chuckled. "Not for long."

There was something about the way he folded her into his arms, something about his resolute tenderness that made the noises fade, at least for the moment. A short whisper of time.

* * *

She was the last parent to arrive at the precinct, where Pete Ferguson was the self-appointed facilitator of an impromptu parent meeting.

"I'm just saying we should nip this in the bud," Pete said, making a cutting motion with scissor fingers. "And if that means suspending a player from the team as a disciplinary measure, so be it."

"Who's getting suspended?" Jane asked, blinking against the bright precinct lights. Why the hell were they conferencing at this hour of the morning? Jane wanted to grab Harper and get the hell home.

"Hi, Jane. Come on in and join us," Pete invited, as if he were hosting a talk show. "What you missed is the fact that your daughter was the instigator in this mess. Because of her, our girls are going to have curfew violations on their records."

"A temporary record," Keiko said firmly. "Officer Haynes explained that to me. If they commit no further offenses, this record will disappear when the girls turn eighteen."

"Regardless..." Pete stretched his arms wide enough to stop a stampeding elephant. "This is a problem, and we all know the source is one young lady in there."

"Can I just point out that Olivia is two years older than the other girls?" Trish held up two fingers, as if to drive home an elementary point. "You'd expect her to set a better example for our daughters."

"That's ridiculous," Linda objected. "Age isn't everything."

"And you were hosting, Pete...Linda," KK's mother piped up. The only black team parent, Cora Dalton usually was treated with deference by other parents, who were afraid of appearing racist in their primarily white community. "Not that I blame you. Kids are going to do what they wanna do. But I'm surprised you two didn't hear these five little lovelies sneaking out the door. If there's one thing our girls are not, it's quiet."

"Olivia's room is in a separate wing, and our house is forty-five hundred square feet," Linda explained. "We didn't hear a thing."

Show-off, Jane thought.

"But I assure you, this is the last time we'll be hosting any of your girls overnight." Linda's mouth puckered in a sour expression. "We don't harbor juvenile delinquents."

"Are you calling my daughter a JD?" Hands on her hips, Cora stood her ground.

"These are good kids," Jane intervened. "Good kids who made a poor choice by going out for a stroll after dark." She looked toward the officer working behind the reception counter. "What's the story on getting out of here? Do we need to sign them out?"

"Not until we figure out an appropriate team punishment." Pete's voice boomed; he would not be ignored.

"Hold on a second, Mr. Pete Ferguson." Cora was on fire now. "You are not the coach of my daughter's team. If there's going to be a team punishment, then Carrie Enderly is the one who is going to make that decision. For now, you figure out your own daughter's punishment, and I will deal with my child. No one else is going to mess with how I raise my daughter, Mr. Pete Ferguson."

Cora's speech took them all by surprise. As a city council member and major contributor to the school district, Pete Ferguson usually got what he wanted in Mirror Lake. Cops and teachers, car dealers and restaurateurs were used to handing this man a proverbial sundae with all the fixings. If Jane hadn't been a schoolteacher herself, and thus compelled to tolerate this difficult man, she would have applauded Cora's defiance.

"I'm with Cora. I'm taking Sydney home." Trish peeled off from the group and went over to the precinct desk.

Norio Suzuki spoke up, the voice of calm. "Cooler heads will prevail after we all get some sleep."

"Amen to that." Jane left the group and followed Trish and the cop to the room where the girls were being held. Olivia was twirling in a desk chair while Emma, Sydney, KK, and Harper were huddled on a low-slung couch, dozing together. All the girls wore the same type of pajamas: colorful cotton boxers topped by a baggy T-shirt. With Sydney stretched across the other girls' laps, the sight was almost comical.

"Wake up, sleeping beauties," Trish called. "Time to go home."

Based on Harper's moan and sullen expression, Jane could tell that she had her parenting work cut out for her.

"Bye!" The girls mustered enough enthusiasm for a round of hugs. "I love you!" they chimed brightly. Was it Jane's imagination, or was the contact with Olivia stiff and forced?

Wishing for a complacent daughter like Emma Suzuki, Jane told Harper to hang out while she took care of the paperwork. One form promised a follow-up call from a social worker; the other threatened a court summons if Harper was caught breaking curfew again. Jane took her time reviewing the legalese. Let the others clear out before them; she'd had her fill of Pete Ferguson for now.

When the coast was clear, Jane went out to the main desk and handed the form to a thin female officer with a dead-fish stare.

"We could have charged them with trespassing," the woman said proudly. "When we came up on them, they were hiding in someone's bushes. Private property. But we decided to go easy on them."

"I see." Jane shoved the pen into a cup on the desk. "Well, thanks for that."

When she turned, Harper stood behind her, annoyance seething in her pretty blue eyes. "Let's go, honey," Jane said blithely. With one hand on her daughter's back, she guided her out the double doors of the precinct.

"I hate cops," Harper carped before the door had even swung shut behind them.

"Don't say that. They're doing their job. They keep us safe."

"That lady cop was obnoxious. She said there was graffiti at Palisades, and she blamed us for doing it, and we didn't go anywhere near the school. Oh my God, they are so ridiculous. You should have seen them trying to track us down through the neighborhood with those spotlights. It was like a chase scene on TV. Like the hoods of L.A. or something. You'd think we robbed a bank or something."

Jane let her daughter vent as they headed up the street. The car was parked behind the precinct, but Jane had already decided that they would head over to St. Olaf's, a French bakery on the town's main square that would be opening any minute now. If she didn't address this now, Harper would scowl at her every time she brought it up over the next few days.

"You did break the law," Jane pointed out, "even if it is sort of a lame one."

"It's so lame. We have constitutional rights. They can't lock us up in our own homes just because we're kids."

Oh, yes, they can, Jane thought as she motioned Harper to turn onto the cobblestone street leading to the square. But now was not the time for a constitutional debate; it was time for Harper to accept responsibility for her actions and learn that laws were not to be broken on a whim. "Why were you walking around so late at night?"

"We had to get out, Mom. There was no air! Olivia's house is so nice, but the rec room where they wanted us to sleep has a musty smell, and I couldn't take it anymore. I just wanted some fresh air, and once we all got out, Olivia said we should go for a walk. She does it all the time. Did you know there's a spot on the top of a hill near Palisades that they call the roundabout? It's kind of high up, and there are no trees around, so you can see the stars really well."

"Yup." Jane knew the spot. Years ago it had been known as a place for kids to park and fool around until the cops stepped up their patrols. "Let's stay on track here. Mr. Ferguson said you were the instigator."

"That is so not true. I swear, it's not my fault, Mom. I wanted to step out, just to the yard, but Olivia said we should go for a walk. She's the one who got us into all this trouble."

"And you think she's afraid to tell her father the truth?"

"Duh. Wouldn't you be?"

"He is a little scary."

"He's such a liar, just like his daughter."

"I thought you were happy to be on the team with Olivia."

"That was when she was going to play shortstop. Now all she can talk about is playing catcher." Harper hugged herself, rubbing her arms for warmth. Despite the pale sky, the cool of night still held the town in its grasp. "Why is she trying to steal my position? That's so unfair."

"I don't know, Hoppy."

"I wish she would move to another town. If she wants to play catcher so bad, she should go to West Green or Hazel Grove."

"That's not going to happen. You know the Fergusons are firmly rooted in Mirror Lake." Everyone gushed over their palace on the lake. "They have a lot of power in this town."

"What am I going to do?" Harper whined.

"You're going to figure out how to play on the same team with her, and stop worrying so much. We talked to Coach Carrie, and as far as she's concerned, you are the team's catcher. Olivia's just going to have to accept that." Jane hustled her daughter past the majestic clock at the center of the cobblestone square and thought of the supreme joke of time.

Years could fly by without a ripple, and then, when you least expected it, time exploded around you like popping corn, making a few seconds stretch into an eternity.

The clock chimed a muted ping that announced five thirty. You had to hate yourself to be up at five thirty on your day off. Or maybe you just resented the person who tore you from a soft blanket of sleep.

"I'm so tired. I just want to go to bed." Harper shivered. "Where is the car?"

"Back that way. We're going to grab some coffee and pastries from St. Olaf's first."

"What? I don't want anything."

"But you love their chocolate croissants."

"I just want to go to bed. I want to go home. You can make your own coffee, Mom. I'm so tired."

You weren't tired a little while ago when you and your friends sneaked out of the Fergusons' house. When you took a stroll to the park. At four a.m. In your shorty pajamas. When you ran from the cops and dove into someone's garden for cover.

Jane knew she wasn't allowed to say any of these things; as the grown-up in this relationship, she had to take the high road. Biting back the bitter response, Jane trudged ahead toward the amber light of the bakery window, a beacon of comfort in the early morning chill. She tugged on the thick, bronze handle, but the bakery door didn't budge. "They're not open yet."

Through the glass, a girl in a white uniform held up her hand, showing five fingers. "She wants us to wait a few minutes," Jane said.

"I don't want to wait." Harper spun away from the door with a whine. "I'm so tired."

"Here. Come sit." Jane put her arm around Harper's shoulder and guided her across the square toward a bench. "Do you want my jacket?"

"No. Someone might see me."

"It's a black leather jacket. It's not that uncool." Jane slipped off her jacket and gave it to Harper.

Handling the garment as if it might burn her, Harper let it rest on her bare knees as she huddled on the bench, cold and a bit pathetic looking in her summer pajamas. Funny that it was okay to be seen wearing boxers and a baggy T-shirt, but beware the leather jacket. Jane longed to sit down beside her daughter and hold her close, working up some warmth between them. A few years ago Jane would have been allowed to snuggle in public, but now Harper would be mortified. That was normal—age appropriate—and yet Jane missed the old days.

It was going to be a beautiful September morning in Mirror Lake. Jane stared off at the cobalt swath of lake in the distance, the green patch of park and trees in the foreground. In another hour or so, vendors from all over Oregon would be setting up carts and booths to sell their wares at the town's Saturday market. Cheese and lavender, organic fruits and vegetables, designer cupcakes and homemade condiments.

"Remember when we used to go to the Saturday market in the summer?" Jane said. "You were so cute, sneaking samples from the cheese lady. I would always buy a block of cheddar from her, but you didn't eat it at home. When I asked you why you liked it so much at the market, you said: 'Everything tastes better when it's free.'"

"Mom!" Harper winced. "That is so embarrassing."

Jane understood; sometimes it was hard to embrace your past.

Pulling her hands into the warmth of her cotton sweatshirt, Jane crossed her arms and breathed in the fresh smells of

morning. Already the plaza was coming alive with city workers. A man in coveralls and an orange vest was power-washing
the paving stones where the market would be set up. Another
man was blowing the plaza clean of debris. On the square, a
city truck crept from one lamppost to another to water the lush
hanging baskets of flowers that decorated every street corner
from spring through autumn. Yes, a well-to-do suburb like
Mirror Lake could be a bit uppity at times, with power-hungry
parents and overly zealous cops, but Jane was grateful for the
good life she had found here.

"Okay, they're open." Harper was off the bench and moving across the square. "Come on."

After they settled at a small table within range of the huge,
warm ovens, Jane initiated the essential conversation points.
"Here's the thing that disturbs me the most about this morning . . . last night. You are refusing to accept responsibility for
your actions."

"But it wasn't my fault." Harper paused to lick a glob of
chocolate from the corner of her mouth. "I told you, Olivia
was the one who—"

"That is exactly what I mean. I don't care what Olivia or
Mr. Ferguson or the man on the moon did. I care about you,
Harper Ryan. You made a bad choice. You broke the law, and
you got caught."

"What do you expect me to do about it now?"

"I want to hear that you're sorry. That you realize you
made a mistake. That it won't happen again."

"I already said that."

"No. You didn't." Jane faced her daughter, refusing to
cower from the fury in Harper's eyes. Why did Harper get
herself so worked up over an apology?

"Fine." Harper scowled down at the table. "I'm sorry,
okay?"

"And you realize you did the wrong thing. Because if you break curfew again, we'll have to meet with the juvenile court." As it was, Jane would be hearing from a county social worker. "I need to know that you're taking this seriously, Hoppy. If this happens again, you could have a permanent police record. It could affect college and your future jobs."

"Okay, yeah. I'm not that stupid. I won't break their stupid curfew again. But I can't believe how mean those cops were to us. Especially the lady. I mean, she checked our hands for spray paint to see if we did the graffiti. And she took our cell phones and looked at our texts. Isn't that a violation of our privacy?"

"Sounds like it," Jane agreed. "But I think it's probably covered under the search and seizure law."

"Then it's a stupid law."

Jane took a long sip of her latte, trying to gather patience. "We need to respect the law, plain and simple. That's what makes a society functional. There are rules designed to protect people, and we follow them. I wish you would stop questioning authority."

"But Mr. Healy said we should always question authority." Mr. Healy had been last year's history teacher. "He said that's what democracy is all about. If people don't keep the government in line, it'll get all corrupt and everything."

"Part of challenging authority is taking action to enact positive change." Jane maintained a calm, steady tone. "Are you going to pursue changing the youth curfew?"

Harper groaned. "I don't care about the stupid curfew. I just want to go home. Can't you see how tired I am?" Her phone buzzed, and Harper brightened as she checked the text message. "Oh my God. Emma says her parents are grounding her. They're talking about two whole weeks. Except for softball. That's so overboard."

"It sounds like an appropriate punishment."

"What?" Harper's periwinkle eyes registered shock. "Am I going to be grounded?"

Jane wrapped her hands around the warm cup as she floated the possibility. Grounding had never been an effective punishment for Harper, as the punishment had only served to make her glum, depressed, and angry. This was a girl who needed outdoor activity and social interaction. Besides, two weeks of restriction would keep Harper from the back-to-school picnic, which was a big event for the entire high school. Held at a park on the lake, the picnic featured competitions in and out of the water as well as a popular local deejay. Last year, Harper had talked about it for days afterward.

"I don't think it would serve anyone to ground you now," Jane said. "But I hope you learned your lesson."

"I did. Thanks, Mama-dish." As Harper tapped a text back to Emma, Jane smiled over the silly nickname that had stuck since grade school. When things were good, Harper called Jane Mama-dish, and Jane called her daughter Hoppy, a name that three-year-old Harper had coined for herself and for the little stuffed rabbit that had accompanied her everywhere. Harper still took that rabbit to bed with her.

The texting activity picked up as Jane finally got around to eating her croissant. By the time she finished, Harper was lobbying to go over to Emma's house after she changed clothes at home.

"I thought Emma was grounded," Jane said.

"She is, but she's allowed to have visitors, and I told her I'd come over to make her feel better."

Jane sighed. "We'll see. Personally, I think you should get some sleep before the game. You need to be in Sherwood at two."

"I'm not tired anymore," Harper insisted, though her pale face with shadowed eyes belied the claim. She looked up from her phone and tilted her head. "I have a question, but you may not want to hear it." She tilted her head, suddenly shy. "Why don't we ever talk about my father?"

The croissant was suddenly dry in Jane's mouth. It took some effort to swallow and speak. "We can talk about him. It's always been hard for me, but time has passed. As they say, time heals wounds."

What a lie. The wounds had throbbed like crazy after she'd watched the documentary recommended by Detective Alvarez. Although the story of Lester and Doug Dixon was spellbinding, the horror of their gruesome crimes had haunted Jane for days. Even Luke had squirmed on the sofa when the program had uncovered the grisly method the men had used to dispose of the young women's bodies.

According to Frank's uncle, Doug Dixon, the first murder had been a crime of opportunity for Frank's father. It had happened in the summer of 1970 in rural Ohio, a state still reeling from the shooting of thirteen students at Kent State and the war that had divided the nation. Lester had picked up a hitch-hiker, a "flower child," whom he viewed as an ingrate, not worthy of life. He drove her to his brother's trailer, where Doug helped him tie her up and subdue her by pressing rags dampened with paint thinner to her nose. The two men took turns raping the young woman, and then they killed her and used a hacksaw to cut her body into pieces. As the family owned a concrete business, they found it easy to dispose of the debris beneath porches and patios that they poured throughout the community.

Doug Dixon claimed that he had been dragged into a life of crime by his brother, Lester. "Once we pulled it off with the first girl and it worked, we just kind of fell into it again. I mean, it was so easy. Those hippie girls, they were easy targets. Lester kept grabbin' 'em, and I helped him, and that's how it went till that one got away." The fourth victim, Audra

Wilks, had escaped from the trailer while the men were off at a bar drinking, and that had ended their crime spree.

The crimes were heinous, but the cavalier way that Frank's uncle recalled the episodes had chilled Jane to the bone. To hear him tell it, the only problem was that the men had eventually been caught.

And the mastermind of it all had been Lester Dixon, the grandfather of the girl sitting across the table from Jane. Her throat worked to swallow a lump of pastry. She washed it down with the now cold latte, glad that her daughter was distracted by a new text message.

"Anyway..." Harper looked up from her phone. "Why don't you tell me stories about him?"

Jane had to steel herself to look into the glimmering blue eyes that reminded her of Frank Dixon. "What do you want to know?"

"I don't know, but you're always remembering stories about me from when I was little. The cheese lady in the market and how I cried when Hoppy lost her ear in the washing machine. And that Cat in the Hop poster that you refuse to take down. But you never bring up stories about my dad. Funny things he did or said." Harper wiggled a hangnail on her thumb. "And you don't have any pictures of him. Sydney thinks that's weird. How come you don't have any?"

"Photos just weren't a priority back then. It wasn't like today with all the camera phones and selfies."

"Mmm." Harper wasn't completely satisfied with that. "Don't you have *any* pictures?"

Jane considered getting one of Frank's photos from the rash of news articles that had accompanied his arrest and trial. Maybe one of the shots where he appeared more handsome than psychotic. She could Photoshop it a little to soften the edges. In a nice frame, it could serve as a keepsake for Harper. Or was that a crazy idea? If Harper ever got tech savvy, she might search the image and learn the truth about her father. "Let me dig around and see what I can find," Jane said.

"And what was he like?" Harper asked coyly. "Like, what made you want to hang out with him at first?"

"Your father was very handsome, and he had a magnetic personality. No one could resist Frank when he turned on the charm." This was all painfully true. Frank was like a narcotic, an opiate that seduced a body into dark unconsciousness. "My mother liked to bake for him, and my father enjoyed talking about cars and other guy stuff with him."

"Ooh . . ." Harper's lower lip jutted out in a pout. "That must have been nice—the whole family together. I wish your parents were still alive. It's not fair that we don't have any family."

"I know; it's hard." Regret flickered deep inside. If only her mother hadn't tried to foist her off on Frank. If her parents had defended her, really listened to her, they might have been able to save her from having to flee.

Jane felt a tug of affection for Harper, who was twisting a strand of her russet hair around one finger. *I will protect you,* she vowed. *I'm doing my best to keep you safe.*

"And what else did you like about him?" Harper asked. "We both know that beauty is only an outward shell."

It was one of the mantras Jane repeated to her daughter: Good looks are not enough. She was glad to hear that Harper had absorbed it.

"Your dad was a surfer. He loved the beach." Or was that a lie? She had never seen him surf.

"Really? So that's where I get my athletic skills."

Jane smiled. "I guess. Your mother almost failed PE in college."

"I still can't believe that, Mom. You were so lame. But a surfer is pretty cool."

While Harper was lost in a text, Jane thought about the one

time she had gone to the beach with Frank. There had been an old building behind his aunt's house, a garage that was so derelict it listed to one side. The foul smell had put her off, but Frank had pulled her inside, insisting that it was fine. "We can be alone in here," he said, scraping the straps of her swimsuit down and taking ownership of her body in an economy of motion. There was a piece of workout equipment—an old weight bench covered in metallic red vinyl—and he'd pressed her onto it and driven into her.

Don't go there now. Jane squirmed in her seat. Not here. Not in front of Hoppy.

But something about the dark, ramshackle building lured her mind back. A sign? No . . . a message written on a beam at the ceiling, either written in marker or etched in, she couldn't remember. She had seen it there when she'd been flat on her back. *Help me,* it pleaded. *Help me.* Who had written it? It felt too desperate and sad to be a joke. And the dark stain on the floor—had it been blood? The sickening smell—what had caused that? Frank had said that he'd chased out a raccoon, but Jane had never really bought his explanation. Maybe Detective Alvarez could make something of the information.

Meanwhile, Harper's crabbiness had given way to a pleasant smile. "I know Dad was pretty young when he died, but was there something he wanted to do in his life? Did he like, want to climb a mountain, or did he dream of a certain career?"

"He had a job." Jane thought it might be as good a time as any to spring this small truth on Harper. "Actually, he was a police officer."

"What?" Harper flicked her hair back. "Are you kidding? Wait . . . you're just saying that to make me show respect to the Mirror Lake cops."

"I am dead serious."

"Oh my God. That's so dramatic. Like a TV show. Emma is going to scream."

While Harper sent another text to her friend, Jane finished her latte and cleared off the small café table. With any luck, that information about her father would be enough to tide Harper over for a few years. Jane had had enough of Frank Dixon for now. She'd had enough to last a lifetime.

Chapter 10

Labor Day was blessedly uneventful. Jane was still in her pajamas at noon, when she woke Harper and Sydney for blueberry pancakes and bacon. The temperature was supposed to reach ninety, but the heat was inviting—the last wave of summer. The girls wanted to go to the swim park, and Jane was happy to soak up some sun.

"Mom, we don't need you to stay," Harper insisted. "There are lifeguards, and I'm almost fifteen."

"But I want to go. It's my holiday too."

Harper let out a growl as she scraped her plate into the trash.

"I promise, I'll set up my own blanket and pretend that I don't know you."

"Like that matters," Harper muttered.

"My mom might be there, too," Sydney said brightly. "You could sit with them, Ms. Ryan."

"That'd be great. But I'll bring a book, just in case."

The swim park was a slice of heaven at the edge of the cold blue lake. Most of the wedge of property on the lakefront was shaded by tall Douglas fir trees that formed a canopy of green overhead. The stone lodge at the park entrance contained rest rooms and a snack bar. Next to the lodge were Ping-Pong tables, shuffleboard courts, and a play structure with slides and monkey bars. Ribbons of pavement looped around the trees, creating paths that led to the lake. The waterfront boasted a kiddie pool, two swim areas sectioned off by wooden walkways, and a waterfront gazebo where paddleboats and kayaks could be checked out.

Harper and Sydney immediately devoured fifty-cent hot dogs and slushies (oh, to burn off that many calories) and then headed to the dock that overlooked the deepest section of the lake. Beside the high lifeguard stand, two diving boards reached out over the lake, relics of a bygone era when water skiers used to soar from platforms in the lake and public pools used to have slides and high-dives. The older kids usually congregated at the diving boards, where they sometimes rated dives, competed, gave tips on how to do a jackknife or a swan dive. And of course, there were the inevitable cannonballs designed to splash everyone sitting nearby.

Right now they were taking turns jumping off the diving board, turning, and catching a football in midair. Harper was currently tossing the ball, though she had been swimming. With her water-slick skin, she reminded Jane of a happy otter. It was amazing how relaxed those girls were around guys. At that age, Jane had been too insecure and too heavy to put herself out there, especially in a bathing suit.

Settled on a blanket in a patch of sunshine, Jane pulled a hat from her tote bag and lost herself in a book. A few couples with small kids were barbecuing across the path, but otherwise the park was fairly quiet. After today, the lakefront park would only be open for special events like the high-school picnic.

After an hour or so Jane leaned back on her elbows and let her book drop to the blanket as she tipped her face up to the sun. This place, the green shade, blue water, easy laughter . . . the town had been a haven for Harper and her. They had dodged a bullet; Harper might never have to know about the road not taken, but Jane would always be grateful to have found Mirror Lake when she needed a safe place to raise a child. The only thing missing today was Luke. She wished he could have come along to chat and laugh, to spread sunscreen on that hard to reach spot between her shoulder blades, to give her the courage to relax in the cold water of the deep, dark lake, where large bass and enormous turtles roamed.

Adjusting the brim of her hat, she glanced over toward the deep-water swimming area to check on the girls. A handful of kids were still diving off the board, and a teen couple sat close on the dock, legs dangling over the water as they watched their friends. Where was Harper?

Her scalp began to tingle as she recognized Harper's neon-green two-piece. That was Harper sitting with a boy, leaning into him. His arm dangled casually over her shoulders, as if he was familiar with the landscape of her body.

Harper liked a boy.

Jane dug her palms into the grass as she steadied herself. Why did the discovery hit her with such a jolt? Harper was almost fifteen. She was a beautiful girl who could hold her own in a conversation.

Maybe it was time for Jane to give up the wide-eyed girl who had dressed up as the Cat in the Hat for three straight Halloweens.

Who was the boy? Jane squinted against the diamonds of light flickering on the lake. Wet teens were harder to identify, but from the build and unkempt dark hair she was pretty sure the boy was Jesse Shapiro, a moderate bad boy of the sophomore class.

Oh, honey, don't make the same mistake your mother did.

But it wasn't fair to put Jesse in the same category as Frank. Although the boy was known for smoking weed, he had a great love for the outdoors and an awesome gift for music. At last year's graduation ceremony he had played the trumpet in a duet that had received a standing ovation. There were worse boys than Jesse Shapiro. And although Jane had never liked the way marijuana made her feel, the pot smokers didn't get violent like drinkers. Was that any consolation? Jane had known some potheads who dropped out of college in the third year, lacking motivation to do much of anything beyond smoking and eating. She didn't want Harper to fall into that trap.

"What a neurotic mother you are," she said aloud. Her daughter was sitting next to a boy, and already Jane was worried about their long-term prospects as a couple. If she could get past the worries, she had to admit that it was a little exciting. Harper's first boyfriend. It was a milestone, even if Jane wasn't supposed to know about it.

The next day, Jane stood at the back of her classroom and did a second count of the literature textbooks on the rolling rack. There weren't enough books to go around, so they were designated for use in class. A good thing, as they weighed a ton, too much to lug around in a backpack.

The bulletin board along the back wall made her smile. Harper had talked her into ordering movie posters from books that had been turned into films: *Romeo and Juliet, The Great Gatsby,* and *To Kill a Mockingbird.* In between the posters, Harper had pinned up the caption: FIRST CAME THE BOOK. The girl was not an academic, but she did get the big picture.

Everything was ready for tomorrow—the first day with the students. The first week was such an important time in a freshman classroom. Orientation. Building self-esteem. Establishing mutual trust. Freshman year was usually a time of physical and mental growth, and Jane was happy to shepherd the kids through novels and writing assignments that sparked fear in their eyes at first. By the end of the year, many of her students were reading for pleasure and signing up for the creative writing elective.

With the classroom squared away, she had some time to spend on her own schoolwork. Jane had completed her coursework for a Master of Education degree at Portland State. She'd enjoyed her classes. Now that her classes were done, her final thesis hung over her head like a heavy cloud bank. She slid a small student desk over to the window, where she could enjoy the sunshine and playing fields while she worked.

She opened her laptop and stared out at the softball diamond. The girls were setting up for a scrimmage, the fun part of practice for Harper. Brandi was pitching, and Emma was up at bat first. After one strike she got a piece of Brandipitch and landed a single. Harper was on deck, pausing to take a swing with her coveted bat, Blue Lightning, before stepping up to the plate. Jane loved to watch her daughter when Harper was in her element, poised to swing. Hoppy swung at the first pitch and connected with a clang.

"Yes!" Jane hissed as her daughter dropped the bat and flew around the bases while there seemed to be some trouble retrieving the ball from the outfield. "She's a home run hitter, and you're never gonna git her. Give it up. Give it up," she chanted, enjoying the moment alone in her empty classroom. Despite her issues with Harper, she was proud of her daughter's athletic abilities. Harper was gifted, but she also worked hard, supported her team, and sacrificed vacation trips and sleep to dedicate herself to sports. No one could say whether Harper's athleticism would lead to a scholarship or a career, but Jane was glad Harper had the satisfaction of achievement to balance her academic challenges. Jane had always been an excellent student, conscientious and attentive. Eventually her work ethic was bound to rub off on Harper.

She opened the file for her current research paper. Dr. Kendris had already approved her topic: Criminal Behavior: A Result of Nature or Nurture? She had always been curious about the topic, and now, with Frank's family history, she had a case that

she could write up. Did genetics play a part in antisocial behavior? Was psychopathy inherited? Harper's involvement in
a few incidents last spring had sparked the possibility that
Harper might share some of her father's issues. Well . . . those
had been Jane's overwrought worries late at night, staring at
the ceiling and wondering if her daughter felt the tiniest shred
of guilt about losing her temper or cutting a classmate off a
party list or taking cash from Jane's wallet. When confronted,
Harper always had an excuse like "That girl deserves what she
gets," or "I knew you would give me the money anyway, Mom."
Jane reminded herself that teens like her daughter were finding their way in the world, pushing the limits, but Harper's
cold, blue stare sometimes frightened Jane when she was
looking for remorse and found none.

Frank's icy eyes.

The appearance of Detective Alvarez had brought Frank's
presence back into her consciousness, although with the distance
of time and miles, her perception of him was more objective. She
now knew that Frank's family was beyond dysfunctional. The
disagreements or addictions that usually caused family strife
seemed minor compared to the violent behavior displayed by
Frank's father, uncle, and grandfather.

"They're all crazy," he'd said of his family. At the time,
she'd assumed Frank was exaggerating, trying to blame his
parents for his own malevolence. She had been wrong about
that. Dead wrong.

Vigilantly, she had watched Harper for signs of her father's
meanness. In the long, late-night hours spent walking her baby
girl through fits of colic, she had worried that the baby's distress
was the beginning of a wicked streak. But the colic had faded
gradually after four months, giving way to a quiet but sensitive
little girl who loved to spend hours in motion, climbing on the
park play structure or tossing a ball toward a hoop. As a
preschooler, Harper had demonstrated independence and self-

reliance. Instead of throwing temper tantrums, Harper dissolved into tears when she didn't get her way. When Jane refused to carry Harper into the grocery store, when Jane had to leave her at preschool Monday morning, when it was time for Jane to leave Harper's bed at night, Harper's blue eyes flooded with tears that tugged at Jane's heart. "It sounds like she has separation anxiety," Marnie told Jane one night when they were talking on the phone. "Who else is she comfortable with? A sitter, or one of her teachers?"

There was no one. Harper was not especially fond of her teachers, and her other attachments with Nancy's sons next door or the children of Jane's colleagues seemed to rely on having Jane present. Inadvertently, Jane had passed on her own feelings of fear and distrust to her daughter. On the recommendation of Harper's preschool teacher, Jane went cold turkey. She refused to pick Harper up and carry her around, even on cold, rainy days. She tried to numb herself to Harper's crying jags. Her only concession was at night, when Harper's sobs tore at Jane from the bedroom door. *I can give you this,* Jane thought, stretching out on the bed beside her daughter and drying her tears. *If it makes you feel safe and secure, I can spare a half hour or so each night.*

Kindergarten introduced Harper to a new school as well as a new friendship group. Emma and Sydney were delightful, their moms a welcome wave of common sense. Harper's behavior was not an issue again until she hit adolescence and suddenly began to pick on Jane and complain about the inadequacies of life. While Jane could accept that her daughter's transformative years would be a difficult time, it was embarrassing when bad behavior flared up at school and the other teachers got an eyeful of the fledgling teen monster, who cursed, whined, and seethed at the slightest disappointment.

Not to point blame, but Jane had been a Goody Two-shoes

when she was growing up—strictly following the rules. On the other hand, Frank had rarely acknowledged his own bad behavior. The rare apologies had been laced with explanations and redirected blame. No guilt. No show of feelings and emotions. And his composure had branded him a hero in the law enforcement community. That calm, cool attitude in the face of people suffering or bleeding around him, the self-possession that people had labeled as courage had actually been the apathy of a sociopath. He really didn't care if a woman died in his arms, as long as the paperwork didn't interfere with his plans after his shift.

Dear God, please don't let my daughter be a soulless monster like her father.

Jane clicked to a photo of Harper. Sparkling blue eyes, heart-shaped face, and a smile that could light up a room. In this shot, the sun was behind her, and her brown hair was aglow in bright golden hues. Jane would be crushed if this beautiful young woman matured into a monster.

But Harper wasn't the only one susceptible to Frank's evil. There was Louisa.

Jane rarely allowed herself to dwell on the child she had given away. Thoughts of Louisa were forbidden fruit, a guilty pleasure, especially when Jane fantasized that the facsimile of her daughter was a model teen who treated her mother with respect. A girl who was kind to all the kids around her. An honest girl who did not blame others when things went wrong. How nice it would be to wake her daughter in the morning and not be greeted with belly-aching about how tired she was. Or to have a whole day when Harper wasn't having a fit about something so terribly wrong in her life like a snub from a friend, a bad call from an umpire, a hangnail that was throbbing. Was Louisa more like Jane—academic and serious-minded, obedient and affable? Jane liked to think that she had given Chrissy and Nick Zaretsky the good child, a daughter who would fill their hearts and thrive in their loving home.

With a sigh, Jane clicked open the 2005 study she'd been using, which was based on an extensive research project involving more than five thousand sets of twins born in the 1990s. A differentiation was made between identical twins, who shared one hundred percent of their cellular code, and fraternal twins, who shared only about fifty percent. The study found that psychopathic traits had a high rate of heritability. "Eighty-one percent," Jane breathed, unable to wrap her brain around the striking statistic. Of course, environment played a role in the way any child developed. The study acknowledged that, allowing that environment could help a child overcome a negative genetic trait.

Even so, the power of genetics was undeniable. One scientist asserted that this evidence debunked the belief that all children were born with a natural innocence. His claim: Some children were born with a propensity for evil.

A frightening assertion. Jane took a deep breath, trying to separate her personal fears from the facts of the study. None of these statistics guaranteed that Harper would inherit the callous lack of compassion Frank had possessed. In fact, one of the traits of a sociopath was lack of emotion, and that didn't fit Harper at all. Of course, Jane would not include Harper in the case study for this paper, for her peace of mind and her daughter's privacy.

As if on cue, the classroom door flew open and Harper dropped her softball bag on the floor. "Why can't anything go right?" She stomped over to Jane, leaving clumps of mud and grass behind her as she crossed the carpet in her cleats. "It's so unfair."

"What happened?"

"Olivia is ruining everything. She talked Coach Carrie into letting her catch in practice, and Carrie thought she did a good job. Olivia is the starting catcher in Thursday's game."

"What?" It didn't make sense. "Carrie told us she was keeping Olivia as shortstop."

"But something happened." Harper raked her hair back, pacing frantically. "He talked to her. Mr. Fergie got to her, Mom. He came to practice and made her give Olivia a try. And now Olivia is catcher. It's so unfair. How can they do this to me?"

"Oh, honey. That's awful." Jane was surprised Carrie had made a move like that without warning her, but she understood the difficulty of dealing with a parent like Pete Ferguson. For now, the only thing to do was soothe Harper.

"Don't you have anything to drink in here?" Harper demanded, checking drawers of the old metal desk. "I'm so thirsty, and I think someone stole my water bottle."

"Get something from the machine in the hall," Jane said.

"I need water!" Harper slammed a drawer closed and stomped across the room. "This is the worst day ever."

"I'm sure you'll get another chance to play catcher."

"No! Not as long as Olivia is around." Looking out the window toward the field, Harper punched a fist against the metal box of the heater.

"Harper!" Jane was not up for a temper tantrum. "Stop it. Just keep your cool about this."

"How am I supposed to do that? Don't you get it? I don't know how to play shortstop, and the outfield is so boring. I can't focus out there, just standing around." Tears were streaming down her cheeks as she turned and paced back to Jane. "Everything was going along fine until Olivia went to that stupid camp. It's all her fault. I hate her."

"Hoppy, we can't blame Olivia for everything," Jane said, trying to divert Harper from playing the blame game.

"Mom!" Harper pressed her palms to her ears in frustration. "What do you not get about this? She is ruining my life, and she doesn't even feel bad about it."

"That's because in her mind it's not about you. Olivia is single-mindedly focused on getting what she wants." *Just as you are,* Jane thought, though this was no time to pick at her daughter; damage control was the primary goal of the moment.

"I don't care what she wants." Harper lowered her voice. "I hate her." The cool glint in her blue eyes was hauntingly familiar to Jane.

Frank's eyes. Harper had his eyes, his malice, his depravity.

"I hate that bitch." Harper's voice oozed venom. "She needs to die."

"Don't say that." There was no tempering the shrill note in Jane's voice. "I know you don't mean it." Jane knew her daughter wasn't like that. The little girl who had spent hours making shots at the basketball net was not a cruel person.

"Why are you telling me what I should say?" Harper's cool tone unnerved Jane. "Don't I have freedom of speech?"

Jane struggled to keep from snapping back some barb about "earning your freedom." It would get her nowhere to argue semantics right now, but she could not have her daughter threatening to kill someone—even if she didn't mean it. "Hate is a strong word—"

"I know what it means, and I know how it feels," Harper bit back as she pulled a coin purse from her bag.

Jane held up one hand. "Fine. You're entitled to your emotions, but you can't go around wishing people dead. Menacing. Even threatening."

"I can wish anything I want," Harper challenged as coins jingled in her cupped fist.

Crossing her arms, Jane held her tongue and glared at the

teenage monster ducking out to the hallway vending machine. *She doesn't mean what she's saying,* Jane reassured herself. Harper hated killing spiders; she wouldn't wish pain on another person.

But she just did, Jane thought, hugging her arms tightly around herself. *She just did.*

Chapter 11

The first few days of school, Jane kept her cool while Harper stomped around like an irate dragon, ready to snap at any obstacle in her path. Jane was sick of hearing about Olivia this and Olivia that. When she asked Harper to take a deep breath and try to keep things in perspective—it was, after all, just fall ball—Harper burst into tears, accused Jane of lacking empathy, and stomped off to her room. Another day, Jane reminded Harper that she had a lot to be thankful for. "You have only one sophomore year of high school to enjoy in this lifetime," Jane pointed out. Harper simply dug into her mac and cheese with a scowl.

When Jane dropped by the PE office to talk with Carrie, the coach was apologetic. "I'm sorry about having to play Olivia as catcher. I know I told you that wouldn't happen, but word came down from the powers that be, and . . . well, I didn't have a choice."

Jane read an apology in the coach's eyes. "Was it Kathleen? Dr. Gallaway?"

Carrie nodded, pressing her teeth into the cuticle of one thumb. "Did you know that the Fergusons donate enough money each year to pay four teachers' salaries?"

"So I've heard." The torn skin around Carrie's thumb was bleeding now. Sad, the pressure schools placed on their coaches. "I've been in your shoes before. Olivia was failing freshman English in my class until her parents clubbed me with their magic wand. The sad part is that Olivia's really the one who suffers the most. She's being taught that you can buy anything you want in life."

"Between you and me? It really sucks."

It was one of those unfair situations that Harper would simply have to deal with. A bitter life lesson.

"Don't sweat it, Carrie," Jane assured her. "Hoppy will learn to deal. And maybe we'll get lucky and Olivia will just give up the dream."

Carrie took a tissue and pressed it to her thumb. "Wouldn't that be nice."

Jane had no choice but to let Harper sulk as she surreptitiously e-mailed Dennis Alvarez and focused on getting to know her new students. The detective told her that she wouldn't be asked to testify until sometime in the spring; with Frank Dixon currently behind bars, there was ample time to investigate and cull evidence to substantiate the other charges. Jane was grateful for the extra time. She still wasn't sure how to explain her involvement in the California trial to Harper, and she dreaded going back to Burnson, dealing with her parents, and the memories the trip would elicit.

Alvarez had found the small house at the coast where Frank's aunt had lived in her final years. One of Frank's cousins had inherited the place, but as far as the police could discern, Frank and some of the other men in the family used it when they went fishing or surfing at the coast. The house had checked out, but the shack behind it had been another story. "That was a good tip. We found blood stains out there," Alvarez had told her on the phone. "I'm thinking that this new evidence is going to help us with many of our cases. Lana Tremaine particularly. It might help us identify where she was held captive."

Lana Tremaine. The young woman was one of Jane's secret motivators. They had never met, but they were on the same team, fighting the same battle. Only Lana wasn't able to speak about what Frank had done to her, so it was Jane's duty to fill in some of the blank spaces. Had Frank developed a greater propensity toward violence in his relationships after Jane?

"We're having forensics go over the evidence," Alvarez said. "But it will be a few weeks until we know anything more."

"Really? That long?"

"Real life is a lot different from those crime shows on TV," he'd told her.

Jane didn't understand the reason for her own impatience. The trip down to California to testify would introduce a huge tangle in her life. Should she tell Harper, or pass the trip off as a teachers' conference?

"I'm leaning toward full disclosure," Luke had said one night during a few stolen moments at his house. "The truth may be hard to handle, but it doesn't come back to bite you in the ass like a lie." That was Luke—honest to the core.

"That's true, but this is a lot for a kid Harper's age to handle. Her father is a criminal. A predatory monster descended from a family of killers. No teen is prepared to deal with that."

"I know a lot of adults who are not prepared to deal with something of that magnitude. But think of the alternative. If you don't tell her now, it'll get worse." He clamped his hands onto her shoulders, massaging the tender muscles strained by stress. "A big bear on your shoulders, growing heavier and heavier."

Jane groaned. "I don't know what to do. I don't know what's right."

"There are no black-and-white answers here, only shades of gray."

"And gray is definitely not my color." She pulled his arms around her body and fell against him. Thank God for the comfort of Luke. When her thoughts raced and ranted, he kept her feet on solid ground.

With the case against Frank Dixon never far from her mind, Jane gladly turned her attention to her classes. She prided herself on her ability to learn the names of her students in the first week, and one of the wonders of teaching high school was connecting to young people at a tenuous period in their lives. She found hope in the fledglings: the struggling students who connected to Shakespeare for the first time, the brilliant skeptics who made her laugh, the emotional dropouts who checked in when the class read *Of Mice and Men*.

One day after school, Jane was in her classroom talking lesson plans with Mary Ellen Kitcher, just back from maternity leave, when Harper marched in without knocking. Emma and Sydney trailed behind her.

"I am not playing in the game today," Harper announced. "I'm too sick to play. Can you take me home right now?"

From the way Emma and Sydney stared away, Jane could tell this poor performance had been rehearsed. "What hurts?"

"I have a headache. And cramps. Really bad. Can you take me home?"

"I can give you some ibuprofen. And if you want I'll make you some tea in the teachers' lounge."

"That's so sweet," Emma gushed.

"I wanna go home," Harper insisted.

"Honey, if the medicine doesn't help, you can sit the game out. But you should be there on the bench, supporting your team."

Harper winced, tears glistening in her eyes. "That's so stupid."

"I know it's hard, but you need to pull yourself together. Your team needs you."

"We do." Sydney gave Harper a bump on the shoulder. "Do you want to walk to Smitty's before the game?" Smitty's was an ancient pharmacy near the school that now sold chips and ice cream.

"I guess so." Suddenly, Harper's cramps weren't so bad. "As long as that new girl isn't lurking by the door. She's so annoying."

"She's in my bio class," Emma said. "She's not so bad."

"She's so cutesy. She asked me which way to go to find the history wing. I told her go back to kindergarten."

"Harper!" Jane interrupted. "Are you bullying a new student?"

"It was a joke, Mom. History . . . go back in time?"

"Not funny. You've always been kind to new kids."

"This girl is different. She bugs me."

"She can't help it that she looks like you," Emma told Harper.

"Don't say that," Harper mumbled. She turned to Jane. "I don't like having a shadow at school, but everyone thinks we look alike. And it's not true at all. She's all frilly and pink. Like she just escaped from Malibu Barbie's beach house."

Sydney let out a goofy laugh, then covered her mouth when she felt Jane's disapproving glare.

"But the new girl is really sweet if you talk to her," Emma said. "And I see the resemblance. If you look at her face, she does look a little like you."

Harper scraped a strand of dark hair behind one ear. "Ew. Ick."

"Now you know how I feel," Sydney said. "People are always asking me if my sister and I are twins, and she's a year younger."

"Well, I don't have a twin." Harper tugged the band from her hair. "I'm an original."

Jane held herself steady, not wanting to show her concern. "What's the new girl's name?"

Sydney squinted. "Isabel-something?"

"Isabel, like a Southern belle." Harper's voice was laced with sarcasm.

"Let's not be unkind," Jane said with a rush of relief. "Isabel is a beautiful name." *And it's not Louisa.*

"Sorry about that," Jane told Mary Ellen after the girls had left. "Harper is having some issues right now."

"I think it's great that your daughter can tell you what's on her mind. Honesty is so important."

"As you can see, Harper doesn't hold back." Jane didn't know Mary Ellen well enough to discuss her long list of concerns about Harper's behavior and her own unsure parenting skills. She didn't know anyone well enough for that. Although Jane had known Keiko Suzuki and Trish Schiavone for years, Jane didn't feel comfortable telling them about her daughter's tantrums or the vile curses that spouted from Harper's beautiful lips, condemning Olivia, the entire Ferguson family, even kind Coach Carrie. Jane was not looking forward to tonight's game.

"I don't know how you do it." Tears filled Mary Ellen's eyes. "I look at my baby, and I hope and pray that she'll be a good person, but there's no telling, is there? I mean, they are born their own people."

"Yes, we're stuck with our genetics. But environment does have an impact." Jane wanted to believe that love was having an effect on Harper; she had to believe that this positive, supportive community would foster generosity in her daughter. She touched the younger woman's shoulder. "All of your nurturing makes a difference. I'm sure you're doing a great job, Mary Ellen."

"But I'm here, and not with her, and I feel so guilty." She pulled a tissue from the box on the desk. "I'm sorry. My hormones are raging. At least, that's what I keep telling myself."

Jane collapsed into a student desk with a sigh. "Mmm. I remember those days. Being a new mother was overwhelming for me. After I had Harper, I didn't work for a year." She had been trying to stay under the radar at the time, and she hadn't had the nerve to put her baby in child care.

"With summer and all, I've had almost six months with Taylor." Mary Ellen blew her nose. "But it's such an emotional quagmire. When I was home, I wanted to be out of the house. Some mornings, I begged Ben to call in sick so that I could take a shower in peace. Take a nap. Breeze through the grocery store on my own. I felt like a servant, a slave. I thought I couldn't wait to get back to teaching. And now that I'm here, I feel so guilty. I miss her all the time."

"They're so helpless when they're little. They need us. And hormones?" Jane shook her head. "I'm convinced that hormones are nature's way of keeping us from abandoning our young."

Mary Ellen laughed through her tears. "That's pretty cold."

Jane smiled, feeling a new bond with the woman. "I have my moments."

Mary Ellen opened her laptop and turned it so that Jane could see the screensaver photo of a pink-faced baby girl. "There she is. . . . My worst nightmare at four o'clock in the morning."

"She's adorable."

"They're all so deceptively cute. They really suck you in."

"That they do," Jane agreed.

Thursday's game did not go well for Harper. She started the game playing shortstop, but clearly wasn't comfortable playing the infield. The wariness on her face said it all. When Carrie switched her to the outfield in the fourth inning, Harper seemed to drift out to sea. Boredom was evident in her stance, glove on one hip, toes of one cleat swooping over the grass. Was she searching for four-leaf clovers?

"Heads up!" came the shout as the ball sailed off the bat of a player from Tigard. By the time Harper looked up, it was too late. The ball hit her shoulder and bounced away as she chased it through the grass. Tigard scored two runs due to Harper's error.

Harper was taken out of the game, and she moved to the end of the team bench, Blue Lightning on her lap. If Harper couldn't use her bat, no one would.

It was painful to watch. Jane had to fight the raw instinct to go to her daughter, enfold her in her arms, and take her away from this emotional broil. Emma and Sydney tried to cajole Harper from her black mood, but that icy blue stare did not falter. Seething hatred, Harper kept her eyes on Olivia, who played well, but could not lead the team to victory.

As the Tigard team ran a victory lap around the bases, Olivia went to retrieve her bag near Harper's feet. Still simmering on the bench, Harper glared at her.

"What's that look about?" Olivia asked. "Too bad, too sad for you."

Jane didn't hear Harper's answer, but she hurried in that direction to defuse the tension.

"This is your fault, you know," Olivia said. "If you hadn't bobbled that fly ball—"

"Shut up," Harper snapped. All at once she rose up with a growl and shoved her shiny bat into Olivia's throat. Later, Jane would thank God that Harper had been holding the bat across her lap; if she'd been able to take a swing with it, the consequences would have been devastating.

Girls and parents swarmed around them. Some tried to pull the girls apart amid the cluster of heat and noise and fury.

"That's enough!" The coach managed to be heard above the din. "I want you and you in my office tomorrow morning."

To their credit, the Fergusons didn't stick around. They pulled Olivia behind the backstop to Linda's illegally parked Mercedes and roared out of there.

"Did you see how she came after me?" Tears glimmered in Harper's sapphire eyes as she accepted hugs from the girls who encircled her. "I had to defend myself. You guys saw that, right? God, she's scary. Next time, I don't know what she'll do." She sniffed, then swiped at her wet cheeks, streaked with dirt and mascara. "She's so mean."

The other girls comforted her with pats on the back and sympathetic remarks like "I can't believe her!" and "Are you okay?"

Harper seemed to revel in their attention, a queen bee. Was that a glimmer of satisfaction in her eyes? Yes, she was gloating.

Jane had seen that look before, but she had to block the memory out. Entitlement and greed. She had seen those demons many times in Frank's eyes.

Chapter 12

Word of Harper's bobbled play was splashing through social media even before Jane made it to the second window at the drive-through.

"Oh my God! They're saying that it's my fault we lost the game!"

"Who is 'they'?" Jane asked.

"I don't know. . . . Olivia."

Jane sank into the seat as she waited for the window to open. "Remember that talk we had about personal best? You'll never be happy if you define yourself by your wins and losses in sports."

"Mom, it's not me; it's them. They're blaming me for losing the game."

Well, it is sort of your fault, Jane thought, *but it's only a game.* "Don't let them get to you. Do your own thing. Why don't you turn off your phone? Have some dinner, get your homework out of the way. I'll help you study for the history test."

"I can't turn my phone off. You really don't get me."

Jane accepted two paper bags of food and thanked the girl at the window. As she rolled away, she stole a steaming fry from one of the bags. "You've got a lot to do tonight, Hoppy. I know you're upset, but you can't let something like this pull you down. And be very careful about getting dragged into a match on Facebook or Twitter. The more you defend yourself, the more attention people will pay to your mistake on the field."

"It wasn't my fault," Harper insisted, and Jane ate another fry, knowing that Harper always needed to have the last word.

That night when Jane went into Harper's room to say good night, she kissed her on the forehead and told her distraught daughter that everything would look better in the morning.

Friday morning, it quickly became clear that Jane had been wrong.

As Jane and Harper walked into school from the parking lot, Jesse Shapiro and Teddy Pitari paused outside the double doors.

Harper's face brightened as if the wattage had been amped up. "Hi." She cocked her head, seductive behind a lock of dark hair that fell over one eye. "How's it going?"

"Hey." Jesse shifted from one foot to the other. He wore faded jeans and skater shoes with holes worn through at the small toe. "I've been worried about you. How's your head?"

"My head's fine." Harper's eyes flashed.

Teddy leaned back warily, as if he were afraid of being punched.

"Oh. Someone posted that you got smacked in the head by the ball yesterday." Jesse scratched his head, scraping back some dark curls. "You sure you're all right?"

"I'm fine." Pulling up her hood, Harper moved past the boys and ducked into the school.

The boys remained cautious, deer caught in headlights.

"She's fine," Jane said, minus the venom. "Don't believe everything you see on Instagram."

Throughout the day Harper sent texts of misery.

Coach Carrie is blaming me for fighting with Olivia when she started it all!!!

I feel really sick. Will you take me home?

Can I just leave?

Ugh . . . everyone is blaming me.

This is the worst day. EVER.

I almost threw up. Really.

"Oh, Hoppy." Jane put her cell phone down with a sigh. Her daughter was such a drama queen, but that was the high school norm. Jane had classes full of them—queens without kingdoms. One of the other teachers attributed it to all the sugar in the American diet. Jane suspected good old-fashioned adolescence.

After school Harper wanted to escape to Emma's house, but Jane wanted her home. "We've got the school picnic to-morrow," Jane said, using it as a crutch.

"I don't even want to go."

"But all your friends are going. Emma's parents even let her out of grounding for it. You'll have a good time if you chill tonight." Harper needed to relax and regain her equilibrium. And Jane wanted a shot at reconnecting with her daughter.

As Jane began dinner preparations, she called Harper down to the kitchen.

"Here." Jane held out a peeler. "Make yourself useful. Wasn't this the year when you were going to learn to cook? Help me out here, and I'll show you how to make the goulash."

"Do you think I have time to cook? Have you seen my schedule, Mom?"

"You're a busy girl, but you're here tonight. Have at it."

Harper snatched up the metal utensil and petulantly sliced a disk of potato peel into the sink.

"Did you patch things up with Jesse?" It was the first time Jane had acknowledged that she knew about the boyfriend.

"I guess. Whatever." Harper poked at a growth on the potato. "Why do potatoes look like warty old witches?"

"Idk my BFF."

"Mom. Stop."

Jane clamped her jaw tight in frustration. When had it gotten so hard to get through to her daughter? When had they lost the ability to have a simple, light conversation without confrontation?

Working the paring knife around the potato, Jane began to carve a mouthpiece for herself. She was going to joke that it was a new device to silence mothers, but when she popped it into her mouth for sizing and saw in the reflection of the window that it resembled horse teeth, her mind skipped ahead.

"Who am I?" Fists on the countertop, Jane galloped along.

"I don't know."

"Owivya." Jane popped the potato out so that she could speak audibly. "Did you ever notice how Olivia runs like a horse?"

"Oh my God, she does!" Harper's sulk began to drain as she started carving horse teeth of her own. Soon, her hood was knocked back as she followed Jane around the counter, neighing and snorting.

They laughed so hard that Jane had to spit out her potato teeth. "Ach! That really makes me salivate."

"Put your teeth back in, Mom, and do a selfie with me. I want to show my friends."

"No! Harper...you can't tell other kids about this. You know it would get back to Olivia, and it's inappropriate, especially since I'm a teacher."

"But it's funny. And my friends won't show anyone." She popped the potato back into her mouth and stretched her cell phone out to focus.

"You can't do that!" Jane snatched the phone from Harper's hand. "Haven't I told you a million times to think twice about anything you send out on social networks? Inappropriate photos have ruined careers. Torn apart friendships." She checked to make sure that the photo hadn't been taken. "Really, Hoppy, sometimes I feel like you don't listen at all."

"Just because I don't follow your every command doesn't mean that I don't hear you."

Not wanting to completely ruin the tenuous connection between them, Jane pretended not to hear the last comment as she poured water over the uncorrupted potatoes and set them on the stove to simmer. "Now, the stew. Here's the recipe. Why don't you pull out the spices while I start browning the meat."

Cooking with Hoppy brought out the teacher in Jane, nurturing yet challenging. Harper was happy to take on the task, measuring and stirring.

"The best thing about cooking is that you get to eat the end result," Harper said. "I wish there was some reward for homework."

"What about knowledge? Or enhancing your mind?"

Harper winced. "Jury's out on that one, Mom. They teach us a lot of stupid stuff. I think I can make it through life without understanding quadratic equations or how a windmill works."

"Mmm." Although Harper's negative attitude toward education needled at Jane, it was clear that Harper's gifts would take her to nonacademic fields. When Harper was on, she was fearless, clear-minded, and kind. Jane could imagine her taking the business world by storm.

"You have a good point," Jane conceded. "The curriculum you learn was originally designed years ago to educate rich young men. It's been tweaked over the years, thank goodness. Otherwise, you would be learning Greek and Latin."

"And I thought Spanish was hard."

While the goulash simmered, Jane sent Harper upstairs to collect the dirty clothes that littered her room. There was a softball practice in the morning before the picnic, and Jane suspected that Harper had nothing clean to wear to either event. As she loaded the machine, Jane explained about washing the dusty uniforms and socks in a separate load and rinsing out stains with cold water. "Okay, Mama-dish," Harper said without looking away from the faces of teen angst on the flat-screen TV.

After dinner Harper brought her plate to the sink—her idea of helping with cleanup. Jane didn't complain as she loaded the dishwasher and started the pot soaking in the sink. *You created this routine,* she told herself. Over the years, Jane had done the cooking and the cleaning, letting Harper off the hook because she had homework or practice or both. It wasn't that Harper sat around wasting time. Many a night the two of them were up late at the kitchen counter, trying to piece together a logical lab report or figure out an algebraic function.

"If I have to be stuck at home, can we buy a movie on demand?" Harper asked.

"If it's something we both want to see," Jane said. Harper knew Jane found it hard to sit through violent suspense films.

To her surprise, Harper chose a Disney movie that had come out over the summer.

"Yay. I wanted to see that." Jane tossed Harper a blanket, and they each settled in at either end of the sofa.

The past two weeks had taken their toll, with rescuing Harper at the police station, school starting, Olivia's power play and last night's dustup at the game. Leaning into the soft cushion of the leather sofa, Jane fought to stay awake and savor the moment with her daughter. Hoppy was a good kid. When light shined from her eyes, it was dazzling. That was Jane's hope for the future: less shadow, and more light.

Chapter 13

The weather cooperated with the picnic plans, allowing a lingering spell of summer with startling sunshine and broad cerulean skies. Manning her position at the gate with Mary Ellen Kitcher, Jane savored a warm spot on the low stone wall.

"This is heaven, isn't it? God's green acres. And look at that sky."

Mary Ellen pushed her sunglasses up on her nose and lifted her heart-shaped face to the sun. "Mmm. Those white jet trails remind me of sugary piping on a cake."

"You're in a festive mood."

"Yeah. And hungry."

The principal had already read them the riot act, warning them about gate crashers. Now they waved through teachers and administrators. A group of phys-ed teachers had just come from a soccer tournament. A handful of staff helped the caterer by carrying in bins of sliced watermelon and foil trays of hamburgers and hot dogs. Half a dozen teachers arrived on bikes, one on a motorcycle.

"Hello, ladies. I see you're already manning our post." Marcus Leibowitz looked crisp and summery in a pink button-down shirt and crisp khaki shorts. Tall and thin, with a sand-colored beard and thick hair tied back in a ponytail, Marcus was a popular advisor and friend to students. Jane suspected that most of the kids didn't realize he was gay, and that seemed fine with Marcus, who lived across the river in Sellwood with his partner of more than a decade.

"We've got it covered, but I'm glad you're here." Mary Ellen looked toward the trees to make sure the principal was still out of hearing range. "Dr. Gallaway warned us about party crashers. Told us to beware of biker gangs."

"Really?" Marcus clasped his hands together. "My heart be still."

"Dr. G does have a flare for the dramatic," Jane said.

Luke came by with a camera and snapped a photo of Jane and Mary Ellen arm-in-arm. He had volunteered to take some photos for the yearbook, since the student photographers tended to stick to their own groups of friends.

"You're a lifesaver," Mary Ellen said.

"I'll do my best. But you might want to run a contest for the best selfies after this is over. These kids photograph every-thing."

Gray Tarkington, the vice principal, trudged up the street with a net sack of balls slung over one shoulder. "Good morn-ing, ladies," he said, his face stern as usual. "Don't even try to make a joke."

Jane tipped her face up to the six-foot-five man, biting back a smile. "Not a word. But you might want to stash that bag behind the snack shack and get some of the students to help you give them out when the time comes."

"Good idea."

A cool breeze tumbled off the lake, rolling up the gentle slope along with music from the deejay's speakers. "I love this tradition," Jane said. "Isn't it great?"

"Can't beat the lakefront." Marcus agreed.

Mary Ellen flipped up her sunglasses, revealing sympathetic brown eyes. "How's Harper doing? Last I heard she wasn't going to come today if Olivia was attending."

"She's coming around. When you're usually the player who wins the game, it's really a come-down to be pointed to as the loser."

"A tough lesson, no doubt," Mary Ellen said. "And kids are cruel."

"Oh, please." Marcus scoffed. "Adults are just as bad. We all suffer the slings and arrows of outrageous fortune."

"Harper's coming with her friends, straight from practice. She made noises about not showing up, but I don't think she could stand to miss it."

A few minutes later, the students started arriving, streaming through the gate. There was no admission fee, but the administration wisely restricted the event to students only.

"Hey there, Austin. Blake. Hi, Palmer." Jane greeted the students with a smile. There was a certain advantage to teaching a freshman class; she got to know a lot of the kids by name in their first year.

Girls traveled in packs, and boys came in smaller groups of two or three. There was a point when the line backed up, and they formed two lines to move things along. This was one of the few events that attracted all grades, pointing up the difference between tall, bearded senior men and smooth-faced freshman boys.

"Don't forget to take lots of pictures for the yearbook," Mary Ellen reminded some of the kids.

When three older guys tried to scoot in through the gate, Jane took them aside.

"This is a private high school function, and most of the kids in there are teens," she said, relieved to notice Luke beside her. "And how old are you guys? Twenty? Twenty-one?"

"Age is relative." The small, Goth-looking kid was the only one of the group whose age was hard to determine; his features were masked by a hood, dark makeup, and the shiny silver stud piercing the skin below his lower lip. "We're here for nostalgic reasons, you know? I went to Mirror Lake. I should still be in school there, but I switched to community college."

"Really?" Luke stepped closer, squinting. "I think you were in my con phys class. Jeremy, right?"

"Yeah." The kid's black lips parted in a smile as he and Luke exchanged a modified handshake. "How you been, Mr. B?"

"I'm cool," Luke said. "How's it going at the CC? What classes are you taking?"

Relieved, Jane left Luke talking with his former student and returned to her post.

When Harper's group appeared at the gate, most of the girls were laden with their bulky canvas equipment bags from practice. They were giggling as they approached.

"Hey, Mama-dish!" Harper beamed.

"Hey, there. You girls look like you had a good practice," Jane said, glad to see their happy faces.

"We did." Harper dropped her bag to the ground. "Olivia didn't show."

"No one knows why," Emma said. "But no one cares."

"But since she missed practice, she can't come to the picnic," Alyssa added.

"That's in the handbook," Harper said, reminding Jane of a six-year-old who crowed about rules. "If you miss class or a practice, you can't attend other activities in the same day."

"My mom checked the student guidelines," Sydney said.

"Did she? Well, sometimes things just work themselves out," Jane said.

"The only problem is our bags," Harper said. "Can you take them to the car, Mom?"

"I can't." Jane couldn't leave her post, but more important, she wasn't about to play servant to a handful of teenage girls. "Take them inside. Mr. Tarkington will help you find a place to stow them by the snack shack."

"Errrr." Harper moaned as she hoisted the strap onto her shoulder. "So heavy."

"It's not far." Jane pointed the way. "Have a good time. Everyone must get wet."

"Woohoo!" Sydney yelped happily, and the other girls joined in as they toted their bags inside.

Jane smiled as she watched them from the gate. Last year, her presence hadn't been an issue, but last week Harper had asked for some space at the picnic. "Other kids won't have their moms there. It's just weird."

Harper had seemed relieved when Jane told her that she'd volunteered to man the gate of the park.

"I'll join the picnic later, but I won't be hounding you or your friends. I promise."

Harper's mouth had twisted in an odd rotation as she mulled that over. "I guess that's okay."

An hour into the picnic, when Mina relieved the other teachers at the now quiet gate post, Jane walked down the shady path. She sipped on a small cherry slushie as she chatted with students and checked out the white board with tallies from the field events. Trying not to engage those X-ray eyes that Harper found so annoying, she gazed down at the waterfront. The striped canvas was tied down, closing off the tent around the dock. Although the kids would use the kayaks for some racing events, the administrators didn't think it was safe to have unsupervised students out on small watercraft during the picnic. Right now kids were lined up on the beach for the orange pass relay race, in which each person passed an orange tucked under his chin to the next contestant's chin, without using any hands. *How did that one get past Dr. G?* Jane wondered with a smirk.

"Mom..."

She flinched at the sound of Harper's voice, feeling caught although she wasn't doing anything wrong. "Hey. Having fun?"

"I was until she showed up. What's she doing here? Did you let her in?"

Olivia Ferguson, damn her. Jane would be thrilled to see that one graduate and leave the school. "She came with a note from her doctor," Jane explained. "Don't let her ruin your good time, Hoppy."

"Don't call me that in front of people. And don't you see what she's doing? She's flirting with Jesse, big-time."

Jane followed Harper's gaze over to the kiddie pool, where Jesse and Olivia sat on the edge, swishing their legs through the water as they talked. "It's probably not as bad as it looks. Why don't you go over and join them. Ask Olivia if she's feeling better and if she's contagious. That should stir things up."

"Nothing is going right. Our team lost the inner-tube relays, and now the new girl wants to come over and hang out sometime. Like we're friends. We're not."

"Where is this new girl?" Jane asked.

Reluctantly, Harper scanned the park and pointed her out by the shuffleboard court. From a distance, Jane saw no resemblance between this girl and Harper. Isabel wore a flouncy short skirt and matching sleeveless blouse with bright pink flats. Her hair was pulled up into a high ponytail with fat silk flowers wrapped around it, with her forehead covered by a pink visor.

"Okay, I don't see how anyone could think you look like her," Jane said. "But then I'm having trouble looking past that crown of flowers."

"It's not funny." Harper's gaze scorched the landscape. "I can't talk to you anymore. Just...later." She turned and jogged off in the direction of the lake.

Whatever, Jane wanted to say. Apparently the annoying parent reputation did not die easily. Catching up with Luke and Marcus by the Ping-Pong tables, she joined in an impromptu match between teachers and students.

The first thing that alerted Jane was the shrill sound of girls screaming. That alone wasn't alarming, but it was followed by male shouting and a stir of activity down at the waterfront. When Dr. Gallaway burst out of the snack shack and went running down to the waterfront with a walkie-talkie in hand, Jane held her paddle up and stopped the match.

"What's going on?" she asked as Luke and Marcus joined her.

From here they could see one of the lifeguards on his feet, whistling for assistance from the tall chair. He was pointing toward the boathouse, outside the zone where swimmers were permitted. The area was full of sharp rocks, boulders, slime, and weeds—undesirable for swimming.

The music stopped, and an eerie silence fell over the park for just a moment. Then the cold, stark adrenaline began to beat in her chest like a fleeing crow. Jane pushed toward the waterfront with Luke and Marcus. The other teachers were consoling students, trying to ease them away from the crowd, but Jane burned with her mission.

Where was Harper?

She passed Emma and Sydney, and Jesse had been up by the snack shack...but no Harper. She listened greedily as kids murmured, spellbound by the horror.

Someone was in the water.

A body. Floating.

A girl.

"Who is it?" Jane asked everyone. "Who? Did you see?"

Like a sparking wire, Kathleen Gallaway popped out of the crowd around the dock and caught Jane's attention. "I need you to go up to the gate immediately and direct the paramedics down here. The ambulance will be here soon. I think they can get their vehicle through a side gate. I'm not sure. Ask the park custodian."

"Of course, but what happened?" And who, dammit? Who was hurt? And where the hell was Harper?

"We found a senior girl unconscious in the water. I already told the dispatcher."

A senior girl . . . not Harper. The hard edges of panic eased, leaving a ghostly numbness.

"Is she breathing?" Jane asked.

"Gray and Phoebe are trying to resuscitate her."

Knowing that Harper was safe, Jane embraced the rescue operation and sprinted up the hill. In a firm, low tone she dispersed the news to other staff members, engaging teachers and responsible students to make sure the main path was clear for the ambulance and to try to calm the students. Her emergency management skills kicked in as she hurried to the window of the rescue vehicle and directed the paramedics to the unconscious girl. Jane walked alongside the vehicle until the way was clear. The students had been moved away from the path that ran alongside the park's edge down to the dock, leaving an obvious route to the drowned girl.

A senior girl.

Suddenly she was trembling in the sunshine. *Don't fall apart now. Hold it together and do your part.* She hugged herself, trying to maintain calm at least until she could see the ambulance on its way. All the emergency workers seemed to arrive at once. Firefighters wheeling fat first-aid kits and oxygen tanks. Paramedics with a stretcher and backboard. Jane directed them down to the dock.

The minutes stretched on.

A female cop, an Officer Norwood, came through the gate and paused when she saw Jane. "Are you okay, ma'am?" The radio on her collar squawked, but Jane couldn't make out what the voice was saying.

"In shock, I think. I'm a teacher at the school, and it's so scary. Do you know if she's okay? I'm not even sure what happened."

Norwood explained that the girl's body had been discovered floating near the boat rental cabana. Some kids on the dock had noticed her first, alerting the lifeguard. The vice principal had pulled her out of the water and started trying to resuscitate her. "They don't know how long she was floating there." Norwood didn't go on, but she didn't need to. Jane understood the inherent concerns: If they did manage to revive the drowning victim, the girl might have already suffered brain damage from oxygen deprivation.

"What a nightmare." Jane listened as the radio chirped again.

"Did you hear that? They've got her breathing."

"That's . . . that's wonderful." Jane pressed a hand to her chest, wishing she could slow her racing heart.

Officer Norwood stepped away as a string of messages came through. The officer responded, then turned to Jane.

"They're bringing her up in the ambulance. I need to notify the parents so that they can meet her at the hospital. Maybe you can help me. Is there a master list of students' names with emergency contact info?"

"Dr. Gallaway has it. She's the principal. I'll help you find her." The dark gloom that had been pressing on Jane began to ease as they walked together toward the main gate. "Who is the girl?"

"They say she's a senior. Her name is Olivia?"

Suddenly Jane stopped walking. She knew of only one senior girl named Olivia.

"Olivia Ferguson," Jane said, and the cop nodded.

"Do you know her?" Norwood asked.

My daughter's rival. Her nemesis.

Jane could only nod.

Chapter 14

"Hey, Mom." Harper's pert smile made Jane's knees begin to melt from under her.

"Harper! I've been looking for you." Jane pulled the girl into her arms and closed her eyes, grateful for the flowery smell of shampoo, the hard bones and smooth skin of her daughter's body. "I was so worried. It's awful." Jane opened her eyes as the teachers she had been talking with backed away. Except for the police and administrators down by the waterfront, the park had cleared out.

"Mom, I'm okay." Harper patted Jane's back, then quickly extracted herself. "You worry way too much. And you promised to keep your distance during the picnic."

"I did, but then this happened, and I was worried about you. Where were you, anyway?"

"Just kicking back with my friends."

"You weren't with Emma and Sydney."

"I have other friends, too, and . . . See? This is what I'm talking about. It's like you're spying on me."

"I'm your mother, and I'm right to worry about you," Jane said firmly. She wasn't going to apologize, but the tension of the day was not Harper's fault. "Anyway, I'm glad you're okay now."

Soon after Olivia had been whisked away in the ambulance, Dr. Gallaway had made the decision to end the picnic. Students were asked to call their parents, walk home, or drive safely. Jane and Luke had stayed on to make sure all the kids found a way home. The principal had been right to end the party. Everyone felt a little wobbly and sick, concerned for Olivia and scared for themselves. Already the rumor was circulating that she had been attacked. Some speculated that she'd been pushed into the water; others said she must have been drunk or high and fallen in. Jane doubted that last theory, but the hospital would screen Olivia's blood for traces of drugs or alcohol.

"So anyway . . ." Harper wrapped a lock of hair around one finger, her voice stretching like sweet taffy. "I was wondering if I could go over to the Westview Apartments with some people."

"What?" Jane blinked. The Westview Apartments had a reputation as a known drug-prone location. The police had found a meth lab in a bedroom there last year, and high school kids seemed to know that it was always possible to score weed on the premises. "Why would you go there?"

"Just to hang out. Teddy lives there, and he says there's a party room that we can use. It's for residents and their friends."

Jane didn't like the sound of this. "Will Teddy's parents be in the party room?"

"His mom's at work, but his grandmother will be there."

"Really? In the party room? So I can drop you off and say hello to her."

"I can get a ride with one of the seniors."

"No."

"Mom!"

"You know the rule. I need to meet the parents, and some adult should be at home."

"That's so unfair." Harper's hands went to her hips. "Don't you think I'm a little too old for a babysitter?"

Jane pressed her cheek to one hand as her gaze fell on the activity down at the waterfront. Someone was stringing a yellow plastic strip around the tree trunks. Crime-scene tape, like on TV. Which indicated that the police were investigating the possibility that Olivia's fall into the lake had not been an accident. A near drowning. An assault. Jane couldn't believe this was happening in Mirror Lake.

"Mom? Are you just going to stand there looking all sad? I hate it when you don't answer me."

You hate so many things.

Jane wanted this day to be over. She wanted a glass of wine. A warm bath. A romantic comedy on TV. A massage from Luke. But she was not going to let Harper slink over to some questionable apartment so that she could have the night off.

"Let's go home, honey." Jane scanned the park for Luke, but she suspected he was up by the gate, hanging with students who needed a ride. The nearly empty swim park seemed deceptively welcoming now. Branches of the fir trees swayed in the subtle breeze, and the late afternoon sun cast diamonds of light on the flickering surface of the water. The lake beckoned, the dazzling voice of nature calling anyone who stopped to listen.

Come to me. Here is tranquility. Here is peace.

"Mom? What is wrong with you?"

Harper's angry voice snapped Jane out of her trance. She hadn't had a lapse like that for years. Dissociating, her therapist used to call it. Jane used to do it all the time when a mind slip was the only way to escape the intolerable Frank and his abuses. "I'm tired, Hoppy. Where's your bag?"

"Up by the snack shack. Mr. Tarkington made us leave them by the back door, even though there are spiders in the bushes there."

"Okay. You need to get your bag and meet me by the front gate."

"I need to tell my friends that I can't come over."

Jane looked around suspiciously. "Where are these friends? Who are we talking about?"

"Teddy and Jesse." Harper was already backing away. "They're waiting out front, by someone else's car."

"Five minutes. And don't forget your bag."

At the gate, Marcus was talking with some students, while Mary Ellen stood talking with her husband Ben.

"We're debating about going for an early dinner since we have the sitter until seven." Mary Ellen shot her husband a hopeful look.

Ben's arms were crossed, his mouth set in a grim line. "Well, we have to eat. Just not feeling very festive."

"She's going to be okay," Mary Ellen said, her eyes glistening with tears. "Olivia's a strong girl. She'll pull through."

Jane hoped that Mary Ellen was right.

"Luke left," Mary Ellen reported. "He's taxiing some students home."

"I'll catch up with him later," Jane said, wishing Mary Ellen would be more discreet. Maybe Harper was right; maybe everyone already knew that Jane and Luke were an item. Still, Jane wasn't ready to make that final move.

"I wonder how long the police are going to be here?" Mary Ellen asked as the three of them looked toward the waterfront.

"As long as it takes to figure out what happened." Ben's voice was cold in that factual way men had of dealing with crisis. He pulled his cell from one pocket. "I'm going to tell the sitter we're going for a bite."

A sour expression puckered Harper's face as she trudged up to the gate. With a flicker of sympathy, Jane forced a smile. So many plans had been ruined.

"See you at school," she told the teachers, pointing the way toward her car. A scowling Harper followed her, probably still stewing about the invitation to the "Drugview" Apartments. Jane popped the trunk and waited as Harper stowed her bag.

"Just saying," Harper began, "when I picked up my bag it seemed way too light. I looked inside and guess what? Blue Lightning is gone. I think someone stole it."

"What?" It was the killing stab of a brutal day. Jane reached for the bag and began to rifle through it, tossing out warm juice boxes and a pack of smashed peanut butter crackers. "I thought Mr. Tarkington was watching the bags for you girls."

Harper opened the passenger door. "I thought so, too." She slipped into the seat and closed the door.

"Harper!" Jane leaned into the driver's side to face her. "Let's go, missy. We need to find that bat."

"I looked. It wasn't anywhere around. Let's just go home. I'll check the lost and found at school on Monday."

"I seriously doubt that it's going to turn up there. Come on. This is not something you can slink away from. That bat cost a fortune, and you need it."

That started the tears. "I already looked, Mom. Geez. What else do you want me to do?"

"Not lose your stuff in the first place."

Sniffing back tears, Harper curled forward.

"I don't get any of this." Jane slid into the seat and stared straight ahead. "It just doesn't make sense for someone to steal it. That bat is so distinctive; no other player in Mirror Lake can get away with using it. And if someone did take it, how did they walk out of the park with it? You can't exactly hide a softball bat under your shirt."

"I don't know. . . ." A small sob broke Harper's voice.

"All right. I'll go look for it."

Walking at a brisk pace, Jane checked the snack shack,

where the gates were rolled down over the counters, but the door was still open. Robin Murphy knew nothing about the softball team stowing their bags out back. Jane checked around the back door, but found nothing. Then she jogged down to the waterfront, where the two top administrators and a few teachers waited. When she asked Gray Tarkington about the bat he was apologetic but distracted. "I didn't see anybody poking around behind the back door, if that's what you mean," he said. "Can we talk about it Monday? I just can't wrap my brain around it right now."

"Of course. I just wanted to check, but I know you've got a million things on your mind." Jane thanked him and asked about the latest update on Olivia.

"She was conscious when she left here, but couldn't tell us her name." He shrugged. "The paramedic said that happened sometimes with a near drowning. They had her on pure oxygen when they left. That's supposed to help."

As Jane hurried back to the car, she wondered if it was possible that Olivia had been drinking or using drugs. Jane had discounted that theory, but how well did she really know the girl? If Olivia had fallen into the water, inebriated...well, that would put her on academic probation for a while. And off the softball team.

Wouldn't that be convenient. Jane frowned, feeling a flicker of guilt for her selfish fantasy. Just a flicker.

"Did you find it?" Harper looked up from her cell phone, apparently in the middle of a text.

"I'm afraid not, but I talked to Mr. Tarkington. He's going to keep an eye out for it. In the meantime..." Jane took out her cell and found the coach's number. "Carrie? Hey, it's Jane Ryan." At first the coach thought she was calling about Olivia. "So you've heard already," Jane said. She shared her limited information, and then told Carrie about the missing bat. "Is there a chance that Harper left it behind at practice?"

"Not today," Carrie said. "I was the last one at the field, and the area was clean as a whistle. It's been an issue lately, getting the girls to pick up after themselves. Those damned water bottles drive me crazy."

Jane hung up with Carrie and started the car. "Coach Carrie says that you didn't leave it at practice."

"I knew that. Are we going home?" The high, chipmunk voice tugged at Jane's maternal instincts.

"Yes."

They drove in silence, moving past the fat trunks of trees and the broad red or pink flowers of rhododendrons.

"Would it be okay if Emma and Sydney came over?"

Jane bristled, annoyed that Harper wanted to squeeze some fun out of the rest of the day. Maybe it wasn't fair of Jane to blame her. After all, the kids had been looking forward to the picnic, and what good would it do for them to sit around and worry about Olivia?

"I'm not up for a sleepover. But if they want to come over for dinner . . ." Jane considered the evening ahead. Maybe getting the girls together would be a welcome diversion for all of them, herself included. "I can make crispy cornflake chicken." It was Harper's favorite.

"Really? So you're not mad at me?"

Jane had to swallow back a quick answer. "I'm not blaming you for how today went." Well, maybe the bat, she amended in her mind. But it wasn't worth bringing her daughter to tears again.

Emma and Sydney arrived with munchies and a few films on DVD. Emma set up the chips and salsa while the girls debated about which movie to watch first. They decided on a romantic comedy, which Jane was happy to watch as she finished preparing dinner at the kitchen island.

The acoustics of the room bounced all sound back to the

kitchen. That included the TV audio, as well as the girls' voices. As Jane slathered honey on chicken drumsticks, she monitored the conversation.

"Some kids say she had it coming," Sydney said.

"That's not nice," Emma objected.

"I'm just repeating what I heard."

"Who said that?" asked Harper. When Sydney named a few names, the girls agreed that they were mean girls. "But Olivia could be pretty mean herself," Harper added.

"You're not supposed to speak ill of the dead," Emma said in a soft voice that gave Jane goose bumps.

"She's not dead," Harper said.

"I know, but it might happen."

The girls were silent for a while, and Jane began to tune in to the dialogue of the movie as she dipped the chicken pieces into smashed cornflakes.

With the chicken in the oven, Jane spread frozen tater tots onto a baking sheet.

"Isn't it kind of funny that she can't swim?" Harper said out of the blue. "I mean, she lives on the lake, plus she has an infinity pool. She could go swimming anytime, but she can't swim. That's ironic, right?"

"My mom says Olivia has a phobia. A fear of water. When she was little, her mom took her for swimming lessons, but she wouldn't get in the pool."

"Is that aquaphobia?" Emma asked.

"I don't know," Sydney said. "Look it up."

Emma found a description on her phone. "Aquaphobia. Some call it hydrophobia, but that's also the name for rabies."

"What? Let me see."

"Oh, it's quite debilitating." Emma read the profile, ending with the information that some aquaphobics avoided bathing or showering.

"That is so gross." The three of them groaned together.

"Was Olivia stinky?" Sydney asked.

"Oh, yeah. She reeked." Harper giggled, and the girls laughed together.

"But I still don't get it," Harper said. "If she hates water so much, why did her parents buy a house on the lake?"

"Yeah. Why even bother to live in Mirror Lake? I mean, we're around water all the time."

"It's all about real estate values," Emma said.

A wise girl.

After dinner the girls went up to Harper's room to listen to some music. Jane was glad for some privacy; she needed to talk to Luke, the sane center of this crazy, spinning world.

"How's it going over there?" he asked. "How's Harper taking it?"

"Surprisingly well, but then again, we're talking about the fall of her arch rival."

"Yeah, well, she's got to feel bad for the kid. Did you see a glimmer of compassion?"

"Barely. She was more concerned with getting to an impromptu party, which I put the kibosh on. But I'm sick about Olivia. Have you heard anything new?"

"They've got her stabilized. No visitors. Marcus stopped by and talked to Pete Ferguson. He didn't see Linda, but Pete's pretty broken up. Rightly so. Olivia's suffered a serious contusion. The doctors are keeping an eye on it. If the swelling increases, she'll need surgery to alleviate the pressure on the brain."

"That's awful." Jane couldn't imagine what Pete and Linda were going through. And Olivia. "Poor kid."

"But it sounds like Pete is staying positive, and overall the prognosis is good."

Jane collapsed onto the corner of the sofa with a grateful

sigh. "Well, at least she's stable and in good hands. Did Olivia say how she ended up in the water?"

"She doesn't seem to remember. Apparently she's disoriented, which is normal for a concussion. I checked out the symptoms on WebMD. Olivia might have a clearer picture of what happened in a day or two."

"So we don't know . . ."

"We don't know if it was an accident or an attack."

A shiver skittered along Jane's spine, and she slid down until her head nestled against the armrest. "That is positively creepy. I wish you were here."

"I wish I could be there to protect. And devour."

She smiled. "Easy there. I've got kids in the house. I don't want to scare them, but I can't stop thinking about Olivia. Did you know she has a fear of water? I keep thinking of the panic she must have felt, and somehow it's worse to think that someone might have deliberately pushed her into the water."

"I want to think that this was all an accident," Luke agreed. "That Olivia tripped and fell into the water. That she was stoned." He gave a heavy sigh. "I want to think that because the alternative might compromise my faith in humanity."

"I know. The prospect of a girl's being attacked in Mirror Lake—I mean, in broad daylight, with all those people around—it's awful."

"The logical explanation would be an accident," he said.

"That's what I'm hoping for."

Her worries were eased by her conversation with Luke. At the very least it was a relief to hear that Olivia was holding her own. Still, the prospect of an attack pressed on Jane's thoughts. When Trish and Keiko arrived to pick up their girls, the quick, murmured exchange among mothers told her that they shared the same worries. What if it had been an attack? Were their daughters safe?

No one is safe, Jane thought that night as she stared out into the black night beyond her bedroom window. *Danger crosses your path and strikes you down. Sometimes the attack is sudden; other times it's slow and subtle, a seduction of sorts, a slowly turning vortex that sucks you in. One wrong move, one poor choice, and you're caught in the trap. No turning back. No chance.*

As she lowered the shade she caught a startling reflection of herself, jaw clenched in a grimace, eyes wild.

Whoa. Slow down; take a breath. She had to stop slipping back to panic mode, back to that numb state of mind that had consumed her in the dark days of her imprisonment with Frank.

The sheets were blessedly soft as she stretched out and pulled back her tight shoulders. Although her nerves were all gummed up, she smoothed back the pages of the cheerful though improbable cozy mystery she'd been reading and gave it a try. The steely nerve of the sleuth was encouraging somehow.

The next thing she knew, the book was flopped onto her chest and Harper stood by her bed. In her boxer shorts and T-shirt, with Hoppy the bunny pressed in the crook of her neck, Harper could have been five years old again.

"I can't sleep."

Jane lifted the covers. "Come on in."

Harper slid in and huddled on her side, facing Jane. The stuffed bunny was tucked under her chin so that Harper's fingers could worry the worn ribbon around the animal's neck, a gesture that had soothed Harper since she was a toddler. That ribbon had been replaced at least three times.

"Do you feel sick?" Jane asked, grateful that her daughter still came to her in the middle of the night. She had never minded the late-night visits when nightmares or charley horses had awakened her girl.

"No, just . . . I don't know."

The light from the bedside lamp cast a glossy glow over Harper's features, and for a moment Jane glimpsed a sliver of both herself and Frank. Could their daughter possess the best of them? Forget about genetic probability, the chromosome for blue eyes or a propensity for evil. Wasn't there some wondrous, creative magic in the emerging form of a human being?

"I can hear my heart beating in my ears," Harper said. "Is that normal? It's beating so hard. I just . . . I feel kind of breathless and rattled."

"That's happened to me before. I hate that feeling. If you let it take over, it will become a full-fledged panic attack." Jane smoothed the dark hair from her daughter's forehead. "You know, fear and anxiety can have a strong effect on a person's body."

"Like what?"

Jane tried to explain the terrifying anxiety that could overcome a person. "I'm not saying you're having a panic attack, but we're all a little freaked out tonight. It's been a tough day. Those were some scary moments when they found Olivia in the lake."

Harper's mouth twisted. "I know. Now I feel bad for her."

At last, a scintilla of compassion. "A lot of people are worried about Olivia tonight, thinking good thoughts and praying. That's what a community does when someone gets hurt. That's one of the reasons I'm grateful to live in Mirror Lake. I know we've got our share of nosy moms and spoiled kids." *Ourselves included,* Jane thought. "But when someone needs help, the people around here do what needs to be done. Good neighbors and friends." She was prattling on, filling the space with fluff to distract Harper, who yawned. It seemed to be working.

"I know. Is Olivia going to die?"

"No." The blunt question was unsettling, but Harper deserved an answer. "It sounds like she's going to survive."

"That's good. I feel kind of bad about how much I've hated her. I'm going to try to be a better person from now on. I mean, I'm not just going to try; I'm going to do it. I'm going to be nice to people. Even obnoxious people like Olivia. Like you always say, I'm going to take the high road and just, like, look the other way when someone annoys me."

"That sounds like a wise plan." Jane had to keep herself from gushing over Harper's epiphany. This was an enormous step in the right direction. "How's that heartbeat doing?"

Harper stopped twirling Hoppy's bow to press a hand to her ear. "It's gone. I can't hear it anymore." She smiled at Jane. "Thanks, Mama-dish. You calmed me down."

"You're welcome."

Harper resettled with Hoppy and closed her eyes. "I'm so tired. Are you going to turn off the light?"

"Yup." Jane reached for the bedside lamp, catching a last glimpse at the tempestuous light of her life before darkness fell over them. Harper had her bad moments—and indefensible, inappropriate actions. But deep inside she had a good heart. Of course, Jane was biased; she would never stop loving her daughter. And if the legend of love was true, eventually it would transform them both.

Chapter 15

The next morning Jane slipped out of bed, trying not to wake up the sleeping girl with dark hair spread over the pillow and an aura of peace settled over her. Jane grabbed her book and headed downstairs for coffee.

"Good morning, Phee-Phee." She opened the back door for Phoenix, who sniffed the grass with little enthusiasm. "We'll go for a walk in a few minutes," she promised. The sky was overcast—a pallid pearl gray that promised rain—but Jane knocked the webs from one of the chairs on the back deck and sat down with her coffee and book. Some mornings in the small yard she fantasized that she was weekending at a country resort. Funny, what a few flowering plants could do for your morale. Privacy, too. The tiger lilies between her deck and Nancy's fence were splendid and dense, a profusion of green dotted with orange flowers, each as fat as a melon.

In the rear corner of the yard were two small flowering pear trees that hosted native birds year round. When Harper had been in grade school, one of the science units that focused on local birds had required Harper to keep a birding journal. Together she and Jane had set up a small birdhouse and hung a suet seed cake from the fence. "When are the birds coming to eat?" Harper had asked. "Aren't they hungry?" It had taken a week or so, but they had arrived in flocks and pairs. Nuthatches and house finches. Tiny black-capped chickadees that seemed to be wearing black hoods. Long-tailed balls of gray fluff that Harper identified as bushtits. What fun that project had been. She had helped Harper with the illustrations, but Hoppy had handled the journals and bird sightings herself. Learning the bird names and characteristics, Harper had realized that memorization was one of her strengths. "All this time, I didn't think I had a strength besides sports," she had told Jane, who now sighed at the memory. She loved that kid.

This morning Jane could hear birdsong, but the only sighting was of a pair of bossy scrub jays. Probably scaring all the other birds off.

Phoenix returned to the deck, circled, and then plopped down at Jane's feet. Over her first cup, Jane organized the day ahead. Harper had a game in the afternoon, but the morning was free. Well, sort of. Harper probably had some homework to do, and Jane had brought home a batch of letters to grade. The proverbial "What I did over my summer vacation" in letter form. As Jane had told the class that they could fictionalize, she looked forward to some outlandish reading.

She was in the kitchen refilling her coffee cup when the phone rang. When she heard Gray Tarkington's voice, a flicker of surprise made her straighten.

"I hope I didn't wake you," he said. "Sunday morning and all."

"No problem." She took the steaming mug back out to the deck. "What's up?"

"I'm calling about Harper's bat."

"You found it?"

"Actually, the police did, just before dark last night. It's an alloy bat with Blue Lightning emblazoned on it, right?"

"That's it." Jane was almost afraid to admit it. "But the police . . . Where did they find it?"

"In the bushes by the boat cabana. So . . . you haven't heard from the cops yet?"

"No." Suddenly, her coffee seemed too acidic to handle. She put the mug on the table. "Gray, what's going on?"

"Look, Jane, I'm probably not supposed to be telling you this, but the cops want to talk to Harper about how her bat found its way to the scene of the crime."

"How would she know? The bat was stolen from her bag. I told you about it."

"I remember. That was one of the reasons I could identify it so quickly."

Jane's mind was spinning. "You know Harper. She would never do anything like that." Like what? Use her bat to conk Olivia on the head?

Even as Jane objected, her words rang false in her ears, reminding her of the vapid parents who defended their wicked little darlings.

"Look . . ." Gray paused, fumbling in silence for a moment. "Harper's a good kid, but everyone knows about the bad blood between Olivia and your daughter."

"Yeah. It's no secret." Hadn't Jane and two dozen other witnesses seen Harper come after Olivia with Blue Lightning in her hands? "But rivalry is one thing. Knocking another kid unconscious . . . that's not Harper. Most of our students wouldn't cross that line."

"I hope not." The distress was apparent in his usually deadpan voice. "I'm sorry, Jane. I don't mean to insinuate anything about your daughter, but I do want the cops to get to the bottom of the attack on Olivia."

"So it *was* an attack? Is that confirmed?"

"I think so, but I can't say for sure. They took the bat as evidence . . . a possible weapon. I'm sorry. Maybe I shouldn't have called. I don't want to give you misinformation. You need to talk to the police."

He was right about that, but the prospect of facing the police right now was like a knife in her gut.

After a conversation with Luke, Jane decided to take control of the situation and contact the police.

"Tell them you heard that they found your daughter's softball bat and that she needs it for this afternoon's game," Luke advised.

"Will they really believe I'm that naïve?"

"Hey, they don't know you watch *Law & Order*. And maybe Gray was wrong. Olivia could have hit her head on the dock as she fell into the water. They'll determine that from the size and angle of the wounds—that part is science, but I doubt the investigation has gotten that far yet. And maybe they've ruled out assault. Who knows? They might just give the bat back to you."

Despite Luke's logic, Jane still found the idea of confronting the police daunting. "Maybe I should hire a lawyer."

"For what? Even if the bat was used as a weapon, it doesn't mean Harper was the person who wielded it. Save your money. Talk to Harper. Make sure she has her story straight; a police interview can be very intimidating, even when you've done nothing wrong."

"That's why I'm worried."

"As long as she doesn't get rattled, she'll be fine."

Jane ended the call with Luke, and then phoned the precinct. A detective named Eldon Drum thanked Jane for calling and agreed to see them this morning. Sick with worry, Jane moved to the stairs.

Waking Harper was never a joyful task. Jane eased the blinds open and started by saying there'd been a change of plans.

Harper must have sensed the tension in her mother's voice.

"What happened?" She opened her eyes and stared sternly at the ceiling.

When Jane told her that they had an appointment at the police precinct, Harper sat up suddenly. "Wait. Why?"

"They found Blue Lightning near the boathouse."

Harper grinned. "They found it!"

"That's the good news, I guess. The police think someone might have used it to hit Olivia. That would make it a part of the crime scene—an assault weapon. I suspect they want to ask you how the bat got there, and where you were around the time when Olivia was found in the lake."

"They're so stupid," Harper whined. "How would I know how the bat got there when it was stolen?"

"That's exactly what you need to tell the police," Jane said, "but in a much nicer tone."

Harper moaned as she plucked at Hoppy's bow. "This is not what I wanted to do this morning."

"Same," Jane returned, using her daughter's shorthand. "But it's better to get this over with. You don't want to miss your game."

"Well, yeah." Harper threw back the comforter of Jane's bed. "Do you think they'll give me the bat back? I really need it today. We're playing Canby."

"I wouldn't count on it." Jane pulled a pair of jeans from the drawer of her dresser, and then turned back to face her daughter. "As I said, they'll want to know where you were when Olivia got hurt."

"Okay." With Hoppy dangling from one hand, Harper plodded out.

"Wait. Where were you?"

"With Emma and Sydney."

Jane shook her head as a queasy feeling niggled at her. "I saw them. You weren't there."

"Yes, I was. God, Mom." And Harper disappeared down the hall.

On the way to the precinct, Jane tried once again to nail down Harper's whereabouts. "It's important that you tell the truth," Jane said, sparing a quick look of concern at her daughter before glancing back at the road. "If you change your answer in any small way, they'll think you're lying. You'll lose all credibility, and they'll begin to question everything you tell them."

Even to Jane, the warning seemed more like a lesson in swindling than an endorsement of trustworthiness. How had she raised Harper all these years without instilling important concepts like honesty and integrity?

"I was with my friends, okay? What do you want me to say?"

"Just the truth." *The real truth,* Jane thought as her fib radar sounded the alarm. She sensed that Harper was hiding something. Time spent with a boy? With senior students? Alcohol? Drugs? She sighed, hoping that she wasn't delivering her daughter to the lion's den.

As they entered the police station there was a moment of awkwardness when Jane acknowledged the female officer at the desk. The cold fish. The woman's bland, flat eyes were uncaring, but they also gave no indication of recognition from the curfew incident. This meeting would be Jane's third or fourth encounter with local law enforcement in as many weeks. You go fourteen years without even a traffic ticket, and suddenly you're a precinct regular. She took a seat in the steel and plastic chair, hoping for another fourteen years of law-abiding peace.

"Mrs. Ryan?" A graying man with a pleasant smile and twinkling eyes hobbled into the small waiting area. His skin tone, a rich mocha, suggested that he was mixed race. "I'm Eldon Drum." He shook Jane's hand, and then turned to Harper. "And this must be the softball star."

Harper glimmered, all blue eyes and shiny braces. "I'm Harper."

"I appreciate you coming in. Your mom told me you have a game later today." He shuffled toward an office, obviously struggling with pain as he walked. "Don't mind me. Bad knees. I'm getting some bionic replacements soon. Titanium! Until then, basketball is out." He eased himself into a chair. "Now I know you play softball, Harper. How about hoops?"

"My favorite sport."

As Harper talked basketball with the detective, Jane took a welcome breath of relief. Compared to old "Fish-eye" outside, this cop oozed personality. They had lucked out.

"So let's talk about your teammate, Olivia." Eldon Drum had a patient yet energetic delivery, like a minister sharing a joke. He showed Harper a photo of Blue Lightning, and she nodded.

"Sure looks like my bat."

He asked her when she'd seen it last, and she gave him the timeline: from practice at the school field to the swim park to stowing the bags behind the snack shack.

"So the other girls brought their bags to the picnic. And they had softball bats with them, too?"

"Most of them."

"Interesting." He scraped back his hair, which curled over his collar in the back. Frank would have had a conniption over that haircut on a cop. He had been a stickler for the elite esprit de corps—a tight, buttoned-down dress code for officers. Annoyed with herself, Jane dug her fingernails into the flesh of her palms. Why was she dredging up a memory of Frank as if he were an authority on law enforcement? Years ago she had worked, purposefully and tediously, to chase him from her psyche; perhaps it was time to reaffirm her commitment to sanity.

While Jane was lost in reverie, the conversation volleyed between Harper and the detective, a smooth, uncontentious match. Eldon Drum did not shed any new light on Olivia's injuries, and although he was cautious about making too many speculations, he believed that she had been attacked.

"That's a frightening thought," Jane said, speaking up for the first time. "I know many of us have been hoping it was just an accident."

"Not from where I stand," Drum said, "though I could be wrong. It's happened before, and it'll happen again. The human condition! Anyhow . . ." He turned back to Harper. "I appreciate your dragging your mom in here today. My job is to gather as much information as possible, and your cooperation is making my job much easier. I'd been wondering why anyone would bring such a nice softball bat to a park without a playing field; now I know why. But I have to say, I can't imagine how that bat got from the area behind the snack shack to the boathouse without anyone seeing. There were hundreds of students in that park yesterday, and so far the kids we canvassed do not recall seeing anyone walking around with a blue and silver softball bat."

"Actually?" Harper's blue eyes were earnest. "There's an easy way to do that without being seen."

What the hell? Jane shot her a scalding look, but her daughter was already explaining how the culprit could have disappeared into the bushes that lined the property's border.

"Show me on the map," the detective said, pushing out of his chair to go to the satellite map pinned on the wall behind him.

Her fingers tracing the dark line of shrubs and small trees, Harper showed Drum a route around the edge of the park.

"Even if you climb the fence to the neighbor's yard, they don't mind," she said. "Kids do it all the time."

Staring at the map, the detective rubbed his jaw. "This I did not know. Wow. That answers that question. Thanks."

"You're welcome."

Jane stared at her beautiful daughter and wondered if the teen was simply naïve or manipulating them all for some mysterious reason.

As the interview wound down, Drum steered the conversation to the question Jane had tried to prepare her daughter for.

"Did you see Olivia in the water?" he asked. "Were you nearby?"

Harper shook her head. "I was hanging out with my friends. We were pretty far from the boathouse."

"Do you want to show me on the map?"

Jane watched as Harper pointed to a spot near the center of the park—not far from the Ping-Pong tables where Jane had been at that crucial time. Harper was either lying or confused.

"Okay. Were these friends girls from the team?" he asked.

"No."

No? Jane bit her lower lip as she reconsidered the lecture she'd given about honesty.

"I was with my friend Teddy Pitari," Harper offered. "And a senior girl. She's not really a friend, but Teddy knows her. Abby Dobler."

Jane had to restrain herself from pouncing on Harper for having poor judgment. As a freshman student, Abby had been forgetful and inattentive—a C minus all the way. And last year, Abby had been suspended for smoking weed in the locker room while the rest of her PE class was outside on the track. She had followed that mundane offense up with a more creative e-blast of herself, topless, to a handful of male teachers. Luke had been relieved that he was not one of "the chosen." The second offense had not earned a suspension, as

Abby had contended that, while she'd posed for the photo, she had not sent it out. Cyberbullying was a tough charge for the administration to sort out; they did not have the resources or the laws to handle the complaint. The whole incident had left Jane feeling sorry for the girl, whose father was in jail and whose mother had not once attended a meeting to defend her.

"But those aren't her usual friends," Jane said, as if that would clear Harper's name in some way. "Her closest friends are Emma Suzuki and Sydney Schiavone."

Eldon Drum nodded sagely. Jane noticed that he hadn't written anything down; she hoped that was a positive sign. He thanked them again for coming in and gave Jane his card. "Call if you have any questions."

She took the card, grateful to have this interview behind them.

"And Harper," Drum said, "I'm sorry I can't return your bat, especially with you having a game today. You think you can blast one out of the park without it?"

"I'm sure gonna try."

"That's the spirit."

Chapter 16

It was hardly a surprise that Mirror Lake won their Sunday afternoon game. Sure, Canby fielded a tough team, but these girls were a well-oiled machine when they were free of distractions like the Ferguson clan. Madison Lowe stepped into the gap caused by Olivia's absence and demonstrated some untapped skills as shortstop. Harper hit two home runs on a borrowed bat and made some phenomenal plays at home.

At the game, the parent contingent was subdued. Jane sensed neither an outpouring of sympathy for Olivia nor a torrent of vigilante fury toward Harper. Some didn't even know about Harper's bat; others didn't seem to be jumping to conclusions, though Jane did notice two moms staring at Harper and whispering behind their hands. She wasn't sure what to make of it, but Luke reassured her with a blunt text:

You're being paranoid.

A greater concern was the possibility of a violent fiend on the loose, most likely a student from the high school, someone passing their kids in the corridors. People were spooked, but with so little reliable information available, they kept the picnic incident out of their conversations.

After the game, Jane had no desire to attend the victory celebration at Pizza Kingdom. She was tired and worried, and there were those assignments to grade, but it was important to save face. "All eyes are on us now," she had told Harper that morning. "We need to stay positive, be friendly, and speak kindly of Olivia."

"Just saying, that sounds really dumb," Harper said. "Who made up those rules?"

"Just be nice."

"I *am* nice. And this is so unfair. I didn't do anything wrong. Just because someone stole my bat, now I'm supposed to tiptoe around everyone. It's just not fair."

"Life is not always fair." Jane tried to keep the frustration from her voice. All things considered, people were giving Harper a pretty fair shake. But Harper didn't see the big picture. On days like this, it was hard for her to see past the annoying zit on her chin.

When Jane walked into the English faculty office Monday, she found one of the teachers ranting about lack of supervision at the picnic.

"There's no denying that a baseball bat is a lethal weapon." Rob Horn was squaring off with Mary Ellen as he used the paper cutter to divide pink papers into small strips. This was the mandate of the last few years; to save paper, teachers now condensed assignments into chunks of tiny print, duplicated them on the same page, and then sliced each printed page into strips that reminded Jane of the blurbs from fortune cookies.

"A lot of things can be used as weapons," Mary Ellen said. "Lacrosse sticks. Polished apples. Paper cutters."

"What idiot let a bunch of girls walk in with baseball bats?" Rob asked.

"I did," Mary Ellen admitted. "They were softball bats, and they were stowed away in big, heavy canvas bags."

"We were both working the gate," Jane added with a level look for Rob, who had always been a little leery of students since he'd left the junior high to teach here two years ago. He frequently commented on the hulking size of the senior guys and the incidents of violence in schools across the nation.

He scoffed. "Then shame on you, too."

"Most of the girls on the softball team came straight from practice," Jane went on. "I guess we forgot to walk them through the metal detector."

Mary Ellen bit back a grin.

"Oh, so funny." Rob's voice was thick with sarcasm. "It's easy to be cavalier about security when you live in the bubble of Mirror Lake."

"Come on, Rob," Jane coaxed. "We're talking teenage girls here. Not a major threat."

"Yeah. Tell that to Olivia." Rob collected his papers, stacking them quickly. "It's all fun and games until someone gets hurt." His face was flushed with annoyance as he strode out of the office.

"Ah, geez." Jane sighed.

"What a load of crap." Mary Ellen stirred creamer into her coffee. "I don't need that. You volunteer to work a school event and suddenly you're supposed to possess superpowers."

Jane tried to laugh it off, but the shadow of the picnic followed her. Later that day in the school library she noticed that a table of parent volunteers went completely silent as she approached. Their staring eyes seemed to drill at her back like hornets as she led her class to the computer room.

On Tuesday Dr. Gallaway stopped by Jane's classroom to ask how Harper was holding up. Jane wasn't sure if she meant under the strain of suspicion or the fear of a maniac on the loose. But she didn't press the matter, and when Jane told her that Harper was fine, the principal moved on. If Kathleen Gallaway had been a more accessible person, Jane would have asked her about the investigation. She was dying to know who had attacked Olivia. But information was sparse. The school said only that they were cooperating with the police investigation, and the police said nothing.

The whole thing bothered Jane more because she knew that something was up with Harper. Of course, she knew that Harper hadn't done it, but had she been involved in some way? An accomplice? It was a concern. Jane longed for answers, but feared the truth.

At least Harper wasn't worried, and that made life pleasant in the Ryan household. Harper liked her new teachers and had high hopes for achieving decent grades this year without "killing" herself. Her spot as team catcher was secure for the time being. She had befriended the new girl and was lobbying for a sleepover to bring all of her friends together.

And she had her first real boyfriend. Jesse had come to the house twice this week to help Harper with her science homework—a presentation on global warming—and the kid knew his stuff. Not just a boyfriend but a student with prowess. Jane had to hide her glee for fear that Harper would discover his inner nerd and dump him.

On Thursday word came that Olivia was being released from the hospital.

"She still doesn't remember the attack," Luke told Jane over the phone. He had been getting information from Gray Tarkington, who had decided it was not wise for a school administrator to talk about Olivia with any of the school parents, even if that parent taught at the school. Gray could be so maddening and frustrating, especially since he knew Jane would get the information in a roundabout way.

"Does Olivia remember being afraid of someone that afternoon?" Jane asked as she paced the backyard, pulling weeds and replenishing the bird feeder. "Was she chased? Is she blaming anyone in particular?"

"Nope. No memory, and she's being gracious about it. As if she's embarrassed that she can't remember. The doctors say that her memory could come back in a week or a month— even a year—but there's no guarantee."

"The police can't be happy about that." Jane thought about Detective Drum with his easy demeanor and bad knees. Would he leave the case on hold and go in for his surgery as scheduled? Would the department drop the investigation for the time being? "I just can't believe that someone could be attacked that way, beaten, and no one heard or saw a thing."

"We don't know that. Just because there's been no arrest, it doesn't mean the police don't have some incriminating witness statements," Luke pointed out. "They may have a suspect in their sights. Maybe they're sitting on him or her until they have enough evidence to build a case."

Jane dropped a handful of weeds into the bin and paced back toward the deck. "It's driving me crazy. I wish I knew who attacked Olivia."

"I think everyone feels that way."

"Everyone isn't under scrutiny the way Harper and I are. I want this to be over." She thought about calling Detective Drum to ask about the case. After all, he had given her his card and told her to call. But she suspected his intention was to get more information from Jane, not to give it out.

Friday was the first home football game of the season, and Harper, who usually could not care less, was suddenly revved up and ready to roar for the Mirror Lake team. Jane suspected that Harper's enthusiasm was fueled by the opportunity to show off her new boyfriend, whom Harper had invited over for a bite before the game.

"I didn't plan to make dinner," Jane said when she came downstairs to find the two of them sitting with their thighs touching at the kitchen counter. "I figured we'd just grab something at the game. They'll have pizza and hot dogs and soft pretzels. How does that sound?"

"I'm good, Ms. Ryan," Jesse said, his dark eyes earnest and huge. Jane was impressed that he looked her in the eye. Some students didn't warm up to eye contact until the fifth week of school.

"I'm so hungry," Harper insisted, hopping off the stool and opening the fridge. "Why don't I cook for you?" she suggested to Jesse.

Cook for him? Jane wanted to say. *You don't even cook for yourself.*

"Do you like mac and cheese?" Harper lifted the box from the freezer.

Now there was something Harper could cook.

"Sure." Jesse shrugged and smiled at Jane. "Are you going to the game, Ms. Ryan?"

"I am. I'll be chaperoning."

"That must be a pain, giving up your Friday nights for a work obligation." This was more than she had evoked from Jesse Shapiro through all of freshman English.

"Sometimes it's a drag toward the end of the season, especially on those cold, rainy nights. But tonight I'm looking forward to it."

As Harper popped the block of macaroni into the microwave, they chatted about the football team and Jesse's involvement in the school band. "We'll be playing tonight from the bleachers," he said. "That part's kind of cool, getting the crowd revved up. But no half-time show, thank God. All that marching makes me feel like a marine recruit."

"Do you wear uniforms?"

"We're supposed to, but you know . . ." He looked down, his hair falling in his eyes. "The dog ate my homework."

Jane laughed and left the two of them to eat while she took Phoenix out for a short run around the block. Once upon a time this big dog had been Harper's main companion and confidante. Jane used to love overhearing Harper singing to Phee. She adored the way her daughter admonished the dog to stay safe when chasing the neighbor's cat. *"You have to be careful in the street, honey. It's dangerous out there."*

But Phoenix had been replaced by the BFFs and now Jesse. Harper's boyfriend. Well, at least she had picked an interesting one.

Jane let the kids walk to school while she stayed behind to clean up the mess Harper had left in the kitchen. Normally she would have made Harper load the dishwasher, empty the overflowing recycling bin, and wipe down the kitchen counters, but she restrained herself from instituting martial law in front of Jesse. She didn't want to embarrass Harper, but how could the girl walk away from splatters of chocolate milk and sticky, neglected macaroni noodles? It was as if she didn't even see it.

It was the perfect night for football—cool and clear, with a smiling, chiseled moon illuminating an inky indigo sky. Jane's annoyance was quickly chased away by the spectacle of Friday night football. The brilliant lights that turned night to day. The booming bass and brass of the school band. The roar of the crowd and the all-American drawl of the announcer's voice. The coziness of burrowing into a fleece jacket to ward off the night's chill.

It was easy to locate Harper, adoring her guy from a spot on the track that surrounded the football field. Along with Emma and Sydney, she flitted along, stopping to chat with other kids, exchanging hugs and laughing. They skipped ahead, shrieked about something, and then raced to the concession stand. Girls.

For the first hour Jane and Mina "patrolled" the area behind the goalpost that backed up to the golf course, talking with kids and, mostly, making sure that they stayed on this side of the barrier marking off the end zone. This part of the field was the unofficial hangout for junior high kids, who came to the high school game in droves, testing the waters of the future. The girls giggled together, munching Pixy Stix and Red Vines licorice. The boys brought Frisbees and footballs of their own, trying to form pickup games on the practice fields. Jane had already learned a few names tonight, knowing that they would be her students in the next two years.

As she strolled past groups of kids, she noticed an elderly woman struggling down the steps of the bleachers, aided by a teenage girl. Leaving so soon? Jane thought. The woman seemed ill or debilitated in some way, though it didn't seem to be an emergency. The girl helping her down the uneven steps could have been Harper with her dark hair and trim shape. Was this the new girl, Isabel? She did have a slight resemblance to Harper. *Although my daughter would never be so patient with an old lady.*

When Jane and Mina were relieved of their post by two other teachers, Jane cut behind the bleachers and noticed a familiar face on the path to the school.

"Detective Drum?" She paused in front of the man watching the game from the summit of the path. "I didn't know you were an Osprey fan."

He dug his hands into the pockets of his jacket. "I'm a fan of Mirror Lake. I was hoping to blend. After last week, we wanted to have a police presence here, but didn't want to upset anyone. One or two cops are okay, but more than that and people get to wondering what's going on. The beefed-up security has the opposite effect; folks start to feel scared."

She glanced toward the back of the bleachers, dark and dense from this angle. "So there are other cops working undercover tonight?"

"Indeed. Protect and serve, that's our first priority."

"It's nice to know we're safe." She steeled herself to ask the question that had been bothering her all week. "I don't mean to pry, but can you tell me if you have any suspects? In the Olivia Ferguson attack, I mean." As if assaults were an everyday occurrence in Mirror Lake.

"We have a few," he said. "One in particular that I was going to ask you about." He swiped across the screen of his cell phone and tapped on it. "This photo came in with a note. It said that this photo was taken near the boathouse around the time Olivia was found in the lake."

The suspect? Jane hungrily scanned the photo.

It was Harper. Her hair was pulled back in a ponytail and she was wearing the turquoise tank top that emphasized her sculpted biceps. Had Harper worn that top to the picnic? Jane couldn't remember.

"Is that your daughter?" Drum asked.

"It looks like her, but I don't really see the boathouse in the background, and I'm not sure she was wearing that shirt that day." She shook her head. "This doesn't prove anything, does it?"

"On its own, no. We have to look at the preponderance of evidence."

Suddenly, Jane saw the puzzle pieces fitting together.

The method was the bat.

The means? Harper knew the exact route to sneak around the perimeter of the swim park, hiding in the bushes so that no one could see her carrying a bat.

The motive? Everyone at Mirror Lake High School knew the answer to that one.

And the tiny admission Harper had made to Jane when she'd crawled into her bed that night. Admitting that she felt guilty. She'd done something wrong. Something about turning over a new leaf in the future.

The big picture gave Jane a queasy feeling in the pit of her stomach.

"It's hard to lend credence to a tip when it's anonymous," the detective said. "We know that these kids are competitive. There's backstabbing, and there's jealousy. All that high school drama. Still, we check everything out."

"And you're investigating Harper?"

"As I said, we pursue every lead."

Expecting disapproval, she steeled herself to meet his thoughtful eyes, but saw only compassion there.

"Take good care of your daughter," he said. "Even living in the bubble, some of these kids make bad choices."

She nodded, despite the sick feeling that her daughter's fate was completely out of her hands.

Chapter 17

Although no one was ever charged with the attack on Olivia, the cloud of suspicion over Harper lifted a bit over the next few weeks as Olivia healed at home and the scandal of the attack was displaced by other high school dramas. A student from a high school across the Willamette River was arrested for homicide after his stepfather had been found stabbed to death, allegedly in retaliation for years of abuse. That was grist for the mill through the end of September. Then, in October, Brett Zilka, a sophomore at Mirror Lake High, was rushed off by an ambulance after cutting his head on the back steps of the school. Rumor had it that he'd passed out after smoking salvia with friends, but as that part was unconfirmed, Brett was allowed to return to school a week later with a gnarly red gash on his forehead.

Catching Brett in the hall one morning, Jane reminded the boy to keep the wound covered with an antibiotic ointment. "That'll help the scar heal."

"Yeah." He grinned. "But it's kind of a badge of honor, you know?"

"Maybe now. But in a few years, it's going to be a little played out."

"I guess."

Watching him swagger down the hall, Jane wasn't sure if he'd learned his lesson from the incident. Brett still seemed to hold that teen notion that he was invincible, and he had the scar to prove it. Life in the bubble tended to encourage that false sense of security.

One Tuesday afternoon in the end of October Jane parked in front of the Suzuki home to pick up Harper. Dismissal had been at noon so that teachers could spend the afternoon working on midterm grades, and Keiko had offered to host the girls after school. But as luck would have it, Tuesday was Harper's day to meet with Mrs. Albertson, the math tutor—a new addition to Harper's schedule, but a necessity. The current geometry curriculum was way beyond Jane's math knowledge, and so far Harper seemed to click with Mrs. A's teaching style.

Jane arrived to find Sydney and Harper in the side yard by the water feature, a dripping circular fountain. Nestled in their team hoodies, they sat on the stone bench, sharing a plastic bowl of popcorn.

"I see two ospreys," Jane called, amused by their matching shirts.

"Hi, Ms. Ryan," Sydney said politely.

"Mom!" Harper jumped up so abruptly she nearly spilled the popcorn. She handed the bowl to Sydney and raced forward to embrace Jane.

"Wow." Jane hugged her, surprised but pleased at the sudden show of affection. "Did you miss me that much?"

"I'm just really happy to see you."

When Harper leaned back, Jane noticed her mouth curled in a sweet smile. What a difference an afternoon off could make. "Where's Emma?" Jane asked.

"She's upstairs with—"

"She's watching a movie," Harper said, cutting Sydney off. "We already saw it, and we wanted to get some fresh air. It's so beautiful out here, with the leaves bursting in color. The crisp feel of autumn." Her words sounded lyrical, almost poetic.

"It is a nice day." Jane stretched her spine and rubbed the back of her neck. "I've been so caught up in getting grades in, I hardly noticed."

"You do work so hard," Harper agreed, admiration shining in her eyes.

"Um . . ." Sydney backed toward the door. "We'd better get back inside."

"I guess it would be too much to hope that you girls got some homework done," Jane said.

"I finished all of mine." Harper's voice was bright, with the tone of a delighted child.

"Amazing."

Jane followed them through the slider to the kitchen, where Keiko was stirring a pot. "Hey, there," Jane called to Emma's mom as the girls bustled up the stairs. "Thanks for taking the girls this afternoon." Jane leaned on the cool granite of the kitchen island.

"It was my pleasure." Keiko tapped the spoon against the edge of the pot, and then looked up at Jane. "They're such good friends. I know we love keeping our girls active in sports, but it's nice to see them having some downtime, too."

"I'm looking forward to a little downtime, myself," Jane said. Weekends had been busy with three softball tournaments: west of Portland in Banks, south in Eugene, and east in Bend, where Oregon's ponderosa pine forest transitioned into high desert. Each trip had been like a mini-vacation, social and active and a great change of venue, but Jane longed for a little cozy solitude. "It will be a nice change, sleeping in on weekends now that the season is over."

"That's true," Keiko agreed. "But basketball is just around the corner. Tryouts in two weeks."

Jane gave an exaggerated groan, and they chuckled together.

"One sport at a time," Jane said. She heard footsteps on the stairs behind her.

"Mom?" The whining tone in Harper's voice was like a splinter under the skin. "Do I really have to go right now? Why don't you just cancel?"

"Because it's geometry, and your frazzled mother can't help you with it anymore."

"I gave up on Emma's math years ago. Good thing her father can help her. That's his strong suit."

"I don't wanna go today," Harper moaned. "We're having fun, and everyone else can stay."

Jane turned to her daughter, who had changed from her team hoodie to a turquoise sweatshirt that brought out the teal hues in her eyes. "You changed your clothes?" She squinted at Harper. "And apparently your mood, too. What happened to the sweet girl I met outside?"

Harper bit back a smile.

"What?" Jane pressed.

"Never mind. Let's just go."

They thanked Keiko and headed out. The grumbling persisted as they got into the car, but Jane tuned it out as she focused on the next few steps of her day. She would drop Harper at the tutor's, then return to school to finish up. Then swing by to pick her up. But what for dinner? Frozen veggie lasagna or tacos? Maybe fish sticks . . .

She was about to back out of the Suzukis' driveway when one last look through the windshield brought her gaze to the window. A ghostly Harper stared wistfully down on them as she pressed a hand to the glass in an enigmatic gesture. A farewell or a warning?

Jane pumped the brakes and squinted. Was it a refraction of the glass, a trick of sunlight—or was she dissociating?

"What's wrong?" Harper said it as a criticism, as in, *What the hell is the matter with you?*

"The girl in the window. I thought it was you, but ..." *But it can't be; you're right here beside me.*

"Mom, there's no one there."

"What?" She shot a look back at the window, but there was only a blank space now. "But she was there. A girl with long dark hair. She was wearing an Osprey hoodie. I would have sworn it was you."

"Let's just go." Now there was disgust in Harper's voice.

Jane tried to put the vision behind her as she drove away. She had a million things to finish today, and she didn't need some strange apparition of her daughter clamoring in her mind.

"Okay, now I feel bad." Harper was facing away, but her scowl was reflected in the car window. "It was just a little game. A joke. Everybody says she looks like me, so we figured we'd see how far we could go with it."

Jane kept her eyes on the road ahead, but her fingers clamped tighter around the steering wheel. "What are you talking about?"

"The girl in the window? That was Isabel, the new girl. And she was the one sitting outside with Sydney when you pulled up. That wasn't me."

"What?" Alarm jangled over Jane's nerves. "But she looks just like you."

"I told you. Only we gave her a makeover today so that she would *really* look like me. She usually wears her hair different, and she likes pink and those flouncy skirts and polka dot explosions. She's a girly girl. But she's okay."

"So you pranked me?" More wounded than angry, Jane struggled to piece the situation together.

"At first we were going to try and fool Emma's mom. We talked about it on the bus ride to Emma's. But Mrs. Suzuki saw Isabel come into the house, and Emma had to introduce her and all, and even without the makeover Mrs. Suzuki commented that we could be sisters."

They could be sisters.

Jane kept her eyes on the road, fending off emotion.

"So we knew Mrs. Suzuki would never go for it. But we did the makeover anyway. And then when you texted to say you were on your way, we decided to try to trick you. Isabel said it would be a real challenge to fool a teacher."

Isabel? No, the name is wrong, and she lives in another state. Still . . .

"What is Isabel's last name?" Jane asked.

"I don't know. Do I have to go to the tutor *every* Tuesday? What about when basketball starts?"

"Yes. Every Tuesday." *Every shitty Tuesday.*

"I was just asking. You don't have to yell."

"I'm not yelling, but I am upset. It's not fun to be the butt of a joke."

"I'm sorry. We weren't trying to mock you or anything. It was more like a challenge to see if we could pull it off."

"Well. I guess you did." Jane's voice dripped with sarcasm. "Are you happy now?" She pulled up in front of Mrs. A's house and punched the gearshift into park with a vengeance. It wasn't a dangerous move, but it revealed the abrasive edge beneath Jane's evaporating composure.

"God, Mom. I said I was sorry." Harper opened the door and yanked out her backpack. "Just get over it." She slammed the car door before Jane could respond.

If you only knew . . . It's taken me years, and I'm still not over it. She'd made a mistake, a huge mistake, and it would overshadow the rest of her life.

With utmost restraint, Jane held to the speed limit on the drive back to school as she kept trying to rule out the one possibility that seemed impossible. Could the new girl, this Isabel, be her daughter?

When she had given Louisa up for adoption, Chrissy and Nick Zaretsky had said they wanted Louisa to keep her name.

"I see it as a gift from her biological mother," Nick had said.

"And such a beautiful name," Chrissy had agreed. With strong, high cheekbones, a dimpled smile, and eyes warm as whiskey, Christina Zaretsky had a motherly way about her that had appealed to Jane when she'd been reviewing profiles of parents eager to adopt. Unlike the other potential moms with hard, angular bodies from hours at the gym or running weekend 10K races, Chrissy appeared plump and soft as a favorite bathrobe. And this would not be her first attempt at motherhood; she had been raising two children back in Russia when their lives were cut short in a train accident. Such tragedy, and yet she had moved on, willing to live and love again.

"Family is everything," Nick Zaretsky had told Jane that day when she'd toured the family's lovely stone and glass house overlooking Puget Sound. "We are lucky to have Chrissy's mother and two sisters nearby, and my mother, she lives in an apartment we built for her out back."

So much family. Any child would be fortunate to grow up in such a beautiful, loving home, Jane had thought. She had never been to Bainbridge Island before, and the fabulous view across the blue water to the Seattle cityscape had won her over.

Chrissy had shown her the nursery, decorated with a menagerie of animals parading along . . . elephants and rhinos, giraffes and flamingos.

"My sister said it was presumptuous to decorate the nursery, but we couldn't resist," Chrissy had said, delicately smoothing a pillow with a pair of round-eyed koalas that had been embroidered by Chrissy's mother. "Not to make any assumptions, of course, but I'm always very positive about the future. My mother used to tell me to write my wishes down and pin them under my mattress. She said that dreams could not become reality unless we pinned them down."

Charmed by the couple, Jane had accepted an invitation to stay for dinner. Everyone had made a dish for the meal, and over a dinner of lamb kabobs, buttery *pelmeni* meat dumplings, and delicious sugared pancakes called *syrniki,* Jane had made her decision. One of her babies would live in this house, in the embrace of this good-hearted family. She imagined her little girl toddling through the breezes that came off the water, learning to walk in this airy family room that opened to the sky. When she grew older, the little girl would make up stories about the people who lived in the glittering gem boxes across the Sound in Seattle. This lucky girl would have adventures with her aunties: shopping and ferry rides and sailing lessons. There would be baseball games with Nick, a huge Mariners fan. And her grandmothers would give her cooking lessons for special dishes that had been passed down through the generations.

Such a good life her baby girl would have with the Zaretskys. The infant who came to live here would be the lucky one, the privileged daughter. The vision of such a charming life made Jane feel a twinge of guilt that she was not giving both children up for adoption. It seemed that Jane was no match for these parents hoping to adopt: couples with personal wealth, community resources, rich family history, and enthusiasm. In her darkest moments she worried that Frank had robbed her of the tools she needed to be a good mother.

Not true, a small voice would whisper. *You can do this. You're the mother. Two tiny lives are growing inside you. They will love you. . . . They will both love you, always, for bringing them into this world. But one will come to love other parents, and that's okay. You're just one woman digging out of a terrible situation. You can only handle one child.*

More than once Jane had fantasized about keeping both babies. She would scribble lists of numbers. The plus column of her savings, the money she had scraped together substitute teaching and temping in Seattle. And then the list of her expenses: food and an apartment rental in Oregon. Car insurance. Bills from the doctors and hospitals, which would not be paid by the adoptive parents if she kept both babies.

"Would you file for welfare?" Marnie had asked Jane one night as Jane added numbers to each column. "You could probably get food stamps."

Jane had already researched that. She had around ten thousand dollars saved—money she planned to use to live on for the first six months or so. "A person with more than two thousand dollars in the bank cannot get food stamps," she said. "Besides, public assistance would put me into yet another database where Frank might find me."

Try as she might to cut the expenses and twist the numbers, the bald reality always shone through. She could barely afford one child; two would put her in a deep financial hole.

She did not discuss the matter of her mental health with anyone, not even Marnie, but she knew she was in a tenuous place, walking a tightrope. One misstep, and the fall would be devastating for Jane and her two babies.

Adoption was the only way to save them all.

And so Jane chose the Zaretskys. They stood out as stable, grounded people—an island of calm in the sea of fear and doubt where Jane had been struggling to stay afloat. She had been living in panic, afraid that, in his spare time, Frank was hunting her down, intent on killing her.

That was why she had decided to leave Seattle. Marnie's support had proven to be invaluable, but sooner or later Frank would find Marnie and then Jane. She couldn't let that happen. She had to keep moving.

And so she had chosen to give one of her babies to the Zaretsky family and move south to Portland, Oregon, far enough away from Seattle that the two girls would not cross paths. It had been a closed adoption; Louisa would not be given Jane's information, and Jane signed away all parental rights. Chrissy and Nick were happy with that; they didn't want to share their baby with an occasional mother. Jane had changed her name in the state of Washington, and spent the last few days before the babies were born searching online for a neighborhood in which to raise her daughter. Somewhere that felt like home, with trees and a main street and a water-front. A slice of Americana with ethnic festivals and a Fourth of July parade. She had found those joys in Mirror Lake; she had built a life here.

And now, a sliver of the past threatened.

Eager to get to the truth, Jane pulled into a visitor's spot in front of the school and went straight to the main office. Keys in hand, she called a few hellos on the way to the registrar's office, where she paused in the doorway, relieved that Carol Delaney was still here. Jane did not have full access to all student records; she would need Carol's help.

"Hey, there." Carol took a slug from a water bottle. "You caught me on my way out. It's too quiet around here without the kiddos."

"Tranquility is good for the soul," Jane teased. "And for getting work done. Listen, do you have a minute to look up a student for me? A potential softball player." A small lie, but she needed some reason, and she could hardly say *my long-lost daughter.* "Her name is Louisa Zaretsky."

"Let's see." Carol sat down, swiveled toward the computer, and clicked the mouse a few times. "Do you know what grade?"

"A sophomore, I think."

Carol's fingers flew over the keyboard. "Hmm. We have one Zaretsky. First name Isabel."

Jane held her breath as Carol clicked open another file. Maybe this girl was a distant relative of her daughter.

"But it looks like her middle name is Louisa. Isabel Louisa."

Slammed by the truth, Jane stared at the screen. This was her daughter. . . . It had to be her.

"What info do you need?"

Jane forced herself to shed the paralysis of panic. "Just her contact info."

"Isabel Louisa . . . That's a pretty name." Carol copied the information in her round script. "I need to tell my daughter. They're looking for names for baby number two."

"I didn't even know you were a grandmother," Jane said, leaning over Carol's shoulder to take in the details on the screen—the impossible morphing into a concrete reality.

Isabel's mother was Christine Zaretsky, but no father was listed. Had Chrissy and Nick divorced? They had seemed like a cohesive couple, so determined to keep their family together.

"There you go."

Thanking the registrar, Jane clutched the slip of recycled scrap paper as she made her way out to the corridor. There, she leaned against the shiny porcelain tile of the wall and dared to look.

Arbor Lane.

The GPS on her phone pointed to a location on the flats,

away from the lake but near the freeway. Although she was tempted to head over there right now, there were grades to finish inputting, and Harper would have to be picked up from her tutor. But as soon as she could get away, sometime this evening, Jane would be paying the Zaretskys a visit.

Chapter 18

From the street, much of the small ranch house was obscured from view by a dense mat of bamboo shooting up from the ground. Probably planted by a novice gardener who had no inkling that the tough stalks would grow wild, tall, and invincible.

Although Jane had not seen any activity inside, the yellow glow from the main window led her to believe that someone was home. Most likely, the daughter Jane had given away was inside that house, and Jane wasn't sure how to feel about that. Staring at the house, she vacillated between feeling like a psycho stalker and feeling like the wronged party in an agreement that, now broken, was going to crack her life wide open. She dreaded Harper's bitter reaction. To learn that your mother had given your sister away at birth and kept it a secret all these years ... It sounded wrong to Jane's ears, even though she knew there were logical, sound reasons for her actions.

Then there was Luke. He didn't deserve the ripples and obstacles Jane had brought to his life. She worried that the story of the daughter she had given away would be one secret too many, that he would see Jane as a bundle of lies, slowly unraveling as the past caught up with her.

And what would happen if the school administrators heard

about this? Of course, they couldn't fire her because she had given a child up for adoption. But upon the unseemly appearance of a scandal, administrators were usually able to find some bogus way to dismiss an employee. Everyone knew the story of the teacher who had been fired for posting "party photos" on Facebook.

It was a sordid mess, one that she had spent a lifetime trying to avoid. And she would have succeeded if Chrissy Zaretsky had stayed put in her lovely Bainbridge Island home.

Holding on to that righteous indignation, Jane marched across the soggy lawn and rang the bell. Her plan was to inform Chrissy that she had been living and working in this town for more than a decade and politely ask the woman to relocate as soon as possible to maintain the privacy of both parties.

But Chrissy did not answer the door.

"Ms. Ryan!" Isabel's smile was effervescent. No longer dressed like Harper, she wore her hair swept back in rhinestone barrettes. The pink cashmere sweater and coordinated plaid miniskirt worn under her kitchen apron were obviously expensive. Isabel stood back and ushered Jane in with all the composure of a fifties housewife. "I didn't expect to see you at the door. Is Harper with you?"

"She's at home." Jane tried to see inside, but a wall blocked her view. "Is your mother here, Isabel?"

"Sure. Come in."

Inside the house was more upscale, with travertine marble floors and eclectic pendant lights shaped like gumdrops hanging over the table in the vestibule. Jane peered around the wall to the living room, but it was empty, as was the dining area behind the living room where sliding glass doors led to the backyard.

"Mom is taking a nap," Isabel offered by way of explanation. "She isn't feeling well."

"That's too bad. I'm sorry to bother her, but I really need to speak with her tonight."

Isabel's smile faded. "Am I in trouble, Ms. Ryan?"

"No. It's nothing you did. Although I have to say that I don't appreciate being pranked."

"I guess Harper told you." The girl's blue eyes grew round. "I'm really, really sorry. I take full responsibility for that. Kids are always saying we look alike, and we wanted to see if we could fool an expert. I can never resist a challenge."

As the girl spoke Jane took in the L-shaped house. An open door on her right revealed a hallway, probably leading to the bedrooms, and from here she could see the doorway off the dining room leading to the kitchen. It was modest and tidy, but a far cry from the house on Bainbridge Island. She turned away and moved toward the built-in bookcases on either side of the fireplace. One photo collage showed Isabel's school pictures from kindergarten through ninth grade, with empty spaces for the last three grades. Most of the other photos featured Isabel, sometimes alone, other times with Nick and Chrissy. Nick's hair had turned to silver, and his face had thinned, but his merry, bold-cheeked smile was unmistakable.

"Is this your father?" Jane asked, lifting a photo in a black frame.

Pressing her lips together, Isabel nodded. "It was. He died last spring. On Easter Sunday."

Stunned, Jane put the photo back. "I'm sorry." She had not expected this; Nick would only have been in his fifties.

"It's been a sad time for Mom and me. That's why we moved here—for a new start. Mom had to get away from the memories."

The block of ice around Jane's heart was melting. "And you? Did you want to come here?"

"It was my idea to move here." When Isabel lifted her chin, tears sparkled in her eyes. "Please don't be mad at me, but I have to tell you the truth. We came here to find you, Ms. Ryan. You see, I know that you're my biological mother."

"What?" Jane straightened.

"After we lost Dad, Mom and I realized that family is everything. My dad used to say that all the time, but I didn't really understand how true it was until he was gone. Mom and I figured that since I have a sister and another mother in the world, it was a good thing to get to know them . . . to get to know you." With pleading eyes, she opened her hands to Jane. "And so here we are."

Jane's fury had dissolved in the midst of Isabel's utter sincerity. This girl, this young woman, her polite, well-mannered daughter. Isabel Zaretsky was the exact opposite of her twin—the day to Harper's night—and this moment gave Jane all the satisfaction that had been lacking in the past fourteen years.

Giving in to the welling emotion, Jane took Isabel in her arms and wrapped her in a hug. "I never thought I would be able to hold you in my arms," Jane whispered.

"I know. Me too."

While Jane ignored the tears filling her eyes, Isabel patted her back. Such a maternal gesture for a teenager, wise for her years.

"I'm glad you're not mad. That would just destroy me right now. I'm in a tender spot with Dad gone and Mom so sick."

Jane stepped back, her hand on Isabel's shoulder. "How long has your mother been sick?"

The girl shrugged. "It started when Dad died. That's understandable. We all felt awful. Then it got bad, and . . . when the doctors didn't know how to help her, the therapist suggested a move."

"Did that help at all?"

"In the beginning. Mom really liked it here. But a few weeks ago, her dizziness and nausea came back." Isabel twisted the string of the apron around her fingers. "She started seeing some doctors here, but they can't figure out what's wrong. I just hope and pray that they find something to help her. I love her so much."

"I'm sure you do."

A scuffling sound came from the hallway. "Isabel?"

Jane had to bite back a gasp. The shell of a woman leaning against the wall barely resembled Chrissy Zaretsky, who had been so vibrant and robust the last time Jane had seen her. Her hair, now thin and a watery gray and white, hung limp on her shoulders, and her damp, drawn face was lined with pain.

"Who is this?" Chrissy rasped.

"My name is Jane. Don't you remember me, Chrissy?" How could Chrissy forget the woman who had given her a child, the light of her life?

Chrissy ran her palm along the wall as if to steady the room. "Refresh my memory."

Was she suffering from early-onset dementia, too?

"Mama, this is Jane, my birth mother. Remember? You and Dad met her and won her over, and then you adopted me."

"Yes, yes. I remember now." Chrissy's dark eyes pinned Jane with surprising fervor. "I suppose we need to talk."

"We do," Jane said, hoping this woman wouldn't put her off because of her illness. Jane had come this far; she wasn't about to back off now with only half of the answers.

"Let's sit." Chrissy pushed off the wall and began to shuffle toward the living room, hunched over her belly as she moved. Isabel hurried to her side, easing her onto the sofa.

"Can you get us some tea, Isabel?" the woman asked.

"Of course. I need to finish the dishes anyway." Isabel turned to Jane. "Would you like some cookies? I baked them with lavender from the garden."

"No, thank you," Jane said, "but tea would be great."

There was a glimmer of her former self as Chrissy stared after Isabel with gratitude and fondness. "Such a good girl. She deserves better than I can give her."

"Don't say that, Chrissy. You love and support her, and I can see that Isabel has turned out to be a wonderful young woman. Respectful and kind." Jane hadn't planned a pep talk, but none of this was turning out as planned. "You are Isabel's mother, and she needs you. That's why it's important for you to take care of yourself. Isabel said you've been seeing some doctors?"

Chrissy waved as if slapping away a gnat. "All the experts money can buy, and so far they can't help me. Gastrointestinal something, they're not sure." She wiped beads of sweat from her forehead with the back of one hand. "I'm sorry about before. I get confused sometimes. Weak and anemic. This disease or whatever it is, it sucks the life out of you."

"It sounds awful, Chrissy. It really does."

For a while they talked about the health issues that had driven Chrissy to leave Seattle. Jane listened sympathetically as the woman described weeks of hospitalization that finally helped Chrissy regain her strength, only to have the same symptoms return again here in Mirror Lake. "And it all came on the heels of Nick's passing." Chrissy pressed a fist to her mouth. "Isabel told you that we lost Nick?"

Jane nodded. "He looks so happy in your photos. What happened?"

"His heart gave out. It was quite sudden. He was seeing a cardiologist, but none of us knew how serious his condition was. After that, the house on Bainbridge Island felt too big, too quiet without him. And so full of memories." Chrissy told Jane about the decision to leave Seattle. Isabel had come up with the idea of moving closer to Jane and to Isabel's twin sister. "She always knew she was adopted, and she knows how important it is to be surrounded by family."

"But we're not really family," Jane pointed out. "Yes, the girls share much of the same DNA, but they have been raised so differently. They're not really sisters. I wish you hadn't brought Isabel here. Now everything is so . . . complicated."

"What else could I do? A child needs a family."

"She has you, and it was a closed adoption. I counted on you to respect my privacy. How did you find me, anyway?"

"A private investigator."

So easy when you had the money. Jane felt compassion for Chrissy, and although sympathy kept her from railing about the unfairness of the situation, she could not let this woman ruin her life. "I'm really happy to see Isabel thriving, but I can't hurt my daughter by breaking the truth about the adoption to her. I just can't open that can of worms."

"I apologize," Chrissy said. "I know we weren't supposed to contact you. But losing Nick was such a blow, and then with this sickness and being in the hospital, I got to thinking. I wondered, where would Isabel go if something happened to me? My little Isabel, she would have no one."

"But you have family," Jane said. "Nick's mother. Your mom and your sisters." And all the money in the world.

"Nick's mother passed away. My mother and my older sister . . . they returned to Europe. Now I have but one sister in the Seattle area, and Anya cannot take care of a child. She has suffered some tragedies, a terrible breakdown that caused her to be institutionalized. She now lives and works with the Carmelite nuns, a peaceful way of life, but very insular. We haven't spoken for years, but even if we mended things, Anya could not manage Isabel. So. I looked at the big picture and saw that Isabel was right. I knew that if things went wrong, we would have to turn to you. And so, here we are."

"I'm not sure what you expect me to do, exactly, but I'm afraid I can't help you. I've got my hands full raising my own daughter." *And I have the rebellious daughter, the one who struggles in school and would not be caught dead serving her mother tea.* "And to be honest, I'm shocked at the way you pushed into our lives, moving to our town and enrolling your daughter at our school. Our girls are becoming friends. Do you have any idea how awkward that is for me? Really, Chrissy. You could have sent a note of warning. You could have called to ask for help. But to just arrive here and insinuate yourself—"

Chrissy cut her off with a firm gesture of warning as Isabel came in with two mugs of tea. "Thank you, dear."

"You're welcome, Mama-dear."

How eerily similar that sounded to Harper's resounding "Mama-dish."

"Do you need milk or sugar, Ms. Ryan? I wasn't sure."

"This is fine, thanks." Jane gripped the hot mug, glad for the reality check of the heat on her palm.

"Are you feeling better, Mom?" Isabel gave her mother a coy smile that reminded Jane of a smug parrot. This expression was not in Harper's repertoire.

"Not so dizzy anymore, and the numbness has gone away. That delicious dinner helped."

"They say that chicken soup is penicillin for the soul," Isabel said brightly.

"And your soup is always soothing." Chrissy lifted the steaming mug to her face. "Isabel is an excellent cook. She has perfected all the family recipes."

"Cooking is fun for me," Isabel said. "I just wish I had more time for it. Now that I'm editor of the newspaper, I'm spending a lot more time at school."

"Editor-in-chief. And she's a good student, too," Chrissy added. "A 4.0 for the past two years."

Jane's heart sank at the realization that Isabel was settling in at the high school, establishing roots. Of course, that was exactly what Isabel needed—just not here in Mirror Lake.

"I'd better get back to my homework." Isabel untied the

apron and folded it into a neat square. "But I'm glad that you came by, Ms. Ryan. This has been a very special night for me. I'll never forget it."

Jane could only nod. It had been an emotional crossroads for her, too, albeit an unwanted one. As Isabel turned to leave, Jane thought of the need to protect Harper.

"Just one more thing, Isabel," Jane said. "Please don't talk about this at school. The adoption was private, and I'd like to keep it that way." *For Harper's sake,* she thought. Poor Harper. So much drama swirling around her, threatening her secure world.

"Of course, Ms. Ryan. I'll do whatever you think is right."

"I told you, she's a good girl," Chrissy said proudly.

Isabel's eyes glimmered as she touched her mother's shoulder tenderly. The bond between these two was obviously strong and affectionate. What the hell was Chrissy thinking, wanting to ensnare Jane in their lives?

The older women waited to continue their discussion until Isabel disappeared down the hall with her backpack.

"You can't stay here," Jane said. "If you return to Seattle, Isabel can pick up with old friends at a familiar high school. Seattle's medical facilities are among the best in the country. Portland's are always seen as a second cousin to them. Seattle is the answer for you. I'm sure things will work out for you there."

Chrissy shook her head. "That is not going to happen." She seemed stronger now, suddenly focused. "There is no going back to the life we used to have. Nick is gone forever, and every corner of Seattle reminds me of him. This is our new home." She closed her eyes as she sipped the tea, then sighed. "I understand your reluctance to be involved with Isabel, and I respect that. I cannot force you to be kind to her."

"I would never be unkind to any kid her age," Jane said, "but you're asking too much of me."

"I am fending for my daughter's emotional happiness, as I know you would do for your daughter if the circumstances were reversed."

It was a study in semantics. Jane cocked her head to one side, struggling to tamp down her annoyance. Why did Chrissy refuse to acknowledge that Jane had her own daughter to protect?

"I need to get going." Harper needed help with her homework, and Jane had promised to help her get started on an awesome Halloween costume. Jane put her mug down and thanked Chrissy for the tea. "You know I wish you the best, but this plan that you and Isabel have for a family reunion is only going to hurt people."

"On that you're wrong, my dear." Chrissy seemed deflated against the cushions, fading into gray once again. "Family is everything."

"But we are not family," Jane said bluntly. "You can't have a family reunion when there was no union to begin with."

Her own words resounded in her mind as she let herself out and drove home to the other daughter, the chosen one.

Chapter 19

That night Jane tried to escape the sickening shadow looming over her as she threw herself into the activity of making a Halloween costume with Harper.

"I was thinking of being a giant Oreo cookie," Harper said.

"Great idea! That's so cute."

"I didn't make it up. I saw it in a flyer for Costume Country. But you can't enter the contest with a store-bought costume, and since this is my last year, I want to score big."

By tradition, sophomore year was the last time students attended the Halloween party at school. Jane didn't know what upperclassmen did on Halloween—she doubted that they sat home handing out candy to trick-or-treaters—but that would be a challenge for next year.

In the mood to splurge, Jane grabbed the stash of cash from the cookie jar and drove Harper to the craft store. An hour later, armed with brown and white felt and pieces of cardboard, they started the project, but lost steam quickly. Jane burned her hand on the hot glue gun, and Harper declared that the big brown circle looked like a "pile of poop." Phoenix's soft woof of agreement made them laugh, but the costume seemed doomed.

"That's it for tonight," Jane said, looking at the clock,

though Harper did not need convincing. She was already stretched out on the couch. "We'll work on it some more tomorrow."

"It's awful," Harper moaned as her fingers tapped out a message on her phone.

"Who are you texting this late?" Jane asked.

"Jesse. He wanted to come over to help, but we got started too late. He says he's got letters for me. I don't know what he means."

"Well, it's about time to turn off electronics and head off to bed."

"Can we throw the costume out and start over on something else?" Harper put her cell on the counter and dug into the cookie jar, where Jane kept emergency funds. "Please, Mom? We've got more than twenty bucks left for something new."

"We already spent money on supplies, and it's an ambitious idea."

"But a flat felt circle is never going to look like an Oreo. It sucks."

"Try to think positive. How can we fix it?"

"It needs texture."

"Let me think about that," Jane said, stifling a yawn. "Hey, maybe we can mold the cookie part from salt dough."

"That will weigh a ton, and I'm not going to wear salt sculptures around my neck."

"Let's sleep on it," Jane said, though she doubted that sleep would come to her now that the past was breathing down her neck.

After Harper went to bed, Jane soaked in the tub. She held her breath and slid down under the surface to escape the world. It didn't work; when she came up for air, her thorny problems were still poking her in the chest. Dressed in her soft flannel pajamas, she burrowed under the comforter on her bed and called Luke. This was a conversation that could not wait until they could be alone together.

"Hey, how's it going?" His voice was bright and cheerful as ever.

"Not so good." Unsure where to begin, she started in the middle of the story. "You know that new girl at school—the one who looks like Harper? Well, the resemblance is there because they are twins. They're sisters, Luke. Isabel was my baby, too. I gave her up for adoption a few days after she was born."

Luke was silent as she told the story, but she didn't feel the sting of criticism or judgment. In the end, he had just one bit of advice: Tell Harper.

"Right now there's another kid walking around the school with some crucial information about Harper's origins and family," he said. "That has the potential to hurt Harper if it gets out and she has no clue. She needs to be armed with the information. Knowledge is power."

"I can't tell her." Jane pulled the comforter over her head and soaked up the soft darkness with the phone pressed to her ear. "I don't know how to tell her. I don't want to tell her."

"You have to. And you figured out a way to tell me. Give her a similar version, minus the part about Frank's chasing you. No kid should have to hear that her father is a psychopath."

"That's for sure. But I don't know about telling her. This is so far out of my comfort zone. Even after all these years, I have feelings of guilt and embarrassment. And inadequacy."

"That's understandable. But trust me on this. You'll feel better once the truth is out. Tell her that she has a sister. She may not choose to act on it, or maybe she will. Put the choice in her hands."

Jane inhaled deeply, grateful that she could breathe again. This was not the end of the world. If she told Harper the truth, she would be giving her daughter a sibling, a sister. Although Jane had not been close to her sister, there had been a time when she and Shelly were a team, a cozy subset in the family, sitting together and sharing a bed when the family went on vacations. She wanted that for Harper.

Decision made, she found sleep.

The next day, Jane reconsidered the situation as she helped her students devise thesis statements for their essays on *To Kill a Mockingbird*. Recalling the way Scout and Jem had maintained lives that were a world apart from their father's social dealings, she wondered if it would be so wrong to keep this secret from Harper. After all, Hoppy and Isabel might not strike up a long-term friendship in the next two or three years. For all Jane knew, their relationship might already be winding down. Maybe it was best to wait.

After school, when Harper came to Jane's classroom to pick up the pieces of her costume, Jesse was with her.

"See what Jesse made for me?"

One by one, Jesse removed four brown ceramic letters from his backpack, spelling *OREO* on Jane's desk.

"He did them in ceramics class last week," Harper explained. "Aren't they the coolest?"

"These are awesome. Good enough to eat." Jane lifted the *R* and found it to be surprisingly light. "You hollowed them out?"

"You sort of have to because big blocks of solid clay explode in the kiln." Jesse dug his hands into his pockets. "Yeah, I modeled it after the cookie, but that was hard because everyone wanted to eat it. The cookie, I mean."

"Isn't it great? It's going to give the cookie texture," Harper said.

"Sure is. How are you going to attach the letters to the felt?" Jane asked.

"Still not sure," Harper answered. "We're going to see if we can get some help in the design studio. They've got all kinds of tools and machines."

"Good idea." As Jane watched her daughter saunter down the corridor with Jesse Shapiro, she realized that she really liked the kid. She also realized that her craft skills, appropriate for assisting her daughter on grade school activities, were now obsolete. How quickly things had changed.

Two hours later, as Jane packed up her laptop, she wondered why Harper had not texted an update. She hoped that Harper and Jesse hadn't wandered off school property without telling her. From the corridor of the art wing, she heard their voices: upbeat and cheerful girls' voices punctuated by Jesse's droll, low comments. From the doorway of the design studio she saw Emma and Sydney leaning intently over a display of papier-mâché fruit that they seemed to be gluing in place.

Harper and Jesse sat together at a high counter, gluing something down to the big circle of felt. Beside them, Isabel worked a sewing machine, feeding white fabric through in a steady stream.

A mixed bag, this crew. Jane was torn, giddy over their goodness and weak-kneed at the horrible potential. The bohemian boyfriend, the secret sister. Was life always a flight from danger, a torrent pushing you to the next precipice?

"Mom! You'll never believe how talented Isabel is. Look at this." While Isabel continued sewing, Harper showed off the brown braiding and felt tiles piled high to make the diamonds, squares, and circles on the face of the Oreo.

The rapid-fire patter of the sewing machine stopped as Isabel smiled up at them.

"And she knows how to sew. She's already fitted the white fabric for me. Pretty amazing, huh?"

"I'm impressed," Jane admitted. No use wishing that all

this creative genius had come from Emma or Sydney—anyone other than Isabel. "It's bigger than life. More Oreo than the actual cookie."

Isabel's eyes sparkled as she basked in the praise. "Harper had the vision. I just showed her how to make it happen." She rose, shaking out the white fabric. "This should fit now. Want to try it on?"

While Harper slid on the white sheath of her costume, Jane asked Jesse what he was planning for the party.

"I don't usually do costumes, but Harper insisted." He took a black cloth from his pocket and stretched it across his face so that the holes lined up with his eyes. "The Lone Ranger."

"I like your minimalist approach," Jane said, earning a sardonic grin.

She spoke with Emma and Sydney about their two-person costume, a clever, eerie dinner table with two holes cut through a plate on the top for the girls' heads to pop through the cardboard.

"It's our heads on a platter," Emma said.

Jane laughed as the girls demonstrated. "Delightfully gruesome," she declared.

Sydney put her hands on Emma's hips, and the two girls swayed together, reminding Jane of the vaudevillian horsehead and tail shtick she had seen in movies. The kids laughed, ribbing each other in a scene that was nothing less than jovial. What more could a mother ask for?

The conversation turned to talk of Isabel's costume, and she admitted that she was not planning to attend Friday's party.

"What? You have to go!" Harper insisted. "The Halloween party is the best one of the year."

"Really," Emma agreed. "I figured you were already done with your costume, Isabel."

Isabel shook her head. "Never even started."

"Well, start now." Sydney straddled a chair next to Isabel. "What do you want to be?"

"I haven't even thought of it, and I have to get home soon. I've got chores to do."

Cooking and caring for her mother. Jane tried to steel herself from emotional reflex, but even the most hardened heart would find some sympathy for Isabel Zaretsky.

"Wow. Your mom must be really strict," Harper said.

"She's not so bad," Isabel said quietly.

"But the party's not till Friday," Emma pointed out. "We can all meet tomorrow to help Isabel with her costume. So what do you think? Maybe a good fairy? Or Dorothy from *The Wizard of Oz*. I've got some ruby slippers in my closet. What size do you wear?"

"I want to be an object, like you guys," Isabel said. "Maybe . . . a glass of milk?"

"Yes!" Harper high-fived her. "And we could go around together, cookies and milk."

Jane forced a smile, disturbed at how this was playing out. Had Isabel deliberately chosen a costume with a theme that would match her up with Harper? Of course. She must have. It was a calculated move, but then Isabel had manipulated her way here from Seattle to find family.

And can you fault her on that? Jane asked herself. She turned away from the kids and paced to the studio windows to stare out at the gathering darkness. Luke had been right. This situation was not going to go away.

On Friday night when Jane arrived at school to pick her daughter up, she found Harper arm-in-arm with Isabel. The judges had found the "Oreo and milk" costume irresistible, awarding first prize to Harper and Isabel.

"We rocked that party, Mom," Harper said. Cellophane

from the "milk glass" of Isabel's costume crinkled as Harper tugged her over to Jane. "Can Isabel stay overnight? We want to celebrate."

"Not tonight."

"Aw. Well, we're giving her a ride home. Her mom can't pick her up."

"That's fine."

The girls shed the large shells of their outfits and stashed them gently in the trunk of Jane's car, joking about how they needed to be preserved in a hall of fame. As Jane drove, the two girls sat together in the back, talking about the party. Typical comments about obnoxious things some girl said, other unusual costumes, and a haunted house made spooky by the senior boys who popped out and grabbed the girls by the arms.

"They're not supposed to touch us," Harper insisted. "I can't believe they did that."

"But it wouldn't have been scary if they didn't," Isabel pointed out.

"Oh, I know. A couple of hanging bats and fake gravestones? That part was lame."

Jane rehearsed her speech as she drove. Each turn was a chance to divert the announcement, each stop sign a moment to pause and think. Oh, how she wanted to put it all off, but things were progressing quickly between the two girls, and Jane would not play her daughter for the fool. Harper needed to have this information, the sooner the better.

"Thanks for the ride, Ms. Ryan," Isabel said.

Jane remained in the driver's seat while Harper helped the girl get her costume from the trunk. A hug was exchanged—a sight that made Jane's insides sizzle with anxiety. And then, Harper climbed into the passenger seat and they were rolling again.

"There's something I need to tell you." Jane stared ahead,

eyes on the road. She had planned to wait, talk over hot cocoa at home, but somehow this seemed easier to say when she could not look her daughter in the eye. "Honestly, this is embarrassing for me. It involves a part of my life that happened before you were born. Some tough decisions I had to make."

"This sounds scary," Harper said slowly.

"No need to be scared. This stuff is history, but it affects our lives today." She reminded Harper of the difficult situation she'd been in when she was pregnant. "Your father was gone, and I had no family. My friend Marnie helped, but I was in dire financial straits."

"I know. And then I came along," Harper said, reciting the family lore. "The light of your life."

"That's right. But there's a bit more to the story. When I was pregnant in Seattle, the doctor told me I was expecting twins."

"You were?" Harper was awed. "So I had a twin? Oh, that's so sad. I always wanted a brother or sister. What happened to my twin?"

"Nothing so bad. I knew I didn't have the resources or support to take care of two babies. So I made the arrangements to give the other baby up for adoption . . . to parents who desperately wanted a baby of their own."

"So it lived?"

"Yes. A baby girl, and her new parents, Chrissy and Nick, were so thrilled to have her, and they were very happy together. But sadly, Nick, the dad, died recently and . . ." Jane's heart thudded oddly in her chest as she turned onto their street. She felt as if she were telling someone else's tale. "Your twin sister and her mother came here to find us because they . . . they want to establish family ties."

"Wait. My sister is here? How old is she? Oh, wait. My twin would be my age. Duh."

It was a relief to have the truth out when they pulled into the garage. Jane cut the engine and turned to her daughter.

Harper's eyes were round as quarters and shimmering with the sparks of connection and discovery. "I can't believe you kept this a secret. A sister! So when do I get to meet her?"

"You've met her, honey. It's Isabel."

"Isabel?" Disbelief and wonder in Harper's voice. "Isabel? Whaaaaah!" A cry of astonishment and delight. "She's my sister? Oh my God. That's why we look alike. My twin. Oh my God, I have a sister! Mom . . . I can't believe you didn't tell me."

Jane took the keys from the ignition and settled back in the seat. It was going to be a long night.

PART 3

I prefer winter . . . when you feel the bone structure of the landscape—the loneliness of it . . . Something waits beneath it, the whole story doesn't show.

—Andrew Wyeth

Chapter 20

In the beginning, Jane held herself back. It seemed that an emotional attachment to Isabel would constitute a betrayal of Hoppy, and Jane knew that first and foremost she must remain supportive of Harper. She kept reminding herself that she had no legal commitment to this girl, that it was appropriate to remain detached and cheerful. She gave Isabel the same level of affection she showed Sydney or Emma, nothing more. On the other hand, Harper gushed over her newfound sister, thrilled to have a friend for life. To save face and privacy, they had decided to tell everyone that Isabel was a distant cousin, and no one questioned the story or cared much.

"That explains why you two look so much alike," Sydney noted, and that seemed to close the topic.

The kids let Isabel in without question. Suddenly Harper, Isabel, and Jesse were a cohesive triad, sitting at the kitchen bar doing homework each day after school. Night after night, Harper finished her homework by dinnertime. She aced a vocabulary quiz and got her first B on a high school math test. Much as Jane loathed admitting it, Isabel and Jesse had helped Harper bring her grades up.

When basketball practice began, the girls lamented that Isabel would not be on their team.

"I wish you could play with us," Harper kept saying. "That would be so awesome."

Isabel claimed to be a total klutz when it came to sports. "But I'll come to every game and cheer you on," she promised.

As mid-November brought crisp temperatures, the bond warmed between the two girls, leaving Jane to feel a bit like the odd man out.

Then the holidays approached, bringing issues without precedent. "Isabel and her mom are going to be alone for the holiday, and Chrissy is too sick to cook," Harper reported. "Isn't that sad?"

"At least they'll have each other," Jane said, "and I'm sure they can find a nice restaurant that serves turkey." The Zaretskys could certainly afford to have a dinner catered; when they had adopted Louisa, they had been among the top twenty wealthiest families in the Seattle area.

"I still think it's sad," Harper said wistfully.

"We've been on our own every Thanksgiving since you were a year old, and we've done just fine."

"I know, but that was before we knew that we had family so close by. My *twin sister*, Mom. Why can't we all celebrate together? It'll be easier for you. Isabel is a really good cook, and I bet she'd be happy to make something. Maybe the mashed potatoes."

"I appreciate your concern, but I'm not up for it."

"Come on, Mama-dish." Harper gave her a playful nudge. "You hate peeling potatoes. Here's your chance for a break."

"I'm happy for the break from school and the chance to spend time with you," Jane said.

"But you always tell me Thanksgiving is a time to count your blessings and pay it forward. Remember when I was little and we brought cans to the food bank?"

"I didn't think you remembered. You were so little."

"I soaked it all up and took it to heart. And now Isabel and Chrissy need our help. I have to help my sister, Mom."

Jane wanted to groan over that painful truth. She appreciated her daughter's altruism, but she had trouble imagining herself as part of a happy family with Chrissy and Isabel Zaretsky. Until recently, when she had visualized her future, she had seen herself doing a figure-eight in alternating revolutions around Harper and Luke. Now, when she looked ahead, the picture was muzzy.

In the end, Jane succumbed to Harper's burst of goodwill and invited Isabel and her mother over for Thanksgiving dinner. How could she deny her otherwise self-absorbed teen this act of philanthropy?

"Thank you for having us," Chrissy said as she slowly made her way into the living room. Her hair shone with ebony color, and the blush on her cheeks hinted at a resurgence of health. The fact that she was walking on her own showed a marked improvement, but Jane erred on the side of caution and held Phoenix's collar. One brisk leap and she could take the woman down.

"Aren't you a nice dog?" Chrissy said as she gingerly lowered herself to the sofa.

"She is a gentle dog, and she sure seems to like you," Jane said, releasing the dog with a warning to behave. The lab trotted briskly over to the older woman and pressed into her legs.

"Oh, yes, yes. Need someone to love you up?" Chrissy leaned down and roughed Phoenix's scruff, giving her a brisk rubbing. In her glory, Phoenix gave a tender whimper of response.

Traitor, Jane thought, though she was not surprised that the dog liked Chrissy. The lab was a good judge of character. Yes, Chrissy had a soft heart and a firm backbone. Years ago Jane had chosen her because she was solid.

The women talked as the girls toted covered dishes in from the car. Savory whiffs of stuffing with apples and sausage, creamed onions, and mashed red potatoes were added to the mouthwatering smell of roasted turkey that suffused the house. Jane offered wine, but Chrissy declined.

"It's been a good week, and I don't want to ruin it by slipping up," Chrissy explained.

"You look great," Jane encouraged her. "The roses are back in your cheeks."

"I don't know about that," Chrissy demurred, "but it's a blessing to get through a few days without those nasty spells." When Jane asked about her symptoms, Chrissy explained that she was often sick with sweating, vomiting, confusion, and intestinal issues. Tingling sensations on her skin gave way to numbness, and her heartbeat quickened and became irregular.

Jane nodded sympathetically. "And the doctors can't give you a diagnosis?"

"I've given up on them, but I'm planning a trip to Seattle to see an acupuncturist who did wonders when I visited my sister last time."

Isabel placed a basket of rolls on the table and came to perch on the rolled arm of the sofa. She looked adorable in her tights, short pleated skirt, and pink V-neck sweater. Years ago Jane would have given anything to get Harper into an outfit that refined; now Jane was resigned to the fact that "dressed up" meant jeans without holes and a shirt without a sports decal on it. "It looks like dinner is served. Are you moms ready?"

"I'm starving," Jane declared. She popped the cap on a bottle of sparkling cider and poured four goblets.

As they sat down together Isabel raised a glass to make a toast. "Thanks for having us. I'm grateful for that." Sincerity glimmered in her blue eyes. "And I'm so happy we can all be here together. Family is everything."

"Hear, hear," Chrissy agreed.

Harper got out of her seat so that she could touch glasses with everyone. "Cheers, family."

Jane let herself smile as the crystal clinked. This odd matriarchy no longer seemed unsettling; they were survivors, the four of them. Strong women. It was time to let go of her anger toward Chrissy; she now realized the woman had come here out of desperation. Was she dying? Jane hoped not. But it was beyond her control.

"Mom, do I like creamed onions?" Harper asked, staring into one of the pots Isabel had brought.

"I'm not sure that you've ever had them, but give them a try. They're delicious."

Isabel beamed with pride as her pale fingers smoothed the tablecloth. "I'm glad you like them." The adulation in her gaze melted the protective shell from Jane's heart. This kid really aimed to please; it was cruel to keep shutting her out.

After dinner Harper invited Isabel up to her room, but Isabel suggested that they clean up first.

"You can go, Isabel," Chrissy said. "I'll help Jane with the dishes."

"But more hands make the work go faster," Isabel insisted, tying on an apron. "I'm happy to help." She went to the sink and started scrubbing a baking dish.

Jane looked up from the dishwasher to see Harper standing with her fingertips in her jeans pockets, her dark hair falling over one eye.

"What do you want me to do, Mom?"

Harper offering to help in the kitchen? It was a first. Jane nodded toward the drawer. "Why don't you grab a fresh towel and dry the pots and pans."

Later, when the two girls were upstairs, Chrissy folded a kitchen towel, a sage light in her eyes. "I was always skeptical about the so-called bond between twins, but there's definitely something special there."

Jane glanced away from Chrissy, not wanting to tell the woman that was just wishful thinking on her part. Despite her research about the special relationship that twins developed in utero, Jane had not noticed an extrasensory connection between Harper and Isabel. No mental telepathy or sympathetic pains. "They do seem to enjoy each other," Jane admitted, "and Isabel has been a positive influence on Harper. Her grades are improving. And I have to tell you that Isabel has always been a model of good behavior around us. You raised her well. Though I'm sure she has her moments around you."

Chrissy pulled her cardigan closer and folded her arms. "Moments?"

"Complaints and tantrums. Sulking and defiance. Most teens tend to vent on their parents."

"Not Isabel."

"Really? She doesn't have a bad day now and then? A case of the blues? Annoyance with a teacher or fury over a social injustice?"

"I've never seen it. She sails on an even keel."

"What about when Nick died?"

"She was sad, but she didn't seem to experience the anger and denial I felt. Or maybe her denial was expressed in the desire to come here and get away from the life we had in Seattle with Nick. Starting over."

"That would make sense. Our hearts and minds heal in different ways." The image of Isabel grasping for a new family life tugged at Jane's heart. The girl had spunk. Jane was reminded of her brief time with Isabel after the birth—her Louisa. Even as an infant, that calm, sure demeanor had been present. Jane had made the right choice to give her up; she could not imagine Harper's surviving the sorrows in the Zaretsky family.

"Isabel is my rock. I'm the one with the worries. This illness had brought me down, and I worry that I've pulled her down with me. But that's changing. Now that she has things to do, so many activities with your Harper, I've hired an aide to come in and help out. A teenage girl shouldn't have to spend every evening cooking and caring for her mother. This is a good thing, to give a young girl some freedom to be with friends and with her sister."

"That sounds like a great plan," Jane agreed. "And Isabel seems to be enjoying her newfound freedom. The other kids have really taken to her."

"And she's all about Harper. Now that they are together, we will never get them apart," Chrissy said. "I'm not a religious person, but it reminds me of that phrase in the Bible. 'What God has joined together, let no man put asunder.'"

Chrissy was right; those two were a match made in heaven. *And I'm the one who tore them apart.*

That night Harper bamboozled Jane into allowing Isabel to sleep over. It certainly wasn't the first pajama party for the girls, but the holiday gave it a special significance that disturbed Jane. Missing Luke, she retired to the solitude of her room. She put a call through, but when he didn't answer she suspected that he was still at dinner or not getting reception at his hotel. He had driven to Spokane to have dinner with his ex-wife Val, their son Matt, and Val's new husband Hans, who was CEO of a huge sportswear company. Holidays with the ex. It sounded like the setup for a dysfunctional Thanksgiving comedy film, but with Luke as the guest of honor, Jane could envision things going smoothly. Vindictive was not something Luke carried in his toolbox. Jane had seen photos of Luke arm-in-arm with Hans at Val and Hans's wedding, both men grinning so brightly they could have been in toothpaste ads.

Ah, Luke, never again. She vowed that they would spend

Christmas together this year. So what if people began to guess that they were involved? The community's lackluster reaction to the revelation that Isabel was a relation had taught Jane a few things. Most people were too caught up in their own lives to notice the ripples in someone else's pond. Some people didn't care that a few rules had been bent, and others celebrated the act of defiance. She was going to have a talk with Mr. Bandini about bringing their relationship out of hiding.

"Hey, Mom." Harper and Isabel stood at the bedroom door. Like a couple in a sitcom, Harper wore flannel pajama bottoms with a sweatshirt on top, while Isabel wore the button-down top as a nightgown. "We thought we'd come keep you company," Harper said, plopping onto Jane's bed.

"Your room is so peaceful." Isabel touched the sheers that swept over the tall windows. "Like a sheltered sea cove. I love the color of the walls. Is that sea foam?"

"I believe it was called Serenity Sea," Jane said, allowing a smile.

"It's perfect," Isabel said, sitting on the bed beside Harper. "Just like you."

"I'm far from perfect," Jane said, though she didn't mind the bit of praise. In fact, she found herself soaking up the wonder in Isabel's eyes. The sheer admiration made her heart race at times. She tried not to compare, but there was no ignoring the fact that she rarely saw anything like that in Harper's eyes. A tough cookie, her Hoppy. The girl, who was currently bent over her right foot, flicking off flakes of nail polish, was often hard on the people around her, and she definitely had a temper. Jane fell into thoughts of the unsettling question of the attack on Olivia, a mud pit of reverie. The culprit was still a mystery to the police, but sometimes when Harper lost her temper, it was easy to imagine her swinging that bat and pushing Olivia into the lake.

Jane shivered, as if to shake off the image. She didn't want to believe that Hoppy had the vinegar and vitriol inside her to lash out that way, but if not her, then who had done it? The police had never named a suspect, but at least Detective Drum had stopped calling.

"I know!" Harper bounced on Jane's bed. "Let's play cards!"

The burst of enthusiasm snapped Jane out of her funk, reminding her of the way Harper could fill a room. This was not a girl who would hurt someone. This was a kid who loved people.

"Do you know how to play hearts?" Jane asked. When Isabel shook her head, Harper offered to teach her.

They sat on the living room carpet, balancing bowls of popcorn in their laps and leaning in around the coffee table to swoop up tricks and sip cider from wineglasses. The game of hearts got the girls talking about their notions of love. Isabel believed that pure love was about loyalty, while Harper thought too many people confused attachment with love.

"I'm not going to settle for anything less than true love," Harper said. "There's no way I'm going to marry a man unless he's absolutely right for me."

"You have a lot of time to figure that out," Jane said. "But there is no perfect love. Relationships take compromise."

"Maybe for you, Mom. But I'm not sacrificing myself for a guy."

Jane patted her daughter's arm. "Good for you, honey."

"Were you in love with our dad?" Isabel asked sweetly.

Jane blanched as Frank's image pierced her thoughts. That winning smile, those mesmerizing blue eyes that she saw whenever she looked at the girls. She had fallen in love with the beautiful package before she knew what it contained.

"Of course she loved him," Harper answered, saving Jane. "But she doesn't like to talk about it. It hurts."

"Oh." Isabel looked back at her cards and extracted one. "Sorry."

For the first time, the picture of possibilities stopped wavering before Jane's eyes as it wiggled into the shape of three heads triangulated in the soft light. A blissful family portrait; the magic of three.

Chapter 21

It was hardly a huge turnout for the traditional tree-lighting ceremony in Mirror Lake's square. Some diehards felt that the day after Thanksgiving was too early to swing into the holiday spirit, and some conservationists had complained that it was a waste of the town's money to light the giant sequoia for six weeks of the year, even with the new LED lights. But tradition lived on. With the high school chorus singing from a makeshift stage, and an audience consisting of two busloads of residents of an assisted-living home, young families, and a few packs of teens and tweens, there were enough people milling about to give Jane a sense of anonymity as she hung out with Luke.

He had given her a recap of his visit to Spokane and was now updating her on Matt's plans to study for a semester in Spain. "But I've been talking a mile a minute and haven't heard a word about your Thanksgiving," he said.

"That's what happens when you drive for six hours straight."

"So how was it?"

"Better than I expected. Isabel makes a mean sausage stuffing, and Chrissy seemed to be opening up to me. I guess she's relaxing around me."

"Good. How is she doing?"

"Better. She was walking on her own, and she seemed to enjoy the meal. Chrissy and Isabel are heading up to Seattle over Christmas vacation. They're hooking up with Chrissy's sister and some old friends. I can tell that Chrissy is really looking forward to it."

"And Isabel seems to be full of holiday spirit."

She followed his gaze across the square to the bench where Isabel, Harper, Sydney, and Emma swayed in time to a Christmas carol from the choir. "That's funny." Jane chuckled. "I'm happy to have her along, but she was raised Jewish. This really shouldn't be her thing."

"Looks to me like she's rockin' the Santa cap. Is Chrissy going to be upset about that?"

"She's okay with it. She was raised Russian Orthodox, but converted to Judaism before she married Nick. Right now Chrissy's focus is more on Isabel's social adjustment than religious connection. Apparently, Chrissy and Nick tried to get Isabel to prepare for her bat mitzvah, but she did not seem interested. All that got pushed aside when Nick was diagnosed, and Chrissy hasn't pushed it since then."

"We can influence our kids in many ways, but we can't control their beliefs," Luke said.

"True, oh wise one."

"Are you making fun of me?" One side of his mouth tipped up in a crooked grin.

"Never. You are the wisest man I know, for sure." If not for the fact that they were both teachers and in a public place, she would have linked her arm through his and kissed him. Mmm. Though it would have been sweet to have that freedom, Jane knew it would curdle her daughter's stomach if Harper caught a glimpse of adult affection. Better to hold back. A little discretion never hurt anyone.

Later, as the event wound down and the crowd began to

scatter, Jane was talking with Trish when Chrissy's black Mercedes pulled up to the curb across the square.

"Isabel?" Jane waved to get the girls' attention. "Looks like your mom is here."

"I'd better go."

"See you later. I love you!" Harper gushed, embracing her twin. Although Harper said this to all her friends, Jane was dumbstruck every time she saw this exchange with Isabel.

"Good-bye, Ms. Ryan," Isabel said sweetly as she trudged across the square.

"Bye." Looking ahead, Jane noticed that the car's driver was not Chrissy. "Hey, there. Isabel?" Jane called, falling into step beside the girl. "Who's that driving the car?"

"Candy," Isabel said flatly. "Mom hired her from an agency."

"I'd like to meet her. Your mother said she's a big help."

"Sometimes Mom is way too nice."

"What do you mean?"

Isabel paused beside the large clock at the center of the square; from here, they were out of sight of the car. "Candy scares me. When Mom is resting in her room, Candy makes me stay in my bedroom. That's so she can go out back and talk on her cell phone and smoke."

"Really? That's not okay. Is she smoking cigarettes?"

"I think so." Isabel's eyes grew wide. "Do you think she's using drugs?"

Jane was a bit surprised by the girl's naïveté. "Probably not. Have you mentioned these things to your mother?"

Isabel shook her head. "She really likes Candy, and I don't want to upset her."

"Your mom likes the fact that this aide frees you to spend time with your friends."

"But I can take care of Mom *and* spend time with my friends. I'm a good juggler. I did it before."

From what Jane had seen, Isabel had a bright future as an efficiency expert. "Your mom is happy to hire a helper to take the burden off you, but maybe this Candy is just not a good fit. Do you want me to talk to Chrissy?"

"Would you? I'm afraid of what might happen if Candy finds out that I was the one who complained. And there's no time for me to talk to Mom alone. Candy stays at night until Mom falls asleep. It's like having a stalker in the house."

"I'll give your mom a call." Jane clapped a hand on Isabel's shoulder, noticing how slight the girl seemed beneath the thick jacket. For a fourteen-year-old girl, Isabel had some heavy responsibilities on these shoulders. "Don't you worry, sweetie. It will all work out."

The endearment brought a flame of pink to Isabel's cheeks. "Thanks, Ms. Ryan."

They exchanged a quick hug, and then Isabel stepped around the clock and headed to the Mercedes.

That night, when Jane shared Isabel's concerns about the aide with Chrissy, the older woman was crestfallen. "I've been so pleased with Candy that I didn't question how she's been treating Isabel. Maybe that's just because I've been feeling better. But, of course, Candy can't really take the credit for that. The doctor says it's my new medication."

"I'm glad to hear that," Jane said. "And I didn't mean to butt in."

"On the contrary! Thank you for intervening. I'm going to call the agency first thing Monday morning and ask for a replacement. And please, feel free to call me anytime Isabel opens up to you. It warms my heart that she knows she can rely on you when she needs help. I'm so grateful that you're a part of our lives, Jane."

Stumbling through a response, Jane ended the call with mixed feelings. While she did not have a sense of family connection with Chrissy, sunny, diligent Isabel was beginning to win Jane over. This kid needed someone to fend for her, and with Nick gone and Chrissy sick, Jane was the only hero in town. For now, she was willing to advocate for Isabel.

December brought a distinctive energy to the classroom as the kids were thrilled at the prospect of time off and weary of assignments and vocab tests. Like her students, Jane was eager for the break. She needed some quiet time with Luke, and it would be nice to spend some one-on-one time with Harper, who tried to spend every waking hour with her girlfriends or Isabel or Jesse or some assortment of friends. In the past few weeks, largely with Isabel's influence, Harper's moods had mellowed. Her grades had gone up. These days her explosive energy, the bright presence that could fill a room, now sparkled with a positive light. Jane missed being close to that. With other people around, Jane was now pushed back to the fringes, a distant planet orbiting the sun. That was probably normal for a mom of a teen, but still, she missed having a close connection with her girl.

Perhaps she was a little jealous of Harper's unrestrained affection for Isabel. The discovery of her twin had evoked a blind generosity in Harper. Sacrifices had been made for Isabel: Plans had been changed, a favorite sweater had been lent, and Harper even gave up her bed one night when Isabel slept over. Cued in on Isabel's interest in Christmas, Harper sympathized with the "deprivation" her twin had suffered by being raised without celebrating the Christian holiday. Jane's reminder of the richness of cultural diversity fell on deaf ears. "Everyone needs a little Christmas," Harper insisted with a snap of blue fury in her eyes.

And so it came to pass that Isabel was included in the caroling, the tree trimming, and the cookie decorating. She accompanied Harper and Jane on shopping trips to the mall. She tied elaborate bows for the gifts under their tree. Harper even insisted that she participate in the "Secret Santa" program at the community center, in which donors purchased and wrapped gifts to fulfill wish lists drafted by needy members of the community.

Somehow, it seemed wrong to sweep Isabel away like that. "It feels like cultural brainwashing," Jane complained to Luke.

"Except that Isabel is into it," he pointed out. "You might say she drank the proverbial eggnog."

It was true. Isabel was savoring every aspect of Christmas. "Thank you so much for letting me share your holiday," she told Jane one night when they were preparing hot cocoa for a group of carolers that included most of the girls' basketball team. "I always knew I was meant to celebrate Christmas. When I was little, I used to pray on Christmas Eve that Santa would come to our house. I wished with all my heart, but it never happened. But now, celebration with you and Harper makes up for all those disappointing Christmas mornings."

"I'm glad you're enjoying it," Jane said. She wanted to point out that Isabel would not be here Christmas morning; Chrissy was taking her to Seattle for a small reunion with Chrissy's sister and mother. Secretly, Jane was looking forward to having Harper all to herself for Christmas. But she didn't press the issue with Isabel, who was aware of the trip. "It's nice that you're open to other customs and beliefs."

"It's more than that," Isabel insisted. "I've realized I'm not really Jewish at all. Christianity is the religion of my heart, and I'm grateful that you and Harper helped me see that."

"Really?" A flash of guilt stung Jane as she wondered if they had taken all this too far. She should have insisted that they celebrate Hanukkah, too. She should have researched other traditions of Russian Jews. "We weren't trying to convert you. Let's not jump to any rash judgments," she told Isabel. "You're still young."

"But I know my heart." Isabel touched Jane's arm in that maternal gesture that defied her age. Her demeanor said that everything was under control: *I got this.* "It's all coming together this Christmas. I received the best gift ever—my sister and my mother. Nothing can ever top that."

Isabel reached out for an embrace, and though Jane took the girl in her arms, guilt circled her. "Listen." Jane leaned back. "That's sweet, but it's not totally true. Chrissy is your real mother. She raised you, and I know she loves you. Very much."

"I know, and I love her, too." Warmth sparkled in Isabel's eyes. "But you're my mother, too," she said in a low voice. That content smile puckered her lips as she lifted the tray of cocoa and carried it out to the kids.

She's right, Jane thought. The realization left her feeling off-balance. Was Isabel expecting a relationship that Jane could not fulfill? It reminded her of the receding tide of Christmas spirit; once the gifts had been unwrapped and the candy stocking-stuffers consumed, the crushed ribbons and crumpled wrappings were a sea of disappointment. She hoped Isabel would have better luck achieving her wishes.

"Is Isabel here yet?" Harper called down the stairs.

"Any minute." Jane was surprised to see that the usually punctual Chrissy and Isabel were nearly ten minutes late.

"What about the pizzas?"

"Luke will go pick them up as soon as Isabel and Chrissy arrive." Jane checked the items assembled on the kitchen counter in preparation for the birthday celebration. Paper plates and cups. Napkins. Juice boxes and water bottles. Plastic forks and spoons, and a cherry-chip cake covered with bright pink frosting in honor of Isabel's penchant for the color.

"Looks like we're all set," Jane said, snitching a dab of icing, "minus one guest of honor."

"Who will be happy to see a very pink cake." Luke patted Phoenix's flank, and the dog leaned into him. "I can't believe Harper let that go. I know she's a chocolate fiend."

"She's been deferring to Isabel on a lot of issues. It makes me pleased to see her unselfishness and guilty to realize I'm not quite as accepting as Harper is."

"Don't beat yourself up. It takes time for revolutionary change to sink in." He glanced at his cell phone. "Speaking of time, it's getting late. Do you want to give them a nudge? Maybe Isabel forgot it's her birthday."

Jane let out a laugh. "That is one thing teenage girls do not forget." She paced to the French doors off the kitchen with the phone pressed to her ear. Isabel picked up on the second ring. "Hi, honey. Are you and your mom on your way over?"

"I don't think so." The words were drawn out, regret as thick as molasses.

"What's wrong?"

"Mom isn't feeling well. I'm sorry. I thought we would be able to make it, but...she says no. There's no way she can drive right now."

"Oh, dear. Harper's going to be so disappointed." Jane stared at the pink cake, thinking how unfair it was for Isabel to miss her party. It didn't seem right for a teenage girl to be stuck serving as a nursemaid on her birthday. "I know you don't have an aide right now, but do you think Chrissy would be okay on her own for a few hours? Do you want to ask her? I'd be happy to swing by and pick you up."

"Really? I would love to come, but..." There was a shuffling sound. "Hold on and I'll ask her."

In Jane's mind, the plan was already forming. Jane would dash over to pick up Isabel, and as soon as she returned Luke could tag team and head out for the pizzas. That would work. She was sorry that Chrissy would miss her daughter's fifteenth, but it was only a pizza party with a few friends. Harper had agreed to keep it low-key because Jane didn't want to draw too much attention to the girls' sharing the same birthday.

"Mom says that would be okay," Isabel said. "She's just going to sleep now."

Jane was already reaching for her jacket and keys. "I'll be there in five minutes."

When Jane came to the door, Isabel was waiting with her coat on. "Thanks for coming for me." She was misty-eyed. "I didn't want to disappoint Harper."

Jane touched Isabel's shoulder. "Harper will be really happy to have you there." Celebrating a birthday together—Jane had thought this day would never come.

"Oh! I almost forgot. I made birthday brownies for Harper."

Jane waited in the living room while Isabel hurried to the kitchen.

"I just need to cover them with foil," Isabel called.

"No worries." Once again drawn to the family photos, Jane was holding a picture of Nick and Chrissy holding baby Isabel when she heard a thin whimper. A creaking board? It seemed to be coming from the door on the right, where a hallway led to the bedrooms. When it happened a second time, more like a raspy moan, Jane pushed open the door and found Chrissy facedown on the floor, her face in a puddle of reddish liquid.

"Oh, my God, Chrissy!" Jane knelt beside the woman who lay eerily still. Was she breathing? Jane turned her on her side and searched her clammy neck for a pulse. "Chrissy, come on," she coaxed. Her body was warm, but her lips had a bluish tint, and Jane could not detect any vital signs. Her chest was still—no sign of breathing.

"Ms. Ryan?" Isabel called.

"Isabel. Quick! Call 911."

One glance from the doorway, and Isabel gasped. "Mom! What happened?"

"She's very sick. Make the call." Jane sensed Isabel fumbling to put the tray on the floor and grab her cell phone. No time to console the kid now.

As the girl called for help, Jane closed her eyes to concentrate. She felt for a pulse, her own heart thumping in desperation. A few more seconds, and she would start CPR, rusty though her skills were. Suddenly, Chrissy let out a coarse gasp and a rheumy breath rattled through her chest and throat. "There you go, Chrissy." Jane fought to maintain a soothing calm in her voice despite the alarm shrieking through her. "Keep breathing, Chrissy. Hold on."

Chapter 22

"Where is her next of kin?" the nurse asked when Jane and Isabel checked in at the desk of the emergency room. They had followed the ambulance to the hospital after Isabel had been unable to persuade the attendants to let her ride with her mother. "Sorry, young lady," the female paramedic had told her. "You have to be eighteen to ride along."

"I'm her next of kin," Isabel insisted, rising on tiptoes to lean in over the counter. "How is she?"

"They're working on her right now. But we need the name of an adult for emergency notification." The nurse glanced over at Jane. "Are you related?"

"I'm not, but Chrissy has a sister in Seattle. She lives in a convent there. Do you have her contact info, Isabel?"

"Aunt Anya." Isabel scrolled through her cell address list and gave the woman the information. "Can I see Mom now? I want to be with her if..." Isabel's blue eyes gleamed with pooling tears. "I'm all she has."

"I need you to wait out here right now," the nurse said. Her voice was firm but not without sympathy. "I know it's hard."

"I don't want her to be alone."

"Right now she's surrounded by doctors and nurses," the woman assured her.

Jane put an arm around Isabel's shoulders and held her close. Hospital protocol could be so dehumanizing, keeping loved ones from the sick people who needed their support, but she understood that family got in the way of treatment.

"We'll be waiting over here," Jane told the nurse as she led Isabel over to the vinyl sofas and chairs.

"My poor mom." Isabel raked back her dark hair, her hand trembling with shock. "And I was about to leave. She would have been all alone. I don't understand why she got out of bed. Do you think she fell?"

Clearly, the girl didn't sense the seriousness of Chrissy's condition. Jane suspected that Chrissy had emerged from her bed to get help when her respiratory system began to shut down, but she knew it would devastate Isabel to hear that theory. "Let's see what the doctor says," Jane said. "Do you want to call your aunt and let her know what's going on?"

"Not yet. I don't want to upset Aunt Anya if this is a false alarm."

Again, denial.

"Do you think Mom's going to be all right?" Isabel pressed her palms to her cheeks. "I don't know what I would do if something happened to my mother. She's all I have left."

Jane pulled Isabel close. "Don't say that. You've got Harper and me, and your aunt in Seattle. You've got a family that loves you."

"That's so good to know." Isabel sniffed. "I love you, too. I'm just so worried about my mom."

"I know." Jane took a deep breath, trying to ease out tension as she exhaled. "The last time I saw her, she was doing well. Was this a sudden thing, or were there warning signs?"

"She started getting sick last week—throwing up—but she thought it was the flu. It's going around, and we think Mom has low immunities now. But instead of getting better, she got worse."

"And you've been taking care of her on your own again. Is she still looking for another aide to hire?"

"I guess. It's all my fault. I should have kept quiet about mean old Candy. At least Mom liked her."

"Don't blame yourself." Jane tried to distract Isabel with offers of a drink or snacks from the machines in the hallway, but Isabel declined.

"Did you tell Harper I'm sorry to ruin her birthday?" she asked, winding a curled lock of hair around one finger.

"Don't beat yourself up. She understands. In fact, she wanted Mr. Bandini to bring her here to be with you, but I reminded her that she has guests to take care of." Jane eased away from Isabel's embrace to dig in her bag for a pack of tissues. "You'll see her soon enough. If they admit your mom, and it sort of looks like that'll happen, you'll be coming home with me."

Isabel sniffed and thanked her.

When the doctor appeared from the emergency room and introduced herself, Jane was unable to read anything but concern in Jill Raffer's fine-boned face surrounded by a cloud of voluminous dark hair. "Your mother is hanging in there, but I have to be honest with you. She's very sick. Her face and limbs are numb. Her heartbeat is slow and erratic, indicating hypotension, and she's suffering from dehydration. You said she had the flu? How long has this been going on?"

Isabel answered the doctor's questions patiently, her round eyes full of rue. "Is she going to be all right?"

"I think we'll get her through this spell, but I'm bringing in a cardiologist, a neurologist, and an internist for consults, and I spoke with Christine's physician, Dr. Malba. He said she has a history of these attacks, though none quite so severe. This is definitely not influenza."

"I didn't know. Mom kept telling me she would be fine. Is she feeling better now?"

"She's breathing on her own, at least, though the bradycardia and hypotension have her in a semiconscious state."

A tear rolled down Isabel's cheek. "Will she wake up?"

"Not tonight. Probably not for a few days. We're looking at twenty-four to thirty-six hours to regulate her heartbeat, and there are tests to run. I'm working my ER rotation, but my specialty is diagnostic medicine. I want to get to the bottom of this. Every mystery gives us clues; it's up to us to catch them."

"None of the other doctors have been able to figure out what's wrong with her," Isabel said flatly.

Dr. Raffer dropped her clipboard to her hip and squinted at Isabel. "It says here you live alone with your mother. Do you have a place to stay for a few days?"

"She's coming home with me," Jane said.

"Can I see my mom?" Isabel's voice now had the high pitch of a young child's voice.

"You can. It might help in her recovery." The doctor's voice was warmer now, sympathetic. "Sometimes even unconscious patients sense when someone they love is near."

As Isabel went down the hall to see her mother, Jane stayed behind and considered their shifting plans. A cancelled birthday party. A few days of Isabel bunking in with Harper. And then there was Christmas to consider. How would this impact their holidays? She doubted that Chrissy would be able to make the trip to Seattle now, and she knew the older woman would be disappointed.

And Isabel? It was up to Jane to make sure she was well taken care of while her mother recovered. Fate had given Jane a second chance. And after what Isabel had been through, the kid deserved some time to be a teen.

*   *   *

It was late when they left the hospital. They went straight to the Ryan home, where Harper met them at the door and threw her arms around her sister.

"You poor thing! Everyone missed you, but we're going to make it up to you with something fun this weekend, after basketball. How's your mom?"

"She's pretty sick." Isabel's mouth puckered, straining, holding back tears.

"Don't worry too much," Jane told her. "Things always look better in the morning."

Isabel nodded. "I'm just so grateful to be here with my family."

"Let's go find some pj's for you to borrow," Harper said. "And clothes for school tomorrow. Right?" Tomorrow would be Thursday; only two school days left until the holiday break. "Oh my God, you're going to look just like me. That'll be hysterical." The girls bounded up the stairs.

Exhausted, Jane looked over the straightened living room, the clean kitchen counters, the man who seemed at home with his laptop on the leather sofa, the dog at his feet.

"You cleaned up," Jane said.

"Well, I didn't want you to see me crying on the cold pizza."

"Missed me that much?" she teased.

"It was a unique experience. I've never partied with three teenage girls before." He rubbed one eye under his glasses. "There were lots of sighs and sorrows for Isabel, but that didn't seem to affect our appetites. Still, I saved a few slices for you and Isabel. Shall I heat them up?"

"That sounds divine." She fell back on the sofa and stroked the dog while they discussed the evening's events.

None of the parents had seemed surprised to see Luke there when they picked up their girls. "I guess the cat's out of the bag," he said.

"Probably a good thing." She relayed the details of Chrissy's condition. "I liked the ER doc. She didn't pull any punches. They can't seem to find what's causing the problems."

"It's confounding in this day and age, with all the medical technology, that they still can't diagnose something like that."

She sat up as he handed her a plate of steaming pizza. "I don't think Isabel had any idea how seriously sick Chrissy was." What a huge responsibility for a young girl. Luke pointed out that sometimes life's difficulties built character in a person. That would account for Isabel's strong moral code. As Jane finished her pizza, she wondered if she had coddled Harper too much, allowing her to be spoiled and temperamental. Maybe. Isabel was raising the bar for Jane and Harper, bringing integrity into their home. There was much to learn from this noble girl.

After school the next day, Jane drove Isabel to the house on Arbor Lane. Isabel needed to pack up some clothes and personal items for herself and Chrissy, who had gained enough consciousness at the hospital to ask for her daughter. As they penetrated the eerie stillness of the house, Jane was sorry that Harper was at basketball practice. Her bright energy would have brought some life and animation into the neat, dreary house.

While Isabel assembled the things she would need, Jane worked on a bag for Chrissy. It felt odd to pull out someone else's drawers and examine the items on the bathroom counter. Toothbrush and whitening gel. Face cream and tweezers. Trying to imagine that she was packing for herself, she pulled together a cosmetic bag and some clothes. She worked quickly, as if that would help her escape the feeling of intrusion.

She zipped up the hard-shell suitcase and rolled it out to the living room, where the family photos reminded her that she was invading someone else's life. The early photos of Nick and Chrissy sparkled with joy and hope and love. But now, on closer inspection, she saw the toll of impending tragedy in the more recent photos: the strain on Nick's face, the disappointment in Chrissy's eyes. Had they been feeling the strain of his illness? Chrissy had said that his death had been sudden, that they had no idea his condition was fatal. Had they been suffering other crises, problems deeper than those most middle-aged parents encountered?

Moving away from the staid photos and stale air, Jane passed through the kitchen to get some air in the backyard and paused when she noticed the sunroom in the back of the house. Set up as a greenhouse, it smelled of rich earth and fertilizer. Beyond the wall of glass, a cold rain dripped from the pearl-gray sky, but it was warm and stifling in here among the rows of herbs, white and purple flowers, and plants. The floor had been swept clean, and small clay pots sat stacked on an aged wood table. It was an odd oasis of life in the airless house.

She was still standing in the doorway when she heard Isabel behind her. "That's Mom's growing room." Alarm laced through Isabel's voice. "She doesn't like anyone to go in there."

"I'm just looking," Jane said. "I didn't know that Chrissy is a gardener. And how does she keep things so green when she's not around?"

"There's a small irrigation system." Isabel stepped around Jane to peer over the herbs. "You didn't touch anything, did you? Mom is very particular about her garden. If you moved something, even an inch—"

"I was just looking. I barely stepped through the doorway."

"Oh. Okay then." Isabel ushered Jane back to the kitchen and closed the door behind them. "That's good. We can't have anything out of place."

Jane had not known that Chrissy was so controlling, but now she was beginning to wonder at the demands she had made on Isabel's time. Cooking, cleaning, and serving as a nurse for her mother. Just because Isabel had not complained did not mean that the duties were not severe. "Would you say Chrissy is a strict mother?"

"I don't know."

"Did you ever feel like your mom was pushing you too hard with chores and responsibilities? You can be honest with me."

Isabel's lower lip trembled. "She said she was teaching me to be a good mother, the way her mother taught her. Cooking and cleaning, sewing and gardening..." Isabel lifted her arm to wipe away a tear that snaked down her cheek.

Jane held her breath, surprised and relieved that the floodgates were opening.

"It's a lot of work, but..." The girl's voice broke on a sob. "But I'm a hard worker."

"Sweet girl." She enveloped Isabel in her arms and stroked her hair. Isabel was due for a rest—they all were. Tomorrow, when Jane met with the social worker at the hospital, she was going to suggest that Isabel stay with Harper and her through the holidays. Chrissy's illness could be an intervention of sorts, a time for Jane to advocate for Isabel and assess her needs. Besides, a little distance would probably help Chrissy and her daughter put things in perspective. This interlude might be a blessing in disguise.

That night at dinner, Isabel spoke of her mother with measured enthusiasm. They had dropped by the hospital, and Isabel had spent a good half hour by her mother's side.

"Mom said that it makes her feel much better knowing I'm being taken care of," Isabel reported as she served herself a helping of broccoli.

"Did she tell you that?" Jane asked. The nurse had told Jane that Chrissy was only capable of one-word answers, but perhaps the woman was more responsive to her daughter. "See that? Even sick, your mom is thinking of you."

"Is she getting better?" Harper asked.

"Oh, yes. She's hoping to come home in a few days."

Again, not what Jane had heard, but she would let Isabel live in denial for now if that got her through the day.

"That's awful, to be all alone in the hospital." Harper gave a shudder as she put her milk down. "Hospitals are terrible places. People die there."

"Harper..." Jane gave her daughter a stern look. This was no time to get morbid.

"Just saying. I don't ever want to go there."

"But you're coming with me tomorrow to visit my mom, right?" Isabel looked from Jane to Harper. "She'll be happy to have visitors."

Harper's pleading eyes beseeched Jane to say no, but Jane simply nodded. "We'll go with you after school."

"But tomorrow is the last day of school," Harper whined. "I was going to the mall with my friends. You can come, too," she told Isabel.

"My mom needs me now. And there's something else." Isabel put her fork down, frowning. "I know this is bad timing, but I've been chosen to take care of the bio lab guinea pigs over the holiday break. I need to bring them home with me tomorrow."

Jane put her fork down. "That is bad timing. I don't think we can have little creatures around Phoenix."

"The thing is, I talked to Ms. Rennert, and she said it would be okay. I've taken care of Squeak and Clover before, and I would never leave them out of their habitat with Phoenix around."

Jane twisted her napkin. Right now, the last thing they

needed was another layer of chores in the house. "Isn't there someone else who can take the pigs? I'll talk to Mina. I'm sure she'll understand if—"

"But I want to take care of them," Isabel said firmly. "There's something so reassuring, something comforting about cuddling a little bundle of fur in your arms."

"Aaaw." Harper was a sucker for easy affection. "Can we take the guinea pigs, Mom? I'll help Isabel take care of them. We didn't have any animals in our class this year. Environmental science is boring. Say yes, Mom. We can keep them in my room."

Rodents for the holidays. The prospect had no appeal for Jane. Still, this wasn't about her; she was responsible for two young women who deserved a say in their lives. The sight of Phoenix sleeping in her bed by the door gave Jane the final push. The golden retriever was obedient, and she had mellowed with age. Besides, it would help Isabel to manage some aspects of her life, allowing her to be more accepting of the things beyond her control. In the end, Jane gave in. "We'll make it work."

That night Jane was awakened by a call from the hospital. Christine had taken a turn for the worse . . . another attack . . . on a respirator . . . touch and go.

"Should we come to see her now?" Groggy and still half asleep, Jane was unable to weigh the tenor of the call.

Not now, but tomorrow. Bring Isabel. Prepare the girl.

"I'll take care of it," Jane promised, not sure what that really meant. Was she supposed to warn Isabel that her mother was dying? Murky images of Chrissy's face and the wispy groan of a breathing machine kept popping through her dreams as Jane fell back into a disjointed slumber.

At breakfast, Isabel took the news in stride. Of course, she did; the girl had been down this road countless times. Jane hugged her and told her everything would work out.

It was a nonsense day at school. Jane had her classes read an excerpt from Charles Dickens's *A Christmas Carol,* which she used as a prompt for a brief essay on what the student would change if, like Scrooge, he could take another look at his life. Rebirth and a second chance . . . The holidays always brought Jane hope, though this year it was tempered with worry over Chrissy's illness.

The final bell had Jane scurrying to the bio lab, where Isabel and Harper had assembled along with a dozen other students. Mina was handing off animals as if she were closing a pet shop. Sand crabs and mice. A ferret and a small boa constrictor that had been found living in the school's ventilation system. Somehow, Mina's classroom had become the shelter for all creatures, furred and scaly.

At least we didn't get the snake, Jane thought as she pushed the elaborate guinea-pig habitat on a cart down the science corridor. Harper and Isabel each had a guinea pig cradled in their arms, one black-and-white and one more of a caramel and white. Mounds of fur with fat faces at one end, twitching noses, and beady eyes. *Please, God, let Phoenix recognize they are not squeaky toys.*

At home they quickly set up the crates in Harper's bedroom as Isabel narrated instructions on the animals' care and feeding. Their cages were to be cleaned once a day, and they would need floor time and plenty of human interaction. A guinea pig could die of loneliness, she told them, prompting a soft cooing noise from Harper as she hugged Squeak to her heart. Change their water. Keep them indoors. Never leave them out around the dog. Keep the bedroom door closed at all times. Make sure they have access to fresh water and grass hay 24/7.

With Isabel well versed in guinea-pig protocol, Jane felt confident that their visit would go smoothly. Once the pigs were securely ensconced, they headed off to the hospital, where Isabel led the way to the intensive care unit, forging ahead through corridors clogged with personnel, wheelchairs, and carts. So brave. By contrast, Harper plodded along with slumped shoulders.

"Come on, honey," Jane prodded her. "We don't want to lose you."

"This is creepy." Harper folded her arms across her chest, scowling. "All these old, sick people. I don't want to be here."

"Do it for your sister. She could use your support."

Although Harper steeled herself and stopped shuffling, when they stepped into Chrissy's bay of the intensive care ward, the girl imploded.

"Mom!" Harper hissed as her eyes grew wide in horror. "She looks like she's dead!"

"Harper!" Jane rasped. "Quiet." Although Jane was embarrassed by Harper's blatant reaction, Chrissy's shell of a body was unrecognizable beneath the mask, tape, and tubes. Her skin tone rivaled the color of the slate sky outside, and the terrible hiss of the breathing apparatus brought Jane back to the disorientation of her morning nightmares.

"Oh, Mama-dear." Unfazed, Isabel went right up to the bed and put her hand over Chrissy's. "I'm here, Mom. Can you hear me? We all came to see you. Ms. Ryan is here, and Harper, too."

There was no movement on Chrissy's face, no shimmer of recognition. In a flash of alarm, Jane wondered if Chrissy was really dying, but Jane shoved the thought away in an attempt to stay positive.

Harper's eyes were round as quarters, and she stared in horror. "I—I can't do this." She turned and hurried out of the room.

"Sorry," Jane said quietly. She had hoped that Harper would stay by her sister while Jane met with the social worker. "Harper has never been in a hospital before."

"She's lucky," Isabel said without looking up from the bed. "But we know the drill, right, Mom?"

Jane hung back for a few minutes while Isabel chatted on. It seemed to bring her a measure of peace to sit with her mother and stroke her arm, talking to her in a soft voice. Jane left them together and went outside to check on Harper.

"I can't stay in there with a dead body." Harper leaned against the shiny tiled wall, shivering and shocked. "Please don't make me go back in, Mom."

"It's okay, Hoppy." Jane took her into her arms, imagining the chasm between them shrinking to nothing as they embraced. "I know it's hard to see someone in that condition. Why don't you come with me upstairs. I've got to meet with the social worker."

"But I don't want to leave Isabel." When Harper leaned away from Jane's embrace, tears shimmered in her stormy blue eyes. "I'm going to wait in one of those chairs by the elevator. That way, if she needs me, I'll be close by."

"That's a great idea." Squeezing her daughter's shoulder, Jane realized she didn't always give Harper enough credit.

Upstairs in a small office cubicle, Sally Pinero explained how the department of social services would try to manage Christine Zaretsky's illness. "Her next of kin is very interested in her condition. Anya Diamant. She's been calling and checking in every few hours."

"That's good to know," Jane said. "I'll make sure that Isabel gets in touch with her aunt today."

"And I see you've been designated as the child's guardian if anything should happen to Mrs. Zaretsky."

Something twisted in Jane's chest. "I have?"

"Isabel brought me the paperwork yesterday." The social

worker opened a folder and removed a document. Some sort of boilerplate contract. "It's wonderful that Christine Zaretsky has all these things in order. I can't tell you how many people come in here without any sort of will or advance directives. It becomes a legal quagmire for their families. But Mrs. Zaretsky laid everything out clearly. Isabel told me she's very happy staying with you. I trust that this living arrangement will work for an extended time if need be?"

"Yes, of course." Jane answered before she had time to process the news. She was Isabel's guardian? It did help explain why the staff had been so accommodating to her, allowing access to Chrissy despite the fact that Jane was nothing more than a caretaker of Chrissy's daughter. But what about the long haul? Given the worst-case scenario, Jane was not prepared to keep Isabel. "What about Chrissy's sister, Anya?" Jane said. "I always thought, if something did happen to Chrissy, that Anya would take Isabel in."

"I don't think so." Sally leafed through the file, shaking her head. "No," she said firmly. "The child's mother has clearly designated you to be the guardian."

Really? She wondered what Chrissy's rationale was, signing her daughter over to someone who had been a virtual stranger until a few months ago. Was this simply because Jane had been Isabel's birth mother?

"And just so you know, if you were to become Isabel's guardian, money won't be an issue. Mrs. Zaretsky has set aside a sizable trust fund to make sure that Isabel is well cared for."

"That's good to know," Jane said, "but I hope it never comes to that."

"We hope for the best." Ms. Pinero's smile was tight, her lips shiny with red gloss. Sort of clownish and depressing. When they finished their discussion, Jane was relieved to slip out of the office, away from contracts that hinged on death and designated the way a life would be led.

Later, as they walked out of the hospital, Jane noticed the way Harper's entire body seemed to blossom and rise when they made it to the safety of the parking garage. "How'd your meeting go, Mom?" she asked.

"That's right. You met Ms. Pinero?" Isabel seemed cheerful, and Jane admired her strength of spirit.

"I did. She told me that your Aunt Anya is very concerned about your mother."

"Of course," Isabel said. "They're sisters. And she told you about Mom's plans?"

Jane wasn't ready to bring it up in front of Harper, but she nodded. "Yes. It seems your mother would want you to be staying with us now, while she's sick." Jane didn't dare speculate any farther down the road; it seemed morbid, even creepy.

"And I'm so grateful to be staying with people I love." Isabel slung an arm over Harper's shoulder, and the two girls rested their heads together so that Isabel's pink beret touched Harper's black skullcap. "My dad was right when he said that family is everything."

In sickness and in health, Jane thought as she started the car and drove off into the gathering dusk.

Chapter 23

Everyone slept in for a lazy Saturday morning. When Jane came downstairs at nine, a layer of frost still clung to the back lawn and the north side of the Tullys' roof. She made a quick cup of coffee and let the dog out back. Hugging her mug, she laughed out loud at the sight of Phoenix treading cautiously over the frozen grass before doing her business and coming back inside.

"Ah," Jane sighed, wiggling her toes in her slippers. Nothing like the first day of Christmas break to sleep in.

Soon Harper was downstairs in her flannel pajamas and fluffy slippers. One of the guinea pigs huddled in the crook of her arm.

"Good morning," Jane said brightly. "Is that Squeak or Clover?"

"Clover. Remember? The C is for caramel color."

"Right. How'd you sleep? Are the pigs noisy at night?"

"They're fine." Harper crouched down and released Clover to the kitchen floor. "It's playtime!"

"Are you sure about that?" Jane glanced over to the living room, where Phoenix was licking her paws in the dog bed by the French doors. "I thought you weren't supposed to release them around a dog."

"Mom, you know Phee would never hurt one of these guys. Besides, we'll be here to keep watch. Careful you don't step on her, Mom." Harper lowered herself to the floor, stretching out on one side so that her body formed a protective curve around the guinea pig, which now stood frozen like a stuffed animal. "What's wrong, Clover?"

The creature's nose twitched, and then Clover moved on, leaving droppings behind. "She pooped," Harper reported. "Right on the kitchen floor."

"Oh, joy." Jane stood her ground as Phoenix, most likely roused by the pig's scent, appeared in the kitchen. A moan squeezed from Phoenix's throat as she sniffed the floor, following Clover's trail.

"No, Phoenix." Harper gripped the dog's collar to hold her back.

"Let's see what she does." Jane kneeled on the floor beside the dog. She sensed no aggression in Phoenix's stance, but she stayed close, just in case.

Meticulously, the dog sniffed along behind the guinea pig, paused at the feces pellets, and lapped them up in one fell swoop.

"Oh my God, that's hilarious!" Laughter bubbled out of Harper, and Jane smiled, mostly at her daughter's colossal amusement. For the next half hour they watched intently as Phoenix befriended the guinea pig, nudging her with her nose and licking the guinea pig's fur as if she were a pup. The tenderness between the two of them struck a chord in Jane; it was as if Phee had found her long-lost child.

Isabel appeared, tugging the pink ribbon on her flowered nightgown. "What are you guys doing? We're supposed to keep the pigs away from the dog."

"But Phoenix loves Clover," Harper said. "You have to see this. Phee was grooming her as if she were Phoenix's very own baby."

"That's sweet, but Clover and Squeak are my responsibility, Harper. You should have asked me first." Isabel's mouth puckered in annoyance.

"Isabel's right," Jane admitted. "We should have asked you first, honey. But now that these two have connected, there's no splitting them apart. I know we have to keep an eye on Phee at all times, and we will, but this is a love affair that needs to be filmed."

"I'll get my cell phone," Harper said, tearing off.

Isabel watched, softening. "They are cute together. I'm going to get Squeak. I bet he's lonely upstairs, all alone." Isabel dashed up the stairs and returned with the black-and-white guinea pig. Jane showed her how to introduce them slowly, and within a few minutes Phoenix had flopped on the kitchen floor with Clover snuggled in the crook of her foreleg while Squeak sat munching a baby carrot near the dog's muzzle.

Jane sat cross-legged with her second cup of coffee, thoroughly entertained.

A few days later as Jane followed Isabel on the well-worn path to the intensive care unit, she wondered if this would be the pattern of the holiday break. Drop Harper off at a basketball practice or a friend's house while she and Isabel paid their respects to Chrissy, semiconscious and unresponsive. The doctors' reports of slight improvements always seemed to be followed by new episodes of heart arrhythmia and respiratory distress. It had to be upsetting for Isabel to see her mother suffer that way, but the girl maintained a positive attitude. Jane hoped that Chrissy sensed the deep faith her daughter had in her recovery.

Up ahead Isabel was talking with the nurse, a tall, rangy man with a receding hairline and large, square teeth. He went behind the desk to check the computer, then shrugged and leaned over the desk, as if to appeal to Isabel on her own level.

But the girl was visibly upset.

"What's the matter?" Jane asked.

Isabel spread her arms wide. "She's gone. They transferred her," she said indignantly.

"To another ward?" Jane turned to the nurse. "That's good news, right? She's out of intensive care."

He shook his head. "Mrs. Zaretsky was transferred to another hospital. She was taken away by ambulance late this morning."

"And no one told me? I'm her daughter. Why didn't you tell me? I would have come earlier to say good-bye." Isabel's eyes were filling with tears.

"She's right," Jane agreed with a reassuring hand on Isabel's shoulder. "And where was Chrissy sent?" To a specialty facility ... or a nursing home?

"All that I know is that the ambulance was headed north to the Seattle area."

"So that Mrs. Zaretsky could be closer to her sister?" Jane asked.

He held up his hands. "Look, I'm sorry, but that's all I know. You need to talk to an administrator upstairs."

It was painful to usher Isabel upstairs to the admin offices, but Jane didn't see any other choice. She herself had no claim to information about Christine Zaretsky, but Isabel was Christine's daughter, and she deserved to be kept informed.

Up in the admin offices, it took forever to sort through the situation. Two days before Christmas, one could not expect the hospital to be fully staffed. While they waited, Jane had to negotiate a ride home for Harper and an agreement to let Harper have Jesse over as long as they stayed downstairs. "Of course we will," Harper snapped over the phone. "God, Mom, you have a sick mind. Don't ever say something like that in front of Jesse."

Sometimes life came at you from all sides. Jane closed her eyes and leaned back in the molded plastic chair of the waiting area. This was not worth picking a battle over; she let the comment slide past and told Harper she would be home soon. Maybe that would keep Harper and her boyfriend on their toes.

It took a while to locate the one social worker on duty, and then he needed some time to get up to speed on the case. Timber Ellsberg, a thirtyish man with receding hair balanced by his well-trimmed beard, was slow but sweet in that blackstrap molasses manner of native Oregonians.

"I just got off the phone with my colleague Sally," he said. "It's her day off, but I wanted to reach out to her because I've never handled a case like this. Neither has she. There have been plenty of times when we were unable to give out medical information to concerned individuals. But in this case, with a minor who is a dependent, it opens up a whole new can of worms."

"I can imagine," Jane said. "But the young lady waiting out there is concerned for her mother. Isn't she entitled to know the medical status and whereabouts of her mother? She came to the hospital today for a visit, and found her mother gone. Apparently hours away."

"Sorry about that. You're right. We dropped the ball on this. We should have notified Isabel that her mom was being transferred, but Sally thought the girl was in touch with her aunt, and none of us expected Mrs. Zaretsky to be moved so soon. None of these are good excuses, I know. Simply explanations."

"We've tried to get in touch with Isabel's aunt. I called her twice, but haven't heard back from her."

He tugged on the diamond stud in one ear. "I can't speak for Ms. Diamant, but I am authorized to give you some information." Nervously working the cuticle of her thumbnail, Jane listened as he told her that Chrissy was still in stable condition. The patient had been transferred to a private hospital outside Seattle that specialized in gastrointestinal disease. As Isabel's guardian, Jane would be able to receive updates from the Cottage Hospital once Chrissy was evaluated there.

"Will we be able to see her if we take a drive up there?" Jane asked. The trip might be a possibility after Christmas.

"You would need to check on their visiting hours and such," he said. "But I wouldn't just jump in the car and head up there."

"No, not a good idea." She squinted at him. "Are we being kept away from Chrissy Zaretsky?"

An awkward smile froze on his face as he looked away from his computer monitor. "I really can't say. But I've seen it happen before. Especially in cases where a wealthy patient is seriously ill. Relatives close in, vying for their inheritance. Not a pretty sight."

Jane winced. "Please tell me that's not the case here. Really? Is that why Anya Diamant isn't answering my call? Does she think she's going to cut Chrissy's daughter out of her inheritance?" It didn't seem likely. Jane suspected that other members of the Zaretsky family had their own financial resources, as she recalled that Chrissy and Anya's father had been an executive for an international oil company. Still, money was a strange motivator.

"I can't say what Ms. Diamant is thinking. Maybe she's simply focused on finding the best treatment facility for her sister."

"I hope so. This is very new territory for me, and frankly, I never signed up to be anyone's guardian, temporary or otherwise. But right now, I'm all that girl has, and I won't let Anya Diamant cut Isabel off from her mother."

"I wouldn't expect you to." This time his smile was earnest. "I'd say she's lucky to have you as an advocate."

"Well, the jury's out on that," Jane said as she rose and hitched her bag up on her shoulder. "And right now I have to explain to that girl outside why she can't see her mother until after Christmas. Got any pointers on that?"

"The truth always works for me."

As Jane headed out to retrieve Isabel, she realized she didn't know the precise truth of the situation. What was Anya's intention, transferring Chrissy to Seattle? Why wasn't the woman returning her or Isabel's calls? She discussed the situation with Isabel and promised to keep trying to contact Anya. Isabel explained that she had never been particularly close to her mother's sister. When Jane offered to drive Isabel up to visit her mother as soon as they got clearance from Cottage Hospital, Isabel demurred, insisting that she didn't want to disrupt the family's holiday.

At home, Isabel seemed to take the new development in stride as she explained the situation to Harper and Jesse.

"The good news is that I get to spend Christmas with you," Isabel said.

"I guess so," Harper said cheerfully.

"That's cool." Jesse dug his hands in the back pockets of his jeans. "But I hope your mom feels better soon."

"Thanks. I think about her all the time," Isabel said, running her fingertips over the piping of the sofa. "This time of year, when school was out, we did so many fun things together. . . ."

Leaving the three kids to talk, Jane went upstairs to work on the laundry. She was hoping to wrap some gifts this evening and bake one more batch of cookies.

"Mom?" Harper found her in her bedroom, folding the mound of clothes on her bed. "How long is Isabel going to stay?"

"I don't know, Hoppy. I've agreed to take care of her until her mother is better."

"But when will that be?" she whined.

"Harper, come on. I don't have the answer to that, and we are the only family Isabel has right now. You've done a great job making her feel at home so far. I'm proud of you. Keep up the good work."

"But I want my room back." Harper sank onto the bed, yanking a shirt out from under her. "All my stuff disappears when she's here, and then she makes a big deal when she finds it. And she's always around."

"That made you happy a few days ago."

"She stares at me while I'm sleeping."

"Really? Does she stay up all night and stare at you?"

"You're missing the point. It's creepy."

"Turn toward the wall. Isabel adores you." Jane plopped down beside Harper and pulled her close. "Come on, old Scrooge. What happened to your Christmas spirit? The season of goodwill and generosity?"

Harper's lower lip puffed out. "I want Christmas the usual way. Just you and me. Family tradition."

"We're extending our hearts and home this year," Jane said. "We already decided to include Luke. It'll be fun, having someone your age around."

In answer, Harper simply pressed her head to Jane's shoulder.

"I love you, too. But I'm also excited about opening our family to others. Change is hard, but down the road, you'll be glad you made the sacrifice."

Harper let out a huge sigh. "Fine."

*   *   *

On Christmas Eve, to satisfy Isabel's zeal for religious experience, they attended a candlelight mass. As the choir sang a hymn, Jane snuck a look at the two girls: Isabel in her red sweater and pleated skirt, with her hair pinned back in a twist, and Harper in a black blouse and gray skinny jeans. Her hair hung long and loose, with dark tresses nearly covering one eye in a dangerous look. In many ways, their personalities had been set at birth. Easygoing Isabel and difficult Harper. But Jane prayed every day that her daughters would defy their genetics, that neither girl would twist and spiral down the dark path that had consumed their father.

Isabel was in the clear, and Jane was grateful for that.

But Harper . . . oh, she had her moments.

Glimmers of those snappish fits had been surfacing again lately. Isabel had been their guest for a week and already Harper was getting testy about sharing her room. She didn't like having Isabel around whenever Jesse came over. She didn't want to share her friends. She didn't have a minute to herself. She kept misplacing things and blaming Isabel. Isabel stared at her too much. Isabel finished Harper's favorite cereal. *Her* cereal, implying ownership. The entitlement of an only child.

"Remember how we talked about sacrifices?" Jane had told Harper that afternoon, speaking in low tones while Isabel had been showering for mass. "Put yourself in her shoes. She has nowhere to go. Her mom is still sick, and there's been a terrible rift with her aunt. The woman has completely ignored our calls. Honestly, I don't know what's going to happen with that situation. But I do know that right now, this Christmas, we are going to do our best to keep Isabel's spirits up. We are going to remind her that she's welcome here. Because right now, we are all she has."

A huge sigh. Rolling eyes. "Fine. But I don't have to like it."

"Do your best to pretend," Jane had told Harper. "Put on a happy face, and maybe your mood will match."

"I should get an Academy Award for this. Or an Oscar."

"Same thing," Jane had called as she made her way down the hall to get dressed.

"Whatever."

Now on her knees, Jane prayed that Harper would learn how to be less selfish. She prayed that Isabel would continue to adjust to the difficulties that came her way. She prayed that neither girl had inherited Frank's sociopath gene. *Let the evil die with him,* she prayed. *Forever and ever, amen.*

In the beginning of December, Detective Alvarez had called to let her know that he had located the beach house that Frank had inherited from his aunt. "Your tip was a good one. Because the house was in another county, we hadn't connected it to Dixon. We found blood stains there that match Lana Tremaine's DNA. Now we have evidence to press charges against Dixon." The detective also told her that the district attorney's office had been granted another extension in the Frank Dixon trial; Jane would not be called upon to testify until the fall. A huge relief, considering everything else that was going on. But the phone call had haunted her with tiny glimpses of Frank in her daughters' behaviors: Harper's blue-eyed fury, Isabel's smug smile. Suddenly Jane saw Frank everywhere, at home, at school, in her dreams. Each day, she reminded herself that the girls were not necessarily infected with his moral depravity. They might be a product of their positive environments, growing into happy, healthy, contributing members of society.

From Christmas Eve through New Year's Day, the holidays were a tumble of family traditions and innovations to accommodate Isabel and Luke and the precious guinea pigs that now enjoyed having floor time downstairs with Phee as a large playmate.

Although Jane had worried about the inequity of Christmas gifts for the girls, no one had mentioned it.

"Finally!" Harper had said as she'd unwrapped the iPad that had been on her wish list. "Everyone else has had one forever."

While Harper's focus melted into the small screen, Isabel had popped up from the paper-strewn floor to give Jane a hug. "A needlepoint sampler. How did you know I've always wanted one?"

"Just a guess. You're so creative with crafts." Jane had priced a sewing machine, but the high cost had forced her to settle for something less expensive. "When I saw this at the craft store, I remembered how my grandmother used to do needlepoint. I remember a few small pillows she made. She said she found it soothing."

"I know exactly what she meant." Isabel nodded. "There's something so comforting about knitting or crocheting. And now it will bring me even more comfort to know that I'm carrying on a tradition my great-grandmother enjoyed."

Behind Isabel, Harper lifted her face from the iPad's screen to flash a sardonic scowl.

Little brat, Jane thought. Spoiled and mocking. Jane was embarrassed by Harper's behavior, but she knew it would be a mistake to call her out in front of Isabel, whose model deportment seemed to irk Harper. On a certain level, Jane understood. She would be annoyed if a smarter, better-behaved version of herself came to town and shadowed her life. It was a little too close for comfort.

Despite the tensions, the holiday season brought Jane moments she knew she would never forget. When the girls sang a carol in harmony. When Isabel made a batch of mouthwatering potato latkes. When Harper scored the winning basket in a game and Isabel was beside Jane to cheer for her sister. When the girls carried the guinea pigs down the stairs and stretched out on the floor to play with them. Suddenly the house wasn't just a place to live; it was a home for their family.

Each day when Jane's calls to Anya Diamant went unanswered, she began to accept the possibility that Isabel might be staying for quite some time. How would that work out? Certainly, Harper would be annoyed, but they could make adjustments. They would have to. As Isabel said, family was everything.

Chapter 24

Jane let out a whoop as she soared down the final hill at Hood Valley. Surrounded by blue sky, sunshine, and white ridges, she was exhilarated by her run down the mountain.

"Look out, world!" Isabel called, moving up beside her on the wide slope.

Their laughter bounced in the thin mountain air as they made an easy turn toward the lodge. The jagged ice peaks of Mount Hood had been intimidating when they drove up to the ski resort, but schussing down the beginner trail with Isabel had been sheer delight.

The ski trip had been conceived as a group activity. Sensing that the train was running off the rails, Jane had planned a ski trip to rekindle family solidarity before everyone went back to school. Although the bond between Isabel and Harper had been Jane's main focus, her plan had been sabotaged when Harper had insisted on going up to the double diamond runs with the more experienced Luke, while Jane, a novice on the slopes, had been left behind with first-timer Isabel.

"You are a quick study," Jane told Isabel as they popped off their skis. "One lesson and you were able to do a smooth run down the mountain."

"It was easier than I expected." Isabel took off the helmet

she had borrowed from Harper, and thick dark hair spilled over the shoulders of the snow jacket. With her hair unbound, she was identical to Harper. "Thanks for sticking with me," Isabel said. "That was fun, Mama-dish."

Jane's smile was tempered by ambivalence. Should she allow Isabel to call her that? It was awkward, especially now that they'd had a report from Cottage Hospital that Chrissy was recovering. They expected her to be released within the next week. Jane estimated that Chrissy might be back in Mirror Lake by the following weekend. That was just a guess; she would have a better sense of scheduling once Chrissy returned her calls. It annoyed her that Chrissy had been dodging them. At first, Jane had fumed over such an ungrateful and inconsiderate lack of response. Then it had occurred to her that Chrissy probably was not getting her messages. She suspected that Chrissy had been temporarily cut off by Anya, whose mental illness seemed to be worse than reported.

"This has been one of the best days of my life," Isabel said as they stacked their skis on the rack. The sun was low in the sky, and it formed a halo around her dark head, forcing Jane to squint into the light. "I'm so glad we found each other," Isabel said.

"I am, too." Jane had to admit the truth. Meeting Isabel had filled the empty spaces that had haunted her at night. "Let's go get some hot chocolate while we wait for the power skiers."

Dusk fell as they drove home from the mountain. The ride took less than two hours, but Jane, exhausted from hours of sun, snow, and exercise, was asleep in the first twenty minutes. By the time she woke up, Luke was turning onto Mirror Lake's Main Street. She glanced behind her to see the girls dozing in the backseat.

"Wow." Jane shifted in the passenger seat. "It's a good thing you stayed awake."

"It wasn't easy. The mountain really takes it out of you."

Luke pulled into the driveway and shut off the car. "Wake up, girls. You're home."

As Harper moaned in the backseat, Jane escaped to the house, moving gingerly on sore legs. Inside, Christmas lingered like a stale scent. The tree was brittle, dust hung from the garland over the window, and the cookies and fudge in the tins on the counter had been reduced to sugary crumbs. And where was Phee? Although the dog usually did not greet Jane at the door, she tended to hang out on the main floor.

"Phoenix? Where are you?" Jane called, scanning the dog's usual spots. When a woof came from above, Jane trudged up the stairs.

The door to Harper's room was open, the first indication that something was wrong. Inside, on the rug beside Harper's bed, Phoenix lay in a heap with Clover nestled in the crook of her foreleg. Phee lifted her head in greeting, but did not bother to get up and come to Jane.

"What the hell?" Jane put her hands on her hips. "You shouldn't even be in here," she told the dog, "let alone playing with the pigs." The cage door was open, and Squeak was huddled in the habitat, tucked in the fleece liner at the far side.

"And I wonder who left this open?"

Probably Harper, the forgetful one. Harper trusted Phee and didn't take the threat of the dog seriously. In secret, Isabel had complained that Harper didn't respect the responsibility of taking care of the guinea pigs. Jane had agreed, although she had decided not to address the issue since the pigs would be returning to the classroom as soon as the holiday break ended.

"All right." Jane kneeled beside the dog. "Let's get you back in your cage before the girls get up here." As she reached for Clover, she noticed the blood. Clover's fur was matted with it, and one of Phee's paws was dark and sticky. "Phee, what happened?" Jane lifted the guinea pig from the dog's embrace and immediately she felt the difference. The creature's little body felt boneless, and its head drooped from a sagging neck.

Clover was dead.

"I didn't do it," Harper whined as a tear trailed down her cheek. "Why does everyone think it was me?"

"We know that Phoenix didn't open the cage on her own," Isabel said in a thoughtful, even philosophical, tone, "and you're so forgetful."

"I am not! Why do you always say that?"

"Hoppy, you've left the cage open before," Jane interrupted.

"When I was there. When I was giving the pigs floor time."

"While you were downstairs," Isabel pointed out.

"Getting some veggies for them, and when I did that I always closed the bedroom door." Harper glared around the room. "Why is everyone ganging up on me?"

In the thick silence that followed, no one wanted to state the obvious. Isabel had not left the cage or door open. Isabel did not make careless mistakes.

They had been round and round, trying to reenact the morning, methodically trying to calculate who had been the last person upstairs. But they had left before sunrise, and even Jane had been too groggy to remember much more than turning off her alarm, slipping on her clothes, and nursing a cup of coffee while the girls got ready upstairs.

Harper created a brief diversion when she tenderly groomed Clover's body for burial and found that there were no bite marks. She reasoned that, if Phee had crushed the guinea pig with her jaw, there would be puncture wounds. But it appeared that the blood had come from Clover's mouth.

"See! Proof that Phoenix and I are innocent!" Harper protested.

Jane turned away to keep herself from snapping. Did Harper really think there was another possible cause of death? As if some fiend had broken into the house and killed one of the guinea pigs for the fun of it?

Checking the tiny body, Luke was sympathetic. "I see what you mean, Harper, but it doesn't really prove anything. Even the pressure Phee applies to a chewy toy is enough to cause internal trauma."

"What?" Harper wheeled on Luke. "You're blaming me, too?"

"It's the only logical explanation. But no one is saying that you did it on purpose." Tears glistened in Isabel's eyes. This had to be hard on her, too. She had worried about something like this happening; she had mentioned it to Jane, but had gotten no support. "Accidents happen."

"But I didn't leave the cage open. I would never do that for such a long time. Why can't you guys see that I'm innocent, and so is Phee? We both loved Clover." Her mouth puckered as she tried to hold back tears. "Stop blaming us."

"We're not here to assign blame," Luke said, placing a palm on the shoebox that contained Clover's still little body. "Do you want to give Clover a small send-off, or should I take care of it on my own?"

"We'll help," Jane said. "No one has to pray or speak, but I want you girls to be involved."

Night was heavy upon them as they tramped to the back of the yard. Jane brought votive candles for the girls, but Harper put hers on the ground and alternately held the flashlight for Luke or took the shovel herself and levered it into the cold earth. They hacked away at the frost, stone, and clay until they could carve out a deep, narrow hole.

Such a pitiful graveside: a shivering Isabel, who clasped her hands around the candle as if positioned for prayer, and Harper, swiping back tears with the sleeve of her jacket.

Well, at least she's feeling the consequences of her actions, Jane thought. Maybe that would help her be mindful of her actions in the future.

"I want to say a little prayer," Isabel said, crossing herself. Jane tamped down a flash of guilt as the girl recited the Our Father perfectly. A quick study.

Luke recited the last lines to a Robert Frost poem, finishing with "miles to go before I sleep." His low voice, smooth and potent as brandy, made Jane fall in love with him all over again.

Harper sniffed and pulled something from the pocket of her jacket. "It's kale, Clover's favorite. I want to put it in the box so she'll have it forever."

A thoughtful gesture, though Jane had hoped for a little less drama and a lot more remorse. A contrite confession would have made this a learning moment, but none was forthcoming.

After the brief burial, as they were heading inside, Harper popped the question: "Can we go to the pet store tonight? We're going to need to buy a new guinea pig."

"Absolutely not." Jane felt her fury seeping into her voice. "You can't just go to the store and replace something you love."

"That's not what I meant." Harper's voice cracked, a wounded sound. "Oh my God, you really think I'm heartless." She kicked her boots into the corner and stomped toward the stairs. "Everybody hates me. I'm just like the worst person in the world."

Jane clamped her teeth together as Harper retreated to her room. She stood at the kitchen counter, blindly sifting through the mail. Luke said good-bye and headed home. Isabel started warming some chicken noodle soup for their dinner.

"Harper's right about getting a new guinea pig," Isabel said as she stirred the pot. "Squeak will get depressed without companionship. But I'll pay for a new one. It's my responsibility, and I have a savings account. I wonder if Harper wants to help pick one out?"

Jane sank onto the couch, feeling like an ogre. "I'm sure Harper would like to help. I'm sorry I snapped before."

"I understand. We're all upset. But do you think you can tell Harper that . . . Well, I don't want to bring the guinea pigs here, ever again. It hurts too much to see something bad happen to something you love."

And Isabel had seen enough of that in the past year. "I'll talk to Harper," Jane said. She reached forward to scratch Phee behind the ears, hoping that Harper would learn something from this sad ordeal. A difficult lesson for all.

Chapter 25

In the cold, gray beginning of January, Jane realized that the honeymoon was over. The period of joyous reunion between her twin daughters had ended. Isabel was now determined to outshine her sister in every way, and Harper was rotten with jealousy over her better behaved twin.

Regardless of Isabel's future living situation, Jane wanted the girls to learn how to get along. Wasn't that her ulterior motive in taking Isabel in—paving the way for a lasting family relationship for the three of them? Realizing that all relationships hit bumps along the road, Jane tried to steer clear of the conflict between the sisters. She encouraged each girl to follow her own path and to stop vying with her twin for favor or accomplishments.

And the girls found individual success.

Isabel had been singled out in the fashion and design class and nominated for an award. Every year, Mirror Lake's design teacher Kendra Pollack required her students to design and sew a dress for the popular Molly doll. Kendra then chose the top creations to submit to the toy company's annual competition for the new face of Molly. This year, Isabel's beaded white tank dress with a pink chiffon skirt that seemed as light as cotton candy had been selected. "She's got a fine eye for the flow of a design," Kendra had told Jane, "and the girl knows how to sew. It's rare for a high school student to have the skills to master working with delicate fabrics." How Isabel managed a project like that while keeping up her other grades mystified Jane. Besides that, the girl helped every night with dinner preparation and cleanup, and her side of the bedroom was always neat as a pin.

"You're an amazing girl," Jane told her when Harper was out of hearing range.

Isabel's cheeks flushed pink. "Thanks, Mom. I think I got it from you."

Fortunately, Isabel's hobbies put no stress on the family. By contrast, Harper's involvement in sports often dominated all their lives, as they ate meals on the fly and spent weekends following the team to games and tournaments. Harper's grades had dipped to Cs once again, and yet the girl was on fire on the basketball court. Although the schedule was demanding, Jane rarely missed one of Harper's games. It was her way of showing support, which Harper barely acknowledged, and it allowed Jane a chance to see her daughter shine a few days a week.

In the thick of a game, it was a wonder to see Harper bob and weave around girls the size of tree trunks. The girl had a knack for finding the holes in the defense and squeezing right through. Fast and low, agile and strong, she danced around the other players and floated into the air, easily lobbing the ball into the hoop. Harper's dance seemed magical—a fluke—and yet she repeated it over and over again against various opponents who simply did not have the speed to stop her.

Harper's explosions on the court sparked pride and joy in Jane's heart. How she loved being in the moment with Hoppy! When her daughter was on the court, Jane was all there for her.

The Seaside tournament was popular among the kids, as it took place in a beach town. That required each team to bunk in at a rented house or hotel, and inevitably the weekend was chock-full of pizza parties, indoor swimming, bumper cars, and ice-cream sundaes.

Mirror Lake finished second in the tournament—the result of a sluggish performance in the final, probably influenced by too much fudge and saltwater taffy. At the awards ceremony the girls were posing for the silver medal photograph when the emcee announced a special award for MVP, voted on by tournament players.

"The MVP Award recognizes outstanding sportsmanship and athletic skill," the short, balding referee said. "And this year the medal goes to a player from Mirror Lake: Harper Ryan!"

Harper's face came alive as she heard her name. She jogged to the podium and made a short, gracious speech about every girl being a winner. Jane was so choked up, she could barely process it all.

Harper needed this honor—this positive affirmation of her skills and hard work. Hugging Harper close, Jane felt confident that this would set Harper back on the right track.

Unfortunately, the euphoria lasted only a few hours. That night at dinner, Harper managed to use her new medal as a put-down of Isabel.

"I know you're proud of your nomination," Harper told her sister, "but compared to my award, yours is sort of bogus. The fashion award is picked by one person, and sometimes Ms. Pollack selects people she likes. The most valuable player is chosen by her teammates as well as opposing players. It's much more meaningful."

"Harper," Jane scolded her. "Both achievements are wonderful accomplishments."

"I know. I'm just saying my opinion. That's all."

Isabel stared down at her plate, pushing grains of rice around with her fork. She had the good grace to restrain herself from confronting Harper.

"This is not a competition," Jane said sternly. Why did two wonderful achievements have to be turned into a contest? "Let it go, Harper. No one is comparing you two."

"Are you kidding?" Harper stabbed at a piece of chicken. "People compare us all the time. That's all they do. Just because we look alike, those idiots expect us to think and act alike."

"*Those idiots?*" Jane repeated. "Who are you talking about?"

"Kids at school. They're so annoying."

"They're not so bad," Isabel said. "I think they really like you, only they're afraid to try and be your friend. They're scared that you won't be nice to them."

"That's stupid. I'm nice to everyone."

"To people you know." Isabel cocked her head, considering. "But I have an idea that could make you really popular. Did you ever think of running for Snow Queen?"

"Ha!" Harper scowled. "It's not my thing. I don't run in that crowd. All the school committees and student government and stuff. Those people aren't my friends."

"But they could be." Isabel's voice was soft but compelling. "I'm going to start a campaign for you, Harper. If people get to know you, they'll definitely vote for you, just like the players in the tournament."

Harper gave a squawk of rejection. "Not my thing."

"In any case, I'm really proud of you girls," Jane said. "You're both amazing."

Isabel smiled, and Harper held up the medal, which she was still wearing around her neck.

"Do you think I could put this on my college applications?" Harper asked. "I mean, do you think recruiters would care about it?"

"Definitely. That's a great idea," Jane said.

"Okay. I mean, it's a good way to get a leg up on the competition." Harper shot a sly look at Isabel, who was finishing her biscuit.

Oh, you little stinker. Apparently, the competition was not so easily diffused.

The girls were both up late that night. Jane quizzed Isabel with notecards Isabel had made for a biology test, and then Jane proofread Harper's essay on heroic qualities in *Star Wars* characters. When the alarm jangled Monday morning, Jane was queasy from lack of sleep. It would be a long day.

After school, Jane was blasting Maroon 5 in her classroom as she graded pop quizzes. Almost done. Then the phone buzzed, and Harper came on with attitude.

"You need to come home and see this, Mom."

Jane braced herself. "Is the house on fire? Is everyone okay?"

"My iPad is ruined. The corner is cracked, and I can't get it to work."

"How did that happen?"

"I don't know. I came home from school, and it was on the floor beside my bed."

"That's a bummer," Jane said. "How could that happen if no one was there?"

"Actually, I know. Isabel must have knocked it off the nightstand when she walked by."

Jane winced. "You know that, or you're guessing?"

"It's the only logical explanation," Harper said, parroting her sister.

"Okay. Look, I'm almost done here. I'll be home in a few minutes."

"Okay. But don't take her side in this, like you always do."

"We'll talk when I get home."

It wasn't even an hour later when Jane arrived to find Harper frantically tearing through her bedroom. The damage to the iPad seemed minimal compared to the clothes, papers, and junk strewn through the bedroom.

"What's going on here?" Jane asked.

"I can't find it." Harper dumped a drawer onto the floor, then got down on her knees to reach under the bed. "She took it. I know she did. That little bitch."

"Whoa . . . What?"

"My medal, it's gone." Harper straightened. "Isabel must have taken it after she smashed my iPad. I can't believe she's that jealous. I'm going to kill her."

"Calm down, honey. Where is Isabel, anyway?"

"At the library." Jane remembered that Isabel was walking to the library for a study session after school.

"Did she see the iPad?"

"I told her about it, and she just shrugged it off. But now, with the medal gone, it's proof that she's vindictive and jealous."

"Not really," Jane said cautiously, not wanting to tip Harper over the edge. "But it is a little suspect. When was the last time you saw the medal?"

Harper remembered stringing it over the edge of her headboard before going to bed. "And it was there in the morning when I left for school. I remember because I stopped and ran my fingers over the *MVP* letters." She shifted from one foot to the other, a bit embarrassed by the admission. "You must think I'm really shallow, getting off on a medal."

Jane shook her head. "It's something you worked hard for, well-deserved." She rubbed Harper's shoulder, then turned back to the room. "I'll help you look. But first, let me text Isabel."

As Jane suspected, their search produced no results, and when Isabel got home, she claimed to know nothing about it.

"Why don't you let me help you look," Isabel said, stashing her backpack in the closet. "I'm a good finder of lost things."

"Especially when you take them in the first place," Harper said, folding her arms.

Isabel shook her head. "I didn't take your medal, Hoppy."

"Don't call me that, and don't lie to us. Tell me what you did with my medal."

"I didn't steal it." When Isabel faced Jane, there was innocence in her round, blue eyes. Jane bit her bottom lip, not sure what to think. "Let me have a look," Isabel said, heading up the stairs.

"Right," Harper muttered to Jane. "And now she's going to go up and magically find it because she stole it in the first place."

Jane sighed. "I don't know, Hoppy."

"Don't tell me you believe her?"

"I don't know what to think right now. But I can tell you that we wouldn't be having these problems if you two would start getting along."

Harper pressed her palms to her cheeks. "Oh my God, you are on her side again! Ever since she came here you got all distant and closed off. You don't believe anything I say anymore, and you treat me like I'm supposed to give up everything for her. My room, my clothes, my privacy, and my friends—it's all fair game for poor little Isabel, whose mommy doesn't care enough to come get her."

"Harper! Quiet. You're being hurtful, and if you don't pipe down she's going to hear you."

"I don't care. I hope she hears me and flips out and packs her bags and goes. It sucks having a sister, especially when she's a manipulative little angel pie. I am so done."

"Honey, I understand that you're upset, and I'll talk to Isabel. But these things are a cry for attention. Isabel is hurting, and it's my job to help her."

"By letting her break and steal my things? Big help you are."

"Of course not. I will have her buy you a new iPad, and I'm sure the medal will turn up soon."

Harper crossed her arms. "And while you're at it, maybe you can pry her little fingers off my boyfriend."

"Jesse?" The idea of Isabel's being interested in a pot-smoking, grungy guy like Jesse was ludicrous, but Jane knew Harper would be insulted by that description.

"She was flirting with him outside the band room. She had her hands all over him. What a slut. Nuzzling up to him to tell him secrets and then giving him a back rub."

"Are you sure it was her?"

"I was there! I saw her from the south-wing lockers. So apparently our prissy little houseguest seems to think what's mine is hers."

"Things aren't always what they seem to be." Jane raked back her hair as she considered this side of Isabel she had not seen. "Maybe they were talking about you. Do you think you could have misunderstood the situation?"

"See what you're doing?" Harper snapped her fingers in the space between them. "Defending her again. Thanks for the support, Mom."

"I'm just trying to sort this out in a rational way."

"You do that. I can bide my time for three years, and then I am out of here."

"Hoppy, don't be that way."

"Yup." Harper turned toward the stairs. "Three years. But right now, I'd better get upstairs before she steals something else of mine."

Feeling like a failure, Jane watched her daughter climb the stairs and winced when she heard Harper shouting at Isabel.

The honeymoon was definitely over.

That night Jane twisted back and forth in bed, floundering for a solution. If she could have simply purchased a new medal for Harper, she would have done so in a heartbeat. But then, that was probably why Isabel had taken it; the medal had intrinsic value. It was priceless.

And then there was the issue of the broken iPad. Although Isabel had offered to pay for it, she still hadn't admitted to knocking it off the nightstand. The standoff made Jane wonder if Isabel was the innocent in this situation; what if Harper had committed the crimes to frame her twin?

Jane rolled over to one side and adjusted the pillow under her head. Was she raising liars, all because of their self-imposed competition? Actually, she wasn't supposed to be raising Isabel; that was a role she had given to Chrissy Zaretsky, who was still incommunicado.

Frustration had driven Jane to call the hospital social worker, who was still responsible for Isabel's case, and beg for assistance. "We've been happy to have Isabel stay with us while her mother recuperated," Jane had said, "but now that Chrissy is recovering, we need a timeframe for when Isabel will be reunited with her mother."

"Of course!" Sally had agreed. "Let me get in touch with Mrs. Zaretsky, and I'll get right back to you."

Two days later, Sally had called without much of an answer. "Apparently reports of Mrs. Zaretsky's recovery have been a bit overly optimistic. I'm told that we're looking at a year or more of recuperation."

"A year?" Jane was starting to feel put upon. Now it seemed like Chrissy was simply buying time.

"Mrs. Zaretsky needs extensive physical therapy and possible surgeries."

"I'm sorry to hear that, but certainly she's well enough to bring her daughter back into her own home now. Isabel is a huge help, and I know that Chrissy has the resources to hire a housekeeper or cook—whatever she needs for daily assistance."

"She's just not ready to handle parenting right now." Sally's voice had gushed with fake sympathy. "But I have good news. She's sending you a check. Ten thousand dollars to offset your expenses."

"What? I'm not in this for the money."

"But I'm sure it will help. It always does. Maybe you can hire a housekeeper or a cook," Sally had suggested.

Jane didn't want to hire anyone; she wanted order restored in her home, and for Hoppy's peace of mind, that meant Isabel's departure. But Isabel wasn't the only one causing the trouble here, and it seemed unfair to banish her so that Harper could reign as the only child once again.

With a sigh, Jane twisted her head around and flopped to the other side. It was wrong to think that getting rid of Isabel would solve the problem. The real key to this situation was establishing an atmosphere of honesty and support for both girls. Her thoughts were interrupted by the rustle of footsteps in the hallway.

"Mom?"

Jane squinted in the darkness. The shadowed glob in the doorway emerged as Hoppy.

"I had a bad dream."

"Come here, sweetie." Jane pulled the covers down, and Hoppy slid into bed beside her.

Snuggling close to Jane's arm, Harper yawned. "I didn't mean that, about wanting to move out. I mean, I'll go to college and all, but this is my home."

"I know, honey. The last month has been kind of crazy."

"Yeah." Harper yawned and faded off.

Jane smoothed the girl's hair away from her face, cherishing the moment of peace between them. In a matter of minutes, the steady whisper of her daughter's breath lulled Jane to sleep.

*   *   *

A good night's sleep restored Jane's faith in humanity, and she felt sure that, by the end of the day, one of the girls would come forward and confess to breaking the iPad and taking the medal. They would sit together for a family meeting, talk, and then finish with a positive resolution. There might even be hugs and tears and giggles.

But disappointment stung as they sat down to Isabel's lasagna with a side of brittle silence.

"How did your days go?" Jane asked.

"Fine," Harper answered over a mouthful of pasta.

Isabel reported relief over a bio test that had gone well. Well, at least she had something positive to say.

After dinner Jane shooed both girls off to do homework while she cleaned up. January marked the end of the semester, and Jane knew that this was their last chance to turn in late work. Harper had a basketball tournament in Bend this weekend, and next week there would be four days of finals.

"I need help with my Spanish," Harper said as she hoisted her backpack on one shoulder.

"I'll be up to help you in a few minutes," Jane promised, "but you can start making flashcards."

"*Sí, señora,*" Harper quipped, heading upstairs.

As she stowed leftover pasta in the fridge, Jane noticed that they were out of milk.

"I'm going to make a quick run to the store," she told Isabel, who was studying on the sofa. "I'll be right back." Jane tucked her license into the pocket of her jeans, and then reached into the cookie jar for a twenty. But her fingertips grazed the bottom of the porcelain jar. She looked inside: empty.

"I just put eighty dollars in here," she said. "Isabel, did you borrow some cash from the cookie jar?"

"No, ma'am."

"It must have been Harper." Oh, well. She would use the five bucks she kept in the car. Jane reached into the cupboard for the spare set of keys, but the hooks were empty. *What the hell?*

"Isabel? Do you know what happened to the spare set of car keys?"

It took Isabel a moment to pull herself away from her focus on the assignment. She lifted her head from her textbook and toyed with one braid. "Car keys? No."

"Okay." Jane trudged up the stairs and repeated the questions to a very annoyed Harper, who claimed to know nothing. *Is this what my life has been reduced to . . . grilling teenage girls for stolen property?* Frustrated, Jane grabbed her purse from her bedroom and marched steadily to her car. She turned up the volume on the radio, trying to drown out her thoughts.

She returned home with milk and a resolution to wait out the thief. Eventually, one of the girls would crack. She had to.

As Jane stowed the milk in the fridge, Isabel brought her textbook over to the kitchen counter. "Did you find the keys?" she asked.

"No. Still looking."

"Oh." She sat on the counter stool. "And the missing money, I guess that's still gone."

"Yup." Jane faced Isabel. "Do you know anything about that?"

"I was wondering if it was one of Hoppy's friends. They're always here. I think they know the code to the garage door."

Jane had suspected as much, but she trusted those girls. "Emma and Sydney have been in and out of our house for years, and we've never had a problem."

"Or Jesse?" Isabel shrugged. "He means well, but sometimes I wonder about what he's up to when Harper isn't watching him."

Jesse's trustworthiness had not yet been established. "The

money is one thing," Jane said, "but why would Jesse want my car keys?"

"Maybe it was the guy who cleans the rugs." Isabel frowned down at the counter. "He might be coming back for your car, when you least expect it."

Jane shook her head. "Have you been watching a lot of crime shows?"

"I just don't want Hoppy to get in trouble."

"If she didn't take them, she won't," Jane said.

"I don't know what she did with the stuff. I searched our room, but she didn't stash it there." Isabel twisted her braid around her finger. "I thought that, if I found everything—the money and the keys and the medal—I thought that we could put the things back together and no one would get in trouble. But when I went upstairs to look, she yelled at me." Isabel paused, her lips pursed in that perplexed expression. "She told me I would never find her medal or the keys or any of the stuff, because it's not hidden in the house."

Jane's mouth gaped open. "Did she give it to Jesse?"

"I think she stashed it at school. . . ."

"In her locker," Jane finished. Of course. It was the one place that was safe from parental view.

"Please don't tell her I told you. She's already so mad at me, and I don't know why."

"She's struggling with all the changes around here. It's not your fault."

"Still . . ." Isabel hugged the textbook to her chest. "I feel bad."

"We'll straighten this out," Jane assured her, though she couldn't quite see her way clear through it yet. She spent that night alone in her room, turning the possibilities over in her mind. She restrained herself from calling Luke, wanting to wait until she had the evidence.

The next day at school, Jane was a lone figure in the wide corridor as she searched out Harper's locker during her free period.

Number 223, outside the library.

Anxiety burned the back of her throat as Jane turned the dial. She had double-checked the combination on Harper's student record. The locker popped open on the first try.

Inside, the beautiful gold MVP medal hung before her eyes, its ribbon strung over a hook.

"Oh, Hoppy." Jane sagged against the locker, taking strength from the coolness of the metal surface. How had it come to this? A petty theft to gain attention. Or was it all designed to cast guilt on Isabel? A ploy to get rid of the other twin.

The car keys sat on the locker's shelf. The money was wadded up and tied off with a rubber band—eighty dollars. It was all there . . . the evidence to prove that Harper was the bad seed.

A cute little liar.

Chapter 26

"But I didn't do it," Harper claimed, pouty and wide-eyed. She had been surprised when Jane had pulled her out of her science class. Now, in Jane's hollow classroom, confronted by the evidence Jane had removed from the locker, Harper's face was a mixture of consternation and horror.

"Then how did these things get in your locker?" The cool calm of Jane's voice seemed to unnerve Harper.

"I don't know. Someone stuck them in there." Harper winced, scratching her head. "I know! Isabel! She knows my locker combination. She did it!"

"Oh, Hoppy, please. Just stop it, now."

"What? Stop what? I'm just trying to explain why . . . She set me up, Mom. She framed me."

Jane shook her head, sodden with disappointment. "The lies need to stop."

"But I'm not lying. I didn't put that stuff in my locker. God, Mom, do you really think I'm that stupid?"

Jane kept her eyes down as she pinched the edge of her desk. "You're a smart girl, and we are going to get through this, Hoppy."

"No, we're not." Harper was on her feet, kicking at an

empty desk. "You're going to take Isabel's side, the way you always do, and I'm going to get screwed all over again."

Jane shook her head. "You won't be punished if you own up to what you did."

"But I didn't do anything!"

Jane was sure that Harper's shrill voice could be heard in Cheree's class next door. "Keep it down. This is not the place to lose it, Harper."

"You're the one who pulled me out of class during the semester review, Mom. Don't blame me when I bomb on the semester exam."

"Fine. Go back to class. Nothing is going to be resolved here." *Not when you keep lying to me.* "And you can consider yourself grounded."

"But . . . what about the tournament? I can't miss it."

The tournament . . . Jane pressed her forehead to her fist. There was no way she could take Harper to Bend with this fiasco unresolved.

But then, maybe it would be better to send Harper off with her friends and take a break. They both might gain some perspective over the weekend. "I'll call Keiko and see if you can tag along with them."

"Okay."

Jane was relieved to see Harper march out of the classroom, though she was no closer to unraveling this tangled mess. Maybe time and distance would squeeze a confession out of Harper. For now, Jane had a class to teach, and she was grateful for the escape.

"It's Friday night. Are you sure you don't want to go grab some dinner with us?" Jane felt a little bad for Isabel, home alone on a weekend.

"We have finals next week." Isabel squinted at Jane as if she were speaking a foreign language. "There's no way I would go out this weekend."

Jane rolled her eyes. "Silly me. Would you like me to bring you a sandwich or some chicken fingers?"

"No, thanks. I'll heat up some leftovers."

"Okay, honey. We're planning to catch a movie after dinner, but I should be back by ten or eleven."

"I'll be in bed by then. Have a good time."

"Call me if you need me." Jane grabbed her bag and bent down to kiss Isabel's forehead, just as she used to kiss Harper when she was younger. It made her long for the simplicity of bygone days, when she had some control over her daughter.

Over green curry rice and chicken satay, Jane and Luke discussed the situation at home. Luke understood Jane's feelings of betrayal. "But I know you'll see your way clear to work it out with Harper. If she stole those things, it's a clear cry for attention."

"If?" Jane held a skewer of chicken over her plate. "You make it sound like there's an alternative, a way that things were magically transported from our house to Harper's locker."

He shrugged. "You said yourself that everyone knows her combination. Look, I know it's improbable, but it's possible that someone set her up. We've both encountered some rotten, conniving students who love to prank other kids. Maybe it was a girl on the team or a friend of Jesse's."

"How would one of those kids get access to my house?"

"Do you know for sure who visits there after school when you're still at work?"

Jane was considering the question when her phone buzzed. She frowned at the caller ID. "Mirror Lake High School. What's this about?"

It was the vice principal, Gray Tarkington, who began with an apology. "I know you've done your share of chaperoning, but we've got teachers down with the flu, and now we're short on supervision for the boys' basketball game this evening. Can you help me out?"

While Gray held on, Jane discussed the situation with Luke, and they decided to forgo the movie and head over to the school. Although they returned to their meal, they did not go back to the topic of Harper, which was fine with Jane. She sensed favoritism on Luke's part, but as he'd pointed out, he had known Harper for a few years now, and he'd grown attached. He liked her fire, her fury, her strong opinions. Jane was touched by his loyalty to her daughter, but that didn't sway Jane's opinion that an intervention was necessary to get Harper back on track.

The check came with two fortune cookies. Jane never ate them, but she couldn't resist cracking each cookie open to read the arcane message inside. "Take another look," she read aloud, "for things are not as they seem."

"The important thing is to not stop questioning." Luke put his credit card in the folder and handed it to the waitress. "I think Einstein said that."

Jane sighed. "He would have had a bright future writing fortunes."

When Jane spotted Marcus Leibowitz in the gym foyer, she figured they were in for a good time.

"Marcus. I'm relieved. I thought we were going to have to really work this gig, but now I know better."

"Don't get your hopes up, doll." He held up one hand to shield the words. "The flu is flinging me home. I just promised to stay until they found reinforcements, and you are it. So . . . let me give you instructions for the changing of the guard." He told them that most of the school was gated off, but they needed to keep an eye on stragglers who tried to drift into dark niches and start their own little parties.

"So we're sitters." Luke gave a grim smile. "And I was hoping to catch some hoops."

"You might catch some action between patrols." Marcus dabbed at his forehead with a handkerchief and sighed. "I have to go before I turn into a rotten pumpkin. Have fun, kids."

With only two other chaperones, they would be spread thin.

"Let's go check the score," Luke said, "then we can divide and conquer."

The crowd seemed tame by high school standards. A few dozen fans were scattered on the visitors' side, and only half the bleachers were filled on the home-team side. Jane suspected that a lot of students were lying low for a study weekend.

"It's a close game." Luke was mesmerized by the quick turnovers that sent players racing up and down the court.

Jane smiled as she left him to check behind the bleachers, where posts and shadows allowed hiding places. No one there. She headed back out and crossed to the visitors' side. From the corner of the gym, she spied a couple sitting on a low bleacher diagonally across from her.

A tangled vine, those two.

They were making out—against school policies, of course—and the girl was leaning into the guy, nearly draped across his lap.

Jane rolled her eyes. How she hated booty patrol.

She tried to catch Luke's attention to send him over, but he was now sitting next to Gray Tarkington, discussing the game. It was up to her. Eyes on the lovers, she made her way across the bleachers. Were they students of hers?

The girl had long dark hair that hung wild over the collar of her black leather jacket, and the guy was sort of a beanpole, thin with scruffy dark hair. Something about his demeanor, cool and loose-boned, reminded her of Jesse Shapiro. And the girl . . . Jane would have thought it was Harper if she hadn't seen her daughter get into the Suzukis' car for the trip to Bend.

Just then the couple stopped kissing, and the girl drew back. Jane paused, staring at her daughter. Blue eyes, dark hair, tight body, and that bubbling laugh that seemed to envelop her being.

"Harper? Harper!" she called across the gym, but her voice was lost in the noise of the game, buzzers, conversations, cheers, and players scrambling on the court.

It was her. Damn it, her daughter had lied again, ditched the tournament, all so that she could come to the school to slut around. Fumbling in her pocket, Jane unlocked her cell phone and called Harper's number. There would be some vindictive pleasure in seeing her react across the gym, a little jolt of alarm, knowing that her mother was calling. But the kissing went on as the line rang on, then switched to voice mail. Jesse was going for her neck now, and where were her hands?

Jane turned away from them and dialed Harper's coach as she strode to the end of the bleachers, making her way over to the couple. Fortunately, Coach Hadley picked up on the second ring.

"Hadley, this is Jane Ryan and I'm calling about Harper, who should be there with you, but obviously ditched her ride. I wish you had called me. There needs to be some—"

"Jane? Hold on. Calm down." Hadley's voice was hard to make out amidst the background noise of a dozen girls. "Harper is here. I don't know why you'd think she's not. We're having a team meeting in the hotel lobby, around the fireplace."

"She . . . she's there?"

"Sitting right across from me. Hold on, and I'll put her on."

A moment later, Harper's voice shined bright. "Hey, Mom. What's up?"

Oh. No.

Harper had done the right thing. She wasn't hopping down from the bleachers, leading Jesse away by the hand. Heading toward the empty team locker rooms.

"Sorry, Hoppy, but I have to call you back." Jane ended the call and picked up her pace, nearly jogging around the boundary of the court behind the basket so that she wouldn't lose the couple completely.

Jesse and Isabel. Isabel pretending to be Harper.

The locker room was littered with equipment bags, towels, and clothes from the team. Jane paused a moment, listening to the moaning sound. The showers.

She found them in a shower stall, still clothed, though the leather jacket lay in a heap on the floor and Isabel's sweater was up over her bra so that Jesse's hands had access to her breasts.

"Stop." Jane grunted, her voice failing her. "Stop it, now." This time, it resounded through the hollow shower room. "Both of you."

Jesse held his hands up and backed away, stunned. "Ms. Ryan." He let out a huff of air. "I'm so sorry."

"What the hell are you doing?"

Isabel stared, wide-eyed, testing the waters. Perhaps she wasn't sure how much Jane knew.

"We're really sorry, Ms. Ryan." Jesse folded his arms, a skinny, frightened kid now. "I just... When Harper's tournament got cancelled we thought..." He glanced at the sexed-up girl who had tried to seduce him and quickly turned back to Jane. "I want you to know, I respect your daughter."

"That's not my daughter," Jane hissed, though the falsity of the claim made her sway against a tiled post. "This is Isabel."

He winced as they both turned to her.

The beautiful face of her daughter, with swollen lips and slightly smudged mascara, transformed from the lazy grin of Harper to the more pert expression of Isabel. "Oh, Mom! You spoiled the joke. Harper and I were playing a little trick on Jesse."

His face went sour as he raked back his hair. "A trick?"

"We wanted to see if you would notice if we switched places. Harper said it would be a real test of whether you really loved her for who she is. The love test." She straightened her sweater—Harper's blue sweater, actually—and cocked her head to one side so that her hair fell over one eye. "I'm afraid you didn't do so well. But we don't have to tell Harper, right? I wouldn't want to hurt her."

Fury roiled inside Jane at Isabel's feigned innocence.

"Crap," Jesse breathed. "This is really twisted, man."

"That's what I thought, at first," Isabel said, "but Harper talked me into it. She said she doesn't want anything short of genuine love. The real thing." She turned to Jane. "Right, Mom?"

Those were Harper's words. Now Jane felt a new confusion spinning inside her at the hint that Harper might have masterminded this whole thing.

"Ms. Ryan?" Jesse's dark eyes burned with misery. "I'm like, freaked out and sort of mortified. I'm gonna go."

Watching him leave, Jane shared his confusion. "Why did you do this?" she begged Isabel.

"Because I wanted Harper to like me again. You've seen how she's been lately." Isabel pressed a fist to her mouth, sniffing. "I'm sorry, Mom. It wasn't such a good idea, was it?"

Jane wondered when Isabel had started calling her "Mom," and when had Isabel and Harper decided to switch places? "So this was planned. Have you ever pretended to be Harper before?"

"No," Isabel insisted. "Well, just that once, the day you came to pick her up at Emma's house."

Not sure what to believe, Jane just stared as a tear rolled down Isabel's cheek. She had always known Isabel to be forthright and truthful, but when she was dressed that way,

Jane saw Harper's face—the face of a liar. But at the same time, Jane was compelled to defend Hoppy, who was having her boyfriend stolen away by her own sister when her back was turned.

Or was that the truth? Jane sensed that it would take some time to get to the bottom of this.

"Come on. I'm taking you home."

Isabel had the good grace to remain quiet in the car. Inside the house, she asked if it would be all right to take a bath and go to bed.

"That's fine, but I trust you to be true to your word from now on."

"I will. I promise. And I'm sorry." She climbed the stairs, eyes downcast, shoulders slumped. The remorse in her demeanor chipped away at Jane's anger, but there was a lot to resolve here, and Jane didn't want to handle Hoppy over the phone.

This would have to wait until Sunday morning.

Jane returned to the high school to finish chaperoning the game. Afterward, she would spill it all out for Luke, her sounding board. Thank God for Luke.

Saturday morning passed slowly, reminding Jane of the old days when her life had been controlled by Frank's whims and furies. She called Sally Pinero, hoping for news about Chrissy's return to Seattle. Luke had pointed out that much of the stress would be eased if Isabel was removed from their home. Of course, Jane got the social worker's machine. Sally didn't work weekends.

Hoppy's team played so well that they had to stay in Bend for the final match, which they won. It was Sunday afternoon when Harper emerged from Keiko's car, smiling and patting a medal on her chest.

"First place, Mom!"

"They played very well this weekend," Keiko said.

"That's wonderful, honey." Jane hugged Harper, emotion welling inside. Harper could be stubborn and boisterous, wild and petulant, but she lived in the moment. Sparkling and genuine. Jane hated to burst her bubble now. "Isabel's inside studying. We need to talk, the three of us."

"Hold on." Harper removed the ribbon from her neck and reached into the car to hand the medal to Emma. "They're keeping it for me. I don't want to take any chances."

"Good idea." Jane thanked Keiko for chaperoning her daughter, then followed Harper into the house.

For twenty minutes, Jane and Isabel listened to anecdotes of the tournament and about the close calls in the championship game. Then, as Harper wound down and searched the refrigerator for something to eat, Jane began to recount Friday night's incident at the school.

As Jane delved into the details, Harper lost interest in her apple. "Is this a joke? Because it's not funny at all."

"It's for real," Jane said. "I saw the two kids making out, and I thought it was you and Jesse."

"Wait. Was it definitely Jesse? Are you sure?"

Jane nodded.

"So who was Jesse making out with?"

"Isabel. Isabel was dressed in your clothes, pretending to be you."

Horrified, Harper let out a little whimper. "You?" She gaped at Isabel. "How could you do that? And to me, your sister!"

"It was your idea. Remember, how you asked me to do the test? To see if Jesse really loved you."

"I never said that. That's stupid!"

Jane kept herself from intervening, wanting the girls to work this out between them.

Isabel stared down at her pale hands. "I didn't want to do it, but when you begged me, I couldn't say no." She lifted her chin, her gaze latching onto Harper. "I'd do anything for you. I wanted to prove that."

"What a load of crap! I never asked you to make out with my boyfriend, Isabel. What kind of weirdo do you think I am?"

"I just wanted to make you happy. I thought..." Isabel's voice cracked as the tears began to fall.

"Now you're crying? I'm the one who should be crying here. You just got with my boyfriend!"

"I should have known. You said we were in this together, but it was a lie. You always twist things around, trying to get me in trouble. Why do you do that to me?" Isabel asked innocently.

"I didn't do shit to you." Harper extended her arms out wide. "I wasn't even here! You can't blame this on me, right, Mom?"

"Isabel needs to take responsibility for her actions with Jesse," Jane said, choosing her words carefully. "But I'd like to know what prompted it. Are you saying that you didn't plan this with Isabel?"

"Well, duh. How stupid do you think I am? Stupid and creepy. Like I'm going to give my boyfriend away?" Harper stomped through the kitchen and tossed her apple into the sink. "This is so crazy. I can't do this anymore." Her cheeks were damp as she grabbed her coat and marched to the door.

"Harper... please," Jane called. "Let's talk this out."

The door slammed in answer.

Jane went outside to follow her, but when she reached the driveway, Harper was sprinting onto the street at the base of the cul-de-sac, a shadow in the January gloom.

Over the next few hours, Jane left countless messages on Harper's phone.

No response.

What would she do if she didn't hear from Harper all night? Calling the police would only alienate Harper further. She began calling team parents. Her second call brought relief.

"Harper is here," Trish Schiavone said. "She said I could tell you as long as I didn't force her to go back home. You won't force her, will you? She's pretty upset."

Jane let out the breath that had been trapped in her lungs. "She can stay there if it's okay with you."

"Sure. When you've got ninety kids, what's one more?"

Jane arranged to drop by with Harper's clothes and her school backpack.

"That's right. It's finals week, but you'd never know from the fun and games around here," Trish said. "That's what happens when you raise athletes instead of scholars."

"They are what they are," Jane said quietly.

She packed Harper's things and left them with Trish. When she arrived home, Isabel had made soup, salad, and homemade buttermilk biscuits, which Jane pronounced delicious.

"Those are from the quick recipe," Isabel said. "One of these days when I have more time, I'll make the layered biscuits."

Jane nodded, exhausted. Her mind was a jumble of lies and accusations, expectations and disappointments. After dinner, she offered Isabel help with her studies, but the girl had it all under control, which was a relief to Jane. A hot shower was soothing. She took a book to bed and fell asleep before she finished the chapter.

That night, when Hoppy appeared in her doorway, a wave of relief swept over Jane. "I can't sleep," the girl said.

Jane pulled back the covers and put an arm around her daughter. "Everything's going to be all right," she said softly, calming her daughter. She was so glad to have her home.

In the morning, Jane went into the girls' room to wake Isabel and saw two empty beds.

That was when it hit her: Hoppy had not come home last night. It was Isabel who had crawled into Jane's bed.

Somehow, that realization haunted her. Although she cared for Isabel, the realization scared Jane, and she didn't know why.

Chapter 27

Monday morning, over oatmeal, Isabel talked about the upcoming Snow Prom in February. "Wouldn't it be amazing if Harper got chosen as Snow Queen?"

"Absolutely amazing," Jane agreed, "especially since the princess court has already been announced." Realizing that this was Isabel's first year at Mirror Lake High, Jane explained how the court was nominated, and then a queen was chosen from the nominees.

"But it could happen," Isabel said. "There's always write-in ballots."

Jane scraped the last of the oats from her bowl. "It's not the sort of thing Harper and her friends get behind. Why are you so interested in Snow Queen?"

"I told you. If I could get it for Harper, she wouldn't be able to be mad at me anymore."

It's so much more complicated than that, Jane thought. Avoiding the issue, she reached down to pet Phoenix. "It's a nice thought," Jane said, "just not very practical."

Isabel shrugged. "You never know."

Jane changed the subject. "Ready for your first finals?"

Isabel gave a thumbs-up. "All set."

Jane appreciated Isabel's optimism on this gray, rainy day.

A mixture of rain and sleet tapping against the back windows had driven Phee under the table, where her tail now tickled Jane's ankle as it swished. Harper's empty chair gnawed at Jane. If Hoppy were here, she would take her breakfast bowl down to the floor so that she could "love me some dog" while she ate. Jane missed her girl.

During her free period Jane called Sally Pinero and got her on the first try. "I need your help," Jane told her. "This is not going to work with Isabel on a long-term basis."

"Right. I got your message this weekend. You know that kind of tension is normal. Petty jealousies and arguments among kids in the home. It happens all the time."

"It's more than that." Without explaining that her two daughters could not live in the same house, Jane gave the social worker an ultimatum. If there was no word from Chrissy Zaretsky in the next twenty-four hours, they would need to look into alternatives for Isabel's care. Translation: She would need a foster home. "I need to know that Isabel's mother is committed to reuniting with her," Jane said.

"A fair demand," Sally admitted, "though tough on me. I share your frustration with Mrs. Zaretsky. She's been difficult to contact. Let me see what I can do."

"Twenty-four hours," Jane repeated.

"Got it. I'll call you back."

Within an hour, Jane had a message to call Sally back.

"No Chrissy Zaretsky, but would you take the next best thing? Turns out her sister is in town to pick up some things from the house. She'll be there most of the afternoon. If you can make it to the Zaretsky place on Arbor Lane by four, Anya Diamant will meet with you."

"Perfect," Jane said. At last, she was getting somewhere.

*　*　*

When Harper stopped into Jane's classroom at lunchtime, Jane longed to fold her into her arms and reassure her. Instead, she smiled and asked: "How are your finals going?"

"Okay. Environmental science was multiple choice, so that was good."

"I'm working on contacting Isabel's mother. Isabel is not staying with us forever; I want you to know that."

"Okay. But I can't stay if she's there, Mom. I'm going to live at Sydney's until Isabel is gone. Sydney already asked, and her mom says it's okay."

It seemed like an overreaction—a bit dramatic—but then Jane had been guilty of her own drama in imagining that she and Harper could fold Isabel into their lives without consequence. Jane agreed that Harper's plan was best for now. They made arrangements for Harper to come by the house after basketball practice to pick up the rest of her things. As Harper headed off to class, Jane tried to tamp down the feeling that she was losing her daughter. She tried to ignore the loss yawning deep inside her as she prepared the final for her next class. She tried, without success.

When Jane pulled up to the house on Arbor Lane, it had all the makings of a crime scene. Squad cars. Yellow police tape stretched across the porch entry. Uniformed officers and plainclothes detectives chatting or searching the lawn and bushes. Squawking radios and the rumble of cars slowing to take it all in.

Detective Drum was one of the cops poking in the bamboo that screened the front of the house. Zipping her coat against the cold, Jane approached him cautiously. "I'm not sure if you remember me. Jane Ryan? My daughter Harper was interviewed over the school picnic."

He nodded, leaning on the rake in his hand. "What can I help you with, Ms. Ryan?"

"What happened here? I was supposed to meet Anya Diamant. Is she okay?"

"She's inside."

"That's a relief. It looks like you've turned this place into a crime scene."

"We're treating it as a possible crime scene." He bent over and poked at the garden bed with the rake.

"What do you think happened here?"

"I'm not at liberty to say, but it's not something you should worry about."

It dawned on her that he didn't understand her connection here. "I'm here about Isabel Zaretsky, Chrissy's fifteen-year-old daughter? She's living with me while her mother recuperates."

That got his attention. "The young lady is living with you?" He straightened and squinted at her. "So you're involved here, whether you know it or not. I hope you've got a hard shell if you're going to talk with Mrs. Diamant."

"What's wrong with her?"

"She's no fan of Isabel Zaretsky. Did you know she's asked the police to press charges against the girl?"

"Against Isabel?" Jane was sure this was a misunderstanding. "For what?"

"Homicide, and attempted homicide." Drum shifted the rake and took an iPad from the inner pocket of his jacket. "She seems to think Isabel killed her father and was trying to kill the mother, Christine Zaretsky."

"Murder? Isabel?"

He glanced up from the screen. "You're surprised. You didn't know about this?"

"No. Of course not. If I'd known I wouldn't have brought her into my home. I..." She covered her mouth with one hand, recalling Anya's lack of mental stability. "Is there evidence?"

The detective poked at a shrub with the rake. "We're here searching right now."

"But Chrissy was sick, and Nick died of a heart condition. He didn't even live here. I don't know what you expect to find."

"Between you and me? I don't know the answer to that either." Drum scratched his chin absently. "This search might be unfounded, but it's not up to me to call it off. Our police chief heard from one of the higher-ups in the Seattle police department, and that got the ball rolling."

"So I shouldn't be worried?"

"So far we've found dozens of prescription medications but no syringes or poisons. We emptied the fridge and took samples from the garden and all the household cleaners. Lucky for us, they didn't live here too long. Didn't accumulate much. Otherwise we'd be vouchering every old can of oil in the garage and soda pop in the pantry."

Jane stared into the dense screen of bamboo that shaded the front window as the sour tinge of disappointment hit the back of her throat. So much for her idea of sending Isabel north to live with her aunt. "Is Chrissy also pressing charges? Isabel's mother?"

"She's not cooperating. Apparently the sisters don't see eye to eye on everything."

Jane was glad for that. At least Chrissy was supporting her daughter. Maybe with help from the social workers Jane could circumvent Anya and return Isabel to her mother. "I'd better go in and talk with Anya," Jane said with a new sense of dread. Clearly, Jane would be perceived as the enemy, harboring a criminal.

Inside, she found Anya Diamant pacing the hall, her arms folded under her ample bosom. Jane recognized Chrissy's youngest sister from their meeting long ago at the Bainbridge

Island house. The woman's deadpan expression made her seem older than her years, as did her clothing. The dark dress worn over black tights and short boots with practical rubber soles gave Anya a witchy appearance.

"Perhaps we should rip up the carpets," Anya said, toeing the shag carpeting at a bedroom threshold. "Or the floorboards. She could have hidden something in the floorboards."

The two cops who were rifling through books in the living room exchanged a look of annoyance. So Jane wasn't the only one who found Anya a bit paranoid.

"Ma'am," said one of the cops, a thin woman with her badge hitched to her fat belt buckle. "This is a preliminary investigation. We don't need to dismantle the house just yet."

It was a rather impressive search for a speculative case, but then Mirror Lake had a reputation for jumping on things with thoroughness. Their unofficial motto was: "No call too small."

"And who are you?" Anya barked, having noticed Jane. When Jane introduced herself, Anya frowned. "I didn't think you'd have the nerve to show."

"I didn't realize I was walking into a crime scene investigation."

Anya's exotic dark eyes sparkled with bitterness. "Then the girl must really have you fooled." She nodded toward the back door. "Come. We'll talk outside."

"How is Chrissy doing?" Jane said, shoving her hands into her coat pockets. Overhead clouds skittered across a field of blue, but occasional winds reminded her that it was winter.

"Her body is healing, but the mind, the mind is wounded. Her thoughts are cloudy, and she doesn't see Isabel clearly. But then, she has always had a sugar glaze over her eyes when it came to that girl. Isabel had her fooled."

"That's not a very kind way to talk about your niece. Isabel is a fifteen-year-old girl who needs you."

"That girl needs an exorcism." Anya scowled, her eyes glimmering darkly. "She has the devil in her."

Jane wasn't sure she believed in Satan, but she deferred to the terror in Anya's eyes. "What is it about her that makes you say that?"

"It's not a look or a birthmark. Nothing so simple. It was what she did to my baby boy, my Gregory."

Was Gregory one of the tragedies Chrissy had mentioned? "What happened to him?"

"He's gone, God bless his soul." Anya made the sign of the cross. "Drowned by Isabel."

Jane saw hands form a circle, a band around the neck. The smallest bit of pressure could cut off respiration, pulling her under. The strange calm beneath the surface, a world of water. And those hands, firmly holding her there.

Frank's hands.

Isabel's hands.

Shuddering, Jane tried to bring her focus back to the moment. "I'm sorry for your loss," she said. "This is the first I've heard of any connection between Isabel and your Gregory."

"Of course, Chrissy never mentioned it. She still doesn't believe it happened. My sister lives in deep, deep denial."

"I think your sister loves Isabel, and if there was a question of responsibility, I understand why she defended her daughter."

"Her daughter? No. Isabel is not blood. She was adopted. My son, my Gregory, he was kin." She took a framed photo from a shelf. "My Gregory. Did you know that Isabel was supposed to be watching him that day?" Jane stared at the photo in Anya's hands—a bright-eyed infant.

"She said she turned her head for one minute and he went under. But I never believed her. I could see that she was jealous of Gregory, seething over every bit of attention he got. She had been the only grandchild, and she didn't want to share. So she killed my baby boy and destroyed my family." Anya explained that the death of their only child had put stress on her marriage. Her husband had started spending more and more time at work. And then one day he was gone. He couldn't live in a house of sorrows. Anya had been lost to depression, ready to die and join her child, when she had stumbled on a facility run by Carmelite nuns. She had found hope and comfort there. She had not taken a vow, but she still lived and worked at the rehab facility. "The good sisters saved my life," Anya said, "and now it is my turn to save Chrissy. That's why she will never see Isabel again."

"But Isabel is her daughter."

"By adoption? That means nothing when the child you have taken in turns against you. I don't know what Isabel did to my sister, but she was making Chrissy sick. I'm guessing that it was food poisoning, maybe from household chemicals. I just know that when Chrissy was around Isabel, Chrissy was violently ill. But when my sister got away from the girl, she began to recover, just as she is now. Do you know that she has not had a setback since I moved her to Seattle? Not a single one."

"That's circumstantial," Jane argued. "There are other factors involved. Maybe it was stress or something in this house. A mold or lead paint. Something that Chrissy is allergic to."

Anya put her hands on her hips. "You won't change my mind. I know Isabel is trying to kill my sister, just as she killed my brother-in-law."

"I thought Nick died from heart failure."

"That was the cause of death, but when the doctors examined him, they learned that he had no heart medication in his system. My sister, she checked his prescription bottles, and do you know what was inside? Little candies. Tic Tacs." Anya lowered her chin and leveled a piercing gaze at Jane. "Who do you think replaced the medication with candy?"

Isabel? Considering Chrissy's devotion to Nick, Isabel was the likely choice.

"You can't prove that," Jane said, though her voice lacked commitment now.

"I don't have to prove anything." Anya tapped her chest with two fingers. "In my heart, I know what is true. There is evil in Isabel's heart. And it is my duty to see that she is stopped."

"But Anya, what if you're wrong? You don't want to make a young girl suffer consequences for something she didn't do."

"I know the truth." Anya beat a fist against her chest. "God in heaven has given me the truth. It is up to me to see that His will is done."

Chapter 28

Reality check, Jane thought as she drove home. Although Anya had been over the top with exaggerations of the devil in Isabel's soul, there was a thread of truth in the accusations that made Jane shiver as she waited at a stop light. She turned the heat up and tried to consider the facts.

Isabel had been on the fringes of some terrible tragedies. The death of her baby cousin. Her father's death and her mother's chronic illness. But sometimes bad things happened to good people, and just because Isabel was involved with these people did not make her guilty of harming or killing them.

And Isabel is a good kid, Jane reminded herself. She was polite and well-behaved. She worked hard in school, and she went out of her way to help other people. If she was telling the truth, her recent inappropriate behavior had been prompted by her desire to please Harper. She had taken on adult responsibilities in caring for Chrissy. Even now, in Jane's house, Isabel did more than her share of the cooking and cleaning.

There was also Anya Diamant's state of mind to consider. The woman had suffered tragedies herself. She'd lost her son and her husband. She'd suffered a breakdown that had transformed her life. And more recently she had buried her brother-in-law and had come close to losing her sister. Jane couldn't help but feel empathy for Anya; but at the same time, she could not trust the woman. Anya's fortitude had rallied the police, but even Detective Drum had admitted that it might turn out to be a wild-goose chase.

Was Isabel a murderer? Or was Anya crazy? Although Jane suspected that the truth lay somewhere between those extremes, the muddle in the middle gave her little consolation.

Back at home, the dining room table was covered with purple material with a paper pattern pinned to it. Isabel worked intently, cutting out pieces of the pattern—a bodice, a flared skirt. Jane didn't mind the project, but the timing seemed odd, right at the beginning of finals week.

"What are you making?"

"It's going to be a dress for Harper to wear to the Snow Prom. The purple is perfect for her, don't you think?"

"It's very nice," Jane agreed politely. She wasn't sure how much to share about her meeting with Anya, but she had decided to save the news until both girls were here. "But I'm not sure Harper is planning to go to Snow Prom."

"She told me she is. With Jesse. She's planning to wear an old dress, but this will be better. I'm going to surprise her with it."

"If it's a surprise, you'd better clear it out of here. Harper will be stopping by after practice in the next half hour."

"Okay, Mom. I'll clean it up." Isabel began folding, calmly, methodically.

As she took a tray of lasagna from the freezer, Jane shook off an odd feeling. Why did it feel strange to hear Isabel call her mom? And why did she slip and say that Harper was coming home when she was actually an absentee daughter, stopping by to pick some things up?

You've got to fix this, Jane told herself. *Put this family back together.* She knew it was up to her, but she didn't know where to begin.

A few minutes later, when Harper tore in like a bull in a china shop, it was about all Jane could do to maintain peace.

"Mom, I'm here for my stuff!" Harper called from the garage entryway. "Do you have it locked in a closet to protect it from the thief?"

"Is she talking about me?" Isabel looked up from her homework with pursed lips.

"Harper!" Jane hurried to the door. "Come in here and don't be so rude. You don't have to stay, but I expect you to be civil while you're here."

With a dramatic roll of her eyes, Harper came in and skulked against the kitchen island. "What do you want me to say? I'm still freaked out about Friday night, and so is Jesse." For the first time she swung around and faced Isabel. "Now that we know you're a psycho, we have a secret code with each other. So don't bother trying that again."

"Of course not," Isabel said. "I only did it for you in the first place. I just want to make you happy."

Harper hunched up and lifted her hands. "Stop that! Just stop. Leave me alone."

"Okay, enough bickering. We have something more important to discuss. Isabel, you know I've been trying to reach out to your mom, and I've been talking with the social workers. Today I met with your Aunt Anya, and I'm afraid the news isn't good."

Isabel's lips swelled in a pout. "Is Mom sick again?"

"Actually, she's still recovering. It sounds like she'll be okay. But your aunt has no intention of bringing you to Seattle anytime soon."

"Aunt Anya never liked me," Isabel said sadly. "It's okay. I don't mind staying here."

"While I was talking to your aunt, she mentioned some disturbing things that you were involved with. Her son Gregory . . . She says you're responsible for his drowning?"

With a silvery calm, Isabel closed her eyes and shook her head. "Aunt Anya is blaming me for her own mistakes. I wasn't even there when the baby drowned. I was at the store with my dad. It was Aunt Anya's fault that Gregory fell in the pool, and the guilt drove her crazy. Do you know that she was in a mental hospital?"

"Yes, I know."

"I feel bad for her. Mom says she lost track of reality."

There was no animosity in Isabel's clear blue eyes.

By way of contrast, Harper looked horrified.

Jane was not sure what to believe anymore. "Anya mentioned a few other suspicious circumstances. She thinks your father's death might have been prevented. He was supposed to be taking medication for his heart, but they found none in his system. Anya thinks you switched his medication for a placebo."

"That's just silly. I loved my dad. Everyone knew that."

"Anya is also blaming you for your mother's illness. She thinks you were doing something to make her sick."

"Poor Aunt Anya." Isabel sighed. "She wants to blame me for everything."

"Well . . ." Harper folded her arms. "If the shoe fits . . ."

"I didn't hurt anyone," Isabel said solemnly. "If I did anything wrong, it was because I tried to protect my mom."

Jane paused a moment, staring down at the counter. "Protect her from whom?"

Isabel let out a heavy breath. "From herself. Have you ever heard of Munchausen syndrome?"

"Is that your new excuse?" Harper snickered. "It sounds like popcorn treats."

Jane had come across it in a psychology class. "It's a psychiatric disorder. People with Munchausen pretend to be sick to draw attention to themselves."

"I can't believe I'm telling you this." Isabel pressed her palms to her cheeks. "This is a huge family secret. But... you're both family, too. The thing is, Mom used to make herself sick so that she could get attention and extra-special care. She would eat weird things like soap and cleansers. I don't even know everything. I just know she made herself really sick."

Harper winced. She didn't seem to be buying it.

"And before that, I... I didn't know it at the time, but I think she also suffered from Munchausen by proxy. I think she was making my dad sick so that our family would get special treatment."

"That's... that would explain a lot of things," Jane said. The revelation should have provided some relief, but she felt tense, her nerves like taut guitar strings being wrenched tighter. "I had no idea your mother suffered from mental illness."

Isabel nodded sadly. "No one ever wants to talk about it. There's such a stigma attached and... I don't want to believe that Mom killed my father. Do you think she would really do that?"

The only thing Jane was sure of at the moment was the cold numbness in her heart. "I don't know."

"Well, I may not know about Munchout Disease," Harper said, "but I know this house has gone cray cray, and I'm getting the hell out of here."

"You're being insensitive," Jane said.

"I'm being practical. I can't believe you made me live in the same room with a killer. Mom, why can't you see what's so obvious? This one is a psycho killer."

"Harper!"

"I'm not a killer." Isabel faced Harper without wrath or anger. "I'm your sister, and I love you. You'll see. Soon, you'll see how much I love you. I'm going to make you Snow Queen, sister dear."

"I don't want to be a freakin' prom queen. I just want to survive high school, and with you around, I'll be lucky to survive sophomore year." Harper went over to the stairs. "I'm packing," she called. "Next family meeting, you can count me out."

"I'm sorry," Jane told Isabel. She followed Harper up the stairs, thinking that she would make her apologize for being insensitive, but when Jane reached the top of the stairs she realized how ridiculous that would be. It was ridiculous to think she was going to rein Harper in at this point. It had taken Jane fifteen years to realize that you couldn't really control another person.

She went to her room and sat on the edge of her bed.

Munchausen syndrome. Why hadn't it occurred to Jane before? To think of the abuses Isabel had suffered, only to land here and receive further abuse from her sister.

Flopping back on the bed, Jane stared at the ceiling and tried to prioritize. She would contact Detective Drum and Sally Pinero to report the accusations about Chrissy Zaretsky. It pained her to think that Isabel was never going to be reunited with her mother. After all, Munchausen by proxy was abuse. It would take a while to determine Chrissy's competence as a parent . . . months, maybe years. Could she keep Isabel here during the investigation . . . throughout high school?

The question made Jane's head hurt.

Her job was to raise Harper. She had made that decision fifteen years ago, and she stood by it. But she'd be damned if she'd let Hoppy dictate whom she could and couldn't help.

For now, she needed to keep her girls safe. Harper would continue to stay with Sydney, and Isabel would have safe haven here.

✻   ✻   ✻

The air in the car sizzled with tension as Jane drove Harper to the Schiavones' house. After a few blocks, Jane broke the silence. "I wish you could be more sympathetic to your sister."

"I wish I'd never found out I had a sister."

Jane sagged back in the seat. "Oh, Harper. Can't you see that Isabel needs our help, now more than ever? She's lived a life of torture."

"Yeah. So she says."

"Why don't you believe her?"

"Maybe because she's a liar and a bully. Did you forget that she set up a whole ploy to make a play for my boyfriend and make me look like a slut?"

"And you really didn't have anything to do with that? Tell me the truth. You never talked about switching places, wearing each other's clothes?"

"Not like that. God, Mom. Why can't you ever believe me? You believe Isabel when she comes up with some excuse, but I always get a million questions."

"That's not true," Jane denied.

"It is! You're always on her side, always making me out to be the bad twin. What can I do to . . ." Overwrought, Harper let out a growl. "Okay, I guess it's safe to tell you now that Isabel almost killed me. Does that make you like me more, Mom?"

"Harper, you know I love you." Jane struggled to keep her voice steady. "Tell me what happened."

"There was one night over Christmas break, when we were hanging out, watching a movie. I think you were upstairs. We were joking around, nudging each other off the couch, and then it got a little crazy and we were wrestling on the floor. You know how that goes. Just goofing around. But suddenly she had her hands around my neck, and she was squeezing really hard."

For the second time that day Jane saw the hands closing in like a vise.

Relentless. Brutal.

She pulled over to the side of the road, threw the car into park, and turned to her daughter. "She was choking you?"

Tears pooled in Harper's eyes as she nodded. "It hurt really bad, but the scary part was that I couldn't breathe. And she told me that she could kill me, just like that. She said it didn't take that much effort if you squeezed the right spot."

"Oh, Hoppy." Jane rubbed her daughter's arm. "I'm so sorry."

A whimper escaped Harper's throat, and Jane held her close for a moment. "You should have told me."

"She said that if I told you, she'd do it again, and she wouldn't back off the next time."

Jane found it a little hard to believe that Isabel had used those exact words. Maybe a veiled threat. But then again, if Isabel had been abused by Chrissy, it was likely that she would carry on the cycle of torment.

"I used to be scared to fall asleep at night," Harper said, her voice rough from emotion. "I was afraid that she would creep over in the dark and smother me while I was sleeping."

"Oh, honey. I didn't know. That was so mean of her. Heartless."

"She's scary, Mom. Aren't you scared to be alone with her in the house? What if she tries to hurt you?"

"She won't. The dynamic is different because I'm her mother. I'm not Isabel's competition. She needs me."

"She needed the Zaretskys, and look what happened to them."

Jane understood Harper's concern, but she knew she was safe. Isabel adored her, but Jane couldn't say that to Harper, who would feel like less of a daughter because she didn't idolize her mother. "Don't you worry about me. You just be sure to listen to Sydney's mom and focus on the rest of your finals this week."

"Okay, Mom." Harper swiped at her tears and sniffed. Jane shot her a sympathetic look and felt a moment of panic when she got a flash of Isabel.

You can't even tell your own daughters apart. Putting the car back into gear, Jane chastised herself as she drove on.

"You are stuck between a rock and a hard place." Luke's voice was a silky whisper. He kept it low to avoid Isabel's overhearing from upstairs. "You have to report the Munchausen. Isabel might feel betrayed, but it's for her own good."

"I know." Jane tucked her feet under her and leaned into his shoulder. Telling Luke had eased the weight of the debacle, but now she felt depleted of energy. "I have to tell. I just can't see beyond that. I'll be cutting off all chances of Isabel's going home. Ending her family ties."

"And you're not in a position to offer her your family in return?"

"I don't think so. Harper is jealous. She might have manipulated Isabel in the switching scheme; I don't know for sure. But she's also scared of Isabel, and rightly so. These girls have been at war with each other behind my back, and I can't really tell who is pulling a power play. But right now, the bottom line is that Isabel will have to leave. And with no family to take her in, what's going to happen to her?"

"No one can say. But you have to take the next step. Call the social worker and the cop, first thing in the morning."

"I just hate to point out a problem that I don't have the solution for."

"It's not up to you to solve every problem. As it is, you've done a lot for Isabel."

Of course—she's my daughter. Jane pressed two fingers on the pressure point between her brows and closed her eyes.

* * *

Isabel was questioned the following day, immediately after school. Fortunately, the social worker and the detective arranged to interview Isabel at the same time, saving her from repeating a lengthy process. Detective Drum explained that he would forward the information to the police department in the Seattle jurisdiction where Chrissy Zaretsky currently resided. "It's not really my case to investigate," he said.

Sally Pinero was another story. As Isabel's advocate, she was going to need to work with psychiatrists and police to investigate the charges and determine the best placement for Isabel in the future. "And since we're working with agencies in two states, my job is exponentially more difficult," Sally explained to Jane.

"But this is a serious business," Jane pressed the social worker, who tended to lose focus. Sometimes she needed to keep Sally on track. "Munchausen is a form of child abuse."

"Of course, and if this turns out to be true, we will do everything necessary to make sure Isabel is protected from her mother."

After Sally left on Tuesday night, Isabel confronted Jane. "Sally told me that I can't stay here much longer, and I understand." Isabel was settled on the sofa with Jane, sewing tiny beads onto a band of white material—a sash for Harper's prom dress. "I know there are some issues between Harper and me, and I know she belongs here, too. But you see, I'm trying to win her over."

"I see that." Jane wanted to slide off the sofa and slither up to her own bedroom. "I'm sorry it didn't work out for all of us."

"I know you are, Mama-dish. But it's not over yet. Harper and I have a special connection; I can tell what she's thinking. Sometimes I think I can even send her little messages."

"Really?" Jane smiled. "I've read about telepathic connections between twins."

"I can definitely feel what she's thinking, and I think she's softening now. She'll come around. Once she sees her beautiful dress and learns that I got her elected Snow Queen, she'll definitely come around."

Although Jane knew that Isabel was setting herself up for an impossible task, she didn't argue. She had pointed out the obstacles before, and Isabel had downplayed them all.

That night, when Jane went to bed, her mind went to the image of Isabel's small, pale hands circling Hoppy's throat. She wasn't sure if the incident had really happened, but flipping it over and over in her mind was not going to prove the verity of it. On impulse, she locked her bedroom door and slid under the covers.

Hours later, the doorknob rattled. "Mom?" Isabel called. "Are you awake?"

The door rattled again, but Jane didn't move. For hours, she remained silent and sleepless. Frozen in place, she stared up at the ceiling and wondered if she had been wrong about her daughters' genetics from the very beginning. Perhaps Frank's evil genes had been passed down to not one daughter but two.

Chapter 29

That week, Jane felt her heart break over and over again as she watched Isabel spend every spare minute crafting an exquisite gown for Harper. Isabel stayed after school to use the sewing machines in home ec, then brought the garment home, where she spent hours adding the details: sprays and starbursts of beads and sequins, ribbon trim along the bodice, and a band of tiny gems sewn into one of the shoulder straps.

The gown had become a dress of dreams, a symbol of Isabel's determination to keep their family together. As Jane watched Isabel push and pull a small needle through the fabric, she found herself sharing in the hope and wondering if Harper would soften, if distance would ease the tension. In fact, Harper seemed in good spirits each day when Jane checked in. She was enjoying hanging out with Sydney, though she craved some privacy. Both mother and daughter looked forward to the weekend tournament in Canby, a short ride from Mirror Lake, though Harper was emphatic about keeping Isabel at bay. Apparently, Harper was not receiving Isabel's telepathic messages of love and support.

The students had no school Friday—a grading day for teachers. Jane was glad to know that Isabel was in the same building, working away in the design studio of the school, though it goaded her that Harper's tournament started at two. Jane would miss the first game. At lunchtime she took Isabel to a nearby sandwich shop, where they chatted and laughed as they ate. A woman at the next table glanced over with a longing look.

I know what you're thinking, Jane thought. *There's a model relationship: a mother and daughter who are in sync with each other.*

It was so far from the truth.

I'm about to abandon my daughter for the second time in her life. Jane put her sandwich down, her appetite gone.

After lunch, Isabel wanted to be dropped at home. "I'm going to make a big batch of cookies for the team," she announced. "If I can't be there to cheer them on, I want to send something nice."

"You don't have to do that. You've been working so hard on Harper's dress."

"But I want to," Isabel assured Jane. "It's all a labor of love."

At three thirty, Jane lammed out of the building on a mission to get to Canby. The essay portion of the exams had taken her longer to grade than she'd expected, but she had finished at last. All her students' grades were posted, and she was good to go.

When she stopped at home to change into her jeans and grab a bottle of water, Isabel stood in the kitchen eating chocolate frosting from a pan on the stove.

"You caught me," she teased, licking a spoon. "I was just finishing off this chocolate icing that I made for Harper. I know it's her favorite." She handed Jane a spoon of her own. "You've got to try it. It turned out really chocolaty this time."

As Jane took a taste, she skimmed the open box of cookies on the counter. A field of vanilla-iced snowmen and two chocolate stars. "Only two chocolates?" Jane asked.

"They're for Harper. I added the cocoa later when I remembered it's her favorite."

"This is delicious," Jane agreed. "It reminds me of my mother's fudge."

"I hope the team likes them." As Isabel slid the lid on the box, Jane recalled Anya's accusation that Isabel had poisoned Chrissy. It seemed ludicrous now, in light of all the meals and treats that Isabel had prepared for them here.

Quickly Jane washed up, changed her clothes, and grabbed a bottle of water from the fridge. "With any luck, I'll be there before the next game starts."

"Tell Harper I'm sending her Michael Jordan brain waves," Isabel said, handing Jane the box of cookies.

"She'll love that," Jane lied, unwilling to dampen Isabel's enthusiasm.

When Jane was stopped at a long traffic light, she checked her cell phone. No new messages. Not even a lame excuse of a text from Sally Pinero. What did that woman do with her time? It was certainly not spent on Isabel's case. Since the interview on Tuesday Jane had not heard a peep from the social worker, who was not only supposed to be investigating charges that Isabel's mother had abused her, but was also supposed to be finding a foster home for Isabel.

Poor Isabel really believed that she was going to change Harper's mind. Jane knew it was a lost cause. Not her stubborn Hoppy.

Jane merged onto the interstate and cruised south until traffic slowed to a crawl after a few miles. She groaned. Friday traffic—she should have expected it. Now she would be late, and Harper would perceive that as a slight, especially now that her stay at Sydney's was losing its charm and Harper was beginning to miss the comforts of home.

Jane turned the radio on to drown out the sound of her growling stomach, suddenly remembering that she had barely touched her lunch. Well, she was hungry now.

As she inched along in traffic, the box of cookies beckoned. Flipping open the lid, she realized that Harper would never know that her sister had baked two cookies for her. She bit into one of the brown star cookies, savoring the bittersweet cocoa frosting. Good, but a little spicier than she remembered. A second bite, and her mouth was tingling. The cookie became harder to taste as a numb sensation came over her tongue. It reminded her of the way the center of a pineapple affected her tongue, and she wondered what Isabel had added to the cookie to cause such a reaction.

What *had* Isabel added to the cookie?

Something horrible.

Frowning down at the remnants, Jane threw them into the box and signaled to pull out of traffic as nausea swept through her, a skittering wildfire. She had to vomit, but please, oh please, not in the car! She opened all the car windows as she signaled again to get over. Someone let her into the next lane, and she managed to edge her car off the roadway as bitter liquid erupted in her throat. The car squirmed onto the gravel, and she threw it into park. Just in time . . . She leaned out of the car and lost it.

Her throat was still thick with mucus, her airways swollen. Suffocating . . . Frank's hands on her throat, closing in.

Fumbling on her phone, she punched in 911.

"Trouble breathing," she rasped. "On I-5, south of Tualatin. Help me, please."

The dispatcher was talking to her, but the woman's voice, firm and comforting, seemed to come from far away. Her mouth was numb now, the edges of her vision growing dark as if someone were burning them away with a thousand matches.

As the circle of light narrowed to a pinpoint, she thought of Harper waiting and watching for her in the Canby High School gymnasium. She thought of Isabel working at the stove, sharing the untainted fudge frosting and slathering on a layer of poison to murder her sister.

Wouldn't that solve all her problems?

With Hoppy out of the picture, Jane would welcome Isabel with open arms.

My mistake saved Hoppy, Jane thought as she faded out. *But please, don't leave her without a mother. I can't go.*

But the pain, the choking pain was too much.

Time to let go.

Chapter 30

The two teens stood on either side of the hospital bed, bookends carved from the same wood but with a few variations in grain that made them distinctive. At the foot of the bed, Luke rested a hand on the white-sheeted ridge of her leg. A quiet reverence filled the room, broken by the beep and click of the monitors and machinery.

Distant and closed off, Harper kept her hands tucked into her hoodie. "What happened to her?"

"They say it was food poisoning." Luke seemed deflated; he hunkered over Jane, his head bowed.

"Mom, can you hear me?" Isabel's face puckered, a sob suppressed. "Come on now, Mom." Fervently she stroked Jane's hand, the part that wasn't encumbered by tape or tubing.

"How did she get food poisoning this bad, this fast?" Harper shook her head. "What did she eat?"

"There was poison in a cookie she ingested," Luke said. "From a box of homemade cookies beside her in the car. The poison is called aconite. It's a chemical found in a plant that can be easily grown here in the Northwest. Wolfsbane is the common name. Some people call it monkshood."

"Who made the cookies?" Harper asked.

Luke adjusted his glasses as he looked up at Isabel. "Didn't you bake them?"

"I baked them but . . . I didn't poison her. I didn't!"

"Here's the thing. The police also found wolfsbane in the greenhouse on Arbor Lane. Quite a few healthy blooms. How did it get there, Isabel?"

"My adoptive mother was growing it. Chrissy. She would dose herself with it to get attention."

Harper winced. "That's sick."

"She *was* sick," Isabel said sadly. "Once she put it in our food, and I got sick. After that, I did all the cooking. I had to."

"But Chrissy wasn't here to poison Jane." Luke rubbed the hairs on his chin, trying to piece it all together. "How did Jane come to ingest it?"

"I don't know," Isabel whispered. "She must have added it to the cookies when I wasn't looking. I can't believe it. She . . . she must have Munchausen too. It's so unfair! Why can't I have a mother who takes care of herself and me? A normal mother who loves me." She sniffed back tears.

"Can I wake her up?" Harper asked. "Is it okay, or does she need to sleep?"

Luke shook his head, moving next to Harper at the head of the bed, where he took Jane's hand. "I'm sorry, but the poison was too much for her system. A machine is keeping her alive right now. The doctors say that, technically, she's already gone."

"Oh, no!" Harper buried her face in her hands and sobbed.

"I can't believe it." Isabel spoke slowly. "Mama-dish . . ."

The curtain moved aside and a man stepped in. Detective Drum nodded respectfully at Luke and folded his arms, a quiet observer.

Wincing, Luke rubbed the knuckles of one hand over his jaw and then bent down so that his face was just inches from Jane's. "I guess this is our chance to say good-bye."

"No!" Isabel cried. "This can't be happening. I can't lose my only real mother. It wasn't supposed to happen this way."

"Because the cookies weren't intended for Jane?" Luke asked. "You baked them for the team, right? The chocolate ones were for Harper."

"How do you—?" Isabel squinted at him. "Stop talking about the cookies! My mother is dying here."

"From a poison you gave her." The detective's voice, low and calm, seemed to rumble through the room. "You made those cookies with the chocolate frosting for Harper. They were the only ones that were tainted."

"Isabel?" Harper blinked. "You tried to kill me?"

"No, I didn't," Isabel snapped. "That's crazy."

"Not so crazy." Eldon Drum stepped forward, a tired frown tilting his lips. "You wanted Harper out of the picture—dead or sick or incapacitated. That way, you could stay with Jane Ryan. You could be her daughter forever. That was what you wanted, wasn't it?"

"I loved my mother, but I would never hurt anyone."

"I beg to differ." Detective Drum sunk his hands in his pockets. "You know we've been investigating those charges against your other mother, Christine Zaretsky. I just came from the Ryan house, where we did a thorough search of your belongings, Isabel, and I've got to say, you have an odd collection of keepsakes that are rather incriminating. Among them was a Ziploc bag of dried purple flowers. Wolfsbane."

"So you did kill my mom!" Harper's eyes were lit with fury.

"I don't know what you're talking about," Isabel said. "Jane must have put it there."

"My guess is that you were growing wolfsbane in the greenhouse, so that you'd have plenty on hand to poison Christine Zaretsky's meals. It's a wonder she survived. And that's not all. We found a prescription bottle with your father's name on it. Heart pills. Some of the medication you stole from Nick Zaretsky and replaced with a placebo."

Isabel crossed her arms. "I never did that."

"Mmm." Drum's mouth twisted in a grim expression. "And the other killing souvenir—and this breaks my heart—a child's pacifier. I'm guessing you pocketed it after you drowned your cousin Gregory. Do I have that right?"

"Go away. Can't you see I'm grieving here? I'm losing my mother."

"You've already lost me." Jane's voice evoked a gasp from Isabel, who stared at the bed in amazement and horror.

"Mom?" The color drained from Isabel's face. "It's a miracle! They said you wouldn't make it."

"Yeah. For a while there I felt like I wanted to die." Jane removed the oxygen mask and reached out to take Harper's hand. "But I knew I had to get through it. I had to be around for my girl."

Humor sparkled in Harper's eyes as she looked down at her mother. "How was my acting? Should I audition for the next school show?"

"Absolutely." Jane smiled at her daughter, the light of her life. "A Tony-winning performance."

"Wait." Isabel's features grew sharp as she stared from Harper to Jane. "You knew? You were all tricking me?"

"I knew you poisoned me. I was hoping to coax a confession from you, but we were unsuccessful."

"But Mama-dish, I didn't do anything wrong. Tell the detective. I'm the best daughter you ever had. Well-behaved and polite. No problem at all."

Harper rolled her eyes, but Jane kept her gaze steady on Isabel. "You are polite and so smart," Jane said sadly. "So much potential, Isabel. But you're lacking a moral center."

"She's the one who's lacking." Isabel scowled at Harper. "I did everything for you. I got rid of that oaf of a softball player, and were you grateful? No."

"*You* attacked Olivia?" Harper edged closer to the bed. "I barely knew you then."

"No one did. But I knew you. I know all about you and your mom. *My* mom, who passed me off at birth like a piece of trash." She wheeled toward Jane. "I would have done anything to make you love me. Anything. I always knew my real mother would be better than the fat, boring Zaretskys, and I was right." Isabel took Jane's hand and held it gently to her heart. "You're wonderful."

Jane shook her head slowly, staring at the girl who was unraveling before her eyes.

"All the things I did for you, and still you loved Harper better. She was going to move back home, while I was going to be sent off. After I helped get her grades up. I got her elected Snow Queen. I—"

"What?" Harper interrupted. "What are you talking about? I wasn't in the royal court."

"But you're going to be queen. They're going to announce it on Monday."

"She stuffed the ballot box," Jane said. "That's why you were spending so much time at school. Not just sewing the dress, but figuring out a way to tamper with the ballots."

Harper winced. "This is really cray cray."

"I cooked and cleaned for both of you," Isabel went on.

"And what kind of thanks do you show me? To send me off to live with strangers?"

Jane suddenly realized why Isabel's tirade looked and sounded familiar.

Frank. He'd always had a way of manipulating the truth.

Isabel was her father's daughter.

Chapter 31

In the weeks after Isabel's arrest, Jane learned that forgiveness was a two-way street. While it was a blessing to be forgiven by someone you'd wronged, the process was not complete until you embraced your past choices and let the burden ease from your heart. And while Harper had been quick to forgive, Jane found it hard to stop kicking herself for all her past mistakes. Countless times, she hugged her daughter close and told her how sorry she was for doubting her.

"Mom, stop apologizing already," Harper insisted one day as they were driving home from a shopping trip at the discount outlets. Harper had a new boyfriend and a new sense of style that involved short dresses and leggings and strappy sandals—a refreshing change that Jane was happy to encourage.

"It's going to take some time for me to forgive myself," Jane admitted.

"You'll get over it eventually," Harper said as Jane steered onto one of the low bridges crossing a canal. Off to the right, diamonds of light gleamed on the surface of Mirror Lake. "Until then, I'm happy to have you showering me with attention . . . and new clothes."

"Oh, that's how that works?" Jane teased, wishing she could let go of the past as easily as Harper had. She couldn't completely shake the feeling that she had let Harper down. *I'm supposed to be your protector, but instead I put you in harm's way.*

Guilt still stung her tongue, bitter as the poison that Isabel had added to the cookie frosting. That damned toxic cookie haunted Jane, probably because it had been intended as a direct attack on Harper. Over and over again, Jane wondered what would have happened if she had passed the treat on to Harper, a special "gift" from her sister. Knowing Harper's habit of gobbling things up, Jane assumed Harper would have eaten the cookie quickly, the poison working its way through her slender body, a lethal dosage for such a small body. The tragic scenario spun through Jane's mind like a video loop until she shut it down with a tool from her therapist.

It did not happen that way. Her therapist's words resounded in her head. *Dwelling on the hypotheticals of the past will keep you stuck there. Accept responsibility for the here and now, and move forward.*

"I still can't believe you would side with a psycho like Isabel," Harper said as they waited at a red light. Although Harper's directness was surprising at times, Jane had learned to admire her daughter's earnestness. "Couldn't you tell she was fakey fake?" Harper asked, her nose wrinkled in disdain.

"She had me fooled." Jane sighed, recalling the real tears she had seen in Isabel's eyes, more than once. The sweet bursts of affection. The twisted facts that pointed blame at others. The pouty lips and endless excuses crafted to portray Isabel as the victim.

"I guess she fooled me a little, too. At least in the beginning. She was so helpful and noble. I thought she was different from other girls, with a little bit of angel in her." Harper popped a piece of gum in her mouth. "I was way wrong. She's a devil girl."

Jane wasn't sure if she believed in the existence of angels

and demons, but she now knew evil to exist. She had seen it with her own eyes, touched it, fallen prey to its piercing claws. "Isabel is evil, all right." *Just like your father,* Jane thought, though she didn't want to go there with Harper now; the girl was still digesting the bombshell of a few days ago, when Jane had shared the distressing details of Frank Dixon's mental illness and criminal past.

"She needs to know," the therapist had told Jane, prompting Jane to spill the truth. Jane had chosen her words carefully, trying to portray Frank as a troubled man without enumerating the details of his crimes. Harper's response had been a rush of empathy for Jane. "Mom, that's so scary for you. I didn't know you were protecting me from him and . . . I can't believe you wanted to keep even one kid after the way he treated you."

Blinking back tears, Jane had answered that she had always wanted a family, and when her babies had been born, she couldn't blame them for their father's poor choices in life. In response, Harper had flung her arms around Jane and squeezed her tight.

This young woman had not inherited the evil of Frank Dixon. Sure, she suffered adolescent angst and the occasional outbreak of bad temper, but that was normal for a fifteen-year-old girl. *How could I not see that?* Jane kept asking herself. She had been overreacting when it came to Harper, seeing ghosts where there were none. She'd made Harper out to be a monster, just like her father, when Isabel had been the one to manifest a proclivity for evil. Isabel had followed in her father's footsteps, killing without conscience. The trials were pending, but Jane knew in her heart that Isabel had killed her adoptive father and young cousin—an innocent baby. The thought of Isabel's putting her hands around the child's neck sent a shiver down Jane's spine. Two dead, and at least three others on Isabel's hit list, with Olivia Ferguson bludgeoned at the lake, Chrissy Zaretsky poisoned, and Harper—Isabel's own twin—in her killing sights.

As final proof of her moral depravity, Isabel had bragged about killing Clover. In one of the depositions, she had coolly explained how she'd smashed the guinea pig's head with a hammer that early morning and set up the scene to make it look like the dog had done it. "It was all so easy," Isabel had claimed, "but when you're smarter than everyone else in your family, you can get away with murder."

It scared Jane to think that Isabel had almost gotten away with her crimes . . . almost. There was some relief in knowing that the girl was locked up in a high-security detention center, awaiting trial and, most likely, a lifetime of incarceration. Jane would have to face her in a courtroom, but there would be no family visits, no letters, no money for treats in the center's commissary. No love lost over the fledgling who had grown up to be a killer.

Jane would be chipping away at guilt for years to come, but in the meantime, Harper had forgiven her, and Luke, God love him, considered her blameless, having watched her navigate the treacherous situation.

"Do you think Isabel is getting bullied in jail?" Harper asked. "I've seen how that works on television. You get bullied and beat up until you assert your territory."

"If I had to guess, I'd say Isabel is probably the one doing the bullying."

"With that sickeningly sweet smile," Harper said. "The way she puckered her lips—"

"Her lips formed a beak," Jane said. "Like a smug parrot."

"Eew!" Harper winced, jiggling her hands. "I used to hate that."

"Me too," Jane said as she pulled into the garage. Mouth-watering scents of lemon and garlic led them to the kitchen, where Luke was making chicken piccata and garlic mashed potatoes. Jane leaned over the kitchen counter to kiss him. "Smells great."

"And I'm starving." Harper dropped her shopping bags by the bar stools. "Shopping makes me hungry. Plus, I played an eleven-inning game this morning with no break."

"You had two cheese dogs at the mall," Jane pointed out.

"I know, but I'm still hungry. When's dinner?"

"This'll be ready by the time you take that stuff upstairs, wash your hands, and put together a salad." Luke smiled at Harper as he turned a chicken fillet in the sizzling oil. In the two weeks since he'd moved in, he had begun to engage Harper in chores, using his charisma and fairness to sell the program.

"Okay." Harper gathered up the shopping bags and dashed toward the stairs. "I'll be right back."

Jane washed her hands at the sink, then nuzzled up to Luke. "What's my dinner assignment, Mr. Bandini?"

"Why don't you open that bottle of Chardonnay in the fridge and pour some for the chef?"

"Will do." She poured wine into a stem glass for herself, and a juice glass—"the old Italian way"—for Luke, then sat down at the counter facing her fiancé. With Harper's blessing, they would be married next week on a dock overlooking the lake. Jane had expected to marry Luke in a simple ceremony—something at the town hall with hired witnesses—but Harper wouldn't allow it. "Mom." Harper had set stern eyes on Jane. "This is one of the most important decisions of your life. I'm not going to let you run off to town hall with Luke like you're going to pay a parking ticket or something."

Jane had squinted at her daughter, wondering when Harper had become the responsible one. The girl was eager to have Jane's relationship with Luke made official, insisting that everyone knew about it anyway. When Luke had talked about his commitment to taking care of Harper as well as Jane, Harper had been the one to suggest that he adopt her.

"That would be my honor," Luke had said quietly, almost reverently, bringing tears to Jane's eyes. The days of hiding and lying were over, and she welcomed her new life as Jane Bandini. She reached down to rough up Phoenix's scruff, imagining the mythological broad-winged bird rising from the ashes, reborn from the destruction of a previous life. Renewal and regeneration. A metamorphosis.

Luke cut off a corner of a chicken breast and extended the fork across the counter. "Taste test?"

Jane leaned forward and closed her mouth over the succulent meat, knowing that it would be nothing less than delicious. She was not disappointed.

Although Jane had been joking that the April wedding might take place under a cluster of umbrellas, the afternoon sky had opened to a crisp blue punctuated by cherubic clouds of cottony white. Before the ceremony Jane had to talk herself through a web of anxiety that had nothing to do with marrying Luke and everything to do with inviting people into her life. After years of playing it cool and low-key, living a relatively solitary life with her daughter, she was now inviting the community to share a private moment. The public spectacle made nervousness flutter in her chest like a trapped bird, but Jane knew that this was the right thing to do. The ordeal that had begun with Frank Dixon was winding to a close, and it was time to move on to the next phase of her life.

Time to rise from the ashes.

Before the ceremony began, Jane cast a nervous look out at the assembling group and was greeted by smiles and sparkling eyes. Harper's boyfriend, Quincy, was escorting ladies to seats. At over six feet, the junior basketball star towered over most of the women, who seemed charmed by his broad smile. Harper's friends Emma and Sydney had brought their parents and siblings. Russell Templer, one of the music teachers, played a bright classical piece on the electric piano, which had prompted the younger Schiavone girls to break into dance behind the rows of chairs. More than a dozen teachers were there with their spouses—a mishmash of the science and English departments. In the front row, Mary Ellen gave a little wave and then leaned down to pick up a pacifier dropped by baby Taylor, who was bouncing on Ben's lap. Jane's neighbors had made it, including Nancy's son Evan, one of Harper's first basketball coaches. Marnie sat off to the side, dabbing at her eyes with her husband's handkerchief as Jason slung an arm around her reassuringly. Tears of joy, Jane suspected; if she let her gaze linger on her old friend, soon she would be misting over too.

When the music changed and Luke took her hands, saying, "You ready to do this, kid?" Jane's nerves melted away.

Gray Tarkington officiated, having gotten an online license from the state of Oregon. His six-foot-five frame seemed like a masthead against the silvery blue waters behind him. Harper was the maid of honor, and Luke's son Matt had traveled from college in Seattle to be Luke's best man, providing a nice sense of family symmetry on the dock.

Their short vows moved as fast as the breeze on the lake, and soon the formality dissipated, giving way to music, dancing, and oven-baked pizzas from the waterfront restaurant. As Jane made her way to the bar with Luke, she marveled over the leagues of tulips that lined the paved walkway. A sea of yellow was framed by red tulip soldiers, and in the distance sumptuous purple flowers reached toward the sun.

"I'd forgotten how early the tulips bloom," Jane said, squeezing his arm. "One of the first blasts of spring."

Luke paused, rubbing his knuckles against his chin. "I'd like to say that I planned it this way, so that we'd think of our wedding day every year when the tulips are in bloom. But the truth is, when you and Hoppy gave the green light to get married, I jumped on the first available date."

She smiled. "How did I ever find you?"

"In this random universe? I'd say we both got lucky."

Taking a sip of champagne, Jane considered how a garden was a metaphor for life. A field of beauty that could make the heart swell with joy, and yet, if you looked closely there were falling petals and some browning stems. Mistakes were made. People were magnificently flawed, imperfect. And yet, last year's fallen leaves served as fertilizer for this year's blossoms. From the ashes, new life arose. Perhaps the tale of the phoenix was more than mythology. One of these days, she would ask Luke about the science of regeneration. One of these days.

Epilogue

The detention center wasn't nearly as bad as everyone made it out to be. She had a tiny room of her own that she kept neat and tidy, and it was a relief not to have to deal with anyone else's dirty, balled-up clothes. Someone else did all the cooking and laundry, and she was allowed books and TV time and anything she wanted to buy from a little menu in the center's store. They had chocolate bars and ramen noodles and her favorite cereal. She'd purchased shampoo that made her hair smell like lavender from the garden. A fat drawing pad and colored pencils kept her busy for hours, drawing flowers and stars and boats and clouds. She was becoming a pretty good artist.

Her first week in detention she had purchased writing paper and stamps so that she could pour her heart out in letters to Mama-dish. Her dear mother. How she missed her! Sometimes she imagined the two of them skiing down the mountain together, cutting loops around each other in a giant chain of love. And the cold, lonely nights here made her long for Mom's warm bed. Isabel had written nearly a dozen letters to let Mom know just how much she missed her. So far, she had not received an answer, but she knew that Mom would write back eventually. Someday, Mom would realize that her little girl was here, waiting patiently to love and be loved.

Until then, Isabel had decided to write to someone else.

Mom had mentioned his name once, while she was having one of those heavy talks with Luke and thought no one else in the house could hear.

Frank Dixon.

Isabel had held his name close to her heart, knowing that someday, in some way, she would find him. It hadn't seemed so important while she had Mom, but once she had arrived here at the detention center, she thought it was about time to reach out to Dad.

It wasn't difficult to find him through the Internet. The picture had taken her breath away.

I have his eyes.

Just seeing him had given her a strong sense of belonging.

There was information about his recent trials, and even the name of the prison where he was living. The United States Penitentiary in Victorville, California. She had clicked on the visiting policies on the prison Web site and imagined herself waiting for him to come to the window. The aura of joy on his face when he saw her for the first time. A big smile. A hand pressed to the bulletproof glass.

Of course, they wouldn't be able to meet while they were both incarcerated. But someday, some way . . .

She smoothed her fingertips over the writing paper and pressed pen to paper.

> *Dear Daddy,*
> *You're going to be surprised to receive this letter from your girl Isabel. That's right, you have a beautiful daughter who shares your dark hair and blue eyes. I can't wait to meet you! I am tied*

up right now, but I hope to visit you sometime in the future.

I am fifteen years old, and my birthday is in December. A Sagittarius—always shooting for the stars. I'm confident and optimistic about life and love, even with all the mean things people have done to me.

So are you shocked? I'll let the good news settle in and write you another letter next week. Until then, I just want you to know that you have a daughter who loves you with all her heart. You and I will make a great team; I can feel it already. After all, family is everything.

TAKE ANOTHER LOOK

Rosalind Noonan

ABOUT THIS GUIDE

The suggested questions are included to enhance
your group's discussion of Rosalind Noonan's
Take Another Look.

DISCUSSION QUESTIONS

1. When Jane Ryan could not imagine herself managing to raise twins on her own, she gave one baby up for adoption. Do twins have a special bond that makes them closer than other siblings? Is it harmful or helpful to separate twins as infants? Do you think parents should encourage twins to have a special bond?

2. Could Jane have handled her escape from Frank Dixon differently? Do you think she would have gotten adequate support from the local police department and district attorney's office?

3. According to the American Civil Liberties Union, one third of the women killed in the United States are murdered by a domestic partner. Do you think restraining orders curtail domestic violence?

4. Colic has been defined as an extended period of uncontrollable crying (three hours in a row for three days or more) in an otherwise healthy baby. Does American society give mothers like Jane tools to deal with colic? Have technological advances assisted women with mothering or would women be better served by relying on basic mothering instincts?

5. In the discussion of nature versus nurture, which do you think plays the most important role in a child's upbringing? Is there a type of home environment that might have steered Isabel to become a compassionate, well-rounded human being? In what ways do our genetics predict our destiny?

6. The author refers to songs by Sheryl Crow, Paula Cole, and Sarah McLachlan to help set the scene for the summer of 1997. Do you find popular references like this to be an asset to a story or a distraction?

7. What parenting lessons does Jane learn through the course of the story?

8. The author opens the novel with Eudora Welty's words: "People are mostly layers of violence and tenderness wrapped like bulbs, and it is difficult to say what makes them onions or hyacinths." How does this apply to the characters of Jane, Harper, and Isabel in *Take Another Look*?

9. At the end of the novel, Jane realizes that "People were magnificently flawed, imperfect." How does this reflect her emotional journey in the novel?

10. If you were casting the roles in *Take Another Look* for a movie, what actors would you choose for Jane, Harper/Isabel, and Luke? If you were writing the script, would you play up the suspense angles of the story or the psychological conflicts?